D1242617

RED-LINE:

TRUST DESTINY

....

J. T. BISHOP

J. T. Bishop
Dallas, Texas

J. T. Bishop
Dallas, Texas
www.jtbishopauthor.com

Publisher's Note: This is a work of fiction. Names, characters, places, and incidents are a product of the author's imagination. Locales and public names are sometimes used for atmospheric purposes. Any resemblance to actual people, living or dead, or to businesses, companies, events, institutions, or locales is completely coincidental.

Book Layout ©2013 BookDesignTemplates.com
Book Editing by Firstlookforauthors.com
Book Cover by Bespokebookcovers.com
Author photo by Mayza Clark Photography

Ordering Information:
Quantity sales. Special discounts are available on quantity purchases by corporations, associations, and others. For details, contact the "Special Sales Department" at the address above.

Red-Line: Trust Destiny/ J. T. Bishop. -- 1st ed.
ISBN 978-0692545638

To Taylor, Alex, Sydney, Colson and Leighton...

It's such a thrill to know you all and watch you grow up. You're smart, funny, strong and beautiful. You meet every challenge, make me laugh, and show me every day how much fun life can be. No matter where your path leads you, I know for sure that you all make the world a better place.
I am grateful to be a witness to it.
Love you all so much!

CHAPTER ONE

....

THE HOT SPRAY of water pelted his skin, turning it red, but it eased his muscle aches and helped him relax. Sliding his hands through his dark hair, John Sherlock Ramsey rinsed away the shampoo and watched the soap run down his shoulders and torso. He reached for the knob and turned it to the off position, stepped from the shower, and grabbed his towel. Wiping away the excess water, he shook the droplets from his wavy hair, wrapped the towel around his waist, and walked toward his locker. On his way, he stopped in front of the mirrors. Studying himself, he raised his hand and traced the scar on his abdomen which peeked out from above the towel. It was raised and pink, but there was no pain. He noted how his body was returning to its former shape. He'd regained some weight and his shoulders, arms and belly were curved with new muscle. Seeing his reflection, he thought back on how lucky he was to be alive.

He headed to his locker and opened it. After an hour of strenuous physical therapy, he felt tired but not exhausted, which was a vast improvement. When he'd first begun this regimen after leaving the hospital over a month ago, he could barely walk back to his car. Pleased that he could now get his clothes on without trembling and needing to sit, he smiled, pulled on his shirt, and slid his pants up with ease. Reaching for his phone, he thought of Sarah. She was having lunch with Hannah, and he looked forward to their anticipated afternoon and evening together. He thought about buying her some flowers and wine on the way home and considered stopping at a local Italian eatery. Picking up a prepared meal that would require only a quick heat in the oven would be ideal if they found themselves more interested in each other than cooking.

Grabbing his shoes with his free hand, he glanced at his cell and saw the lighted notification bar, telling him that he had messages pending. He typed in his passcode and felt the first pangs of anxiety when he saw a recent text from Hannah and two missed phone calls. He opened the text message.

Waiting for Sarah. Is she with you?

A cold shiver ran through him, and he sat and quickly put on his shoes. He grabbed his wallet and keys, closed his locker, and accessed his voicemail. Both messages were from Declan, his stepbrother and the man responsible for Sarah's security since her Shift two months earlier. Picking up his pace, he left the workout area and headed out into the parking lot.

He listened to the first message.

"John." It was Declan's voice. "Call me. I need to know where you and Sarah are." There was a brief pause. "I just..." There was a long pause. "...just call me," Declan said again, and the message ended.

Ramsey reached his car, unlocked it, threw his bag in the back seat, and sat.

He deleted the first message and listened to the second. Declan's voice returned. "John? Where are you? I need to reach you. Call me."

Pushing back his growing fear, he closed his voicemail and started the engine. He began to return the missed calls when his phone rang. It was Declan.

He answered. "Declan?"

"John?" There was a pause, and Ramsey could hear his brother release a relieved breath. "Where are you?"

"I'm leaving therapy. What's wrong?"

"Is Sarah with you?"

Ice cold hit his midsection. "No," he said. "She was supposed to have lunch with Hannah."

Declan didn't respond.

"What's wrong, Declan? Where is she?"

"She never showed at lunch. She's not answering her phone. I got an alert from Marco, but I haven't been able to reach him, either. I'm heading to his last location now."

Ramsey fought to keep his panic at bay. "Where?"

"Sullivan's. It's a restaurant over on the east side."

"I know where it is. I'll meet you there." Afraid of the answer, he hesitated before asking the next question. "What is it, Declan? What are you getting?"

Declan paused again, and Ramsey knew his stepbrother didn't want to answer. "We'll find her, John. I'll see you at the restaurant." Declan hung up before Ramsey could reply, and Ramsey knew then that his worst fears were realized. Sarah was missing.

He threw the car in reverse and punched the accelerator. Still holding the phone, he hit the button to call her, but listened as the phone rang several times and went to voicemail. Sarah never answered.

**

Twenty minutes later, after breaking most of the traffic laws, Ramsey pulled into the parking lot of Sullivan's. He saw Declan's car, and his stomach flipped when he saw that it was parked next to Sarah's. It was still too early for the dinner crowd and the lot was open, but he parked in front of the building's entrance and jumped out of his car. Running inside, he started to confront the hostess when he saw Declan in the bar area to his right. Turning abruptly, he went in to meet him.

"Anything?" he asked, trying to remain calm.

Declan stood near a booth and seemed to be focused on it "Feel that?" he asked.

"Feel what?"

Declan studied his brother and must have realized that Ramsey was in no state to tune into much at the moment. "He was here."

Ramsey grimaced. "Dammit, Declan. Where the hell is Sarah?"

Declan withdrew from whatever held his attention. "I talked to the hostess, but she just came on duty. She didn't see anyone matching Sarah's description. She's looking for anyone who may have been here earlier."

"And Marco?"

"Still nothing. They both made it here, but what happened after that..."

"Why the hell was she here? Wasn't she supposed to meet Hannah somewhere else?"

"I don't know."

"But you got an alert from Marco, right?"

"I did."

When Sarah had returned home after Ramsey's hospital stay a month earlier, she and Declan had agreed that her security would continue, since neither could assume that Y would keep his word and remain at a distance. In the event that Sarah needed help,

Declan had set up an alert system that would notify him and his team if something occurred.

"When did you receive it?" asked Ramsey.

Declan checked his watch. "A little over an hour ago. I called you and Hannah both, hoping that Sarah was with one of you. Hannah told me that Sarah had never showed at lunch. She'd texted her but never received a response."

"Where's Hannah now?"

"I told her to go back to work. She wanted to come here, but until I knew it was safe, I didn't want her here."

"Did you talk to Leroy?"

"Yes. I asked him to notify the Council. As far as I know, he's talking to them now. We've got to get as many resources on this as fast as possible."

Ramsey's tension mounted, and he voiced his fear. "It's Yates, isn't it?"

Declan nodded. "That's what I'm sensing."

"Damn it." Ramsey stared at the booth Declan had focused on, imagining Sarah seated there. "Where would he take her?"

"Sarah has been to his house. I assume he would take her there. But we don't know where that is. All we know is that it's about an hour away from the hospital, it's big, and it's on the coast."

Ramsey ran a hand through his hair, trying to stay calm in order to think. He did Sarah no favors by panicking. Pulling his phone out of his pocket, he proceeded to do what he'd been doing since he'd gotten in the car. He dialed her number, praying she would answer. Listening to the soft tones as Sarah's phone rang, he heard the sound of buzzing nearby.

Declan heard it, too. Dropping down low, he looked on the floor beneath the adjacent table and pulled out the source.

Ramsey ended the call when he realized Declan was holding Sarah's phone. "Oh God," he said.

Declan accessed the screen and read the text messages. His face looked grim.

"What?" asked Ramsey.

"Her messages. She's got one from Hannah asking Sarah to meet her here."

"But Hannah said she hadn't talked to her."

"Exactly."

They both stared, realizing the implications.

"Hell," said Ramsey. "He lured her here." Declan continued to read the list of texts, and Ramsey felt his brother's energy constrict. "What?" he asked.

Declan looked up from the phone. "The last message. Sarah received a text from Hannah asking where she was. Sarah began a reply, but never finished it."

Now Ramsey couldn't help but feel the fear slam into him, but before he could answer, a man approached them. A bar towel was thrown over his shoulder and his nametag read "Dave."

"You two looking for someone?" he asked.

Ramsey had to restrain himself from overreacting and demanding answers. He made himself take a breath as Declan took over the questioning.

"Yes...Dave," said Declan, seeing the man's nametag. "We're looking for a woman. Tall, with shoulder-length dark brown hair and bangs. We believe she was here, in the bar, earlier."

Dave answered quickly. "Yeah, I saw her."

Ramsey turned. "Where is she?"

Dave shrugged. "I don't know. She left with her fiancé. She was sick."

Ramsey didn't think he heard right. "Her what?"

"The guy she was with," answered Dave.

Ramsey walked up close. "What do you mean, her fiancé?"

Dave took a step back as Declan stepped in between his brother and Dave. "Sorry, Dave," said Declan. "Don't mind him." Declan eyed Ramsey but then spoke to the confused bartender. "Why don't you start from the top? Tell me what happened."

Dave watched Ramsey, who stared back, before returning his attention to Declan. "She got dizzy or something. He helped her into a booth because she looked like she was going to faint. The guy said she had a medical condition and asked me to get a damp cloth for her. I did, and he wiped her face. She was really pale and didn't look good."

"She didn't say anything?" asked Declan.

"Not to me, she didn't."

"And why the hell did you say that was her fiancé?" asked Ramsey, stepping in even closer.

Declan held up his hand to put up some sort of boundary between Ramsey and Dave.

"Because he said so," said Dave.

Ramsey set his jaw. "And what happened to her?"

Dave pulled his bar towel off his shoulder. "He carried her out."

"He what?" Ramsey almost shouted.

"John...." Declan stepped in to prevent Ramsey from grabbing at Dave.

They made eye contact, and Ramsey knew he had to rein it in. He let out a deep breath and stepped away.

Declan turned back to Dave. "You said he carried her out?"

Dave answered, although he kept an eye on Ramsey. "Yes. I think she was too sick to stand and walk. He said he was taking her to the doctor. She wasn't objecting."

Ramsey stopped pacing. "Was she even conscious enough to object? How do you know he didn't give her something?"

Dave raised a hand. "Hey, man. Neither of them had anything to drink. She'd only been here a few minutes. He didn't seem like a bad guy. He was taking care of her, you know?"

"Do you have any idea who he was?" asked Declan.

"Who?" asked Dave.

Ramsey grunted and rolled his eyes.

"The man, Dave," replied Declan. "The one who carried her out. Have you seen him before?"

"No, never seen him before."

"What did he look like?"

Dave huffed. "Tall, slim build, blond hair, fancy suit."

"Hell..." said Ramsey.

Declan pulled out a card. "Can you do me a favor? If that man comes back in here in the future, will you call me?"

Dave took the card. "Sure. I'll call you." His forehead creased. "Is she going to be okay?"

Ramsey stopped pacing but didn't say anything.

"Yes," said Declan. "She'll be okay. Thanks for your help."

Dave nodded and stepped from the room.

Ramsey sat in the closest booth, facing out. He hunched over and closed his eyes. Willing himself to calm down, he pictured Y picking up a scared Sarah, whom he'd undoubtedly drugged, with her unable to get away. He could almost hear her in his head, praying and desperate for his help, but he had not been there. The guilt curdled his stomach. Why had he let her come here on her own? Why had he ever agreed to let her out of his sight? He cursed himself.

"John?"

Ramsey opened his eyes to see Declan sitting across from him.

"Stop what you're doing."

"What am I doing?" he asked.

"I can feel it all over you. You're blaming yourself."

Ramsey turned in the booth. "You're damn right I am. I knew he wouldn't leave her alone." He rubbed at his temples with his fingers, trying to get the image of Sarah out of his mind. "I never should have left her."

"Then you'd be missing, right along with Marco."

"Maybe," Ramsey said, dropping his hand, "maybe not. At least I could have been there."

Declan clenched his hands together. "Listen to me," he said. "He wanted to get her alone, without you. If it hadn't been today, it would have been another. He knows what this is doing to you, and he did it intentionally. He knows you'll feel guilty. He's counting on it."

Ramsey swallowed hard. "We have to find her, Declan."

Declan reached over and squeezed Ramsey's wrist. "I promise you. We will."

Ramsey nodded as Declan's phone rang and he picked it up. "Yes?" Declan looked at Ramsey. "It's Leroy."

Declan talked to Leroy, but Ramsey only heard half of what was said. Sending out a silent message to Sarah, he hoped that in some way she could hear it. He told her to stay strong, that he would get to her soon, and prayed that somehow, the message would find its way to her.

CHAPTER TWO

....

SARAH LAY IN bed, hearing the cry of seagulls. She cracked her eyes open, and a sharp pain lanced through her head when the sunlight from the window made her squint. She had no idea where she was, but she felt warm and comfortable despite her headache. Shifting, she opened her eyes some more, but moaned as another blinding pain pulsed behind her lids.

"Sarah?" She heard her name. "Are you awake?"

She tried again to focus, but the lull of sleep lured her, and she wanted only to close her eyes and drift off again, but the voice wouldn't let her.

"Hey, sleepyhead. You awake?"

Managing to open her eyes a bit more, her vision began to clear. She was in a bedroom. Blinking her eyes a few times, she tried to engage her brain. She wanted to talk, but no words would form.

"Honey?" The voice spoke again. "Can you sit up? You need to take your pill." Blinking a few more times, she turned her head to see who was talking. A man sat on the side of the bed, looking down at her. He reached over and brushed the hair away from her eyes. "You all right?"

"Where am I?" she managed to croak.

"You're home. You're safe. Do you remember?"

Sarah furrowed her brow, not sure what he referred to. Looking around the room, a faint memory returned. She'd been here before. A memory surface and she remembered the man. His name was Yates. She tried to think about why she felt so miserable, but the fog in her brain wouldn't clear. "What's wrong with me?"

Smiling down at her, he said, "Take it slow. The doctor said your memory would come and go."

She frowned. "My memory?"

"Yes. After the accident."

"I had an accident?"

"Yes," he said patiently. "You had a car accident a couple of months ago. You hit your head and suffered a mild brain injury. As a result, your memory's been affected. The doctor said it would come back slowly, although you will continue to have these spells."

She squinted. "I feel dizzy."

"Yes. You get lightheaded, and then the headache hits. It takes you out for a few days."

"A few days?" Sarah tried to sit up, but it hurt to move. She groaned, and he put a hand on her shoulder.

"Easy," he said. "You're not over it yet. You need to take your pill." He held out his hand.

She saw that he held a small yellow pill. Her attempts to think made her head hurt more. "How long have I been out?"

"Since yesterday."

Needing to use the bathroom, she moved to sit up despite the pain that seemed to find its way to every muscle in her body.

"Go easy," he said.

Pushing the covers off, she sat up. The curtains in the room drifted as the wind blew, and she had a hazy memory of the view of the ocean. Leaning over, she put her head in her hands.

His hand moved to her shoulder, and he rubbed it. "You need to go back to sleep."

"I need to go to the bathroom."

He held the pill out to her with a glass of water. "Take your pill first and then I'll help you."

She eyed the pill in his outstretched hand. "Is that supposed to help this headache?"

"Yes. Doctor's orders."

The memory of seeing a doctor did not surface, but at the moment all she cared about was her pounding head. She reached over and took the pill from him. After taking the water he offered, she tipped her head back and swallowed the pill.

"Good girl. Now let's get you up and to the bathroom." Standing, he took her hand and helped her up.

She accepted his assistance and left the bed, but swayed on shaky legs.

"You okay?" he asked.

His warm body felt good close to hers, and she leaned into it, needing to feel safe.

He put his arm around her and held her against him. "Can you walk?"

She nodded her head. Smelling his familiar scent, she took a breath to steady herself. "Yes. I can walk." When she felt strong enough, she pulled away, but he stayed close in case her balance wavered. As they moved toward the bathroom, she saw the double sinks and large mirrors on the walls. Heading into the toilet area, she closed the door as he waited outside.

"Are we suddenly shy?" he asked.

Not knowing what he meant, she didn't answer as she used the facilities and then returned to wash her hands. He remained where he was, watching her.

"Sarah?" he asked. "Do you know who I am?"

She met his gaze through the bathroom mirror. "Yes," she said. "You're Yates."

His smile lit his face. "Yes, but do you know who I am?"

She didn't say anything because she wasn't sure what he meant. "I'm your fiancé."

Turning off the faucet, she tried to think. She knew him. She knew this house, but everything else was a giant blank. Another pain sliced through her, and she closed her eyes and moaned.

"You need to get back to bed." He moved up beside her, put his arm around her, and bent to pick her up. He lifted her into her arms.

She put up no resistance. All she could do was lean her head into his shoulder. He carried her back to the bed as a new wave of dizziness hit and she grabbed at his shirt. Shutting her eyes, she tried to keep her stomach from lurching.

He must have felt her pain, because he brought his chin down to rest on her head. "Easy, honey. It will pass soon. You need to rest some more."

Having no will to argue, she felt him lower her.

Yates put her back into bed and covered her again. "Sleep, Sarah," he said. "You'll feel better when you wake up."

She felt his fingers stroke her cheek as she drifted off again.

....

CHAPTER THREE

L EROY SAMPSON, RAMSEY's best friend and a former Protector, stood at the door to his home office, watching as Ramsey dozed on the couch, finally giving in to pure exhaustion. After twenty-four hours of mindless searching, Ramsey had acquiesced to Leroy's insistence that he lie down.

Leroy's house had become an impromptu command center. Declan had taken over the dining table with his laptop and maps, giving instructions to those assigned as to where to look for Sarah. The Council had garnered as much reliable assistance as they could find and had dispatched a group of people to blanket the area near where she had disappeared, each with a sketch of Yates and a picture of Sarah, in hopes of locating at least one of them. So far, they'd had no luck.

Ramsey had joined in on the search, hitting every commercial property close to the restaurant, but he'd found nothing. He'd then headed to the coast and randomly walked to any door he could access to ring the doorbell and ask if anyone recognized the people in the pictures. After a long day with no results, Leroy had located Ramsey and managed to convince him to return to the house and eat something, even though Ramsey had little appetite. He'd insisted on going back out, but Leroy explained that not many omeowners were going to answer their door to a bedraggled stranger after dark, especially in the affluent areas where he searched.

Ramsey eventually relented, and he'd returned with Leroy to Leroy's house where he could hear the updates Declan received from the other people in the field, although by then, the search had ended for the night, with plans to resume again in the morning.

That evening, the three of them had determined the next areas to cover in the morning and who to send where. Hannah had contacted Leroy and Declan, telling them that she had taken leave of her current home healthcare assignment and wanted to help. She'd been there for a few hours but left, planning to return the next day. Leroy's wife, Olivia, had made food for all of them, but they ate little. Declan had disappeared in the early am hours to catch a few hours of sleep, and Leroy had tried to get Ramsey to do the same, but after another argument, Leroy had given up and headed into his own bedroom.

After a few hours of restless slumber, Leroy had emerged again only to see Ramsey still in the living room, looking over the maps of the neighborhoods they would search that day, as if they had missed something. Declan was in the kitchen, but he only shook his head as Leroy joined him, unsure himself what to do with his brother.

Now, four hours later, Leroy had finally managed to get Ramsey to eat a few bites of lunch and go into the office to lie down, but only by promising to wake him if anything happened.

After ensuring his friend slept, Leroy closed the door, determined to let Sherlock rest for a while. He prayed they'd find Sarah soon, knowing that his friend would kill himself looking until he found her. He walked into the living area, where Hannah sat and Declan hung up the phone.

"How is he?" asked Declan. His jawline was shadowed with stubble.

"Finally asleep," said Leroy. He walked to the couch and sat.

Declan rubbed his eyes. "I don't know what to do with him."

Leroy sighed. "You and me both."

"I can't blame him, though," said Declan.

"No," said Leroy. "I know how I'd feel."

"Yeah."

Hannah listened to them. Holding a cup of coffee in her hand, she voiced the concern no one wanted to mention. "What if we don't find her?"

Declan dropped his hand from his face. "That's not an option."

"We'll find her," answered Leroy, not wanting to think of the alternative.

Hannah shook her head. "You know, we have to think about this."

Declan spoke through a yawn. "What do you mean?"

"I mean we have to think like he...Y does," she said. "Right now, we're in reaction mode. We're just out searching the streets, which doesn't exactly offer the highest probability of success."

"Agreed," said Declan. "But what else do you suggest we do?"

"I don't know," said Hannah. "But Y's up to something. He has a plan. He knows we're looking for her. And if he plans on staying around, then he knows we'll eventually find her."

"He's right about that," said Declan.

Hannah gripped her mug. 'Well, he's not going to just give her back."

Neither Declan nor Leroy answered.

"He wants to hurt Ramsey, make him suffer," Hannah continued, thinking out loud. "He knows what Sarah's absence is doing to him."

"What are you saying?" asked Leroy.

Hannah sat forward. "I'm saying Y doesn't have short-term plans. He wants Sarah. He's always wanted her. He's..."

Declan straightened. "What, Hannah? What are you not telling us?"

Hannah sighed. "Sarah told me a few things about her meeting with Y, when Ramsey was sick."

Declan stepped closer. "I always wondered if she'd told us everything. What did she leave out?" he asked.

Hannah paused. "That he felt entitled to her, as if she belonged to him. Since they're both the last two Red-Lines, he believed that if he'd gotten to her before Ramsey, that she would have wanted him instead."

"Not surprising," said Leroy, "considering the ego on the arrogant bastard."

"But she doesn't want him," said Declan. "What's he going to do? Force her to comply? He doesn't strike me as a guy who likes a woman who doesn't want him."

"What do you do when you want someone who doesn't want you?" asked Hannah.

Declan tipped his head. "You think he has a way of changing her mind?"

"He's a Red-Line, Declan," said Hannah. "He sent some sort of toxic poison through a mirror to kill Ramsey. Don't you think he may have other talents as well?"

"Creating a poison and getting a woman to fall in love with you are two totally different things," said Leroy. "I suspect the first is easier than the second."

Declan stared off. "He took her blood."

"I know," answered Hannah.

"What are you saying?" asked Leroy. "That he's got some way of brainwashing her?"

Declan sighed. "I don't know. Why would he take her blood, though?"

"Think it through," said Hannah. "What better way for Y to get what he wants? He manipulates Sarah and makes the man he hates, and who loves her, watch as she chooses Y over him."

Declan cursed. "I'd say that's effective revenge."

"You think he could do that?" asked Leroy.

"He's well motivated," said Hannah. "I'd say yes. Besides that, he doesn't just want to keep Sarah for himself and make Ramsey suffer."

Declan's face furrowed. "What else does he want?"

Hannah hesitated. "Children."

Declan's posture went rigid and Leroy took a second to absorb the implications.

"Listen to me," said Leroy, pointing. "Regardless of whatever we think right now or what Y may have up his sleeve, none of us is going to voice a single word of this theory to Sherlock." He'd always referred to Ramsey by his middle name, much to Ramsey's dismay. "You understand?"

Declan swallowed and rubbed at his temples. "He won't hear a word from me, unless there comes a point where he needs to know."

Leroy eyed Hannah.

"At some point, if we don't find her, we'll have to tell him," she said.

"Then we'll deal with it when the time comes, but for now, not a word. The man's struggling enough as it is." His authoritative air left little room for discussion.

Hannah nodded. "Okay, Leroy."

**

A few hours later, Ramsey emerged from the office looking worn and tired, as if his sleep had only added to the weight on his shoulders.

Hannah looked up as she was speaking on the phone. She'd been helping Declan follow up with those out on the street searching for Sarah. As people called in, she noted their progress and then sent them to wherever Declan indicated next. Declan and Leroy were sitting in the kitchen, looking over maps of potential new areas to search.

Hannah hung up the phone as Ramsey walked to the table.

"Any news?" he asked. His sunken, unshaven cheeks and puffy eyes portrayed his weariness and worry.

"Nothing new," she said, and watched him deflate. "When's the last time you ate a solid meal?"

"I'm not hungry." He stood by the couch. "What can I do?"

She told him what he didn't want to hear. "You can go take a shower and get something to eat."

"I can shower and eat later. Where's the next search area?" He searched for his keys.

"We've got plenty of people looking, Ramsey. You need to rest."

Ramsey's fragile nerves stretched thin. "Dammit, Hannah. I don't need to rest. I've rested enough. I can't just sit here. I have to go out and look for her."

"You're not going to do her any good if you collapse while you look. You have to keep up your strength."

He continued to look for his keys. "Forget it. I'll head out my own."

Leroy and Declan came out of the kitchen at the sound of Ramsey's voice. "Sherlock?" asked Leroy.

"What, Leroy?"

"You need to take it easy. You're pushing yourself too hard."

Ramsey's last reserves snapped. "Will you all stop telling me what to do? While I'm here resting, Sarah's out there dealing with who the hell knows what. I'll rest when she's back here safe." He searched the room without success. "Where the hell are my keys?"

"John," said Declan.

"What, Declan?" Ramsey retorted as he swiped at some papers.

**

Watching his brother dig through a pile of discarded maps, Declan stilled himself and tried to project some measure of calm toward Ramsey.

"Stop doing that," said Ramsey, he yelled. "I don't want or need your interference."

Declan remained passive. "John," he said. "She's going to be okay."

Ramsey's head whipped back at him. "How the hell do you know that? You don't know where she is or what she's going through. God knows what he's doing to her."

Declan didn't let Ramsey's outburst stop him. "She's going to be okay."

Ramsey stopped for a second, but his manic energy wouldn't still. "You can't be sure of that. If she fights him or refuses to comply, he could hurt her."

Declan kept up his affirmation, knowing that Ramsey needed to believe in something. "She's going to be okay."

Declan's words seemed to pierce through the wall of fear that Ramsey had erected. He stood as if he carried a hundred pounds of weight around his neck. His frantic, searching gaze managed to stop long enough to find and hold Declan's. "You don't know that."

Declan didn't hesitate. "Yes. Yes, I do. I feel it in my bones."

Ramsey studied him, and Declan sensed his brother feeling for any indication that Declan might be lying, but Declan didn't waver. Ramsey's fatigue hit him, and with quivering legs, he sought and found the armrest and lowered himself down onto the couch. Releasing a deep breath, he clasped his shaking hands together to keep them still.

"Sherlock," asked Leroy, "you okay?"

Ramsey didn't answer but sucked in deep breaths of air as if he couldn't get enough. His body trembled and he blinked as if dizzy. He leaned forward and closed his eyes.

Hannah was up and sat next to him on the couch. "Hey, what's wrong?" she asked. She reached for his arm and felt his skin.

"I don't know," he answered. "I can't seem to get enough oxygen." His breathing picked up, and he turned pale. He squinted and held his chest.

Declan and Leroy kneeled beside him. "Take it easy," said Declan.

"I think you're having an anxiety attack," said Hannah. "Leroy, do you have a paper bag?"

Leroy stood, headed into the kitchen, and returned with a brown paper lunch bag. He handed it to Hannah.

She took it and opened it. "Breathe into this," she told Ramsey.

He did as she asked, breathing shallowly at first, but then deeper, and his breathing began to slow.

"Feeling better?" asked Hannah.

Ramsey opened his eyes. "A little," he said into the bag.

"Take your time. Are you dizzy?" she asked.

"Yes."

"It should pass in a minute or two. Just keep breathing." She kept watch over Ramsey. "You're lucky I'm a nurse." She patted his hand. "You'd have never made it this far."

Ramsey's breathing slowly returned to normal and he lifted the bag from his face. "Me and Sarah both," he added. He was still pale. Despite his cool skin, beads of sweat popped out on his forehead.

"I know you're not hungry," said Hannah, "but something in your stomach would help. You need fluids, too."

He rested the bag in his lap. "I'm fine."

"You look terrible," said Leroy, studying Ramsey's haggard face. "If Sarah walked in here right now, she'd give you an earful for not taking better care of yourself."

"God, I wish she would." Ramsey dropped his head. "I don't know what I'm going to do if..."

"Stop thinking like that," said Declan. "I know it's easy to think the worst and your imagination is running wild, but you have to remember something. He's not going to hurt her. He wants you to suffer, but not her. Even if she refuses to do what he wants, he won't harm her. But what he will do is hold her until he drives you stark raving mad, which I suspect is a big part of his plan."

"Well," said Ramsey, "It's working."

"Don't give him the satisfaction of falling apart," said Declan. "You do what you need to do to find her, but you have to take care of yourself in the process. You keep going like this, and you won't last long enough to enjoy it when we bring her back."

"And I don't want her yelling at me for not taking care of you while she was gone," said Leroy.

"I've seen her temper," said Declan. "Nobody wants her angry."

Ramsey smiled softly. "No," he said. "Nobody wants that."

"Olivia made some soup," said Leroy. "Think you could handle some?"

Ramsey sighed and sat back on the couch. "Okay," he said, finally giving in. "I hear you. I'll try some soup."

"Good," said Leroy, heading into the kitchen. "I'll bring you some water, too."

Hannah kept an eye on Ramsey. The phone rang, and she rose to answer it. "You stay where you are," she told him. She picked up the phone and followed up with another searcher calling in to report his progress.

Declan continued to monitor his stepbrother, and when his earlier frantic energy did not return, he sensed that Ramsey had achieved some measure of acceptance. He hoped that meant Ramsey would be a little easier to handle. He began to rise from his kneeling position.

"Declan?"

Declan stopped in mid-crouch. "What?"

"You meant it, didn't you?"

Declan sank back down and put a hand on Ramsey's shoulder. "Yes, I did. She'll be okay. I wouldn't lie to you. "

Ramsey said nothing, but Declan watched his lost look return. "Hey," he said. "If you eat all your soup and take a shower, I'll give you my piece of Olivia's chocolate cake."

Ramsey's lost look faded. "You don't eat chocolate cake."

"I know, but Leroy does."

"You're taking your life into your hands."

"I'm willing to do it if it will help you feel better."

"That must be one hell of a piece of cake."

Leroy walked into the room, holding a bowl of soup and carrying a tray table. "Anybody touches that last piece of cake, they'll pull back a stump."

CHAPTER FOUR

....

S ARAH DREAMED OF dark eyes and hair. She moved as if she were made of fog, undulating and wispy. Snaking through the darkness, she saw images—of a man who searched for her—appear and disappear. His nervous energy and taut nerves vibrated the air, and her fog-like presence shimmered in various shades of red and orange. Feeling his energy shift, she observed him as his legs turned shaky and his breathing turned shallow, and the fog that was her faded to hues of grays and browns. The urge to curl around him tugged at her, and her presence surrounded him, but his fear remained. Continuing to drift, she watched an unexpected smile light his face. The fog around her turned blue as his energy stilled, but then flared a vivid pink when a wave of love escaped him and pierced her. She reached out to him, but something distracted her, pulling her away. Feeling a pressure on her shoulder, she opened her eyes. Despite her desire to hold onto the tendrils of the dream, they slipped away like the last rays of light before the sun sets and were lost to her as her memory of the dark-eyed man vanished.

The ache of his absence lasted only for a moment, and then she found herself back in bed, her head still hurting, but now able to keep her eyes open without pain. The bedside lamp was on, and she could hear the surf, but the room had grown dark. She had no idea of the time, and she blinked, trying to remember where she was.

"Feeling any better?"

Hearing the voice and remembering the hand on her shoulder, she turned her head and saw Yates sitting with her. She focused in on him, trying to think.

Seeing her apparent confusion, he asked, "How are you?"

Her muddled mind began to clear, and she remembered where she was – a bedroom, no, her bedroom; the bedroom she shared with Yates. "Slowly coming back, I think," she said.

"You had me a little scared. This was a bad episode." He squeezed her hand. "How's your head?"

She shifted in the bed, pleased that her body did not resist. "Still pounding, but I can at least move now without wincing."

"That's good. Feel like sitting up? There's some water if you want some."

Orienting herself, she started to lift up. She had to take her time, because her head hurt with the movement. Managing to sit upright, she pushed back and leaned against the headboard of the large bed. She noticed she was wearing pajamas.

"Where did I get these?" she asked, feeling the material.

"I thought you'd be more comfortable. I didn't know how long you'd be asleep." His thumb caressed the back of her hand. "Do you like them? I bought them for you yesterday."

"They're soft," she said. "Comfortable, too."

"As pajamas should be."

"How long have I been out?"

He glanced at the bedside clock. "About thirty-six hours."

She rubbed her temples. "It feels like it."

"You want to lie back down? Sleep some more?" He handed her a water glass with a straw, and she drank from it.

"No, not right now." Her gaze traveled around the room.

He took back the water and put it on the nightstand, then moved on the bed and sat facing her. Still holding her hand, his thumb moved to her palm, and he began to trace over it in slow circles. "Good. You think you can eat something?"

"Hmm. Not sure."

"It would be good to get some nourishment."

"Sorry. I'm just not sure I can keep it down."

"You feel sick?" He continued to apply gentle pressure to the inside of her palm.

She closed her eyes, and the room spun. "Dizzy," she said.

"Take some breaths. It'll help."

Doing as he suggested, her head started to clear and her balance returned.

"Better?"

"Yes." The movement of his fingers against her palm helped her relax, and he smiled at her. "What?" she asked.

"I can feel you."

"Well," she said, "you are holding my hand." She glanced down at his fingers entwined with hers.

"True." His thumb continued to gently rub her palm. "You don't mind, do you?"

Feeling his touch, Sarah felt something in her shift, as if a lever had moved from one side to the other, and she began to feel a whisper of heat build on the inside of her hand. Out of nowhere, her appetite ignited and her stomach growled.

"Hungry now?"

The heat grew and traveled past her wrist and up to her elbow. She relaxed even more as it made its way up her arm and into her shoulder and neck and down into her torso. Her body warmed as her muscles eased. Sighing, she leaned her head back against the headboard. "What's on the menu?"

He grinned. "Whatever your heart desires." He frowned for a moment. "Except for hamburgers. Julian didn't buy any, so don't ask for hamburgers."

Smiling back at him, the warmth enveloped her and the heat bloomed in her belly. Feeling it travel down further, she suddenly wasn't thinking of food any more. Moving her own hand, she trailed her fingers alongside his, and she met his gaze. "What else is on the menu?"

His eyes never wavered from hers. She felt his uncertainty, but also his desire. When he didn't react to her question, she stilled her hand. "What?"

He studied her in the lamplight. "You're beautiful."

The circular motion of his thumb against her palm made it hard for her to concentrate. "I am?"

"Yes." His eyes caressed her face. "I can't believe you're mine. You take my breath away."

The heat churned in her now. "I hardly think I look all that desirable at the moment."

"You're always desirable to me."

Her breathing picked up and the heat increased, and a sudden need for him overcame her. Her next words to him surprised her. "Show me."

He hesitated, and she waited as he seemed to make a decision. Moving closer, he leaned toward her and brought his face up to hers. The anticipation of his kiss made her heart thump, but he surprised her when his lips moved away from hers and up to her forehead, where he gently kissed her.

"What?" she asked when he pulled back.

"Don't think I'm not tempted," he said, "because right now it's taking everything I have not to take you in my arms and devour you, but I have to honor your request."

"My request?"

"Well, both of ours, actually."

"What do you mean?"

His free hand came up and stroked her cheek. "After the accident, we postponed our wedding until you were better. Remember?"

She tried to think, but it made her head flare. "It's a little hazy."

"You had a severe concussion and with your memory loss, we..."

"We, what?"

He sighed. "Even though you were improving, you still had these relapses. We decided it would be best to wait until we married before we were intimate again."

Sarah tried to remember. "We did?"

He gave her a sad smile. "I know. What were we thinking?"

"Why did we do that?"

"Well, at first it was doctor's orders. You were injured. Then, once you began to improve, you still had periods of migraines and memory loss. I didn't want you to wake up in bed with me and not know who I was."

She considered that. "I admit that would have been awkward."

"Yes, definitely." His fingers continued to graze her cheek, and the heat in her intensified. He remained close enough that she considered pulling him near and kissing him despite whatever agreement they had made.

"So," he continued, "after some long discussions, we decided that we would marry when you felt ready, and if we waited, then it would be romantic, as if it was the first time." His hand dropped from her cheek. "Plus, it serves as motivation to get married sooner rather than later. We've already postponed it once."

"You're saying that we decided to wait?"

Despite his hesitation, his eyes conveyed that it was taking every ounce of control not to touch more than her cheek. "Considering you don't remember the conversation, I'd say you're still recovering."

"But what did the doctor say? Did he say I'd remember everything?"

"He couldn't be sure."

"Well, don't you think we're setting ourselves up for a long wait?"

He shrugged. "To be honest, this is the first time you've even brought it up. You haven't really been in the mood."

Still feeling the heat in her belly, that revelation surprised her. "Then maybe we should consider this a marked improvement."

"Maybe we should."

The desire to be with him grew, and she heard herself ask, "So, what do you say?"

"About what?"

"About getting married? Maybe it's time to move our timetable up." A brief flare of warning tugged at her, and the urge to pull away almost stopped her, but it evaporated before she could act on it.

Watching him study her, she sensed something stir within him, and he smiled as if he'd conquered the world. "Perhaps we should." He paused. "But only if you're sure. I told you I'd wait, no matter how long it took. And I meant it."

The heat began to wane, but she still felt its pull. "Waiting is for hospitals and traffic." She let go of his hand and stroked his arm. "I'm ready to move forward." She paused. "I want to be your wife."

Feeling the power that her words had on him, she held her breath as he leaned close and kissed her forehead again, lingering there. This time, though, his lips moved down to kiss her nose and then lowered again to hover near her mouth. Waiting, she looked into his eyes and blinked when she thought she saw his blue eyes turn a chocolate brown. Staring at the strange transformation, she was unsure of what to think, but then his lips moved in and met hers, and the strange occurrence passed. The kiss lingered and held, and she kissed him back. Her desire flared, but before it could escalate, he pulled away.

"Okay then," he said, exhaling a deep breath. "If you're sure, then I'll make the arrangements." He hovered near her. "And the sooner, the better, because I look forward to continuing this..." His hand came up again to touch her face, and then he trailed his fingers down her arm, causing tingles where he touched her. "...after we marry."

The heat bubbled up again, and she brought her palm up to cup his cheek. "At least I know I'm marrying an honorable man."

He hesitated. "There are a few out there who would disagree with you." His fingers rested over hers.

"I doubt that," she said, "but who cares? The only thing that matters is the two of us."

His blue eyes flared. "I couldn't agree with you more, Sarah." Hearing her stomach grumble, he chuckled. "Now how about we go raid that refrigerator?"

**

Several hours later, Sarah stretched. After Yates had scrambled up some eggs the previous night and they'd both eaten, her lethargy had returned, and he'd insisted she go back to bed. He didn't want her to trigger another headache. Now, after a solid night's sleep, she felt invigorated. Awakening alone, she rose from the bed and entered the bathroom to study herself in the mirror. Her face still showed the remnants of sleep, and she needed a shower. Thinking about her clothes, she caught sight of the closet door through the mirror. A brief memory flickered of the room, and she remembered the size of it.

She walked inside. It was as large as she recalled, but now it looked fuller. Clothes filled the closet, and by the looks of it, they were mostly hers. She raked her hands over the hanging items and recognized many of them, although several still had tags on them. The center console held nothing but shoes. She saw many that she recalled wearing, but others that had had no wear at all. She didn't remember being such a clotheshorse.

Finding something to wear, she entered the large walk-in shower and turned on the spray, making it hot enough for steam to coat the mirrors. She sighed as her weariness and fatigue from the past few days began to lift. After finding her shampoo and bath products, she lathered up and rinsed. Once clean, she grabbed a towel and wrapped it around herself. The mirrors were steamed over, and she flipped on the fan and opened the bathroom door to help the air clear. She jumped when she saw Yates standing there, holding a glass of water.

"You scared me," she said.

He turned his lips up in a smile. "Sorry. I just wanted to check on you."

"Why didn't you come in?"

He looked her over. "Because I didn't trust myself."

His stare made her feel warm, and she blushed. "Probably a wise choice."

He didn't keep up the banter, but instead held the water glass out to her. "You need to take your medicine." His other hand held a yellow pill identical to the one she'd taken yesterday.

"I do?" she asked. "How long do I have to take this?"

"Until the doctor says otherwise. I don't need you falling ill again just as we're about to say our vows."

Reluctantly, she reached for it and swallowed it with the water.

"How are you feeling?" he asked.

"Much better."

"Good. I've got a delicious pancake breakfast waiting on the patio. Get dressed and join me."

"Pancakes? You're turning into quite the cook."

"I can't take credit. Isabelle made them."

"Isabelle?"

"You likely don't remember her. I just hired her. She cooks and keeps up the house. Between her and Julian, they maintain the domestic duties, which gives me more time with you."

That made her think of the closet. "By the way, why do I have so many clothes in the closet? I don't recall buying them."

He gave her a sheepish grin. "You can blame me for that. I love to buy you things while I'm out. It's a bad habit."

"Well, I think I'm set for now. I could wear a different outfit every day of the year and still not wear everything that's in there."

"I admit, I've been a bit of a shopaholic, but when it comes to you, I can't help myself." He nodded. "But I see your point. I'll refrain from buying any more clothes." His eyes lingered on her towel. "And speaking of clothes, you need to put some on before I forget our agreement."

Smiling, she looked down at herself. "Much as I enjoy tempting you, I'll get dressed."

He tipped his head toward the bathroom counter. "Oh, and your necklace is on the countertop."

Not understanding, she said, "My necklace?"

"Yes." He pointed. "Right over there. Your necklace with the hummingbird."

She felt around her neck. "I thought..."

"What?"

Looking over at the counter, her eye caught a twinkle of light and she saw it sitting next to the far sink. "I don't know. I thought it was missing."

"No," he said. "It's where you always keep it before you go to bed."

She tried to think, but the pill was taking effect and her mind went hazy, and it was harder to focus.

"I'll be downstairs," he said. "Don't take too long. You don't want the pancakes to get cold."

"Okay. I'll be right down." For the briefest moment, Sarah felt uncomfortable, as if she were out of place, but then the sensation disappeared. Feeling her hunger for breakfast, she dropped the towel and began to get dressed.

CHAPTER FIVE

....

L EROY WALKED INTO the dining room, where Ramsey
sat amid a pile of papers, rubbing his head.
"Here," said Leroy. "Take this."

Ramsey looked up. "What?"

Leroy held out two pills. "It's aspirin."

Ramsey stared at the pills and then reached for them, swallowing them down with the water. "Thanks."

It was mid-afternoon, and now forty-eight hours into Sarah's disappearance. After his apparent anxiety attack the previous day, Ramsey had remained at Leroy's house. For some reason, he'd felt close to Sarah at Leroy's, as if she knew he was there, and in some non-physical way, he'd felt her nearness and didn't want to lose that connection to her.

Declan's team as well as those sent by the Council were still out looking, and he continued to hold onto the fact that she would be found, and that Y would not hurt her because his main goal was to hurt Ramsey instead. Ramsey told himself that constantly in order to keep the fear at bay, but as the hours passed, his doubt grew, and it was all he could do to stay put and wait.

He stared at the map again. The search area now extended in a wide circle away from the midpoint, which was Sullivan's. It was a large area to cover, and he knew it could take weeks to fully check the area. Sighing, he thought of Sarah and sent out his own signal, telling her to hold on and that they would find her.

Leroy sat next to him. "Declan should be back soon."

Declan had left to meet with the Council, updating them on their progress. "Yeah," Ramsey answered.

They heard the front door open and close. "It's me," they heard as Hannah came into the room.

They watched her put down two bags and take off her jacket. "What'd you get us?" asked Leroy.

"Sandwiches. Help yourself." She pulled out cellophane-wrapped food and placed it on the table. "Anybody thirsty?" She walked into the kitchen.

"Just a water for me," said Leroy. None of them had managed to eat breakfast, other than coffee. He pulled out a ham and cheese for Ramsey, who showed little interest. "Here, Sherlock. Eat."

Ramsey pulled himself out of his daze to see Leroy holding a sandwich out to him. "Why are you always giving me food?"

"What kind of question is that?" asked Leroy. "It's the same reason I insist you sleep. You're not much good without either. Now eat something."

Ramsey reacted as if on auto-pilot. He took the food and put it in front of him, staring blankly at it.

Leroy reached over and unwrapped it for him.

Hannah returned with two waters and placed one in front of Leroy. Seeing Ramsey had some already, she kept the other one for herself.

Sitting in silence, Hannah and Leroy began to eat. Ramsey took a few bites, but with little enthusiasm. He barely tasted his sandwich, and as much as he hated to think about it, he wondered how much longer he could hold out like this, with no news or indication of Sarah's whereabouts. Two days had felt like two years. He didn't want to know what four days or ten days or, God forbid, ten months felt like. His thoughts were interrupted by the sound of the front door opening and Declan's voice in the house.

"Where?" he heard Declan say. Declan walked into the room holding his phone. Ramsey immediately sensed Declan's energy, and the two of them made eye contact.

"Down by the coast?" Declan asked.

Ramsey stood. Declan made a gesture signaling that he needed a pen. Leroy got him one and Hannah handed him some paper. "Give me the address." He held the phone to his ear with his shoulder and wrote. "Text it to me, too. Thanks, Sylvia." He ended the call. "They got a hit on the sketch of Yates."

"Where?" asked Ramsey.

"About an hour away. Down by the coast. Guy in a coffee shop recognized him."

Ramsey moved to find his keys as Leroy stood to find his jacket.

"He didn't know his name, though."

"I don't care," said Ramsey. "I want to talk to him."

"Okay," said Declan. "Let's go." He glanced at Hannah. "You stay and hold down the fort. Call me if you get any updates."

"You let me know if you learn anything," said Hannah.

"We will," said Declan, following Leroy and Ramsey out the door.

An hour later, Leroy pulled into the parking lot of the "The Big Cup" coffee shop. A coffee cup with pink neon steam blinked from the window. Ramsey had the car door open before Leroy could put it into park. Declan jumped out of the back seat and Leroy joined him, and they followed Ramsey in and up to the counter, where a woman wearing an orange uniform shirt with a monogrammed coffee cup on the pocket stood to take their orders.

"I'm looking for a man named Jonah..." Ramsey looked at Declan.

"Jonah Duncan," Declan finished. "He works here?"

The woman behind the register stared at the three men. "Any of you want any coffee?"

"We don't want any coffee," said Ramsey. "What we want is to speak to Jonah Duncan. Is he here?"

Her curious gaze drifted back behind the counter. "I think he's on break."

"Can we speak to him?" asked Ramsey.

"You want me to get him?"

Ramsey tried not to show his impatience. "Yes."

"Please," finished Declan.

Another employee walked by, and the woman by the register said, "Fran, would you get Jonah?"

The woman named Fran stopped. "Why? He's on break."

"Somebody wants to talk to him." The woman nodded her head at the men at the counter.

Fran narrowed her eyes at them. "You guys want any coffee?"

Ramsey grunted, and Declan answered, "No, thank you. We'd just like to talk to Jonah."

"What for? You guys the police?" asked Fran.

Ramsey almost launched himself over the counter. "We are not the police. Would you just get Jonah?"

Declan put a hand on his arm, and Ramsey restrained himself.

"Jonah's not in any trouble," Declan continued. "We're just looking for someone, and we're hoping Jonah can help us." He flashed a twenty-dollar bill. "We'll make it worth his time."

Fran studied them and the money and must have decided they were telling the truth. "Fine," she said. "Hold on."

The first woman watched the exchange, and as Fran walked away, she looked at Declan. "Someone came in earlier asking questions. Did someone go missing? Is this like one of those CSI cases?"

Leroy sighed as Ramsey rolled his eyes.

"Yes...Linda," said Declan, reading her name tag. "You could say that."

Linda's eyes perked up. "I love those shows. You know, I just came on duty. You want me to look at your pictures?"

Just then, a short, pudgy man came around the corner. His baby face gave him the appearance of a teenager, but he had to be in his mid to late twenties. "You guys looking for me?"

"Yes. Are you Jonah?" asked Declan.

"Am I in trouble?"

"No, you're not in any trouble," said Declan. "You mind if we talk to you for a minute?"

Jonah eyed the clock on the wall. "I got five minutes left on my break."

"That's all we need." Declan pulled the pictures from his pocket. "Someone came by earlier with these pictures. I was told you recognized this man?" He held the picture out, and Jonah, along with Fran and Linda, leaned over to look.

Jonah studied the picture. "Yeah, I recognize him. He comes in for coffee sometimes in the morning. Wears a nice suit. That's why I remember him."

"When's the last time he came in?" asked Ramsey.

"Uh, I don't know. Last time I saw him was probably a couple of weeks ago. I only work two mornings a week, though. He may have come in at another time."

"You know his name?" asked Declan.

"No."

"Does he pay with a credit card?" asked Leroy.

"No. He always pays in cash."

"Cash?" asked Ramsey.

"Yup, Big bills, too. That's another reason he stands out. I have to get change from the safe."

"What about the woman?" asked Declan, showing them Sarah's photo. "Have you seen her?"

Jonah studied the picture. "No. Never seen her."

Ramsey scanned the front of the shop. "What about cameras. Do you have cameras?"

"Are you kidding?" asked Fran. "We can't get the owner to buy us cups for the employee room."

Linda snorted. "Ain't that the truth."

Ramsey's frustration mounted. "You mean to tell me that we can't find out who this man is?"

"I can tell you who he is," said Linda.

That got their attention. "Who?" asked Declan.

"I was here last week, covering for Manny. You know he got sick, right?" She shot a look at Fran.

"Yeah, poor Manny," said Fran, frowning. "I think he's still in the hospital."

"I know. And he's got no insurance," said Linda, shaking her head.

"You know," said Fran, "Martin's thinking of throwing a fund raiser to help him out."

"Martin is? That's a great idea." said Linda. She leaned a hip against the counter. "You know, I heard he broke up with Sheila. So sad."

Ramsey was ready to yank Linda over the counter. "The man?" he asked.

"Oh, yeah," said Linda. "Well, he came in and ordered coffee. Then he struck up a conversation, which was odd because the place was busy. I thought he was cute and all, you know? The tall, beach boy thing, but smart with that suit and all." Her gaze met Declan's. "You know the type?"

Declan paused. "Not really."

Ramsey thought he'd been tortured enough these past two days, but now he realized how much further torture could go. "And?" he prompted.

"So, he's talking and I'm answering, thinking maybe he's interested, but then realizing that he's just chatty. I mean what guy like that goes for a girl behind a coffee counter, right?"

"Don't sell yourself short, honey," said Fran. "You're a great catch."

"Thank you, sweetie," said Linda, smiling at her friend.

"Oh, for God's sake..." said Ramsey.

"Ladies," interjected Leroy, his own impatience rising. "I apologize for my friend, but the woman in the picture has gone missing and we think this man may be responsible, so we need whatever help you can give us as quickly as you can. Her life may depend on it."

Both women's eyes widened. "This really is a CSI case, huh?" asked Linda.

"The man?" asked Leroy, pointing at the picture. "Who is he?"

Linda returned to her story. "Well, when he left, he tipped me."

"So?" asked Declan.

Linda said flatly, "It was a hundred-dollar bill."

"What?" asked Ramsey, right along with Fran and Jonah.

"Yeah. I couldn't believe it, so I says to him, 'If you're gonna give me that, you might as well give me your number, too.' Thought I'd be bold, you know?"

"What happened?" asked Fran.

"He gave me his card."

"He did?" asked Ramsey. "Where is it?"

Linda shrugged. "I threw it away."

Ramsey couldn't believe it. "You what?"

"Why?" asked Fran.

"There was nothing on it."

"What do you mean?" asked Declan.

"The only thing on it was his name. No contact info or nothing." She crossed her arms in front of her. "I looked him up online, but found nothing, so I threw it away. Guess he was messing with me."

Fran shoulders dropped. "He doesn't know what he's missing, Linda."

"The name, Linda," said Ramsey. "What was his name?"

She stared up at the ceiling, thinking. "It started with a Y. Yane...Yale...no...Yates. That's it. Yates."

"Yates who, Linda?" said Declan. "Think."

Linda tapped her chin. "Yates...Yates...something. I think it had an 'r' in it."

The air in all three men seemed to deflate. Ramsey slumped and gripped the counter.

"No, wait," she said. "I think I remember. Reddington. That's it. Yates Reddington. I'm sure of it."

**

Sarah watched the waves roll into the shore, break, and rake against the sand. Eyeing the horizon, she admired the hues of pink and orange in the sky as the sun descended. Standing out on the patio of the house, she listened to the seagulls, and the breeze fluttered her hair. She'd spent most of the day just wandering, walking through the house and the extensive grounds and familiarizing herself with her surroundings. Some of it she'd recognized, but other areas were foreign to her. She'd met and spoken with Isabelle, or Izzy as she preferred, who was the cook and housekeeper. She'd met the groundskeeper, a somewhat shy fellow who looked at her as if she'd risen from the grave. She remembered Julian, and she'd made a point of speaking to him as well. If she was going to live in this house, then she ought to know everyone connected to it.

Although why she remembered so little concerned her. Yates had explained that they had not spent an extensive amount of time here prior to her accident, which would explain her lack of memory, but as she gazed at the ocean, she realized that there were other pockets of history lost to her, and it began to bother her.

Feeling a presence behind her, she smiled when she felt arms encircle her. After breakfast, Yates had disappeared into his home office in the basement, and he'd reappeared only for lunch. He'd allowed Sarah some time to herself in order to help her adjust back into her routine, although what that routine was, she had no idea. Bits and pieces of flashbacks occasionally sparked, but they made no sense, and she couldn't put any pieces together.

"What is it?" he asked, sensing her questions.

She rested her hands over hers. "I still have so much missing."

"What do you mean?"

"I mean I don't remember things. Things I should know."

"Like what?"

She continued to gaze at the ocean. "Like how we met."

"You don't recall?"

"No."

He pressed his chin against her ear. "We met in a coffee shop."

"We did?"

"Yes. I took an empty seat at your table and struck up a conversation." He held her close. "Remember?"

A vague image of him sitting across from her at a table flashed in her mind. "Yes. I think I have a vague recollection."

"Good. What else?"

"How long have we known each other?"

He paused. "Honestly? I feel as if I've known you my whole life. But if you want to get exact, we've sort of had a whirlwind romance." Taking one of her hands, he began to gently rub his thumb over her palm.

"How long is a whirlwind?" she asked, feeling herself relax. She leaned back against him.

"Six months."

"Six months?"

"Well, we didn't get serious until a few months in."

"Wait. You mean we've only been seeing each other for a few months?" She couldn't help but feel surprised.

He didn't answer immediately. Instead, he turned her around and led her to a nearby bench, where they both sat while he continued to hold her hand.

"Sarah, there are a few things I should discuss with you before we go any further with this."

That made her sit up. "What?"

"I hesitated bringing them up because it upsets you, but if we're going to marry, you need to know everything."

Her hand squeezed his as his thumb rubbed over skin. "Tell me."

Yates looked out over the ocean. "You've been through a lot recently. And it's not just about the accident."

Her anxiety notched up. "Is this about me being a Red-Line?"

"You remember?"

"That part is hard to forget. I'm still getting used to it."

"Do you remember when you found out?"

Sarah squinted and held her head. "Someone told me, but I don't remember who."

"I can tell you who."

"You can?"

Turning serious, he said, "Sarah, not long after we met, I realized who you were. You were special. I could tell. You and I are basically the only two remaining Red-Lines, plus we have similar origins, so it made sense why we hit it off so quickly. But when it came time to tell you about who you were and what you were about to experience, it was taken out of my hands."

"What do you mean?"

"There is a Council made up of members of our Community who were not in agreement with how your case should be handled."

"Council?" Her memory flashed on a stylish woman with silver-white hair. "Morgana?"

His eyes widened. "See, your memory is improving."

"What did the Council have to do with it?"

"They did not agree that I should tell you. And before I realized what was happening, they had taken you and assigned a Protector."

"A Protector?"

"Yes. Do you remember him?" The pressure of his thumb against her hand increased.

She had no recollection of a Protector. "No."

"His name is John. John Ramsey."

For a split second, Sarah sensed the familiarity of the name, but the pressure on her hand distracted her and the moment of recall vanished. "I don't know him."

"Sarah." He faced her on the bench. "The Council felt it best if he told you about your impending Shift and helped you through it. He was assigned. I had no idea where you were or how to stop him."

"Stop him?"

"Yes. He did as he was instructed. He got you successfully through it, but he..."

"He what?"

"He became attracted to you. He developed some sort of obsession. His friends helped him, and I couldn't get to you because he took you and hid you."

"Hid me?"

"He wouldn't let you leave."

Another brief flash hit when she recalled yelling at a man, feeling intensely angry. She'd gone to her room and slammed the door. She blinked as the memory faded.

"You tried to escape, but he brought you back. Finally, though, you managed to get out. You took a car, but in your haste to escape, you lost control and had your accident. That's when I found you again. You were in the hospital, and I've been nursing you back to health ever since." Sighing as if the story exhausted him, he closed his eyes. "It was the worst time of my life. Not knowing where you were, or what he was doing to you."

Memories of beeping machines and stark hospital rooms sparked in her mind, although she had no memory of being ill. "I don't remember that."

His eyes opened. "The doctor said it would be unlikely if you ever remembered the accident or the immediate aftermath. It's not uncommon with a traumatic head injury."

She sighed, wishing she could recall the events of her past. "What happened to him?"

"Who?"

"This John Ramsey person."

"I don't know. After I found you, he disappeared. Probably realized he'd lost his chance with you." His gaze drifted. "I hope to God I never see him again. I don't know what I'd do."

"Hey," she said, feeling his anger. "I'm here, aren't I?" She put her hand on his cheek. "You got the girl, remember?"

He smiled. "Does this mean you still want to marry me?"

Heat slid up her arm, and warmth spread through her midsection. "The sooner, the better."

His thumb stroked her hand. "I've made arrangements with a justice of the peace. You told me before you weren't big on large ceremonies. Is that still okay?"

Sarah couldn't agree more. "Absolutely. The simpler, the better. Can I invite Rachel and Aunt Gerry?"

His face fell.

"What?" she asked.

"Just be prepared. They don't know about me."

"They don't know about you? Why not?"

"You didn't tell them."

"I didn't?"

"When we initially met, we kept it a secret. And then you suddenly learned you were a Red-Line and a member of an alien species, and things became a bit more complicated."

That did ring a bell. She couldn't reveal her true nature to her best friend and aunt. "Yes, I can see why."

"But if you want to invite them, I won't stop you."

"Well." She considered it. "Maybe it would be better to tell them after the fact."

"Whatever you want."

Sarah nodded. "Then I guess it's official." She leaned in close. "We're getting married."

His lips moved close to hers. "How's this weekend sound?"

She kissed him. "Terrific."

CHAPTER SIX

....

RAMSEY SHOVED HIS seat back and stood, then turned and pushed the chair back in, slamming it hard into the table. The table shook, and Leroy jumped with the sound. "Hey, watch what you're breaking, Sherlock. Olivia will come after you if you chip the furniture."

Ramsey barely heard him as he raked his hands through his hair. "How can we not find this guy?"

The three of them sat at Leroy's dining table, the day after speaking with Jonah and getting Yates's full name. Hannah had gone to lie down an hour earlier after sleeping little the night before. They'd been on the computer looking for answers for several hours, getting little sleep themselves as they followed every lead. The searchers continued to look, now asking people if they knew a Yates Reddington and showing his sketch. So far, they'd had no luck on either front.

Declan had the laptop open in front of him. "He obviously owns nothing in his name."

Ramsey paced. "How does a guy with his kind of money not show up on the internet?" He looked at the time. It was now nearing seventy-two hours since Sarah had been taken.

"He must have a hell of a team that ensures he stays off of any web search." Declan closed the laptop, frustrated over their lack of results.

Leroy rubbed his tired eyes and ran a hand over his shaved head. "What about the Council? Have they had any luck?"

"I gave them the name, but I haven't heard anything." Declan closed his eyes. "Reddington."

Ramsey narrowed his gaze at him. "What is it?" He approached the table. "Something's on your mind."

Declan snapped back to attention. "That name. For some reason, it rings a bell, but I can't place it."

Ramsey leaned over and put his hands on the table. "Well, think. Use those superhero gifts of yours and figure it out."

Declan turned stony. "What do you think I've been doing all morning?"

"Well, think harder, damn it."

"You know," answered Declan, his own temper sparking, "if you would stop jumping down everybody's throats every time we moved the wrong way, it would help."

Ramsey banged his hand down. "What do you want me do, Declan? Knit myself a scarf while I wait to find out what this man is doing to the woman I love?"

Declan erupted. "That's not what I mean, and you know it."

"That's enough." Leroy stood. "You two don't need this right now. I know we're all strung out and tired, but pull it together. We're close, so don't lose your cool."

Declan dropped and held his head. "Sorry."

Ramsey turned and walked away, taking a breath as he collected himself. "No, I'm sorry." He paused for a moment. "It's just this waiting."

"I know," said Declan.

Leroy sat again, satisfied the crisis had passed. "You know, Sherlock, I can sympathize with your mother. Did you snap at her like that?"

Ramsey glanced at him. "Let's just say I didn't make it easy on her."

"I can imagine."

"Mother..." Declan said, his eyes furrowing.

"What?" asked Ramsey.

Declan's eyes widened. "Mother," he said again as he pulled his laptop open and began typing.

"What are you talking about?" asked Leroy.

"Did you remember something?" asked Ramsey.

"Edward Bright," said Declan.

"Who?" asked Leroy.

"Edward Bright," repeated Declan, flipping through files on the computer, searching for the right one.

"The man who tried to take Sarah on the street?" asked Ramsey.

"Yes, and Yates's pseudo-father, according to Sarah," said Declan. "We did a full background check on him. That's where I remember the name." He found the file he was looking for. "Here it is."

"Reddington? You remember the name in connection to him?" asked Ramsey, moving closer as Declan read.

Declan's gaze moved over the file. "Here." He pointed at the computer.

"What?" asked Leroy. He stood and moved behind Declan.

"Edward's mother," said Declan. "Her name was Emily Reddington."

"His mother?" asked Ramsey. "But what's the connection to Yates?"

"I don't know," answered Declan. "But if Yates was close to Edward..."

"Maybe he was close to his mother?" asked Leroy.

Ramsey pursed his lips as realization dawned. "That's it. He took her name." He spoke to Declan. "Where is she?"

Declan kept reading. "She died ten years ago."

The energy drained from the men. "Damn it," said Ramsey, walking away. "Can't we catch a break?"

"But I know where she is."

"Where?" asked Leroy.

Declan tapped at the screen. "The Peaceful Palms Cemetery. She was buried there four years ago."

"But she died ten years ago," said Ramsey.

"Exactly," said Declan. "She was moved and given a very expensive headstone. I doubt the plot she's in is cheap, either." He raised a brow.

Ramsey understood. "He paid for her plot and tombstone."

"And they likely have a record of it at the cemetery," said Declan.

"And a next of kin information?" asked Leroy.

They froze for a moment before Declan was out of his seat and Ramsey was headed for the door.

Leroy headed for the guest room. "I'll tell Hannah."

**

Two hours later, they had an address. They'd managed to find the manager of the funeral home and cemetery, and after relaying a very touching story of how they'd known Emily as children and were hoping to find her extended family, the man had relinquished the address, making them promise that they would deny any link to him if someone asked how'd they'd found it.

Now they were close to the house they'd been searching for. Leroy drove as Ramsey gripped the door handle with white knuckles.

Sensing Ramsey's relief at finding the address but feeling his worry, Declan began to wonder how to best handle this situation. He doubted they'd even be allowed onto the property.

"John," he said from the back seat.

"What?"

"You need to consider a few things before we get there."

"Like what?"

"He's not going to let us walk in and take her back. We may not even be able to get inside."

Ramsey stared straight ahead. "I know."

"We can't just barge in."

They entered an upscale community and drove past large estates, almost all of them bordered by high walls. "That's exactly what he wants," said Ramsey.

Leroy glanced over at him. "What do you mean?"

"He wants to torture me. He'll let us inside. I'm just not sure what will happen after that."

"We have to play this safe," said Declan.

"I'm not leaving without her. I'll play his game if he wants, but if she's there, we're getting her out."

"We can't risk her getting hurt in the process," said Declan.

"He has to know we'd come for her," said Leroy.

"He does," said Ramsey.

"Just don't do anything stupid," said Declan.

"If you get a chance to get her out, then do it," said Ramsey. "Don't worry about me."

"We're not just going to stand there and let you throw yourself to the wolves," said Leroy.

"She's the priority," said Ramsey. "Get her out first."

Declan and Leroy didn't respond, but their eyes met in the rearview mirror.

"We're here," said Leroy, approaching a tall, Spanish-style stucco wall with a driveway which led up to ornate iron gates. He turned, pulled up, and stopped before an intercom that sat among the manicured shrubs lining the driveway. He rolled down the window. "Here we go," he said, pushing the button.

They waited for an eternal ten seconds before hearing a voice answer. "Yes? Can I help you?"

Leroy sat quiet for a second until Ramsey solved his muteness problem when he leaned over and answered, "John Ramsey to see Yates Reddington."

Leroy barely stifled a groan.

"Great," said Declan. "That ought to set the stage."

"It's not like he doesn't know it's me," said Ramsey.

There was silence on the intercom before they heard a buzzing and the gates in front of them began to open. Leroy moved the car forward up the driveway.

"See? What'd I tell you?" asked Ramsey.

Declan felt a cold feeling move through him as he began to realize that perhaps they were walking into more than they were ready for. Yates had prepared for their arrival. Declan felt the impulse to tell Leroy to turn around, but knew they had already come too far to turn back.

Leroy drove up the long driveway, passing tall, heavy-trunked trees and uniform green grass. A large fountain with cozy cherubs spewing water greeted them as they approached the front entrance. He stopped the car. Ramsey opened the door and got out, looking up at the large Spanish-style estate with its tiled roof and large carved wooden doors.

Leroy and Declan stepped out of the car, and Leroy whistled. "Big house."

"I've seen bigger," said Ramsey, walking up the pavestone steps, with Declan and Leroy behind him.

"Just try and stay cool," said Declan.

"I'm as cool as ice cream," answered Ramsey, ringing the bell.

54

Leroy and Declan both released pent-up breaths as the door opened and a short man with dark hair and a goatee welcomed them, although Declan could feel from the man that he was almost as anxious as they were.

"Please come in," he said. "We've been expecting you."

"You could have called," said Ramsey. "It would have been easier." He walked past the man and entered the house.

Leroy and Declan followed.

They found themselves in a large foyer with high ceilings and a staircase with an intricately carved banister leading to the second floor. The interior was mostly white, with white furniture and large contemporary pieces of art decorating the walls. A doorway led into an extensive kitchen, den, and dining area where a large, brightly colored fresh flower arrangement took center stage. They could see into the living room, where big picture windows stood open, and they perused a spectacular view of the ocean as the curtains blew in with the breeze.

As they studied the view, a man walked in from the living area. He was dressed in casual brown pants and a white cotton shirt, and sandals adorned his feet. His hair was ruffled, although it still looked perfect, as if it were intentional for it to look slightly tossed by the breeze.

Putting his hands in his pockets, he regarded his guests. "Thank you, Julian."

Julian nodded and made a quick retreat from the room.

"So," he said, "I see you found me."

"You knew we would," answered Ramsey.

The man smiled and Declan knew this was Yates. "Did my little trail of crumbs finally work? How is Linda, by the way? Did she make you some coffee?"

Seeing Yates for the first time, Declan felt a wave of malevolence emanate from him. He stilled himself, trying not to recoil, but Yates narrowed his eyes as if sensing his discord. "So, we finally meet."

Declan met his gaze but said nothing.

"I wish I could say it was a pleasure," said Yates.

"I don't," answered Declan, feeling a hatred for the man well up inside him.

Yates only grinned before speaking to Leroy. "And Sampson. Ramsey's eternal long-suffering friend." Leroy stared back with unreadable but intense eyes. "Still watching out for him, I see."

Leroy stood quietly as if to keep the situation calm, but the tension in his posture and his set jaw was evident.

Getting no response from Leroy, Yates turned his attention back to Ramsey. "All healed up? How's the belly?"

Ramsey didn't take the bait, but instead got straight to the point. "Where is she?"

Yates just stood with his hands in his pockets. "I'm afraid you've wasted your time. You've made a grave error."

Ramsey pointed, his body rigid. "You've made the error. Where is she? What have you done to her?"

"I've done nothing. Nature just took its course."

Ramsey stilled. "What do you mean?"

"I told you she would come to me of her own free will, and she has."

"You're a liar," said Ramsey. "You drugged her and you took her."

"She fell ill," said Yates. "I merely helped her and brought her back here. She's been recuperating ever since. She's been free to leave at any time."

Ramsey narrowed his eyes. "You can play all the games you want, but I know Sarah. She would never stay if given the choice."

"Wouldn't she?" asked Yates. The smug grin never left his face.

"What are you saying?" asked Declan.

"Oh, come on, gentlemen. Look at this logically. She was never going to stay with any of you." Yates waved a hand at Ramsey. "You were a temporary distraction as she made it through her Shift. Then afterword, you pretended to protect her, when I was never after her in the first place. You're the one who tried to control her. But she knows who she is now, and she knows who I am." He paused. "And she's chosen me."

Ramsey sneered. "Really, Yates? You expect me to believe that? I wasn't sure at first, but now I am. You are as stupid as you look."

Yates did not argue, but quieted as if sensing something. Declan felt it too and the hairs on the back of his neck stood up. "Well," said Yates, "if I'm so stupid, why don't you ask her yourself?"

The room was quiet for a second, but then Declan heard the sound of a door opening and closing from nearby. "Yates," they heard from behind the stairs, "I've got a great idea. The beach. We should have the ceremony on the..." Sarah came around the corner and stopped. "Oh," she said. "I'm sorry. I didn't realize you had company."

Ramsey froze. Declan did the same and looked her over. She appeared at ease and comfortable in loose-fitting white cotton pants and a green narrow-cut T-shirt. She wore flip-flops on her feet, her hair kissed her shoulders, and her tan face revealed she'd spent some time in the sun.

"Sarah?" Ramsey asked. He started to approach her, but stopped, and Declan sensed what he'd felt – Sarah's apprehension.

Sarah's eyes rounded in surprise, and she glanced at Leroy and Declan. "Do I know you?" she asked, walking over to Yates, who put his arm around her.

Ramsey paled. "Sarah," said Ramsey. "It's me."

His worst fears realized, Declan shared a bewildered look with Leroy.

"It's John," said Ramsey, in disbelief. "John Ramsey."

She tensed and leaned into Yates. "Oh," she said.

"Sarah," said Yates, "Why don't you go upstairs? I'll take care of this."

"Sarah?" asked Declan, praying for his brother's sake that if he reached out to her that some memory would spark. "Don't you remember us?"

She squinted as if her head hurt. "Is your name Declan?"

Relief washed through him, and he heard Ramsey take a breath. "Yes, that's it. I'm Declan."

She stared at Leroy. "And you're Leroy?"

Leroy nodded. "Yes, Sarah."

"Sarah, it's me, John." Ramsey waited for her to remember him.

Putting her hand to her head, she rubbed her temple. "What? Are you here to take me back?"

"Yes, Sarah," said Ramsey, his voice hopeful. "To take you back home."

She held on to Yates. "But I am home."

Ramsey stood stunned, his mouth open. "No, you're not. This is not your home."

She recoiled at that. "I'm not going anywhere with you. I don't know you."

Ramsey's shock turned to anger. "What has he done to you?"

"I think that's enough," said Yates. "You're scaring her. You should leave now."

Ramsey ignored him and Declan had to steel himself against his brother's shared outrage and panic. "You're wearing your necklace," said Ramsey.

Declan saw the twinkling hummingbird necklace around Sarah's neck.

Ramsey jabbed a finger at Yates. "You bastard. You used it against her." Yates offered no expression and Ramsey turned his attention back to Sarah. "Sarah, listen to me." Declan heard the desperation in his voice. "You can't trust this man. He's done something to you. He's not who he says he is."

Sarah continued to look at him with that awful blank stare.

"John..." said Declan, but Ramsey couldn't stop.

"What did you do?" yelled Ramsey at Yates.

"I told you," said Yates. "She loves me. She's always loved me."

Ramsey's control crumbled. "You son of a bitch. I'll kill you." He moved forward, and Yates stepped back, holding Sarah as Leroy and Declan stepped in to stop Ramsey's progress. "I swear to God," said Ramsey, struggling to get past Declan and Leroy.

"Sherlock, stop," said Leroy, holding his struggling friend.

Declan held on, too, knowing if he let his brother go after Yates, they would all suffer the consequences.

"Get out of my house or I'll call the police," said Yates. "Julian?"

Julian stepped out of the shadows. "Yes, Mr. Yates?"

"Call nine-one-one."

Julian left the room as Ramsey tried to launch himself again at Yates, stopped only by Declan and Leroy, who had him around the chest and arms. "You think the police are going to stop me?"

"John," said Declan, trying to reach him. "We have to go."

"I'm not leaving without you, Sarah." He continued to struggle. "Please," he said, his anger turning to fear. He softened his advance. "Please tell me you know me. Tell me you remember who I am. It's me. It's John."

Her arms around Yates, Sarah looked frightened. "I don't know you, but I know what you tried to do. Please leave."

Stricken, Ramsey went still, his eyes haunted. "No," he said.

Sarah pulled away from Yates. "I'm going upstairs," she said, and walked away without acknowledging him.

Ramsey tried one more time. "Sarah..."

But she ignored him. Taking the stairs at a quick pace, she reached the top, turned into a hallway, and disappeared.

Ramsey began to deflate, every muscle in his body giving way and Declan and Leroy eased their hold on him.

"I told you," said Yates, looking satisfied. "Guess you weren't as impressive as you thought you were."

Ramsey steadied himself. "I'll find out what you did to her."

Yates didn't hide his satisfaction. "You do that."

His fury returning, Ramsey struggled against Declan and Leroy, who pushed him back. "Let me go."

"No," said Leroy, breathing hard but holding on. "That's exactly what he wants. You go after him, and the police will show up and haul you off. Then you'll have that to deal with, too."

Declan and Leroy shoved Ramsey back to the front door, where Julian, who'd reappeared holding a cell phone, held it open for them.

Ramsey refused to go quietly, though. "This isn't over. I'll be back for her."

Yates followed them to the door. "I'm counting on it."

"You hurt her," said Ramsey with menace, "and I'll kill you."

"Hurt her?" asked Yates, with amusement. "I would never hurt her. Sarah and I are going to live a long and happy life together."

Ramsey made one last lunge at Yates, but Declan and Leroy held fast. "Damn it. Let me go."

"John," said Declan, "this is not the time or the place. We have to leave."

Ramsey looked at him with torment in his eyes. "I can't leave her here."

Declan felt his insides twist at his brother's devastation. "We have to."

They'd made it through the door and down the pavestone steps. Getting him back to the driveway, Declan finally felt his brother's strength begin to ebb. Declan spoke to Leroy. "Get him in the car."

Leroy took over and managed to push Ramsey back toward the vehicle. He got the door open and tried to get him to sit. "Get in the car, Sherlock."

"Leroy," said Ramsey, pleading "She's here. She's in the house. We have to get her."

"I know," said Leroy, with painful conviction. "But not today. Soon, though. I promise."

As Leroy took care of Ramsey, Declan turned and headed back toward the entrance where Yates was watching from the top of the stairs. He stopped at the bottom of them.

"You need something?" asked Yates. "Looking for your pride, maybe? I think you left it somewhere in the house."

"You may have won today," said Declan, "but this won't last."

Yates smiled, and Declan felt the urge to lunge at him, too. "You underestimate me," said Yates. "I've planned for every eventuality."

"You're overconfident. She's a Red-Line. At some point, she'll figure out what you're doing. And she'll remember."

Yates scoffed. "Don't you have a rejected brother to take care of?"

"It's not just him you have to worry about. Don't think you've seen the last of me either."

Yates walked down the stairs. "And don't think I've forgotten what you did to Edward."

Declan didn't flinch at his approach. "He should have stuck to science instead of kidnapping. He deserved what he got."

Yates went still, and Declan sensed his anger. "Too bad Hannah couldn't make it to this little party. She missed out on all the fun."

Declan's heart thumped and his own temper fueled. "You leave her out of this."

Yates's expression hardened. "Let me make one thing perfectly clear. Sarah is with me now. You and your friends meddle in my affairs, and you'll learn quickly what I'm capable of."

"And what about you?" asked Declan.

"Me?"

"When Sarah figures out what you've done, you'll learn what she's capable of." His gaze never wavered. "And I pray I'm there to see it."

Yates chuckled. "Well, then, you better hope that happens in the next twenty-four months," he said, reminding Declan of the remaining time left for Gray-Lines if they didn't recover their serum. He narrowed his eyes. "On second thought, make that twenty-two months. Time goes so fast." He tapped at his watch. "Tick-tock, tick-tock."

Declan didn't say a word, but set his jaw, and let his eyes do the talking.

Yates tossed out a hand. "Now take your lovesick brother and get off my property." He turned and walked back up the remaining stairs. With a last glance, he said, "Come back again and next time I won't be nice." Disappearing through the threshold, he slammed the door shut behind him.

.

CHAPTER SEVEN

S ARAH PACED THE bedroom, trying to quell her restless energy, but all she could see in her head was that man and his eyes, pleading with her. She shut her own eyes as another crack of pain pulsed behind her eye, and she had to sit. She hugged herself, and after a few minutes, the pain subsided. She heard the bedroom door open, and she looked to see Yates come into the room. He took a seat beside her.

"Are you all right?" he asked.

As she clenched her eyes shut, her head flared, and he took her hand and began to massage her palm.

"Just relax," he said. "It will pass."

Sitting with him, her tension eased and her head started to feel better. She opened her eyes. "That was him?"

"Yes," he said. "That was him."

"Why was he here? How did he get in?"

"He was here for you. He believes you love him. I told you he was obsessed."

Her agitation increased. "But how did he and his friends get into the front foyer?" She stood and resumed her pacing.

"Sarah," he said, "you should relax. You'll trigger another episode."

"Answer my question." Her energy racing, she faced him, and a vase on the nightstand quivered and then shattered into small pieces.

Yates eyed the remains of the vase but said nothing. Finally, he stood and approached her. "I let them in."

"But why? To upset me?"

"No. Quite the opposite. To upset him."

"But what for? You said he hadn't been around since the accident. Why all of a sudden did he show up now?"

"Because, Sarah, he's been searching for you."

"What?"

"He's never stopped looking for you. I thought by letting him in and showing him that you wanted me, that maybe he'd back off."

"You don't think that maybe you should have told me that?"

"I wasn't sure if he'd actually come here or not. I didn't want to worry you."

"What do you think I'm doing now?" Breathing deeply, she tried to assimilate everything that had occurred.

"I'm sorry," he said, sounding sincere. "I thought that if he heard it from you, he'd leave us alone. But I should have told you."

"You're damn right you should have told me."

Her head dropped as another lance of pain hit her, and he was by her side instantly. "You need to relax." He guided her to the bed and took her hand again. "I think it worked, though. Did you see his face? He won't be coming by again anytime soon."

His calm touch soothed her; the pain in her head eased and her muscles started to unwind.

"That's it." He sat behind her and massaged her neck. "What were you saying earlier about the beach?"

Closing her eyes, she felt her tension melt away. "About the what?" she asked, her mind calming.

"The beach. You said something about it being the perfect place?"

"Oh...for the ceremony," she said.

"You mean the wedding?"

"Yes," she said, feeling almost drowsy. "We should get married on the beach."

"I think that's a great idea. You're right. It's perfect."

She sat still, feeling his energy move from him into her, but before her mind became too hazy, she couldn't deny what she'd felt downstairs. When John Ramsey had pleaded with her and she'd seen his eyes, she had not sensed the energy of control or obsession, but instead an overwhelming need to protect her, and in addition to that, his total and complete love for her. She couldn't get it out of her head. But sitting there, as Yates kneaded her neck and her mind slowed, the memory became fuzzy and within minutes, winked out and went dark, and the memory of John Ramsey was lost to her again.

**

The car ride was excruciating. Ramsey sat in the back, eyes closed, replaying the events in his mind over and over as he tried to find some explanation for Sarah's denial of him. Considering a possibility, his eyes shot open. "Maybe he's threatening her."

Declan and Leroy had until then remained quiet, allowing the emotions of the last several minutes to subside and giving Ramsey time to deal with Sarah's rejection.

"What?" asked Declan.

Ramsey sat up. "Maybe he told her to play along or he would hurt us. Maybe she didn't have a choice."

Declan made eye contact with Leroy.

"She must have played along to protect us...or me." Ramsey stared out the window. "That's the only explanation." He turned back. "We'll have to go back. Maybe we can sneak in somehow...get her out."

"John..." said Declan.

"What?"

"There's another possibility you need to consider."

"What is that?"

Declan hesitated. "That she has no memory of you."

Ramsey made an uncomfortable laugh. "That's not possible. How could she not know me? I mean...she knew you and Leroy."

"She knew our names, but I don't think she knew much else."

Ramsey clenched his hands. "That's not possible. It's ridiculous. All the time we've spent together, everything we've been through... No. I don't believe it. And I don't believe she wants him either. She's pretending. It's what she would do if she thought I...or any of us...were in danger."

"That may be true," said Declan, "but—"

"But what?"

"Sherlock..." said Leroy from the front seat. "We think he may have done something to her to make her forget."

Ramsey shook his head. "How could he do that, Leroy? How could he make her forget?"

"He's a Red-Line," said Declan. "He almost killed you with some toxin. He likely came up with something to affect Sarah's memory. It may be the reason he wanted her blood."

Ramsey didn't buy it. "You're telling me he took her blood and came up with some concoction that's erased her memory of me?"

"Yes," said Declan.

Ramsey thought about it. "Maybe I can accept that her memory has been affected and that somehow she's forgotten me, but what I can't accept is that she loves him. That's not possible." Declan and

Leroy stayed quiet. "What?" He looked between the two of them, feeling the chills return. "What are you not telling me?"

Declan sat back, his shoulders slumped. "We think that maybe she thinks she does."

Ramsey dropped his jaw. "Oh, come on. I don't care what he drugged her with, she couldn't possibly..." Declan looked at him solemnly. "What is it? You felt something, didn't you? What did you feel?"

Declan swallowed. "She loves him. I don't know how or why, but she feels..."

Ramsey widened his eyes and his stomach dropped. "Just say it."

"She feels the same way about him as she felt for you."

The air in the car suddenly seemed ten times heavier. "*Felt* for me?" Ramsey asked. "What are you saying?"

"Sherlock..." said Leroy. "Whatever this is, whatever hold he has on her, we're going to stop it. We'll figure it out. It can't last."

Ramsey didn't move as the implications of Sarah's change of heart occurred to him. "But...if that's true, then..." Declan watched him with knowing eyes. "Oh, God...she's not..." He went rigid. "Is she...?"

"John..." said Declan.

Ramsey gripped the seat in front of him. Setting his jaw, he stared blankly at the floor. "Stop the car." He could barely draw a breath.

"Sherlock—"

"Stop the car, Leroy," he yelled.

Leroy turned and pulled into an empty parking lot in front of a vacant building. A "For Lease" sign hung in the front window. Ramsey jumped out, forcing a deep breath as images of Sarah with Yates plagued his mind, understanding with horror that Sarah believed she loved Yates and that he loved her and all that implied. Barely able to see straight, he leaned his hand against the car and tried to stay upright.

Declan and Leroy exited the car.

Ramsey held his stomach. "Oh God. He's not...she can't be."

Declan and Leroy stood helpless, as Ramsey came to terms with the fact that Sarah was likely in an intimate relationship with Yates.

"John..." said Declan.

"When?" asked Ramsey.

"What?" asked Declan.

"When did you suspect this?"

"Sherlock..."

"No, Leroy." Ramsey wanted to throw up, but he pushed it back as his anger erupted. "When did you consider this? Was it just now, in the car?" Something in him knew that was not the case.

Declan released a held breath. "We thought it might be a possibility."

Ramsey whirled on Declan, his rage and hurt fueling him. "You thought?"

"Sherlock, it was just a theory. We had no idea..."

"Looks like your theory is no longer a theory," said Ramsey. "How long did you plan on keeping this from me?"

"We weren't keeping it from you," said Declan. "We didn't see the point of telling you a theory."

"She's sleeping with him, Declan," he shouted. "Don't you think maybe you could have prepared me for that possibility?"

"You were worried enough," Declan yelled back. "Did you want that on your shoulders, too?"

"That is not the point." Ramsey grabbed at his head, trying to make sense of it all. He knew they had only wanted to protect him, but now it only felt like betrayal, and he needed to vent his outrage.

"Sherlock...listen."

"Don't tell me to listen, Leroy." He paced back and forth, trying to grasp the situation, but failing. "God, what is happening?" He clasped his hands behind his neck and stared up at the sky. "How is this happening?"

"We'll figure this out," said Declan. "We'll get her back."

But Ramsey couldn't see it that way. He looked with dismay at his brother. "Will we?" He dropped his hands. "And what happens if we do? Huh? What happens to Sarah in the process? Who exactly will I come back to? Something like this—"

"Don't forget who she is, John."

Ramsey shot out his hands. "She's a Red-Line, damn it! I know that. She's also half human. It will devastate her." He bent over, his hands on his knees, and dropped his head. "Damn it."

Nobody said anything for a few seconds until Declan broke the quiet. "She'll have you to help her through it. She won't be alone. As long as she's alive and well, you two will find a way."

Ramsey didn't move, but continued to stare at the ground. "Maybe..."

"Maybe what?" asked Leroy.

"Maybe she's better off..."

"Stop it," said Declan. "She's not supposed to be with him. She's supposed to be with you."

Ramsey snapped his head up. "But she's not now, is she?"

Neither Declan nor Leroy could answer him.

"What if bringing her back to me means hurting her, traumatizing her?" asked Ramsey.

"You don't have a choice," said Declan. "You know she would never forgive you if you left her there. She'd rather deal with the consequences and be with you than remain where she is, no matter how it may feel for her right now."

Ramsey couldn't get the images out of his head, and he shut his eyes against the visions and resumed his pacing. "I can't get back in that car." He took a shaky deep breath as he tried to pull it together.

"Then we'll walk with you," said Leroy.

"No," said Ramsey, turning away. "I don't want any company." He walked toward the street.

"Where are you going?" asked Declan.

"Does it matter?" He walked to the intersection, looked both ways, and crossed, leaving Declan and Leroy behind him.

CHAPTER EIGHT

....

S EVERAL HOURS LATER, Leroy hung up the phone. "No answer," he said.

"Where the hell is he?" asked Declan.

"I don't know."

"He just walked off by himself?" asked Hannah.

"Yes, he did." Declan walked to the window and put his hands in his pockets. Now that they knew where Sarah was, they'd called off the search for her, although they still had people out looking for Marco. With Sarah located, though, the three of them were left to figure out what to do next.

"He needs to hibernate for a while. Give him time." Leroy said it for his own benefit just as much as theirs.

"And she remembered nothing?" asked Hannah. "I don't believe it. How is that possible?"

"Nothing other than our names," said Leroy. "She didn't know Sherlock at all."

"My God," said Hannah. "I can't imagine what that did to him."

"Yeah, well, it wasn't as bad as us having to tell him that Sarah loves Yates." Declan kept staring out the window. "And watch as he figured out what that implied. I never want to feel that again."

Hannah glanced at Leroy, who sat unmoving at the kitchen table. "How long do we wait before we go looking for him?"

"He's a big boy," said Leroy. "He'll come back when he's ready."

Declan dropped his head. "There's something else that's bothering me."

"What?" asked Leroy.

"Did you hear what Sarah said when she came into the room, before she knew we were there?"

"What did she say?" Leroy thought about it. "Something about the beach?"

"She said the beach would be the perfect place for the ceremony."

"The ceremony?" asked Hannah.

"Yes," said Declan.

"What ceremony?" asked Hannah.

"Exactly."

Leroy sucked in a breath. "You don't think..."

Hannah came to the same conclusion. "She's not going to..."

"Marry him?" asked Declan. "It's the logical conclusion."

"Dear God," said Leroy. "Every time I think this can't possibly get any worse, it does."

"She wouldn't," said Hannah. "She's only been gone for four days."

"I can't explain it," said Declan, staring out the window, "but, yes. I think she just might."

**

Ramsey heard his phone ring and forced his eyes open. He didn't know where he was, but those blissful few moments of forgetfulness disappeared when his memory roared back and he realized he had not been dreaming. Sarah was gone, and worse, he wasn't convinced he'd be able to get her back. Blinking his eyes against the soft sunlight that filtered into the room, he saw Sarah's things.

He'd walked for hours the previous day, thinking of her and their time together, replaying the events in his mind leading up to this moment, until the moon had risen, and finally paying attention, he realized he was in Sarah's neighborhood. Finding his way to her apartment, he jimmied her lock, entered, and had fallen asleep in her bed. He'd had no dinner, but he didn't want to eat. His phone had rung several times, but it was always Declan or Leroy, and he had no interest in talking.

Eyeing the clock on the nightstand, he saw that it was eight o'clock in the morning. It surprised him that he'd managed to sleep. The phone continued to ring, and he wondered how he still had battery power. Picking up the phone, he noticed that he had only one bar left, but more importantly, he didn't recognize the number on the display. Visions of Sarah calling him flashed in his head, and he answered it.

"Hello?" he said, clearing his throat.

"Mr. Ramsey?"

"Yes?" He sat up in bed. "Who is this?"

"It's Julian. Perhaps you remember me from yesterday?"

A vision of the short, dark-haired man flashed in his head. "Yes. What do you want?" He couldn't help but feel some measure of hope that maybe this man wanted to help.

"Mr. Yates asked me to call."

The cold lump in his chest returned. "What does that bastard want?"

"He felt remiss that he had not invited you to the ceremony."

"The ceremony? What are you talking about?"

"Miss Sarah and Mr. Yates are to be wed."

Ramsey gripped the phone. "What the hell are you talking about?"

"This morning. It's a lovely day for it."

"This morning?"

"Yes, they're having an early service out on the beach before they head out on the honeymoon."

Ramsey couldn't make himself think. "Service? Honeymoon?"

"Yes, sir. Mr. Yates thought you should know."

A million questions shot through Ramsey's head in a split second. "What time?"

"Pretty soon, actually. I think..."

Ramsey hung up before Julian could finish. He grabbed his jacket and ran out the door. Realizing he didn't have a car, he cursed himself. He considered calling a cab, but he didn't know if his phone's battery would hold out that long and he didn't have the luxury of waiting.

Remembering a hotel nearby, he ran for it, hoping he could find a cab there at this hour of the day. He raced down the block and turned the corner, and seeing the hotel across the street, he pushed himself faster. A yellow cab sat out front. A car horn blared at him as he ran blindly, ignoring the traffic, but he made it there safely and jumped into the back seat, breathing hard after his sprint.

"You the guy going to the airport?" asked the cabbie.

Ramsey tried to catch his breath. "Forget that. I need to you to get to an address as fast as possible."

"Hey, I'm supposed to pick up some dude going to the airport."

Ramsey leaned forward. "Screw the airport," he said, pulling out some cash. "You get me to where I need to go, and fast, there's a hundred-dollar tip for you."

The cabbie eyed the cash Ramsey was holding and started up the car. Ramsey gave him the address and sat back in his seat, praying he would get there in time.

**

Sarah blinked her eyes in the sun. She'd had an anxious sleep the previous night, with visions of the strange man named Ramsey plaguing her dreams. Remembering only bits and pieces, she recalled him searching for her, saying her name over and over, and her frozen in place, unable to move. Not a surprising dream, she supposed, considering the circumstances, but what bothered her about it was that she felt fairly certain that if she'd been able to move, that she would have likely looked for him too, wanting to find him. She didn't understand why she felt that way, because she didn't want him anywhere near her.

"You look beautiful."

The voice startled her. She focused, then saw Yates standing next to her. Glancing down at herself, she swayed in her simple white lace dress and smelled the bouquet of white and pink roses in her hand. She stood barefoot, her toes wiggling in the sand as the wind blew tendrils of her hair that had fallen around her face. "Do I?" she asked.

"Yes."

Perusing him, she admired his white suit and shirt and the pink and white roses pinned to his lapel. He, too, stood barefoot in the sand, and in front of them stood a beautiful latticed archway, shrouded with intricately placed pink and white roses and long, white stretches of tulle blowing in the breeze.

He took her hand. "You ready?"

Giving his palm a squeeze, she said, "Yes."

Izzy stood behind her, all too happy to be part of the ceremony, and as Yates turned and looked, Julian walked out onto the sand and went to stand behind Yates.

"Everything good?" asked Yates.

"Just fine, sir," said Julian, smiling at his boss. His gaze moved to Sarah. "You look lovely, Miss Sarah."

"Soon to be Mrs.," said Yates.

"Thank you, Julian," said Sarah as Yates held her hand and massaged her palm.

"Then let's do this," said Yates. He eyed the man standing beneath the archway, who was waiting for the go-ahead. Yates had found a local justice of the peace, who, with a little persuading and with an offer of a monetary reward well worth the man's efforts, had agreed at late notice to come to the beach early and perform the ceremony. "We're ready when you are, Judge Ellerby."

The judge began to speak, and the ceremony began. Handing her bouquet off to Izzy, Sarah took both of Yates's hands in hers and recited her vows, then listened as Yates recited his. His gaze never leaving hers, he reached for the ring, which Julian offered, and holding her hand, he slid it on to her finger while repeating the judge's words. Sarah did the same after taking the ring Izzy held out to her. And then, as quickly as it had started, the ceremony ended and Sarah heard the judge say, "You may kiss the bride."

And just before their lips touched, Sarah shivered when, looking up at Yates, she saw brown eyes instead of blue.

....

CHAPTER NINE

THE CAB PULLED up to the entrance of the long driveway. The cabbie rolled down the window, prepared to hit the intercom, when the gates opened on their own. Ramsey didn't stop to consider the reasons behind it. "Drive," he said. "Up to the door."

Once the gates opened, the cabbie did just that. He pulled up to the entrance just as Ramsey dropped the cash in the front seat and jumped out. The cab forgotten, Ramsey ran up the stairs and rang the doorbell numerous times. When no one answered, he pounded on the door.

Finally, it opened and Julian greeted him with a smile. "Mr. Ramsey. Good to see you again."

"Screw the pleasantries, Julian," said Ramsey, pushing inside. "Where is she?" He saw no one in the foyer and headed into the living room. "Sarah," he yelled.

Shutting the front door, Julian watched Ramsey walk through the house. Ramsey strode into the kitchen, but saw nothing. The house was quiet. He came back into the foyer, where Julian was waiting. Looking upstairs, Ramsey asked, "Is she up there?" but Julian stayed quiet.

He took the stairs two at a time. "Sarah," he called again. Moving down the hallway, he looked into the various rooms. When he saw what appeared to be the main bedroom, he entered it. The room was clean and the bed made. Walking back into the closet area, he stopped short when he took in the clothes. Many items belonged to Sarah, but they were clothes that had been in his closet, where she'd moved them only a week before. Stopping briefly, he touched one of her sweaters and brought the material to his nose to inhale her scent. Studying the area, he saw empty hangers and other clothing he did not recognize. Turning, he left the bedroom and raced back downstairs. Julian still stood in the foyer.

"Where is she?" he asked him.

"Mr. Ramsey, it's too late," said Julian, but Ramsey was already moving toward the back of the house.

"Mr. Ramsey..."

"Sarah." Ramsey searched everywhere, his fears growing when he found no one in the house. Spying the patio, he found and opened a back door. He could hear the sound of seagulls and the pounding of the surf. "Sarah!" he yelled again into the wind.

"Sir," said Julian behind him. "I'm afraid the ceremony is over."

"Tell me where she is."

Julian regarded his watch and then stared out toward the beach as if reminiscing. "Probably taking off by now, I would imagine."

Ramsey followed his gaze and saw the rose-covered archway in the sand. White slices of tulle blew in the ocean breeze. His mind couldn't grasp what his senses were telling him. "No." The impact of it hit him. He eyed Julian. "You're lying."

"It was lovely and she looked beautiful." Julian watched as Ramsey absorbed the shock. "She'll be home from her honeymoon in a couple of weeks, though. I'll let her know you stopped by."

Ramsey was dumbstruck. Every hope he'd held for Sarah's return vanished, and the realization that he'd lost her hit him as his heart slammed against his ribs and his chest constricted. The only thing left to him was rage. It ignited in his belly and worked its way up into his torso, and then his mind went white with fury.

"You son of a bitch." Without thinking, he advanced on Julian, but before he could get his hands on the small man, something hard came down on the back of his head and everything went dark.

**

Declan spoke wearily into his phone. "Okay. Keep looking," he said. Ending the call, he sat at Leroy's dining table. "That was Mary. She finished in her area. I sent her to the next one." He kneaded his tired eyes. They'd spent yet another near-sleepless night, worrying now about Ramsey instead of Sarah. He had not returned since his departure from Leroy's car the previous day, and he did not answer his phone, which now went straight to voicemail.

"Where else would he go?" asked Hannah, who sat across from Declan.

Leroy sighed as he paced the room. The day outside had turned to night. They'd already checked Ramsey's house and Sarah's apartment. They'd found the bed at Sarah's slept in, but no Ramsey. "I don't know, Hannah," he said. "In the past, if he had trouble, he'd come here."

"Maybe he got drunk, and he's sleeping it off somewhere," she said.

"It's possible," said Declan. "But I think he would have been back by now. Or at least been in touch with one of us."

Leroy kept moving. "It's not like him to get drunk at some bar and pass out. He'd go home to do that."

"Not if he doesn't want to be found," said Hannah.

Leroy and Declan scrutinized her. "I mean," she said, "I know what he may have done in the past, but this is a little different."

Declan shook his head. "No, there's something wrong. I can feel it."

"Me, too," said Leroy.

"Would he have gone back to Yates's house?" asked Hannah.

Declan's head bobbed up as if that were a possibility, and Leroy stopped pacing.

"You think?" asked Declan to Leroy.

Leroy didn't stop to wonder. "You have the number?" he asked, pulling out his cell.

"What, you want to call Yates?" asked Declan.

"At this point, I'd talk to the devil himself," answered Leroy.

Declan searched his phone. "Be careful what you ask for."

"Just give me the number."

Declan gave Leroy the number he'd received from the manager at the cemetery a day earlier.

Leroy dialed and waited. "Hello?" said Leroy when someone answered. "Yes, I'd like to speak to Yates Reddington." Leroy stared at Hannah and Declan. "This is Sampson Leroy calling. I'm looking for John Ramsey." Leroy's posture straightened, and his face tightened. "Excuse me?" he asked, his eyes widening. "He was there?" Leroy paused. "The wedding?"

"Oh, no," said Declan.

Leroy turned rigid, and his voice hardened. "And who the hell told him about the wedding?"

Declan cursed and Leroy's tension kicked up another notch and then turned into full-blown anger.

"You're a liar," said Leroy into the phone. "What the hell did you do?" He paused. "How about you suggest where we might look?" he asked, eyes shutting and voice raising.

Hearing that, Declan stood.

Opening his eyes, Leroy responded again. "Your boss should know that we are not going away." There was another short pause. "You do that," said Leroy before he hung up the phone and shoved it in his pocket. "That bastard."

"They told him, didn't they?" asked Declan. "Sarah and Yates got married, and they told him."

"No," said Hannah.

Leroy was furious. "They called him this morning. Told him about the impending ceremony. He rushed over there, but it was too late. Yates and Sarah were gone. Julian apparently told Sherlock, and according to him, Sherlock lost it and got violent and attacked him. They called the police, but Sherlock ran off. They're still looking for him."

Declan didn't hide his smirk. "He's lying."

"Of course, he's lying."

"Why would they do that to him?" asked Hannah.

"He's turning the screws," said Declan, "Yates is making John suffer as much as he can."

Leroy managed to rein in his anger and refocus. "I asked him where we might look."

Declan grabbed his keys. "What did he say?"

"Said we should look down by the Rail House area."

Declan shook his head. "That's mostly bars and nightclubs," he said, reaching for his phone.

"I know, but it's a place to start," said Leroy. He picked up his jacket and slid it on.

"I'm coming with you," said Hannah.

"You should stay here," said Declan. "It's safer."

"I will not stay here. There's nothing I can do here." Her gaze met Declan's. "Besides, he's my friend, too. And if he needs medical attention, I can help."

Declan hesitated, but then nodded. "Fine," he said, "but if there's any trouble, you stay in the car."

"Yes, sir," she said, grabbing her jacket and following him and Leroy out the door.

A steady beat of deep-toned muffled music reached his ears, and Ramsey cracked his eyes open, the throbbing in his head intensifying. His sight blurred, though, and he shut his eyes again as a ripple of nausea hit. Biting back the impulse to vomit, he tried to take a deep breath and waited for his stomach to settle. After a while, the nausea eased and he opened his eyes again. Feeling a chill, he realized that he was sitting outside and by the aches and pains in his body, he was in an uncomfortable position. Finally managing to focus, he realized that he was sitting on concrete, with his back and side against a hard surface, and across from him was a brick wall from another building. Trash littered the ground, and turning his head, he saw that he was leaning sideways against what appeared to be a dumpster. A rocket of pain sliced through his head, and he gasped, raising his hand to the back of his skull and feeling his matted and sticky hair.

He tried to remember how he got here, but his brain wouldn't function. Looking around at his fuzzy surroundings, he determined that he was in an alley. Other dumpsters dotted the dirty back street and sat like discarded empty boxes behind the back doors of what appeared to be commercial businesses, most of which were likely bars and clubs, if the pounding music was any indication. As if to confirm his theory, one of the distant back doors opened and he watched through obscured vision as a skinny black man carried out a large trash can. Loud music played as the back door remained open and the man raised the can to dump out a pile of garbage into one of the dumpsters. Finished, the man turned and went back inside, closing the door behind him, and the alley went still again.

Ramsey reached for his phone but then remembered the dead battery. A sudden flashback made him think of Sarah, and then the nightmare of the last few days came surging back. Her disappearance and memory loss, his long walk, the phone call, and rushing back to Yates's house to find Sarah was no longer there. He sucked in a painful breath. Then he remembered why. She'd married Yates. She was on her honeymoon. His distress returning, he wished he could shut out his memories. Knowing she was with Yates now, he pictured Yates touching and holding her. His stomach rebelled and he leaned forward, despite the aches in his body, and was reaching to steady himself when he heard something metallic clatter to the ground.

Swallowing the bile in the back of his throat, he searched for the source of the noise and went still when, in the soft glow of the moonlight, he saw a knife covered in blood. He forgot about the need to be sick. Where had that come from? Feeling shaky, he sat back again and studied the knife, lying there as if accusing him. Ramsey knew it must have fallen from his lap when he'd sat up. He studied his hands and froze in horror when he saw his fingers covered in blood. A bubble of panic set in when he connected the dots. A bloody knife and bloody hands. What the hell had happened? Fear sharpened his senses, and he sniffed the air, grimacing when he recognized the pungent smell of alcohol. Studying himself and his dirty clothes, he realized that the smell was coming from him. He reeked as if he'd taken a bath in tequila, which wasn't even his preferred drink. Yet he had no recollection of drinking, and he didn't feel hungover.

He tried to put the pieces together, but all he could do was think of Sarah, and he couldn't help but wonder how everything had fallen apart so fast. What had he done wrong? Dropping his bloody hands, he leaned his head back, trying to understand, but it hurt too much to think, and he closed his eyes.

A few moments later, he heard the sound of footsteps. Opening his eyes, he saw a beam of light bounce along the walls of the alley. Watching the light encroach his spot beside the dumpster, he began to comprehend what would happen to him if the police found him like this. He swallowed and watched as the beam sharpened, and he gave himself over to his fate. If the cops found him, what would it matter? He'd already lost the only thing he'd cared about.

The light grew closer, and he held his breath, knowing that whoever was wielding it stood just around the dumpster. A figure emerged from behind it and turned the beam in his direction. Ramsey shut his eyes as he tried to prevent the light from splitting his head in two. He heard an intake of breath and some shuffling, and then a voice.

"I found him," said a female. "He's in the alley behind the piano bar."

The flashlight beam moved away, and Ramsey peered through his eyelids to see a woman crouched beside him.

"Ramsey?"

He focused in on the face. It was Mary from Declan's security detail.

"You all right?" She reached for his arm and stopped when she saw the knife. Looking him over, her face furrowed when she saw the blood and likely smelled the alcohol.

Ramsey winced as his head flared. "I've been better."

"What happened?"

He considered that a worthy question. "Your guess is as good as mine."

"Okay. Stay still. Help is coming." She stood and aimed the beam down the alley. "Stay here. I'm going to look around."

Ramsey tried to shift his body on the concrete, but his muscles protested and he stopped. "I'm not going anywhere."

Heading further down the alley, Mary disappeared from sight. Ramsey wondered where she was going, but his attention was diverted when he heard a car approach. It sounded as if it stopped just down the alley, and he heard car doors open and close.

"Where is he?" A distinct voice, which he recognized immediately as Leroy's, boomed through the air.

"Against the dumpster," he heard Mary yell back. "Don't touch anything."

Footsteps approached, and then Leroy, Declan, and Hannah were there.

"Sherlock..." he heard as Leroy squatted next to him.

Declan kneeled close. "You okay?" He noticed the knife. "What happened?"

Ramsey wished he could pull himself up, but he didn't have the strength. "Mary and I covered that already. I have no idea." His muscles strained as another wave of nausea hit him and he fought another urge to be sick.

"Let me see him," said Hannah.

Declan leaned back, his eyes darting between the knife, Ramsey's hands and surrounding area. Frowning, he stood and looked down the alley to find Mary.

"Take it easy," said Hannah. Ramsey gasped as she checked his head and found the wounded area. "Wow. Somebody popped you a good one."

"He okay?" asked Leroy.

"He's got a concussion, I'm sure." Ramsey grunted as she checked for broken bones or other damage. "Can you move?" she asked him.

He let go of a groan. "Only if absolutely necessary."

"What happened to your hands?" She picked them up and looked at them.

"I don't know," he said. "It's not my blood."

She put his hands down. "You been drinking?"

"Hannah..." asked Leroy.

Ramsey answered despite Leroy's objection. "No, I haven't. I may smell like it, but I don't recall drinking."

Hannah studied him. "You didn't drink or you don't recall drinking?"

"Hannah, now is not the time to interrogate him," said Leroy.

Hannah took Ramsey's wrist and felt his pulse. "I'm not implying anything, Leroy, but from a head-injury perspective, it's important to know. If alcohol is dulling his senses right now, his injuries could be worse than I suspect."

"I'm not drunk, although I wish I was," said Ramsey.

Mary's voice interrupted them. "Declan... I need you down here."

Declan, who'd been waiting for her to return, headed down into the alley.

Finishing her examination of Ramsey, Hannah sat back. "We should get you to a hospital," she said.

"No, no hospital," said Ramsey.

"Sherlock," Leroy said, "you need to be checked out."

"I've had enough of..." Ramsey stopped and shut his eyes as his head and vision spun again.

"Take it easy... Just relax," said Hannah.

"No hospitals, Leroy," Ramsey said, fighting the dizziness. "I'll be okay."

**

Down the alleyway, Declan approached Mary, who was standing beside another dumpster just a few businesses down from where Ramsey was lying. She aimed her flashlight beyond where he could see.

"What is it?" he asked.

"It's not good," she answered, nodding her head in the direction of her beam. He stood in disbelief when he saw Marco's body crumpled against the brick wall of the alley. The man lay covered in blood, staring in wide-eyed silence.

"Oh my God. Marco..." said Declan. He'd not prepared himself for this. He knew Yates was a dangerous man, but he had not anticipated this level of corruption. It took him a moment to collect himself.

"Did you see what was next to Ramsey?" asked Mary.

Declan pulled himself together at her question, and it dawned on him what lengths Yates was willing to go to destroy his brother. The knife, John's bloody hands, and the reek of alcohol flashed in Declan's mind.

"How do you want to handle this?" asked Mary.

His focus became clear at her question, and he moved into action without regard to the consequences. If his suspicions were correct, then the police were already on their way.

"Initiate a clean-up," he said. "You know what to do. Move fast, though. We don't have much time."

Mary flipped off her light and instantly headed down the alley.

Declan returned to where Ramsey lay against the dumpster, still looking dazed. He moved close as Leroy looked up.

"What's wrong?" Leroy asked.

"We have to get him out of here," said Declan. "Now."

As if on cue, the soft sound of sirens could be heard in the distance.

"They're not coming this way, are they?" asked Hannah.

Declan moved to Ramsey's side. "Help me lift him, Leroy. Hannah, pull the car up. Hurry."

A split second passed and the implications becoming obvious, Hannah jumped up and headed to the car and Leroy moved to Ramsey's other side. Together, he and Declan got Ramsey by the arms and hauled him up. He grunted in pain and they supported him until Hannah drove up and they carried him to the car and set him down in the back seat.

"Hannah," said Declan. "You get in the back seat with him. Leroy, you drive. Slowly, stay at the speed limit. Do not get pulled over."

Hannah jumped out of the driver's seat and joined Ramsey. Leroy slid in behind the wheel. "What are you going to do?" asked Leroy.

"I'm going to help Mary."

"With what?"

"I'll fill you in later. I'll meet you back at the house. Now go."

"You be careful," said Leroy.

"I will. Just get him out of here."

The sirens grew louder in the distance.

Leroy drove off. Declan returned to the scene and picked up the bloody knife with the tail end of his jacket. He hurried back to where Marco lay and where Mary had pulled up her own car and popped the trunk.

He disposed of the knife inside it. "You ready?" he asked.

"Yes."

They both leaned over and gripped Marco by the arms. They lifted his lifeless body and lowered him into the dark space of the trunk. Both watched the dark alley as they did so, praying that no one showed at that moment. They successfully got him in, and Mary shut the trunk and slid into the driver's seat while Declan assessed the scene to make sure they had not missed anything.

"Come on," said Mary, hearing the sirens wail as they neared. "We're out of time."

Declan searched the brick walls of the alley, looking for cameras, then walked up to the passenger side and got in. Mary hit the accelerator and they left the alley behind

CHAPTER TEN

....

S ARAH STRETCHED HER neck and rubbed her shoulders. The long plane ride and jet lag, plus her lack of sleep the previous night, had drained her. After the ceremony, they'd traveled by private jet, and several hours later, they'd landed and a limousine had picked them up. During the flight, she'd had no idea where they were headed, but the moment they began to descend, she'd watched from the window and she knew where they were—Paris. It had been a dream of hers to come here, and looking down as the plane neared, the beauty of the city took her breath away.

They'd arrived at the hotel and checked into their room—a magnificent penthouse suite with heart-stopping views of the Eiffel Tower and surrounding city. She thought they would relax, but he surprised her and, guiding her into the closet, told her to change. Her jaw dropped when she saw the elegant red designer cocktail dress and red strappy high-heeled shoes. Along with that, he handed her a jewelry box. Opening it, she stared wide-eyed at a stunning diamond necklace.

When she didn't move, he took it out of the box. Still in shock, she took off her hummingbird necklace, and he draped and fastened her gift around her neck. She'd argued it was too much; she had no need for such expensive jewelry, but he refused to hear it. An hour later, they were seated in an exclusive French restaurant.

She wore her new dress and necklace, and he wore a stylish black suit with a black and white tie. He ordered for her in French, and the waiter delivered and popped open a ridiculously expensive bottle of champagne. Yates raised his glass and toasted to their marriage, and they spent the next three hours enjoying a seven-course meal.

It had been a day of remarkable firsts, but now, returning to their room, she could barely keep her eyes open. All the activities and excitement, and now a full stomach and several glasses of champagne, had taken their toll. Kicking off her shoes, she couldn't wait to get comfortable. Looking into the closet, she saw that their bags had been unpacked and all her clothes now hung in the closet.

Reaching behind her, she unzipped her dress. Before taking it off, though, she rubbed at her neck. Another hand joined hers, and she realized that Yates stood behind her. She dropped her hand as she let him massage her shoulders.

"Tired?" he asked.

"Yes," she said.

"It's been a long day."

"But a good one," she said as she closed her eyes and he continued her neck massage.

"I can show you how to conserve some of your energy."

Relaxing at his touch, she asked, "What do you mean?"

He moved his fingers to the base of her skull and massaged the muscles there, making her sigh in delight. "As Red-Lines," he said, "it can be hard at first to manage the amount of energy that we have access to. It can sap your strength if you don't know how to pace yourself."

"Really?"

"Yes." He leaned in close, and she could feel his breath on her neck. "There's a lot I can show you if you're interested."

Her back rested against his chest. "I'm interested," she said. "I think I have a lot to learn."

He trailed his hands down her back and encircled her waist. "You've actually done quite well for someone so new to your role," he said into her ear.

Her heart skipped when she felt his lips on her neck and his hands moved over her belly. She didn't feel so tired anymore.

"Better?" he asked. He kissed her shoulder, and she realized then that he was sending her energy. She could feel it course through her.

"Thanks to you," she said, and she sent him some of her own.

He laughed softly. "See," he said, "you're already pretty advanced."

"I have some skills," she said, and she turned in his arms.

Wrapping his arms around her, he brought her up close. He dropped his head and touched his forehead to hers. "God," he said. "You're so beautiful."

Sarah stilled as images of another man, saying the same words, flashed in her head but then vanished just as fast. She sucked in a breath.

Yates raised his head. "What? What's wrong?"

Sarah blinked, trying to recall what she had seen in her mind. She stared off for a moment because it felt important and she wanted to remember.

"Sarah, what is it?" He trailed his hands up and down her back in lazy movements, directing more energy into her and noticed the moment she came back. "Where'd you go?"

She shook her head as his hands on her body brought her back to the present. "Sorry. I guess it's the jet lag and champagne. It's making me a little loopy."

He pulled her against him, and she wrapped her arms around him. "You ready for bed?" he asked, his lips finding her neck.

Her fatigue diminished, the heat began to build, and she found herself wanting him. She pulled away from his embrace, and he let her go with reluctance. Reaching up, she tugged at her dress, and it shimmied down her body and fell to the floor. She stood in front of him, wearing little more than her diamond necklace.

"I thought you'd never ask," she said, and she stepped out of the dress and into his arms, meeting his eager kiss.

**

Leroy emerged from his bedroom, feeling better after catching up on some much-needed sleep. Heading into the kitchen, he spied the coffee pot, but seeing Hannah asleep on the couch, he turned and pulled a blanket off a chair and covered her with it. She didn't stir. Moving back into the kitchen, he picked up the pot and began to fill it with water.

"Morning..." The quiet voice startled him, and he turned, sloshing the water in the pot.

Declan stood in the doorway.

"You're going to give someone a heart attack one day," said Leroy.

Declan gave him a slight smile. "Sorry." He noticed what Leroy was holding. "I hope you're making a full pot." He moved into the kitchen and sat at the breakfast table.

"All the way to the brim," said Leroy. He added the water to the machine and the grounds to the filter and started it up, then went to sit next to Declan. Seeing the bags under his eyes, he asked, "Did you get any sleep? What time did you get in?"

Declan wiped at his face. "About two a.m."

Leroy frowned. "What happened out there?"

Declan dropped his hand. "We had to do a clean-up."

"A what?"

"Measures that have to be taken to prevent discovery."

"Discovery of what?"

"Do I smell coffee?" Hannah stood at the kitchen entrance with the blanket wrapped around her.

"Did we wake you?" asked Leroy.

"It's fine," said Hannah. "I need to go check on Ramsey anyway. I've been asleep since the first time I looked in on him, which was several hours ago."

"You needed the rest," said Declan.

"I needed to check on him during the night. He's got a concussion."

"He's okay. He's got a hard head," said Declan.

"I don't doubt it, but I still need to be sure he's all right."

"Let him sleep a little more. He needs it," said Leroy.

"And I doubt that waiting a few more minutes will make a difference," said Declan. "Sit and have some coffee. Let him have a few more moments of rest before he has to wake up and face his demons again."

Hannah agreed with a yawn. "I'll give him five more minutes."

Declan slid into another chair and Hannah sat beside him. They yawned together until the coffee machine beeped. Leroy got coffee mugs and poured each of them a large serving from the pot.

Hannah took a sip. "That's good. Thanks."

"You're welcome," said Leroy, sitting back in his seat. He spoke to Declan. "So, now that we have caffeine in our veins, tell me what sort of discovery you were preventing."

Declan sipped his own drink and put it down. "John's potential arrest for murder."

Leroy choked on his drink, and Hannah let a chuckle escape. "What are you talking about?" she asked.

"Are you joking?" asked Leroy, coughing.

"No, I'm not," said Declan. "Mary found Marco's body in the alley just down from John. He'd been stabbed."

Leroy and Hannah sat open-mouthed.

"There was a knife next to John," said Declan. "And his hands were bloody."

"You're not saying he did something, are you?" asked Leroy.

"Of course not," said Declan.

"But somebody was trying to make it look like he did," said Leroy.

"Yes."

"Why?" asked Hannah. "Who? Yates?"

Declan nodded. "Yes, Yates. He's intent on putting John through the wringer."

"The man has tunnel vision," said Leroy. "But I suppose Sherlock in jail would keep him out of his hair."

"I doubt a murder rap would have stuck," said Declan. "The body was several days old and the blood on John's hands was fresh. I doubt if it was even Marco's. Plus, John smelled of alcohol..."

"But he wasn't drunk," finished Hannah. "A blood alcohol test would have proven that."

"Still, it would have been a hell of a mess to explain everything to the police," said Leroy, "who, by the way, just happened to show up at the last minute."

"Exactly," said Declan. "Yates is playing with us. Someone made the call right when we found him. They set the whole thing up."

"What about Marco?" asked Leroy.

"Mary and I drove him to an autopsy lab run by our people. Although it's pretty obvious what killed him." Declan sighed. "I talked to Morgana before I got in this morning. She'll call and notify Marco's family today. And I told her the situation with John."

"What'd she say?" asked Leroy.

"You know her," said Declan. "All business. She said to keep her informed."

"Keep her informed?" asked Leroy. "Sarah has lost her memory, married Yates, and they're kicking Sherlock in the teeth every chance they get, and she wants us to keep her informed?"

Declan didn't answer him.

Leroy gripped his mug. "I'll keep her informed. How about with my foot right up her—"

"Leroy..." said Hannah. "She's just doing her job. She can't afford to get emotionally involved."

Leroy was not appeased. "I'm not asking her to come over here and tuck him in. She could at least show some measure of warmth."

Hannah didn't argue. "Well," she said, "speaking of that, I'm going to look in on him." She stood, draped her blanket over the chair, and walked out of the kitchen.

"So, what do we do now?" asked Declan, rubbing his temples.

Leroy huffed, still angry over Morgana. "I have no idea." He held the bridge of his nose. "Sarah's gone, Sherlock's a mess, Marco's dead." He stopped and stared at Declan. "I'd say we've got a few problems."

"I'd say more than a few," said Declan.

Hannah came back into the kitchen. "Where is he?" she asked.

"Who?" asked Leroy.

Hannah rolled her eyes. "Ramsey."

"He's in the bedroom," answered Leroy.

"No, he's not."

"What, you two forget where you put him?" asked Declan.

"He's in the bedroom," said Leroy, standing.

"No," repeated Hannah. "He's not."

Leroy stomped out of the kitchen with Declan right behind him. "Hannah, if you're playing games with me..."

"I'm not playing any games."

Leroy entered the bedroom and stopped, seeing the empty but rumpled bed. "Where the hell is he?"

"That's what I asked," said Hannah.

"Oh, hell..." said Declan, his shoulders slumping, "don't tell me we lost him again."

"He was right there," Leroy almost shouted.

"I know that," Hannah almost shouted back. "But he's not there now."

Leroy's frustration grew. "I can see that."

Hannah's own fatigue began to take its toll. "Don't yell at me. I didn't lose him."

Leroy glared. "You were supposed to be checking on him."

"Hey," said Hannah, her voice pitching higher. "Don't put this on me."

"Take it easy, you two," said Declan. "He can't have gone far."

Leroy groaned and took a breath to calm himself. "Sorry."

Hannah took her own deep breath. "It's okay. Let's just figure out where he is."

Leroy stepped out of the room. "I swear when I find him, I'm gonna wring his neck."

Hannah followed. "I'll hold him down while you do it."

**

Ramsey had returned to his house two hours earlier. He'd awakened at Leroy's, his head still hurting, but seeing everyone asleep, he'd found his car keys, snuck out, and returned home. The moment he'd walked in the door, though, he'd realized his mistake. Reminders of Sarah were everywhere. He'd barely been in his house since her disappearance, and now, looking around, he saw the cup she'd drunk from, the dishes she'd eaten from, and the chair she'd sat in, still pushed outward from the table as if she'd just stood up from it. A tube of her lipstick sat atop the kitchen counter, and he swore he could smell her perfume.

Feeling the misery of her absence, he made himself go to the bedroom closet, and he saw exactly what he'd suspected. Her clothes were gone. He looked around his bathroom. Her toiletries, her cosmetics, and her shampoo from the shower were all missing. At some point since the time she'd disappeared, someone had come into his house and removed her things, likely in an effort to support whatever story Yates was feeding her.

Ramsey stared at himself in the mirror. He'd finally mustered the courage to remove the sheet that he had used to cover it. After his hospital stay and near-fatal poisoning, Sarah had shown him how to block Yates from accessing him through the reflective glass. He thought of that night, when he'd had his nightmare, and how Sarah had held him and soothed him. He remembered confiding in her about his fears, but now the worries he'd had about Yates using the mirror to get to him seemed like ancient concerns. He gaped at his appearance. Dark shadows of stubble peppered his jaw, his cheeks were sunken, and his hair was dirty and matted. His forehead was scraped, and he had a bruised cheek. But his bloodshot eyes were the worst; they held a haunted look.

He stepped away from the sink, not wanting to look anymore, and headed into the bedroom, where he opened the drawers. All of Sarah's items were gone, save one. The bottom drawer still contained one article of clothing—the Wonder Woman costume. He reached for it and pulled it out, then held it tightly in his hand. One of the appliqued stars from the bottom portion came off and fell to the floor. Watching it fall, he felt his hands start to shake, his legs quiver, and his emotions surface, but he pushed the pain back. He threw the outfit back into the drawer and slammed it shut. Feeling as if weights were tied to his body, he picked up the lonely star and held it. Ramsey moved back into the living room and sat on the couch, then noticed the cracked coffee table. His head still hurting and his vision blurry, he shut his eyes, trying to shut out more than just the physical pain.

But he couldn't. Visions of her in his house and in his bed tortured him, and worst of all was imagining her with Yates. Finally, he stood, dropping the star and letting it drop to the floor. Seeing a book on the end table, he grabbed it and threw it, and it hit the wall with a satisfying thunk. That fueled him, and he started reaching for anything he could find. He threw pictures, pillows, chairs, and—moving into the kitchen—dishes and glasses. He destroyed anything not linked to Sarah. The items shattered as they hit the walls and floor, making him even angrier. If he could have pulled the cabinet doors off their hinges, he would have done it. When he ran out of items in the kitchen, he headed to the hall closet and, breathing hard, grabbed everything he could, yanked it out and demolished it. He slammed the vacuum against the wall, pulled the coats down and kicked at them. He found a box of old pictures, dumped them out on the ground, and stepped on them, feeling nothing but rage as they crumpled beneath his shoes. He spied his overnight bag, pulled it out, and flung it across the room. His skin glistening with sweat, he felt ill. His belly twisted, and he could barely see straight, but he kept going. Destroying everything seemed to be the only thing that helped to manage the burning sickness in his gut.

When he'd removed everything from the closet and there was nothing left to throw, he stopped. His heart raced and he gulped in air. He began to sway and held the wall to stay upright. Finding his balance, he turned and went back to the kitchen as shards of broken kitchenware crunched beneath his feet. Spying an untouched bottle of vodka, he cracked it open, poured a shot into a plastic cup and knocked it back, feeling the heat slide down his throat. He poured another glass, and just as he was about to drink that one too, he noticed a small white envelope on the floor in the hallway. It stopped him cold. Leaving the cup and bottle on the counter, he walked over and picked it up.

John was hand-written on the front and Ramsey remembered Declan handing it to him in the hospital. When he'd been ill and near death, Declan had read him a note from his mother. In it, she had given Ramsey a letter from his father which she had found amongst her things. She'd never opened it, and neither had Ramsey. Too ill to read it at the time, he'd planned to read it later when he had the strength, but he'd found it to be too difficult. He had left it in his overnight bag.

Holding it with shaky fingers, he leaned back against the wall in the hallway and slid down until he sat on the floor. Then he slid his finger under the flap, opened it and pulled the letter out.

My dear son,

I know the road ahead will not always be clear, but know that I am always with you. And if you ever find yourself at the end of your rope, with nowhere else to turn, please remember to Trust Destine. I promise it will lead you in the right direction.

I love you forever,

Dad

Ramsey studied the letter through blurry eyes. The feelings he'd fought so hard to contain now welled up within him, and he sucked in air, trying to calm himself. But the tide of emotions would not be held back, and he slid sideways onto the floor, curled up, and sobbed.

CHAPTER ELEVEN

··

THE POUNDING WAS distant but gradually grew in volume. Realizing it wasn't his head, but his front door, Ramsey didn't move. He couldn't bring himself to care. He'd stopped crying, but his physical and emotional outbursts had left him drained. The pounding continued, and he thought he heard his name, but he couldn't be sure. Footsteps approached and crunched on the broken remnants of his possessions, and then Leroy was there.

"Sherlock?" Leroy kneeled down next to him.

Holding the letter in his hand, Ramsey was still in the fetal position, the tears drying on his face.

"Hey, can you hear me?" Leroy asked. Ramsey heard the worry in his voice.

Declan came up and crouched next to him, opposite of Leroy. "John? Hey, you okay?"

Hannah walked up behind them. "It's hitting him. I'll get him some water."

Leroy leaned over and tried to get Ramsey's attention. "It's Leroy, Sherlock. I'm going to sit you up."

Ramsey made no indication of consent, but Leroy didn't let that stop him. He took Ramsey's arm and gently pulled as Declan pushed up from the other side. Ramsey let himself be dragged up, but he made no effort to help. Another tear trickled down his cheek.

Hannah came back with the water. "Hannah brought you something to drink," said Leroy. "You thirsty?"

Ramsey didn't answer. Clenching his eyes shut, another wave of emotion washed over him and he tried to hold it back, but it was as if the gates had opened and he had no way of shutting them. Fresh tears ran down his face.

"John," said Declan. "Please don't give up. You've got to hang in there."

Ramsey managed to say a few strangled words. "I've lost her."

Leroy squeezed his shoulder. "No, you haven't."

Ramsey made himself look at Leroy. "Yes, I have. She's married to him. She's..." He couldn't finish.

Leroy stared back in anguish, and Ramsey knew he had no idea what to say. Finally seeming to make up his mind, Leroy looked him over. Ramsey still wore the clothes he'd had on for the last two days, and his hair was matted with dried blood. "How about we get you cleaned up, huh?" he asked. "You'll feel better after a shower."

Ramsey didn't reply. Leroy regarded Declan, who nodded at him, and together, the two of them lifted Ramsey.

Leroy took the letter from his hand and handed it to Hannah. "Come on, big guy," he said. "Let's get some of that grime off of you and put you in some clean clothes."

**

Leroy and Declan half carried and half walked Ramsey into the bathroom. Trying to stay busy, Hannah began to clean up some of the mess in the living room. She put the furniture back in place and found a broom and began to sweep. Thirty minutes passed before Declan came out of the bathroom.

"How's he doing?" asked Hannah.

Declan stood as if he'd carried a load of bricks for a mile. "Not good. He doesn't even want to engage." He sighed. "Leroy's helping him get dressed."

Hannah nodded. "He's on overload right now. He's exhausted, dehydrated, underfed, and almost had his brains knocked out of him. I'm surprised he's lasted this long."

Declan sat at the table. "Yeah, I know. Still..."

She knew he was dead on his feet. The last few days had affected all of them. "Ramsey will come around," she said. "He can't stay quiet forever." Declan still looked unconvinced. "Just tell him Morgana's out here. That'll get a reaction out of him."

Declan couldn't help but chuckle. "That's not a bad idea."

She set the broom aside. "I occasionally have a few good ones."

His gaze found hers. "Yeah, you do." The eye contact between them held, and the air in the room began to warm. "You're a special lady, Hannah," he said.

Hannah swallowed, and she felt her cheeks flush. "Well, I don't think my ex-husband would agree with you." She went back into the kitchen and found something to do. When she looked back, she was relieved to see Declan's eyes on the room, and not her.

"You've been busy," he said.

"I figured I'd make myself useful while you two got him cleaned up," she said from the kitchen.

Declan spied the letter on the table. "What's this?"

Hannah came back to the table. "It's the letter he was holding."

**

Declan unfolded the sheet and read it. He understood then what had caused his brother to crumble. Having just lost his own dad, he felt the emotional weight of the words. He heard the bedroom door open and saw Leroy walk out with Ramsey, who was looking much better in a change of clothes, his skin and hair clean. Leroy stood beside him in case he needed help, but Ramsey made it to the table and sat without assistance.

"Feel any better?" asked Declan.

Ramsey stared back at him with the same dull look. "Death might be an improvement."

Declan glanced at Leroy, but Leroy's face expressed little encouragement.

Hannah put a cup of water in front of Ramsey with two white pills. "Take them. It'll help."

Ramsey put up no argument. Instead, he threw back the pills and took a swallow of water, then put the cup back on the table and held it in his hands.

Leroy took a seat. "Declan and I were discussing earlier what to do next."

Ramsey didn't appear to hear him as he continued to stare at his cup.

"We need to find a way to get through to her," said Leroy, waiting for a reaction. "Hey, you listening?"

Ramsey made no response.

"I think we should all go to Disneyland," said Declan, trying to push his brother's buttons. "They say it helps."

Ramsey remained passive.

"Sherlock," said Leroy. "We need to talk about this."

"There's nothing to talk about." said Ramsey.

Leroy smacked a hand on the table. "Damn it, yes, there is."

Ramsey did not push back but continued to sit unaffected, the emotion he'd displayed earlier now gone. "No, there isn't." He closed his eyes. "I'm tired. You should all leave. I just want to go to bed."

Leroy's eyebrows furrowed. "What, so you can stay here and feel sorry for yourself?"

That earned Leroy a scowl from Ramsey. "You can think whatever you want to. I don't care anymore."

"Is that what your dad would want?" asked Declan, holding up the letter.

"Put that down," said Ramsey, finally exhibiting some fire.

"What does he say?" asked Declan, looking at the paper. "Trust Destine? Is that what you're doing?"

"It's trust destiny, you idiot. Now give that to me." Ramsey leaned across the table and yanked the letter out of Declan's hands.

"Destiny?" asked Declan. "That's not what it says."

"Not that it's any of your business," said Ramsey, "but he always told me to trust destiny. That's what he meant."

Declan raised a brow. "You're sure about that?"

Ramsey was no longer passive. "Why in the hell would he tell me to trust destine? That makes no sense." He stood. "Now do me a favor and get the hell out of here."

Declan ignored his outburst. "Why doesn't it make sense?" he asked. "It was your grandmother's name."

Ramsey stared at Declan as if he'd lost his mind. "My grandmother's name? What is wrong with you? My grandmother's name was Rose."

"That's what everyone called her," said Declan, "but her given name was Destine."

"It was not."

"Yes, it was."

"How the hell would you know that?"

"Because she told me, you idiot."

Ramsey stood rooted to his spot. "She told you?"

"Yes. When I first met her. She told me everyone called her Rose, but that her true name was Destine."

Ramsey squinted. "Declan, have you been hit in the head?"

"You're the one with the head injury," said Declan. "If anyone's crazy, it's you. Believe me, I should know."

Leroy and Hannah shared glances, and watched the exchange between the brothers. Ramsey looked completely perplexed.

"She never told me her name was Destine," he said. "Don't you think she would have mentioned it to her grandson? Why would she tell you instead?"

"I don't know," said Declan, throwing up his hands. "Maybe it's my good-natured charm. God knows you could use some."

Ramsey reread the letter. "Trust Destine," he said. He furrowed his brows. "What am I supposed to do with that? How do I trust a woman who died three years ago?"

"You've still got her things, don't you?" asked Declan.

"Her things?" asked Ramsey.

Declan nodded. "Yes. You know. Stuff she used to own? She had a storage unit."

Ramsey's eyes widened.

"Do you have access to it?" asked Leroy.

"Yes," Ramsey said. "When she died, I received the key. I put some of her items from the house in the unit because I didn't want to sell them, but I've never gone through her stuff to see what else was in there." He stared at the letter. "It was just a few boxes and some furniture, but not much else." He glanced back at Declan. "But what does that have to do with anything?" he asked. "How is it that we're thinking about my grandmother when we've got bigger problems to deal with right now?"

"Because you don't want to deal with them," answered Leroy. "And keep this in mind. Your father told you to trust destiny. What are the odds that you opened that letter when you did, and Declan was here to clarify the name?"

"I'm not a big believer in coincidence," said Hannah.

"Neither am I," said Declan.

Ramsey continued to stare at the letter.

"Maybe your dad is trying to tell you something," said Hannah.

Ramsey's lethargy faded. He straightened, took in the three pairs of eyes staring at him, and scratched his head. "Anyone care to join me on a trip to the storage center?"

Leroy stood. "I thought you'd never ask."

"We're stopping for food on the way," said Hannah.

"I'm not hungry..." Ramsey stopped short when they all froze in mid-motion and looked at him. "All right, you win," he said. "We'll stop."

Hannah pointed. "And you'll eat something, or I'll hand feed you myself."

His shoulders drooped. "Yes, ma'am."

**

Ramsey rolled the door to the storage area open and the lights flickered on, revealing boxes stacked in a corner, and various items of furniture pushed into the small space.

He remembered the last time he'd been here. He'd brought in his grandmother's desk not long after she'd died and he'd moved into her house. Ramsey had not needed it, and it had no monetary value, but he couldn't bring himself to sell it or throw it away. It sat exactly where he had put it three years ago. "Any idea where to start?" he asked the others.

"I'd say the boxes," said Leroy.

"It's as good a place as any," said Declan.

**

The three men began to pull out the furniture that blocked their way. Hannah watched them move the desk out into the hallway of the storage area, as well as a table and chairs.

"These were your grandmother's?" she asked, running her fingers over the wooden table.

"Yes," said Ramsey.

"Why are they in storage?" she asked. "These are antiques."

Ramsey moved a chair out of his way. "I don't know. She kept them here. I never saw them in her house. They must have sentimental value."

"They have more than that," said Hannah. "These would catch a pretty penny at an auction house." She admired a large armoire that was pushed up against the wall. It was taller than she was. She popped open the door, smelling the musty odor of stale air. "This is beautiful."

Ramsey grabbed a box. "You want it?"

She stared over at him as he handed the box to Leroy. "What?" she asked. "I can't take this. It's worth thousands, I'm sure."

"It's just sitting in a storage unit, Hannah. Someone should enjoy it. Besides, I'm not going to sell it."

"But you'd give it away?"

"I'd give it to you," he said. "It's the least I could do."

"She'd have wanted you to have it," said Declan, as he opened a box. "She would have liked you."

"She'd have admired your pluck," said Ramsey.

"That sounds like something she'd say," said Declan.

"Still, it's too much," said Hannah.

"The offer stands whenever you want it," said Ramsey, pulling out shirts and pants from a box. "There's nothing in here but old clothing."

"Nothing of interest in here either," said Leroy, closing his box.

Declan accessed his box and found several photo albums. He lifted one out and opened it. "Is this you with your mom and dad?" he asked.

Ramsey stopped and leaned over. "Yeah, that's me."

"You were a cute kid," said Declan. "What happened?"

Ramsey sneered at him. "Just keep looking, smart ass."

Declan chuckled and put the box of albums aside to bring back with them.

Ramsey handed Declan another box as Leroy dug into a new one. Hannah worked her way over to a vanity table in the opposite corner of the unit. A small bench sat pushed up beneath it. She pulled it out and sat on it. Looking into the cloudy mirror atop the table, she envisioned an older woman sitting there, running a brush through her silver hair. It was another lovely antique piece, and she wondered how old it was. Out of curiosity, she opened the drawers. Inside one of them was a hairbrush, much like the one she'd envisioned. She pulled it out. It was silver with soft bristles, and she could only assume it had belonged to Ramsey's grandmother. Running her fingers over it, she wondered about its history.

"Nothing in this one either," said Leroy.

"Or this one," said Declan.

"This one's a bust, too," said Ramsey.

"Any more?" asked Leroy.

"That's it," said Ramsey, closing his box. "Looks like this was a wild goose chase."

"Uh, Leroy?" said Hannah.

Leroy looked over at Hannah. "What?"

"Would you come look at this please?"

"What is it?" he asked, moving toward her.

Hannah handed him the tarnished antique brush. "Is that what I think it is?" she asked.

"Well, if you think it's a hairbrush, then yes," said Leroy.

Hannah frowned. "Other side."

Leroy turned it over and ran his fingers over the cool metal. His eyes widened.

"What?" asked Ramsey.

"It can't be..." said Leroy, peering at Hannah.

"It looks pretty similar," said Hannah.

"It's more than similar."

"What?" asked Declan.

"What are you two looking at?" asked Ramsey. He and Declan moved closer and Ramsey took the brush from Leroy. "Something odd about a hair bush?"

"The back of it," said Leroy.

Ramsey turned it over. Engraved on the back was an ornate letter D in calligraphy.

He smirked at Declan. "This backs up your story that her name was Destine."

"It's not a story," said Declan, who took the brush from Ramsey and began studying it. He went still for a moment. "It was hers, though."

"What's the problem?" asked Ramsey.

Hannah raised a brow at Leroy and Leroy pointed at the brush. "The Eudoran Mirror has that exact engraving on the back."

"You mean this?" Declan asked, pointing at the D.

"Yes, that," said Leroy.

"Well, I'm sure it's not that uncommon for antique items to have engravings," said Ramsey.

"The exact engraving?" asked Leroy. "With the same initial?"

"Back in the day," said Hannah, "cosmetic items like this came as a set. There was a brush, a comb—"

"And a mirror," finished Declan, understanding dawning. His eyes rounded. "Are you saying—"

"That the Eudoran Mirror at one point belonged to Sherlock's grandmother?" asked Leroy. He nodded. "Yes, I think that's what I'm saying."

Ramsey stared at the brush, then shook his head. "Oh, come on. That's not possible."

"Why not?" asked Declan.

"Because..." Ramsey ran a hand through his hair.

"I think your dad is definitely trying to tell us something," said Hannah.

"But what?" asked Leroy.

"I'm completely baffled," said Ramsey. "How is this even possible?"

Declan held the brush, running his finger over the elaborate letter D. "I don't know," he said. "But I bet you I know who does." He met Ramsey's look.

Ramsey's eyebrows rose, and he grabbed the hairbrush. "Come on," he said. "Let's go."

CHAPTER TWELVE

·····································

D RAKE SET HIS glass on the coffee table and sat back on the couch in Morgana's office. "It's a disaster. The whole thing."

Morgana took a sip from her own glass. "I agree the situation is not ideal."

"Not ideal?" answered Drake. "Things couldn't be worse if you poured gasoline on them and lit a match."

"You do have a flair for the dramatic, Drake."

"I guess when you come to terms with the fact that your life expectancy has just decreased by several years, you tend to think the worst."

"Some choose to think otherwise."

"Not me."

A loud banging from the front door stopped Morgana's response. She swiveled toward the sound.

"Who's that?" asked Drake. "Expecting someone?"

Morgana stood as more banging could be heard. "No." She walked to the doorway of her office and looked down the hall toward the front door. Ronald, her valet, appeared.

"Come on, Morgana," said a loud voice from outside the door. She recognized it immediately as Ramsey's. "I know you're in there." The banging came again.

She nodded at Ronald, and he headed for the front door as she went to sit down. "Apparently I have guests," she said to Drake.

Seconds later, Ramsey filed into her office, followed by Declan, Leroy and Hannah.

"Well," she said. "To what do I owe this unexpected pleasure?"

Ramsey eyed Drake on the couch. "Drake," he said.

"Ramsey," Drake replied.

Ramsey addressed Morgana. "Don't bother getting up."

"I won't," she said. She looked him over. "You appear to be doing well, despite your near incarceration."

Ramsey's eyes narrowed. "My what?"

"I'll explain later," said Declan from behind Ramsey.

Ramsey held up the brush. "I found something you might find interesting."

Morgana eyed the item in his hand. "Based on your appearance, I'd say you need it more than I do."

He walked up to her. "I don't know about that," he said. "I thought perhaps you might like the engraving."

She put her drink down, took the item from him and turned it over in her hand. Seeing the engraving, she stilled. "Where did you find this?"

"In my grandmother's things."

"What is it?" asked Drake.

Morgana held the brush for a moment longer before handing it to Drake. He took it and his eyes widened. "Is this what I think it is?" he asked.

"I don't know, Drake," said Ramsey. "That's what I'm here to find out."

**

Ramsey watched Morgana stand, pick up her glass, and walk to the window. After setting her drink on the desk, she put her hands in the pockets of her neatly pressed pants.

"I'd say the time has come to tell him," said Drake.

"Tell me what?" asked Ramsey.

Morgana studied the yard as if lost in thought.

"Come on, Morgana," said Leroy. "What the hell is going on?"

After another few seconds of silence, Morgana turned to face Ramsey. "I knew your grandmother," she said.

"You what?" asked Ramsey.

She took her hands out of her pockets. "Take a seat," she said. "All of you."

Ramsey started to argue, but then thought better of it as Hannah and Leroy went to sit next to Drake. Joining Declan, he sat in one of the chairs across from Hannah and Leroy. "Okay," he said. "We're all comfy now. Tell me."

Morgana paused, as if wondering where to start. "I met her when I was a child."

Ramsey waited while she appeared to collect her thoughts.

"I went to school all over the world. My father never believed a child should be raised in one place. When I was twelve, we lived in France and I went to an exclusive grade school. It was there I met Destine."

Nobody said a word.

"We became fast friends, in fact, best friends. We spent most of our time together. But her father, like mine, kept moving. Within two years, she was in Switzerland and I was in Spain. Nevertheless, we always kept in touch."

She reached out and picked up her glass in order to take a sip. It was the first time Ramsey had ever seen her exhibit any nerves. He could swear her hand was shaking.

"Anyway," she said, putting the glass down, "at the time, I had no idea who she was. I knew she was Eudoran, but like the rest of us, she never spoke of it." Morgana stared off for a second. "Years later, after school, I became an attorney and went to live in the U.S. I'd heard she'd married an American military man and had a child. They lived in Europe on various military bases. When her son...your father... was old enough, they sent him here to go to college. He met your mom, and you were born. After Destine's husband died, she moved to the States to be closer to you and her son. It was around the same time I became a councilwoman and retired from the legal profession." She picked up her glass again, but didn't drink from it. "It was then that I learned her secret."

"Her secret?" asked Ramsey.

"What do you mean?" asked Declan.

Morgana hesitated, but then eyed Ramsey. "She was a Red-Line."

"She was a what?" asked Ramsey.

Declan, Hannah, and Leroy sat up in surprise.

"No, she wasn't," said Ramsey.

"Yes," said Morgana. "She was. No one knew it, though. She'd kept it hidden all her life. How she did it, I don't know. I knew then why her father moved around so much. He was keeping their secret."

"Their secret?" asked Ramsey. He couldn't have been more surprised if he'd seen a space ship land in Morgana's back yard.

"They were both Red-Lines—Destine and her father. They'd been in hiding for years."

"But how?" asked Leroy. "Why?"

Morgana took a heavy swig of her drink. "Because if their true identities were known, their lives would be at risk. Destine's father couldn't take that chance. His child's protection was his priority."

"Why were they at risk?" asked Ramsey.

"Because..." said Morgana. "The woman who piloted the ship that went down, Varalika, the one who jettisoned the serum and coded the Eudoran Mirror?"

Ramsey nodded.

"Destine was her daughter, and Destine's father was her husband." Morgana's gaze sharpened. "So that makes you, John Sherlock Ramsey, Varalika's great-grandson."

The silence in the room was disturbed only by Ramsey's intake of air.

"I'll be damned," said Leroy.

Ramsey was speechless.

"He's what?" asked Declan. "Are you serious?"

"Unbelievable," said Hannah.

"Oh, it gets better," said Drake.

Morgana eyed him into silence.

"But..." Ramsey tried to think of what to say. "How come I didn't know that?" He shot a hand out. "Why didn't Dad tell me? How come she didn't tell me?"

"As I said, Ramsey," answered Morgana, "it was a secret. Hence the not telling you part."

"That's a hell of a big secret to keep," said Ramsey.

Morgana tipped her head. "Indeed."

"Why were they in danger?" asked Declan.

"Because Varalika's ship did not go down by accident."

"How do you know that?" asked Ramsey.

Morgana swirled what was left in her glass. "All I know is what Destine told me."

"And what did she tell you?" asked Leroy.

Morgana went to her desk and leaned back on it. "I didn't learn who she was until she moved to the States and we picked up where we left off, resuming our friendship. After she returned, I knew there was something she was hiding. I could feel it. I was on the

Council by then and had learned of the precarious position our people were in, but I had no idea that Destine, or Rose, which is the name you knew her by, played a part in it." She paused. "She finally confided in me during the time you were sick as a child, Ramsey."

"Sick?" asked Ramsey.

"You were three years old. You'd contracted viral pneumonia."

Ramsey thought back. "I vaguely recall my dad telling me about that."

"They had you in a hospital. Your grandmother was so worried. She'd been by your bedside night and day. When the crisis passed, I took her home. We started drinking. She rarely drank, but with all the stress and fear, she couldn't sleep. She needed to relax. I opened some wine, and two bottles later, I knew her story."

"And what was her story?" asked Ramsey.

Morgana paused. "Varalika was not the only passenger on the ship. Her husband and daughter were also on board, although the manifest showed she traveled alone."

"Why is that?" asked Leroy.

"I can only assume she didn't want anyone to know they were with her," said Morgana. "Based on what I understand now, I believe she was aware of something that put her life in danger. She brought her family on board to protect them. Only the ship was compromised. She dumped the cargo and landed as best she could, but she was injured and did not survive, although Destine and her father did."

"They believed that whoever came after Varalika would come after them?" asked Declan.

"Yes," said Morgana. "If this person knew they were alive, they were potential targets."

"But how did they survive?" asked Hannah. "They were Red-Lines with no serum."

"They had serum," said Morgana. "Destine's father must have taken measures and brought some on board. He took it with them when they abandoned the ship."

"And her Shift?" asked Ramsey. "How did she get through it?"

"Her father did much the same as you did with Sarah. He put her somewhere safe, found some discreet people he trusted to help him, and got her through it. She had serum, though, which helped. After that, she had to be even more careful. A Red-Line after their Shift is even harder to hide, but her father taught her how to cloak herself and how to contract her energy so as not to be felt. Otherwise, she would have been found by our people in no time."

"She learned well," said Declan. "I never felt an inkling of energy fluctuation in her."

Morgana nodded. "By the time you met her, she'd been doing it for years. It was second nature to her."

"Wait," said Ramsey, raising a hand. "You're telling me that the mirror that Varalika had, the one that everyone's been trying to read, belonged to my grandmother, whose real name was Destine?"

"Yes," said Morgana. "It was a gift from her parents. She brought it with her on the ship."

"Then why didn't she read it?" asked Leroy.

"Yeah, why didn't she?" asked Hannah.

Morgana studied her drink. "She did."

"She did?" asked Declan.

"Yes," said Morgana. "The moment I heard her story, I knew the mirror belonged to her. She had no idea the position we were in and had no knowledge that Grays lacked serum. When I told her the situation, she of course agreed to read the mirror, but she made me swear to tell no one who she was or anything about her involvement."

"But why?" asked Ramsey.

"She still feared for her life and for her family's. She didn't want anyone hurting you if her true identity were discovered."

"Was she still in danger?" asked Declan.

"She couldn't be sure," said Morgana, "but she didn't want to take the risk. So, I agreed to her request. One week later, I snuck her in after dark and let her read the mirror."

"What happened?" asked Ramsey.

Morgana stared off. "It was extremely traumatic for her. She felt and sensed everything from the accident, including her mother's death. It was all I could do to calm her down."

"Did she see the serum's location?" asked Declan.

"She confirmed it was on board, and she knew her mother dumped it, but she couldn't see where. Her mother wouldn't tell her."

"What do you mean her mother wouldn't tell her?" asked Leroy. "They weren't having a conversation."

Morgana took a shaky sip from her glass. "Yes, they were."

"What?" asked Ramsey.

Morgana walked to the bar and added more liquor to her drink. "I've never seen anything like it. She was talking to her mother as if she were there, which I guess from Destine's point of view, she was."

"What did she say?"

Holding her beverage, Morgana returned to her stance against the desk. "Her mother told her to stay away and not come back; there were some things Destine was not meant to know. But before Varalika left, she told Destine that the mirror would reveal its secrets one day. When the time was right. But that it would require another mirror to read it."

"Another mirror? You mean there's another mirror out there?" asked Declan.

Morgana took another heavy sip of her drink, looking like she needed it. "Not in the way you mean. I knew Destine understood, but she needed some time after the encounter to regroup. It took her a while to recover from the incident, but when she did, she told me what her mother meant."

"Which was?" asked Ramsey.

"She didn't mean another mirror as in a piece of reflective glass. She meant another mirror of herself."

Ramsey shook his head. "I don't understand."

Morgana put her drink down and crossed her arms. "When Destine read her mirror, she saw her mother dying, clutching the mirror in her hand and her father lying with her, desperate to save her, but knowing he couldn't. Her mother told him to leave and take Destine and protect her. He had no choice but to leave her there. All of that energy went into the mirror as she held it, and now that energy requires like energy to read it."

"Like energy?" asked Declan.

"Basically, the person who reads the mirror must mirror Varalika—a Red-Line female in distress, her husband, or rather the man she loves, by her side."

"What?" asked Ramsey.

"How did you plan on recreating that scenario?" asked Leroy.

Morgana flicked her gaze toward Leroy. "We didn't have any plan. I was sworn to secrecy, but Sarah was eighteen months old at the time, so we had one part of the equation. We just needed the other part." She looked at Ramsey. "Which is where you come in."

"Me?' he asked.

"Yes, you."

Ramsey sat up. "What role do I play in this?"

Morgana walked over to the cabinet beside her desk. She opened it, pulled out another bottle and poured a drink. She put the bottle away and made her way to Ramsey and handed the glass to him. "Considering everything," she said, "you may need this." She walked to the window. "Let me preface this by saying that your grandmother and I had no plans to intervene. We simply put things in place and let nature take its course."

Ramsey held the glass, his hands suddenly shaky. "Morgana...what do you mean?"

She stared out at her yard. "You should know something about female Red-Lines, Ramsey."

"What is that?" he asked.

"They're extremely smart and they know what they want. And when they want something, they usually get it."

"What are you talking about?"

She swiveled her head in Ramsey's direction. "Destine and I knew Sarah was the one chance we had to save you."

Ramsey held his breath. "Me?"

"Yes. Keep in mind your grandmother knew your life was at risk. She was extremely motivated to find the serum. So even though our entire race was threatened, her sole intention was to protect your future."

Ramsey clutched his glass. "Okay."

She faced the group. "We put our heads together to think things through, and we came up with an idea."

"What idea?" asked Ramsey.

She paused. "To see if you and Sarah would fall in love."

Ramsey dropped his jaw.

"Why?" asked Declan.

"Because Varalika was in love with Destine's father when she died. What better way to mimic that than to have Sarah in love with Varalika's great-grandson. That's a pretty similar energy, if you ask me."

"You arranged this?" Ramsey asked. Unsettled, he took a swig from the glass Morgana had given him. "How could you possibly do that?"

Morgana sighed. "At the time, you were both children, but we knew that if no other solution presented itself that the two of you were our best hope. Based on the amount of serum remaining and the time it would take to wait for you both to grow up, it was going to be close. We had to pray that Sarah's Shift did not come too late." She stopped for a second. "It was Destine who guided you toward becoming a Protector. I questioned whether you would succeed in the role, but Destine never wavered in her belief in you. As usual, she was right."

Morgana paused again. "Before she died, Destine made me promise to reveal nothing to you. She insisted that I only arrange for you two to meet. She suggested that Sarah's Shift would be the best timing. When the time came, I made sure you were her Protector. After that, I was to step back and stay out of it. I had to leave the rest of it alone, she said, or it would affect whether or not the mirror could be read. It would know the difference between real and false energy."

"I don't believe this," said Ramsey.

"What's so hard to believe?" asked Hannah. "It makes perfect sense. It's no different than any other grandmother who wants their grandchild to be happy. All they did was introduce you to her. You guys did the rest."

"And it didn't take long, either," said Declan.

"No, it didn't. You liked her from the start," said Leroy.

"She liked you, too," said Hannah.

"I'd say it was destiny," said Declan.

"I was pleased with the results," said Morgana. "You two were instantly attracted to each other, as if it was meant to be."

"I'm glad I made it easy for you," said Ramsey, putting his drink on an end table. "but in case you haven't noticed, things have gone downhill recently." He paused. "I don't have her anymore."

Morgana studied him. "Regardless of the circumstances, you and she are still very much intertwined."

He grimaced. "She married him. I'd say her future's just taken a drastic turn."

Morgana stepped away from the window and neared him. "On the contrary, her future is still linked to yours as long as you still love her."

Ramsey tensed. "Of course, I do."

"Good," said Morgana. "Then you won't mind what I have to tell you next."

"Next?" asked Ramsey. His questioning eyes held Morgana's piercing ones. "What else could there be?"

Morgana took a moment before she spoke. "Female Red-Lines follow certain...shall I say... practices when they find a mate. Destine believed if you two hit it off that Sarah might initiate these practices with you."

"Mate?" asked Ramsey. "Is that what I am now?"

"Yes," said Morgana. "Someone they wish to take as a partner. The method by which they claim their mate is called a Binding."

"A Binding?" he asked.

She nodded. "When a female chooses someone, a Binding is initiated. It happens of its own accord. Sarah had no idea that it had a name or a purpose. She simply acted instinctively. If the female takes no action to stop it, then it will proceed accordingly."

"And what sort of process does this entail?" asked Ramsey, knitting his brows.

Morgana studied him. "An intense period of sexual activity begun by the female, usually lasting anywhere from twenty-four to forty-eight hours."

Ramsey sat dumbstruck. An image of Sarah standing in front of him in a Wonder Woman outfit popped into his head. "It was more like sixty," he said, "but who's counting."

Declan and Hannah smiled, and Leroy chuckled.

"You're telling me she took me as her mate?" Ramsey asked.

Morgana found her drink and picked it up. "She did."

Ramsey hung his head. "Funny. It seems she's smitten with someone else."

"For the moment," said Morgana.

"We have a theory about that," said Drake.

"What theory?" asked Ramsey.

Drake leaned forward. "That this man Yates somehow mimicked the Binding process with her. Made her initiate it with him."

Ramsey shut his eyes. "Oh, God," he said, dropping his face into his hand.

"Drake, we can't be sure if that's the case," said Morgana.

Drake ignored her warning tone. "Come on, Morgana. We all know what Yates wants. Let's not ignore the elephant in the room."

Ramsey lifted his head. "What elephant?"

"Let's not make any hasty assumptions," said Declan, looking at Leroy and Hannah. "Nobody really knows what he wants."

"That's right," said Hannah.

"Let's go back to this Binding theory," said Leroy.

"No, wait a minute," said Ramsey. "What does Yates want?"

"Children," said Drake.

"Drake—" said Morgana.

"Oh, come on, Morgana," said Drake. "The man needs to know. And you're taking forever to tell him."

"Children?" Ramsey let word sink in. "Children?" He felt the color leave his face.

"Sherlock..." said Leroy.

Ramsey stood. "No, Leroy." He faced Morgana. "Is this what you're trying to tell me? That he's initiated this Binding process with her in order to have children with her?"

"Sit down," she said, unaffected by his shock. "I'm not done."

"What else is there to possibly say?" Ramsey sputtered. His lips kept moving, but no words came. He tried to breath, but his chest was so tight he could barely suck in air. "They're on their honeymoon, for God's sake. She could be—" He stopped, unable to say the word.

"Dammit, Morgana. Don't you think he's been through enough?" asked Declan.

Morgana maintained her calm. "Everybody relax, especially you, Ramsey," she said. "I'm telling you this for a reason."

"Why?" he asked, feeling his strength leave him. He held onto the wall for support. "You getting a kick out of this? Seeing me at my lowest?"

She ticked up a brow. "Don't be absurd."

"Then why?"

She knocked back the remains of her drink and set the glass on her desk. "Because she can't possibly be pregnant with his child."

That got his attention. "Why not?"

"Because she's already pregnant with yours."

Ramsey's had expected a myriad of answers, but that was not one of them. "Wh...what?"

"What are you talking about, Morgana?" asked Leroy, saying the words that Ramsey failed to utter.

Morgana narrowed her eyes at him. "A Binding is not just about taking a mate, it's also about continuing the line."

Ramsey could only stare. "The line?"

"Yes. A Red-Line binding results in pregnancy every time."

"But..." Ramsey struggled to find his tongue. "But she used birth control."

"You think a little pill is going to stop thousands of years of genetic instinct?"

"But she's not just a Red-Line. She's half-human."

She shrugged. "I doubt that matters."

"You doubt?" he asked, pushing off the wall. "So that means you're not sure?"

Morgana squared her shoulders. "Considering all the changes in her since her Shift? All the abilities she's exhibited? I'd say her Red-Line is showing. That combined with the sixty hours you say you two spent together? I'd wager my savings that the two of you are expecting."

"A baby?" He shook his head, still in disbelief. "She's going to have my baby?"

"Congratulations," said Hannah.

Leroy stood. "Sherlock, you okay?"

"Maybe you better sit down," said Declan.

Ramsey blinked, and sat, grabbing at the chair handle to support himself. "I'm okay," he said. "Just give me a second." He found the drink on the end table and shot it back.

"If what you're saying is true," asked Declan, "and I'm about to be an uncle, then how do we get Sarah away from Yates without him hurting her or the baby?"

That snapped Ramsey back to attention, and he waited to hear the answer.

"It may take a little maneuvering," said Morgana, "but I believe it can be done."

"How?" asked Leroy. He walked over to the cabinet and found the bottle of liquor Morgana had just accessed. "You mind?" he asked.

"Help yourself," she said.

Leroy grabbed Ramsey's empty glass and poured more liquor into it. He put the bottle away and offered the glass to Ramsey. "Here," he said. "You need another one."

Ramsey, still in shock, didn't disagree. He took the glass, his fingers trembling. "Thanks."

Leroy went back to his chair.

"He may have been able to initiate the Binding process with her by removing her memories of Ramsey," said Morgana, "but I suspect that whatever methods he's using will only last for the short term."

"Because she's a Red-Line?" asked Declan.

"Exactly," she said. "You can't manipulate that kind of energy for any length of time without it starting to unravel. It will eventually backfire."

"But he's got to be expecting that," said Declan. "He must have something in place in case that happens."

"My guess is he's planning on getting her pregnant. Once that happens, then she's bound to him forever," said Morgana.

"Or worse," said Hannah.

"What do you mean?" asked Morgana.

Hannah sat forward. "If she comes out of it and doesn't want him, then maybe he'll just want the baby."

"You mean after he gets the child, he won't want her anymore?" asked Leroy.

"He wants her," said Ramsey.

"I know he does," said Hannah, "but if she fights him..."

"When she comes out of it," said Ramsey, "she'll fight him."

"We have to find a way to get her out of there," said Declan, "preferably before it comes down to a battle between the Red-Lines. That could be disastrous."

"Not only that, but we have to find a way to get the two of you to read the mirror," said Morgana.

"Two?" asked Ramsey. "As in both of us?"

"Yes," said Morgana. "We have to mirror Varalika's energy. She was with her husband when she coded the mirror. That, and..."

"And what?" asked Ramsey.

Morgana raised a brow at him. "There's something else that's important to know about Varalika's death."

"What's that?" asked Ramsey.

"Your grandmother felt it when she read the mirror," said Morgana. "Varalika was pregnant when she died."

"No," said Hannah.

"She was?" asked Ramsey.

"Well, if that's true," said Declan, "then..."

"...then if we can get Sherlock and Sarah together and have her read the mirror," said Leroy, "then we've got a great shot at finding that serum."

"Don't forget the distress part," said Drake.

"Oh, I think we've got that part covered," said Ramsey.

"How do we arrange this?" asked Leroy as Morgana came back to her seat. "I suspect you have some ideas?"

Morgana eyed Declan and Leroy. "You said when you saw her, she remembered your names?"

"She did. Declan and Leroy's," said Ramsey, taking a swig of his second drink.

"So, she hasn't lost her memory of all of you." She sat back.

"No, I don't think so," said Declan. "But we don't know how much she remembers."

Morgana pointed. "We'll start there."

"Where's there?" asked Ramsey.

"He hasn't been able to shut all of you out," she said, "so we send one of you in to start jogging her memory."

"One of us?" asked Declan. "Who?"

Morgana looked at Hannah.

"Me?" asked Hannah.

"No, I don't like it," said Declan.

"She's perfect," said Morgana. "She simply plays her role as best friend, but in a non-threatening way. You play along with her story, but you just add in some helpful details along the way. My guess is that Sarah will take it from there, and with your help, she'll start to remember."

"It's too dangerous," said Declan.

"I'll do it," said Hannah.

"Hannah..." said Declan.

"We'll keep an eye on her," said Leroy. "If we think there's a problem, we can pull her out."

"Like we got Sarah out?" asked Ramsey. He glanced at Hannah. "Declan's right, Hannah. Yates is a Red-Line. If he gets one whiff that you're helping Sarah to remember, we don't know what he'd do. And as much as I'd like to say we could protect you, we can't."

"What are we supposed to do then? Sit back and let this man take what he wants?" asked Hannah.

"I'll do it," said Ramsey. "It's my risk to take. I'll find a way to get through to her."

"You push her too fast," said Morgana, "it could do her more harm than good. We have to take this slow. We don't know what methods he's using to keep her under his control."

"I want to do it," said Hannah. "She needs my help. If it were me, she'd be there. Besides, what this Yates has done to her pisses me off. We can't let him get away with this."

"He's not going to," said Declan.

"Isn't he?" asked Drake. "Just how do you expect to stop him?"

Morgana gripped the arm of her chair. "Drake, do you think you could refrain from thinking the worst?"

"And do you think you could face reality?" asked Drake. "The man's a Red-Line. He's shown what he's capable of. You'll never be free of him, and neither will Sarah, unless..."

"Unless?" asked Hannah.

"Unless he's no longer around to hurt us," said Declan.

"Precisely," said Drake. "So before you undertake this plan of yours, you need to prepare yourselves to do what needs to done. And figure out how you plan to do it."

"What are you saying, Drake?" asked Ramsey.

Drake set his jaw. "You know exactly what I'm saying. But I'll spell it out for you. You want her back, you're going to have to kill him to do it. Anything less, and he wins."

CHAPTER THIRTEEN

....

DRAKE'S WORDS REVERBERATED throughout the room as each of them considered how far they were willing to go to protect their own. Their thoughts were interrupted by the ringing of the doorbell.

"I have no problem with that," said Ramsey, ignoring the bell. "Get me close enough to him and I'll do whatever it takes."

"Me, too," said Declan. "I'm with John."

"I'm in, too," said Leroy.

"It's okay if you're not, Leroy," said Ramsey. "You have Olivia to think about."

"Olivia is not the only important person in my life, Sherlock," said Leroy. "I won't be able to live with myself if you and Declan are taking all the risks. That's not the kind of man I am. Olivia will be fine. I'll ask her to go stay with her sister for a while."

"I'm in, too," said Hannah.

"Hannah," said Declan, "you don't have to do this. Of all of us, you're the least likely to be targeted by him. It's better you get out before this gets ugly."

"Don't tell me what to do, Declan," she replied. "I'm a big girl. And like Leroy says, I'm not going to sit around and watch you all take the risk. I've been in this since the beginning, and I'll see it through to the end. Like it or not." She held his gaze until he nodded, unable to do much else.

Ronald appeared at the doorway.

"Yes, Ronald?" asked Morgana. "Who was at the door?"

"The police are here, madam. They'd like to speak with you."

Everyone went quiet. After a second of silence, Morgana stood. "No one leaves this room." She'd moved back into her authoritative role. "Who drove here?" she asked.

"Me," said Leroy.

"That's your car out front?"

"Yes."

"Good. I'll be right back." She turned and left the office, closing the door behind her.

"Oh, hell," said Drake. "This can't be good."

"The police?" asked Ramsey. "Why would they be here?"

Declan met Leroy's gaze. "Sherlock," said Leroy, "in the alley last night..."

"What?" asked Ramsey.

Declan huffed out a sigh. "We found Marco's body," he said. "Not far from where we found you."

Ramsey froze. "Marco's body? He's dead?"

"Yes," said Declan. "He'd been stabbed multiple times."

Ramsey thought back. "My God. The knife. My hands." He looked at his palms. "What did I do?"

Drake rolled his eyes. "I wouldn't say that to the police."

"You didn't do anything," answered Leroy. "Yates just wants to make it look like you did." He addressed Declan. "Why would the police be here? Did we miss something?"

Declan groaned. "I don't know. I guess we need to hear what Morgana says."

"You think they're looking for me?" asked Ramsey.

"Let's not jump to conclusions," said Leroy. "Let's wait and see what happens."

"This is all I need," said Ramsey, dropping his head back into his hand. "A murder rap." He snorted. "It's almost funny."

"You are not going to be charged with murder," said Declan. "They have no body and no weapon. They probably just have a few questions. That's it."

The office door opened, and Morgana returned, sitting back in her seat.

"Well?" said Drake. "What is it now?"

She eyed Ramsey. "They're looking for you."

"What?" asked Declan. "Why?"

"Figures," said Ramsey.

"What do they want?" asked Leroy. "Sherlock didn't do anything."

"Relax, all of you," said Morgana. "They're looking for Marco, too. He's been reported missing."

"It's Yates," said Declan. "That bastard is pulling the strings."

"Why do they want to speak to me?" asked Ramsey.

"And how did they end up at your door?" asked Leroy.

"Because he's listed as an employee of mine," said Morgana. "He's done security for us in the past."

"What did they say about John?" asked Declan.

Morgana spoke to Ramsey. "They want to ask you some questions. They didn't go into specifics. They just said they think you might have some information about his whereabouts."

"It's more than that, I'm sure," said Ramsey.

"Maybe, maybe not," said Morgana.

"What do I do now?" asked Ramsey. "How am I supposed to help Sarah and hide from the police at the same time?"

Morgana crossed her legs and interlaced her fingers. "You are not going to hide from anyone."

"And what happens when they drag me down to the station?" asked Ramsey.

"They can't do that without a warrant, but should you be taken anywhere, you keep your mouth shut and call me."

"And if they just question me like they did you?"

"You simply answer their questions, just as I did."

"Questions?" asked Ramsey.

"Yes," she said. "When's the last time you saw Marco?"

Ramsey thought about it. "Uh...the day Sarah disappeared. He had her security detail."

"That's what you say," said Morgana. "Just don't elaborate."

"But how does he explain Sarah, or her need for security?" asked Hannah.

Morgana shrugged. "Sarah was a girlfriend. You've since broken up. Marco was initially your security. You'd been stabbed recently. But Marco followed her that day, not you. Keep it simple."

Ramsey frowned. "But then they'll want to talk to Sarah."

"Let them talk to her," said Morgana. "That could play to our advantage."

"And how is it that his girlfriend is now married to someone else?" asked Declan. "Doesn't that seem suspicious?"

Morgana adjusted her sleeve. "Let Yates deal with that one. Ramsey has no knowledge of what Sarah's done since she left."

"I don't want any suspicion to fall on her," said Ramsey. "They do enough digging and they'll find that Marco followed Sarah to Sullivan's."

Morgana nodded. "And she left with a man who carried her out, unconscious."

"That leads them to Yates," said Declan. "Assuming they can find him."

"Exactly," said Morgana. "The man, in his zeal to get to you, Ramsey, may be digging his own grave."

"I doubt it," answered Ramsey. "I suspect Yates can get himself out of a hole when he needs to."

"Which brings us back to our original topic," said Leroy. "How do we get rid of him?"

"It won't be simple," said Morgana. "Keep in mind he's a prominent businessman."

"Prominent?" said Declan. "We couldn't even find his name on the internet."

"The Council has done some digging since you learned his last name," said Morgana. "Despite his ability to keep a low profile, he's the founder of XYZ Laboratories, one of the biggest medical technology companies in the nation, and he's a very rich man. Killing him is not the issue. It's killing him without suspicion. Therein lies the rub."

"Great. Now we're in some sort of Shakespearean drama," said Drake.

"Shakespeare should be so lucky to write this story," said Ramsey.

"Let's just hope the bad guy dies in the end," said Leroy.

"He will," said Morgana.

"And that he doesn't take any of the good guys with him when he does," said Hannah.

None of them disagreed.

CHAPTER FOURTEEN

·····································

YATES SAT AT his desk in his home, staring up at the computer monitors where bits of data and formulas splayed across the screen, which would have looked more like a jumble of tiles from a Scrabble game to any lay person. But he didn't study the data. His mind traveled elsewhere. Arriving home a week earlier from his honeymoon, he recounted his successes and delighted in his satisfaction. He and Sarah had enjoyed a wonderful time together. The idea of extending the trip had crossed his mind, since he knew Sarah wanted to see Italy, but he chose not to when he realized he'd only brought a limited amount of medication for her. He couldn't run the risk of running out. Smiling, he reminisced of their trip. She'd completely forgotten about Ramsey and appeared to have few lingering effects from the serum he'd given her, which he'd created after studying her blood chemistry and that of Ramsey's, which he'd obtained during Ramsey's stay in the hospital.

Based on what he knew of female Red-Lines, he understood that when they found a mate, they had a powerful and instinctual urge to bind with them. Arnuff and Emerson had told him little about this process, but he knew enough to realize that Sarah had come close to initiating the process with Ramsey, and he'd had to act fast before she claimed him as her own. Fearing that Ramsey's recovery would only bring them closer, he'd been glad to hear from Julian that the exact opposite had happened; Ramsey had distanced himself from Sarah. Pleased at the news, Yates had buried himself in his lab, anxious to complete the creation of the drug that would make Sarah turn from Ramsey and choose him instead. It had been a risk. In time, he knew Ramsey would realize his mistake and find his way back to Sarah, and Yates needed to act before that occurred.

After weeks of long work days and sleepless nights, he'd finally completed his testing of the drug. Despite his efforts, he knew the dangers still existed. If Sarah had received too much of his concoction, she could have forgotten him as well. Too little, and his plan was a failure. But as usual, he'd planned perfectly, and his experiment continued to work. With just a little help from the pills he gave her and the energy he used to mollify and distract her, Sarah had become his wife and lover while Ramsey, to Yates's delight, had watched all of it unfold.

He chuckled, recalling the moment when his adversary had stood stunned when Sarah did not recognize him. Yates would carry that image with him for some time and revel in the beauty of it. But he also derived just as much joy from anticipating the look on Ramsey's face when he would one day, hopefully soon, reveal that Sarah was carrying his child. The excitement of that sat with him like an excited toddler eager to hold a puppy.

Yates kept a steady eye on Sarah. She showed no signs of recall and she continued to take her pills, but she'd asked recently about being reexamined, wondering when she could forego the medication. He'd have to find a doctor to support his findings, but he knew that would be the easy part. Few disagreed with him, and if they did, he handled it accordingly. No, the bigger problem would be Sarah herself. He'd started working with her during their honeymoon, teaching her the ways of manipulating energy and how to use it to her advantage. He'd shown her how to expand and contract it, allowing her to reveal or hide herself and her thoughts. He'd taught her how to read objects and people, using that knowledge to make deductions and conclusions that could aid her in various situations. And with every lesson, he sensed the power in her. She'd picked up everything the first time, as if she'd always done it.

Yates knew that eventually her extrasensory skills would awaken the memories within if he didn't act to prevent that from happening. So he had returned to the lab, looking for the next solution— a serum that would make her his forever, with no remaining trace of Ramsey or his friends, while leaving the Sarah he knew intact. The fact that she could be pregnant had to be considered. He'd replaced her birth control pills with placebos, so it was just a matter of time. Sitting back in his seat, he stared at the screen, pleased with himself as he envisioned their bright future together.

**

Sarah walked through the kitchen. She'd just spent the last hour sitting on the patio, eating lunch and enjoying the day, but she'd done it alone. They'd been home for a week; the honeymoon in Paris and areas of Southern France had been both mesmerizing and unforgettable, and Yates had introduced her to the beauty, culture, and food of the French people, but at the end, she'd been ready to return. Yates had flirted with the idea of staying and going to Italy, but something about it made her uncomfortable. She didn't tell him that she'd wanted to leave because she didn't want to disappoint him, but something inside her stirred and she'd wanted to return, as if she was missing something. Yates only suggested the idea of extending the trip once, perhaps realizing that he needed to return as well, and considering all the time he'd spent in his basement office since they'd been back, he must have had plenty of work to catch up on.

He had been downstairs since the early morning, and now, after she'd spent the day walking the beach and then organizing her closet, she needed to get out of the house. She'd been almost housebound since coming home. Worried about the possibility of another episode occurring, Yates insisted that she take her time before venturing out, but she'd had no problems since their honeymoon and she felt fine.

Leaning against the counter, she opened her hand. Inside it was the small yellow pill she'd been taking every day since her last episode. Yates insisted that she take one each morning. Doctor's orders apparently, though she could not remember any doctor. The bottle sat next to the salt and pepper shakers on the countertop. The pills had a label on them with a name written across in typeface— "XYZ Labs. Dr. Samuel Downey." Yates explained that after her injury, he'd gone to work with the professionals at his lab to see what would help and this Dr. Downey had studied her test results and had recommended the yellow pill, stating apparently that it would help her with anxiety as well as her migraines. If taken over a period of time, it might also help with her memory issues. She didn't know about any of that, but she did know she didn't like the way it made her feel. She'd asked several times to be reevaluated, and Yates had agreed, but no subsequent appointment had been made. Now, looking at the pill in her hand, she toyed with the idea of discarding it.

"Hi."

The voice startled her. Yates stood in the doorway to the kitchen. "You already eat lunch?" he asked.

She eyed the clock. "It's two o'clock. I ate about an hour ago."

He widened his eyes. "It is? I'm sorry. Time got away from me." His gaze moved to the pill in her hand. "Have you taken it today?"

She closed her hand. "Not yet. I was just going to."

"You should have taken it earlier." He walked to the cabinet and pulled out a glass. He filled it with water from the dispenser at the edge of the counter. "Here," he said, handing her the glass of water.

Sarah knew that now was not the time to argue with him, so she took the glass and swallowed the pill.

"Good," he said, taking the glass and putting it in the sink. "How about I set up an appointment to meet with Dr. Downey next week? We'll get you checked out. Maybe he'll be okay with changing your prescription."

She couldn't help but perk up at that. "Really?"

He smiled. "Yes. I know you're tired of taking them, but I need you to be well, so just be patient, all right?"

She nodded. "Okay." She sat at the breakfast table, putting her hand in her chin.

"What?" he asked. "What's bothering you?"

She glanced over at him. "I'm bored."

"You're bored?"

"Yes. I'm in this big house. You're holed up downstairs. I'm bored. Plus, these pills make me feel like I'm walking through a fog." She sighed. "Sorry. I know I'm complaining."

He studied her for a second. "Come with me."

Her eyes tightened, but she sat up. "What?"

"Just come with me." He motioned for her to follow, and she did. He walked to the door under the stairs that led to the basement area. It was not an actual underground basement. The house being on the beach, it sat up on stilts a good fifteen feet above the ground. The basement sat below it.

"You're really going to let me into your private lair?" she asked. She had yet to see his office and lab.

"Of course," he answered. "Why not?"

"I got the impression it was the man cave, with no women allowed."

He held the door for her. "You're the one exception."

Walking over the threshold, she saw steps leading down into a dark hall. He hit a switch and the stairway brightened, revealing white walls and a simple staircase. At the bottom, she turned and saw a door to her right. Yates walked past her and took out a set of keys and unlocked it. Stepping back, he let her pass and walk inside. He reached in and flipped on the lights. She was impressed by the size of the room. The far corner illuminated a large wooden rectangular desk, with various stacks of paper and folders arranged neatly on its perimeters. Lined up next to each other, three impressively sized flat-screen computer monitors took center stage on the imposing desk, which had a worn cushioned brown leather chair pushed up under it. She could see a keyboard beneath the top of the desk in a hidden compartment.

Opposite the desk in the other corner was a large stainless-steel cabinet with a combination lock. Its size required much of the wall space. The middle of the room appeared to serve as a laboratory work space. There was a sink and a wide counter, with a small refrigerator and cabinets beneath and various machines and pieces of laboratory equipment that Sarah could not identify sat atop or next to it. Beakers, pipettes, microscopes, and Bunsen burners were about the only items she recognized, although everything else looked scientific enough. The only warmth in the room came from the soft sea-foam color painted on the walls. To the far right of the room, just next to where the large cabinet ended, stood a closed door.

"Well," he asked. "What do you think? Not that exciting, really."

Sarah walked around the room, touching objects as she moved, feeling the energy of each and seeing jumbled formulas and scientific jargon race through her mind. It meant nothing to her.

"It's bigger than I imagined," she said.

"It was smaller originally, and there was beach access. I had them enlarge the area when I bought the place."

She moved up next to the locked cabinet. "Is this where you keep all your secrets?" she asked.

He nodded. "To some degree, yes. In my business, it's best to keep what you're working on under wraps. You can never be too careful."

She walked up to the closed door beside the cabinet. "What's in here?"

"Open it."

She did and looked inside to see a small twin bed and nightstand with a lamp. Across the room stood another door which led to a small bathroom.

"I've spent more than a few all-nighters in there," he said. "Back before I had a beautiful wife who shared my bed."

She closed the door. "You don't have any windows."

"I consider it a basement area."

"You're on a beach. Why not build it where you can have a view?"

"It's too distracting. I need to come down here and focus. I can't do that if I'm staring out at the waves."

She held the corner of the countertop. "And here I thought you were down here playing video games and watching sports."

He grunted. "I didn't get where I am doing any of that."

"No, I can see that."

Walking over to the large cabinet, he said, "I want to show you something."

"What?" She watched as he moved the dial to the combination lock back and forth until she heard an audible click, and he popped the doors open. She got a quick view inside as he pulled out a small box from above and put it on the workstation. Before he closed the doors again, she saw various other boxes and binders stacked inside and what looked like a square shaped trunk on the bottom shelf, which also had a lock on it.

"What's that?" she asked, eyeing the small container he'd taken from the cabinet.

Sliding the opening mechanism over, he opened the box, revealing what appeared to be a syringe and vials of solution. "You're not the only one who has to take their medicine," he said.

She cocked her head. "Is that what I think it is?"

"Yes," he said. "It's Red-Line serum. I have to take it to survive." He reached for the syringe-like device and took it out. There was no needle. It was designed so that vials of prepared serum could be inserted and he only needed to slide in a new vial whenever he took a new injection. The instrument had a vial already in place. He lifted his shirt and placed the needleless tip against his abdomen. He pushed against the tube that held the vial, and she heard a click, and then the serum slowly disappeared as it entered his body. Once it was gone, he released the pressure and pulled the device away from his skin. He popped out the empty vial and replaced it with a new one, throwing the old one away.

"How is it that you have serum?" she asked. "I thought it was gone."

"Not all of it. This belonged to Arnuff and Emerson. They kept some in order to survive."

"They did? And no one knew?"

"They lied. It came naturally to them."

"How often do you have to take that?"

He closed the box and opened the cabinet, returning the box to the shelf before closing and locking the cabinet again. "Usually about once a month, depending."

She leaned against the counter. "Depending on what?"

"How I feel, usually. Sometimes, if I've been working a lot of late hours and getting little sleep, I might give myself an extra dose. There have been a few times when I've needed more."

"Like when?" she asked.

He crossed his arms in front of him. "Once, when I was a teenager, I had a slight altercation."

"Slight altercation?"

"Yes," he said. "I got pissed off. I reacted in a way which resulted in unpleasant consequences."

She squinted at him. "What does that mean?"

His posture tensed. "I threw Arnuff up against a wall, and he retaliated by sending me into the path of an oncoming car."

"What?"

"It wasn't going that fast."

Sarah couldn't believe it. "He threw you in front of a moving vehicle?"

"Arnuff didn't have much tolerance for an aggressive teenager."

"But why? What did you do that was so bad?"

Yates scowled. "I hated him. I called him a weak old fool. Told him I was better and stronger than him." He stared off. "He decided to put me in my place."

Sarah shook her head. "How bad was it?"

"Three broken ribs and a fractured leg. Some internal injuries. Luckily, Red-Lines heal fast, especially when they have serum to help. I took it every day for two weeks."

"And Arnuff?"

"What about him?"

"Did he apologize?" asked Sarah. "Feel bad for what he'd done?"

"He was gone the next day. I didn't see him again for another month. I was healed by then."

She felt the pain he tried to hide. "I'm sorry."

"Don't be. He found out later that what I said was true." His anger flared.

"What do you mean?" she asked.

"It's not important anymore. He's out of my life." Shaking off the past, he walked up next to her and put his arms around her. "And now you're in it, which is all that matters."

She encircled her arms around him, and they held each other.

"How much serum do you have?" she asked.

"Oh, I'll live to be a hundred, I'm sure. Don't worry about me. Arnuff and Emerson had enough saved to take care of the family for a while."

"Good," she said. "I don't plan on being a widow."

"You won't be." He kissed her nose.

She smiled. "Thank you."

"For what?"

"For sharing that with me. For sharing your space with me."

He hugged her. "I'll share everything with you. What's mine is yours."

She pulled back. "I still have a problem, though."

"What's that?"

"I'm still bored."

"Oh, that."

"Yes, that. I need to get out of this house."

He shrugged. "What do you want to do?"

"I don't know. I'd like to see Rachel. See my aunt."

"Sounds fine to me."

"I could go back to work."

"No."

She pulled out of his arms. "Why not?"

"Because you don't need to work."

"It's not about needing to work. It's about having something to do."

"I don't want you working right now. You're still recovering."

Sarah stepped back. "But I feel fine."

"I know you do, but that can be deceiving."

"Well, then, I need to go back to the doctor. Let him check me out. I'm sure he would clear me."

"When he clears you, then that's fine. But not until then."

Sarah didn't understand. "Why are you so worried?"

He gripped the side of the counter. "Sarah, I almost lost you once, and it scared me to death. I know you're eager to return to your life, but I don't want you taking it too fast."

She took a breath, trying to stay cool. "I'll take it slow, but I need to venture out once in a while. At least go out and shop or get a cup of coffee."

"I'd love to take you shopping. You want to go out to dinner tonight? I'll have Julian make reservations."

"No, that's not what I mean."

"What do you mean?"

She put a hand on her chest. "I mean me going out on my own. Driving. Going on errands. Doing things around the house."

"But we've got people for that."

She rolled her eyes. "I know that, but I'm perfectly capable of cooking a meal or doing laundry or going to the grocery store. If you're not comfortable yet with me working, at least let me contribute."

He raised the side of his lip. "You really want to do the laundry?"

She sighed. "Anything is better than me standing around and staring at the walls. I want a car, too."

"Well, that's easy. I've got six of them."

"I mean I want the car keys."

"We have a driver."

She groaned. "But I don't want a driver."

"Why not?"

"Because I am perfectly capable of driving."

"I know, but why do it when I've got somebody to do it for you?"

"You're deliberately trying to irritate me, aren't you?"

He crossed his arms. "No, I'm just thinking of your safety."

"My safety?"

"Yes."

"You expect the bogeyman or something? In case you haven't noticed, I can take care of myself."

He didn't answer immediately. "I know that," he finally said. "It's just..."

"Just what?" She was waiting for him to answer when it dawned her. "It's him, isn't it?"

"Who?"

"You're worried about that man, Ramsey, aren't you?" She knew she was right. "What? You think he's going to show up and I'm going to fall for him?"

Yates's face hardened. "That's not funny."

"I can handle him."

"Sarah, he's not someone you can trust."

"Listen, I am not going to sit in this house and live in fear. That's not who I am, and it's not who you married."

He waved a hand. "It's because of him that you ended up with a head injury. If something else happened or he tried again to get to you..."

"You said yourself that you thought he finally got the message. He knows now that I'm with you. And if he showed up and tried to convince me otherwise, I'd set him straight."

Yates paused. "You would?"

"Yes. Without hesitation."

He appeared to gauge whether or not he trusted her to be out on her own.

"You've taught me a lot," she said. "Remember?"

"Yes, I know, but there's more to learn."

"I know enough. Ramsey's a Gray-Line. I can handle him."

Yates hesitated. "Okay," he said. "I hear you. I'll try to ease up a bit."

"Good."

"But I still want Nelson to drive you."

"What for?"

"Because I'm paying him. He ought to do something while he's here."

"Then let him drive you."

He reached up and took hold of her shoulders. "Sarah, please, humor me for now. You want to go out and get a cup of coffee or go grocery shopping or meet Rachel for lunch, fine. I'll live with that. But for now, use Nelson. I'll feel better if you do."

She weighed whether it was worth continuing the argument. Considering that he'd agreed to her leaving on her own, she decided to live with it for now, but she hadn't forgotten his other concession. "All right, I'll use the driver provided you make an appointment with that doctor. Today."

He held up his hands. "Fine. You win. I'll call him."

"Thank you."

He reached out and took her back into his arms, pulling her close. "You drive a hard bargain."

Sarah encircled his waist with her arms. "Yeah, well, I don't give in so easy."

His lips found her neck. "I can see that," he said.

"And I'm not giving up," she added, feeling her body warm as she hugged him back.

"On what?" he asked as he nibbled her skin.

"Finding myself again. One of these days I will." She found his ear with her tongue and flicked it.

She felt him still for the slightest moment before he resumed his attention to her neck and jawline. "I know, Sarah," she heard him say in a whisper. "I know."

CHAPTER FIFTEEN

....

R AMSEY STARED OUT the window of Leroy's office, the potted plants the only witness to his quiet contemplation. Hannah had left thirty minutes earlier, with Declan behind her and Leroy was talking on the phone in the kitchen. After almost four long, painful weeks, they finally had some activity. Declan's team had placed a small, inconspicuous camera across the street from the driveway of Yates's house, so they knew the moment Yates and Sarah had returned. But it had been another week before Sarah finally ventured out without Yates by her side. She'd left for a short period three days ago, but she'd had a driver, and she'd only been gone for an hour before she'd returned. Seeing that, they'd begun the preparations to put Hannah in place. Declan had arranged for a car to watch the street, and when Sarah left again, they planned to follow her. As she ventured out more often, they hoped the appropriate opportunity for Hannah to appear would reveal itself.

He prayed this would work. He didn't like putting Hannah at risk any more than Declan did, but if they played it smart, he hoped their plans would keep them all safe. Even so, he knew it was a long shot at best. His experience as a Protector had taught him that all plans were only guidelines, and that most of the time, you had to reevaluate when nothing went the way you thought. He figured this would be no different.

Ramsey had chosen to stay at Leroy's for most of the three weeks. Occasionally, he'd sleep at his house or Sarah's apartment when he felt the need to be close to her or just be alone, but he couldn't stay long at either place. The memories pulled him into dark places, and he couldn't afford to fall apart again. When they got Sarah out, he needed to be ready in case something went wrong and he had to rely on his instincts. He couldn't do that without focus. And he couldn't focus if he sat in depression all day.

The police had found him during one of his stays at his house. He'd kept his cool and answered their questions as Morgana had instructed. They'd looked about as interested in his answers as a nurse asking a patient's height and weight. He suspected that they were only following the established routine, and without any suspicious activity to alert them to the possibility of foul play, they had written off Marco's disappearance as just another case that had no explanation. He could only hope it stayed that way.

A noise from behind him drew his attention from the window. Leroy was standing at the door to the office. After waiting a few seconds, Leroy walked up and stood next to him, staring out the window as Ramsey did.

"You okay?" Leroy asked.

Ramsey stood pensive. "Yeah."

"You've been quiet for a man who's learned he's about to become a father."

Ramsey took a second before he answered. He'd thought of little else since hearing the news. "Guess I don't want to get my hopes too high."

Leroy stayed quiet.

"I mean, we don't know anything for sure," said Ramsey, staring out absently over Leroy's manicured yard. "Morgana left a bit of wiggle room. She may not be pregnant." He paused. "At least, not with my child." It was hard for him to say.

Leroy played with the leaf of a potted plant by his side. "What does your gut tell you?"

Ramsey shifted his stance and stared at his shoes. "That she's pregnant, and it's mine, and it scares the hell out of me."

"Because?"

"Because if Yates finds out, I don't know what he'll do."

Leroy put his hands in his pockets. "He won't find out."

"How can you be sure?"

"Because the only way he'll know is if Sarah knows, or one of us tells him. I'm not worried about the latter, and the former should only happen once Sarah's memories return."

"That's another thing. If her memories return and she's not out of there..." Ramsey shuddered.

Leroy looked over at him. "You know at some point, you're just going to have to trust destiny."

Ramsey couldn't help but smile. "Guess I should follow my own advice, huh?"

"You know that's what your dad would tell you."

Ramsey studied the backyard again. "It's just that there are a lot of moving pieces to this puzzle. One wrong move..."

"Have you stopped to consider how many moving pieces were required to get you and Sarah together in the first place? Hell, Morgana and Destine have been planning this since you were a child. And it worked."

"It worked until Yates showed up."

"Then you have to trust that he showed up for a reason. Regardless of his motivations, he's a part of this just as much as we are."

Ramsey released a held breath. "I guess easy and simple is too much to ask for."

A squirrel ran across the yard and skittered up a tree trunk, and Leroy nodded. "Sometimes easy and simple don't lead us where we need to go. There are benefits in the hard and long path, too. We just don't see them till the path clears and we cross the road to the other side."

Ramsey regarded the bubbling water fountain in Leroy's yard, seeing it for the first time. "As long as on the other side there's Sarah and the baby."

"You have to let that be and just trust. Hard as it is."

Ramsey looked away from the churning water of the fountain to meet Leroy's gaze. "And if this were Olivia instead of Sarah, would you still say that?"

Leroy's face showed the tumult of emotion at the question. "No," he said. "I wouldn't, but you would."

Ramsey couldn't bring himself to deny it. He returned his gaze back to the yard. "Since when do you have a water fountain?"

Leroy took advantage of the change in subject. "Six months ago. It was here last time we grilled outside. You were here."

"Oh."

"I can tell you were impressed."

"Sorry."

"How's my plant?" asked Leroy.

"Your what?" asked Ramsey.

"My plant," said Leroy. "The one I gave you for your birthday."

Ramsey recalled Leroy's gift. "Considering I haven't watered it since this all started, I'd say it's pretty withered."

"I'll get you a new one."

"You really should reconsider."

"I won't give up hope, and neither should you."

They watched as the sun's rays brightened the lawn and reflected in spotted beams in the gurgling water.

"I'm tryin', Leroy," said Ramsey. "I'm tryin'." His thoughts traveled to Hannah, and he wondered if she'd made contact.

"I know you are, Sherlock. I know."

Sarah opened the back door of the sleek Mercedes and slipped out of the soft leather seat. Leaving her bags in the back, she spoke to her driver, Nelson, feeling silly that she had to be driven to the local coffee shop. It was bad enough that he'd dropped her off at the shopping center, but now to make him wait while she grabbed a cup of coffee felt foolish. "I'll be right back, Nelson."

"Take your time, ma'am." He glanced at her from the front seat. "I'm just going to park over here. You can sit and relax if you'd like."

Sarah did like the idea of just sitting and enjoying a cup of coffee. "Okay, I just might do that. Thanks."

"Sure thing. Enjoy yourself."

She went inside, and after perusing the menu, ordered a long overdue latte with an extra shot and found and sat in an oversized chair. The bell on the coffee shop door chimed, but she paid little attention. They called her name, she picked up her drink and returned to her seat. Taking a sip, she sat back and sighed, reflecting back on her breakfast conversation with Yates. While spearing a bite of poached egg, she'd watched him place one of her pills by her plate. A pang of annoyance had flared in her gut and he'd caught it.

"You called the doctor?" she'd asked him.

"I told you. He's out of the country. He'll be back next week. I'll call and schedule then."

"But I thought you were going to try and find someone else?"

"I considered it, but he's the most familiar with your case. He's the one you should see."

It was at that moment that she'd felt something from him she had not felt before. It flickered in her, and she couldn't ignore it. Dishonesty. "Why don't you want me to see the doctor?" She'd opened up her senses, and he'd closed up.

He drank from his coffee cup. "Don't be ridiculous. I want you to see the doctor. I just want you to see the best one."

Sarah considered her options. Although he masked his feelings, she still felt the distinct pangs of resistance. He was hiding something, but she chose not to confront him. He slid her orange juice glass closer to her. "Take your pill."

She picked up the pill, put it in her mouth, and took a swallow of orange juice. Smiling, he stood and took his plate to the kitchen sink. "Please don't be mad," he said. "I promise, as soon as I can get you to the doctor, I will."

She said nothing as he walked over, leaned down, kissed her on the forehead, and left the kitchen.

Once she was sure he'd gone, she'd lifted her hand to her mouth and spat out the pill, staring at the slightly dissolved disk before throwing it away.

Now, as she sat in the coffee shop, she wondered if perhaps she had overreacted. Not taking the pill had been her way of retaliating, but now she debated the wisdom of that choice. Would it only hurt her in the end? When she returned home, she could take another pill. But what would it hurt if she didn't take it for one day?

Her thoughts were interrupted by a series of mumbled sounds. Glancing over at the small table opposite her, she watched a woman rummage through her large purse. "Where is it?" she heard the lady say. "I know I put it in here."

As the woman dug through her bag, something nagged at Sarah. The woman had long, straight auburn hair that fell over her shoulders, and her voice was familiar. "Ah," said the stranger as she pulled out a cell phone. "Here it is." She sat up and Sarah saw her face.

A memory surfaced of a woman leaning over her, wiping a cool cloth across her face. And then another of being helped to dress and of her lying in a bathtub with this woman watching over her. "Hannah?" she asked.

The woman looked up, her gaze meeting Sarah's. "Sarah?"

Sarah held her stomach. An unexpected well of emotion rose up, and tears sprung into her eyes. She didn't know why seeing this woman evoked so many feelings, but the discomfort disappeared as fast as it came and then she just felt happy to see her. "Yes, it's me," said Sarah.

With her bag now slung over her shoulder, Hannah walked over, holding her own coffee. "It's so good to see you."

"Please. Sit," said Sarah, motioning to the seat opposite her.

"Thanks. I will." Hannah sat and dropped her bag to the floor and then placed her cup on the small table between them. "It's been a while. How are you?"

"I'm..." Sarah was suddenly tongue-tied. Her thoughts were jumbled, and she took a second to focus.

"You okay?" asked Hannah.

Sarah blinked. "Yes. Sorry. Don't know where I went." She shook her head. "What was I saying?"

Hannah smiled. "I asked how you were."

"Oh gosh, yes. I'm fine, thanks. How are you?"

"I'm great. I just took a job not far from here, but I had some time, so I stopped in for some much-needed coffee."

"I understand," said Sarah. "How's..." She stopped herself when she realized what she was about to say.

"How's what?" asked Hannah.

Sarah remembered Hannah's connection to other men in her life, men she'd wanted to forget, although at that moment, she couldn't recall why. She didn't know why she felt so confused.

"Nothing," she said. "Never mind." Sarah could almost read Hannah's mind, sure that her friend thought she'd lost her marbles.

"I heard you got married," said Hannah.

Sarah pulled herself out her wandering thoughts. "What? Oh, yes. A month ago." She waited for the obligatory congratulations, but none came. Hannah took another sip of coffee. Sarah picked up on a feeling of dislike or discomfort, but couldn't tell which. Perhaps it was a combination of both. "Something wrong?"

Hannah picked up her cup. "Just surprised is all."

"Surprised? By what?"

"That it happened so fast."

"The wedding?" Well," Sarah hesitated, "it's just that after all that happened, we didn't want to put things off, you know?"

"All that happened?"

"Yes," said Sarah, surprised. "The car accident. My memory loss. That awful experience with..." She stopped, realizing that Hannah knew Ramsey. Something in her head pounded, and she rubbed at her temples.

"You all right?" asked Hannah.

The pounding eased. "Yes, thanks."

"Car accident, huh?" asked Hannah.

"Yes. Poor Yates was worried sick. Especially when I woke up with memory loss. I've been trying to get it back ever since. Thankfully, I remembered him."

"Thankfully," murmured Hannah.

"I guess when I realized how close I'd come to losing him, I decided to move forward with our commitment. Time is short."

"Did you see a doctor?"

"Of course. I was in the hospital when I woke up after the accident."

"But since then?"

Sarah gripped her coffee cup, surprised that this subject had popped up again. "Not yet, no."

"Really?"

"Yates is very particular about who I see." She found herself defending him. "He's got important connections, considering the business he's in. You know he's the founder of XYZ Laboratories?"

"Yes, I know."

"There's a doctor assigned to my case, but apparently he's in high demand. I've had trouble getting in to see him again."

"Even with Yates's connections?"

That observation pricked at Sarah. "Strangely, yes. But I guess if you're out of town, you're out of town. He'll be back next week."

"Good."

"Besides, he gave me some pills to take. They're supposed to help with the headaches and anxiety."

Hannah's eyebrows rose. "Pills?"

"Yes. I have to admit, though, I'm getting tired of taking them. I've never been very good when it comes to medication. Especially when I feel just fine."

"Then stop taking them," said Hannah.

Sarah widened her eyes. "Stop taking them?"

Hannah studied her cup. She took a second before she answered. "I'm a nurse, Sarah. I've worked with hundreds of patients, many of them with head injuries. In fact, my current patient is dealing with the same thing. She fell down a flight of stairs and suffered a concussion. Now I admit most of them have not suffered memory loss, but there is one thing in common among all of them."

"What's that?"

"The only thing they've ever been given for headaches is aspirin."

"But they're more than that. They're migraines."

"When's the last time you had a migraine?"

Sarah had to stop at that. The last migraine she'd had had been just before she'd married. She'd had headaches since then, but she assumed that the bad ones had been kept at bay by taking the little pill.

"It's been a few weeks."

"And are you anxious?"

"Anxious?"

"Suffering from anxiety?" asked Hannah. "After your marriage and long honeymoon?"

Sarah detected some sarcasm in Hannah's tone, but didn't comment on it. "No," she answered. "No anxiety, really. Just some adjustment issues."

"Normal, considering."

"What are you saying, Hannah?"

**

Declan had warned Hannah to keep her feelings as sheltered as possible, since he suspected Sarah could easily read her. She worked hard at it now. Sitting there, listening to Sarah, she felt disgust when she realized the extent of the lies Yates had spun to keep Sarah under his thumb. She wanted to tell Sarah everything, reveal all the nastiness that Yates sought to conceal, but she couldn't. Not yet. Sarah couldn't handle it, and Hannah didn't want to be responsible for causing her friend to spiral downward with no way to bring her back. Hannah knew she was taking a risk by making Sarah question Yates's motives. It could backfire, and Sarah could end up shutting her out. But she had to do something.

"Just that Yates's concern for you may be doing you more harm than good."

Sarah narrowed her eyes. "Are you saying my husband wants to do me harm?"

The defensiveness in Sarah's tone was obvious. Hannah treaded carefully. "Not intentionally, no. He's your husband. He's worried about you."

"Of course, he is."

Hannah considered another option. "What's written on the pill bottle?"

"Excuse me?"

"The bottle of pills you take. There's a prescription label. It should tell you what you're taking, the dosage, the doctor's name."

Sarah paused. "Dr. Downey is the doctor's name."

"And the dosage? What's the name of the medication?"

"I don't know."

"You don't know?"

"No. There's nothing else written on the bottle."

"Oh, that's strange."

"Yates went through his own channels, working with a doctor he knows through his business. He read my test results. Studied my hospital charts."

"Regardless, any prescription would have this information. You should know what you're taking."

Hannah waited as Sarah considered that. She figured Sarah would either accuse her of maligning Yates and stomp out of the shop—and all hope of connecting with Sarah would be lost—or she'd accomplish what she'd set out to do, make Sarah think twice.

Sarah played with the lid of her coffee cup. "Hannah?"

Hannah held her breath. "Yes?"

Sarah paused and seemed to come to a decision. "If I brought you one of these pills, would you be able to tell me what it is?"

Score. Hannah fought to control her emotion. "You're sure about that?" She had to be careful not to appear too anxious. "I'm sure if you ask Yates, he'll tell you. Or this Dr. Downey, whenever you manage to meet with him."

She must have said something that convinced Sarah to move forward, because Sarah looked at her with an expression of total conviction. "Can you meet me here tomorrow?"

**

Declan fought the urge to strangle Hannah. He'd followed her back to Leroy's after her successful encounter with Sarah and now he was listening as she updated all of them on their conversation.

Ramsey stood with his hands in his pockets, his posture revealing his tension. Leroy sat next to Hannah on the couch while Declan paced in front of the fireplace.

"What the hell do you think you're doing?" Declan couldn't help but ask.

"What am I doing?" asked Hannah. "I'm finding a way in. He's told her all sorts of lies. I can't just come out and tell her who she is. I've got to find some way of making her question her assumptions. Help her start to remember. If we can get her off those pills, I don't think it will take long."

"If she goes back and tells him that she met with you, then that's it," said Declan.

"I don't think she'll do that," said Hannah.

"How can you be sure?" asked Leroy.

"Just by the way she acted. I think something's got her suspicious."

"This is a huge risk," said Declan.

"It's a risk we have to take," said Ramsey. "Hannah's right. We have to find a way in."

"But if we move too fast, then it could blow up in our faces," said Declan.

"But if we move too slow," said Leroy, "then we may lose our advantage. If Sarah is already suspecting that Yates is keeping secrets, then we have to use that. If we can make her see that she's at the bottom of the rabbit hole, maybe we can get her out of there."

"But at what cost?" asked Declan. He looked at Hannah. "You know he'll retaliate."

"We all knew that going in," she said. "And we all agreed to accept the risk. It's not just me he'll come after. It will be all of us."

"My fear is he'll suspect her memories are returning," said Ramsey. "He already drugged her once. He could do it again." Ramsey shut his eyes and bunched his fingers into fists in his pockets. "God, I wish we could just pull her out of there."

"We can't," said Hannah. "I saw her react when she started to think of..."

Ramsey opened his eyes. "What?" he asked. "Me?" Hannah didn't say anything. "React?" he continued. "How did she react?"

"Don't think the worst," said Hannah. "She held her head as if she had a headache. I suspect that as her mind tries to remember, she feels pain or pressure. It's why we can't do this all at once."

"But if she stops taking those pills? That won't hurt her?" asked Leroy.

"I can only guess the pills are keeping her mind dull, even foggy. It's probably why she wants to stop taking them. Once she goes off them, it might take only a few days before she starts to experience the effects."

"A few days?" asked Ramsey. "So if she's not taking them, she could feasibly begin to remember this week?"

"I'm only surmising," said Hannah. "But as a Red-Line, her natural instinct will be to find an energetic balance, and with the energy she accesses, it makes it probable that her body and mind will lead her in the right direction and the rest will take care of itself."

"What do we do then?" asked Declan. "We can't possibly predict when she'll remember. Or even if she'll be on our side if she does."

"What do you mean by that?" asked Ramsey.

Declan chose to be honest. His brother needed to be prepared. "You have to consider the possibility that she may learn of Yates's deceit, but at the same time, not regain all of her memories. Or that one may happen before the other."

"Declan..." said Hannah.

"Wait a minute. Are you suggesting she may never remember me?" asked Ramsey.

"That's not what he's saying, Sherlock," said Leroy. "Is it Declan?" He eyed Declan with a warning look.

Declan knew that no one wanted him to broach the subject, but if things were happening faster than anticipated, he'd rather have his brother ready instead of broadsided the way he had been weeks ago. "We don't know, John, we don't know how much she'll remember. If she simply realizes that Yates lied and used her, then we've got a pissed-off Red-Line, but if that's all that happens—"

"You mean she dumps Yates but doesn't want me either?" asked Ramsey.

"I want you to consider the possibility," said Declan.

"She'll remember you, Sherlock," said Leroy.

"But if she doesn't?" asked Declan.

Ramsey's jaw clenched. "Then I'll deal with it. But first and foremost, we have to get her away from him."

"And if she's pregnant?" asked Hannah.

"I can't deal with that until we have confirmation that she actually is," said Ramsey. "Until then, I can only handle so much."

"Then we move forward," said Hannah. "And I'll meet up with her again tomorrow."

CHAPTER SIXTEEN

ARAH FLIPPED ON the faucet at the kitchen sink and began to clean the pots and pans she'd used to prepare the meal. After seeing Hannah that morning, she'd replayed the events in her mind to assure herself that she was doing the right thing. She'd considered telling Yates that she'd bumped into Hannah that day, but something told her he'd be displeased. She didn't want to go behind Yates's back, but she couldn't ignore the feeling that something wasn't sitting right. Her mother had taught her not to ignore those messages. When intuition spoke, you listened.

Deciding to keep her mind occupied, she'd asked Nelson to drive her to the grocery store and she'd bought the items necessary to make her mother's favorite meal—Vinegar Chicken. The last time she'd made it, it had been for Aunt Gerry, over a year ago. She'd tried to call her aunt when she'd returned from her honeymoon, but had been unable to reach her. A vague memory surfaced of Gerry telling her she would vacation soon, and Sarah assumed she was on one of the twice-yearly cruises she enjoyed.

She'd called Rachel, too. They'd had a long conversation, but Sarah found herself unable to tell her coworker that she'd married. Sarah knew Rachel's reaction would be complete shock. She'd never met Yates, and Sarah didn't feel like having the long conversation over the phone. Besides, Rachel had been visiting with the family of her boyfriend Todd, so they'd agreed to meet up the following week. Sarah decided she would tell her then.

Yates had been down in his office all afternoon. He didn't know she was preparing dinner, and she wanted to surprise him. When the oven timer sounded, Sarah placed the last dish in the drainer, forgoing the dishwasher. Izzy and Julian had both offered to help with the meal, but she had declined. She needed to stay busy, and to be honest, she missed cooking. Turning from the sink, she grabbed the oven mitts and opened the oven. The sound of sizzling and the smell of the cooked chicken made her smile as she took out the dish and placed it on the counter. She dropped the mitts, closed the oven, and went to check the boiling pasta on the stove.

She stirred the pasta and tasted it, then decided it needed a few more minutes. She opened the cabinet above her and began to pull plates down to set the table. Remembering the wine, she opened the refrigerator and removed the bottle Julian had picked for her from the wine cellar. It occurred to her that she should have taken it out sooner, but it would have to do. She began to pull out silverware from one of the drawers and turned to place the utensils along with the napkins on the table. Reaching for the wine glasses, she stopped when the smell of the chicken made her stomach lurch. Leaning against the counter, she put the wine glasses down as beads of sweat popped out on her brow. Her stomach flipped again as the once-pleasing smell now made her gag.

Nauseated, she dashed to the bathroom on the opposite side of the den, barely making it in time before the remains of her lunch from a few hours earlier came up. Holding her hair back, she retched into the toilet as her stomach recoiled. The smell of the chicken drifted into the small bathroom, and she closed the door to keep the stench from reaching her. She continued to gag until her belly calmed. As the discomfort began to ease, she sat back on the floor and took long deep breaths, waiting for her stomach to settle. Once she felt a little better, she stood and stared at herself in the mirror, noting her pallor. What had come over her? She turned on the water and rinsed out her mouth, washed her hands, and splashed her face with water. Not wanting the pasta to over-cook, she hurried back to the kitchen, but the smell of the chicken induced another wave of nausea. Pausing at the dining table, she realized that she would not be able to complete the meal, much less eat it. She left the kitchen and walked toward the back of the house.

Julian sat in his small office, writing something. She knocked at the open door.

"Yes, Miss Sarah? What I can do for you?" He stood from his desk.

"I'm sorry to bother you, Julian. I know I told you to take the night off, but I need you to finish the pasta."

"Ma'am?"

"The pasta is on the stove. I need you to get it. The chicken is prepared, and the wine is out. Tell Yates dinner is ready."

"Aren't you going to eat, Miss Sarah?"

"God, no," she said, feeling her stomach churn at the mere men-tion of food. "I'm not feeling well. I'm going upstairs to lie down."

"I'm sorry to hear that."

"Tell Yates to eat. He can check on me later. I don't want dinner to get cold."

"Yes, I'll tell him."

"You'll need to get the pasta now, or it will be overdone." Feeling the urge to be sick again, she didn't stop to wait for his response. One hand clutched at her belly, Sarah moved back through the house and up the stairs, and made it to the bathroom just as an-other wave hit her and she found herself retching again.

**

It was fifteen minutes after Hannah's scheduled meet-up time with Sarah at the coffee shop, but Sarah had not arrived. Hannah checked her watch for the millionth time, as if that would change anything, and she thought of Declan sitting in his car down the street. No matter how hard she'd tried to convince him that he didn't need to follow her, he wouldn't give in. Hannah knew that he worried about her and that he didn't like her involvement in all of this. She tried to convince herself that his actions toward her resulted only from his natural protective instincts, but she couldn't deny that it was more than that. Her mind drifted back to the look they'd shared at Ramsey's house, and the warmth it had induced within her. She tried not to think about it, because she had no intention of starting anything with him. After her failed marriage, the thought of a serious relationship made her want to curl up in a ball on the floor. But she hadn't been able to forget that moment between them at Ramsey's. Hoping to prevent it from happening again, she'd made a deliberate effort not to be alone with him since.

Checking her watch one more time, she noted that Sarah was now twenty minutes overdue. Hannah's stomach sank. Had Sarah changed her mind? Had she begun to doubt Hannah's motives? If she had, then Hannah didn't know how she would reconnect with her without creating suspicion.

Continuing to sit with her now-empty coffee cup, Hannah waited as the twenty minutes turned to thirty. Dismay flared in her chest, and Hannah knew then that she had failed. Something had triggered Sarah to back off. Ramsey would be devastated at the news, the little progress they'd made now gone. Hannah was preparing to leave when her phone rang. Seeing the display, she breathed a sigh of relief when she saw Sarah's name.

"Hello?" she answered.

"Hannah?"

"Yes, Sarah. You okay?"

"Yes, I'm fine. I'm sorry I'm not there. I haven't been able to leave."

"Why not?"

There was a brief silence on the line. "Hannah, can I ask you for a favor?"

Hannah sat up. "Of course." There was another pause, and Hannah sensed Sarah's uncertainty. "Sarah, you still there?"

"I need your help."

Sarah's voice sounded steady, and Hannah wondered what had happened to keep her from their meeting. "What kind of help?"

"Your medical expertise. I need you to examine me."

Hannah didn't expect that. "Examine you? I'm not a doctor, Sarah."

"I know, but that's all right for now. I just want your opinion."

"Sarah, what's wrong?"

"I can't explain right now. Can you do it? Is there someplace we can go? Whatever's easier for you. The hospital? A clinic? Your house? I'll meet you wherever it's easier. Please, Hannah."

Hannah questioned the reasonableness of Sarah's request. She could only do a cursory examination; she wasn't trained to make any sort of diagnosis. Yet she stopped herself from telling that to Sarah. Sarah obviously needed to discuss something, and this would be the perfect opportunity to spend more time with her. If she felt Sarah needed a doctor, then she could handle that when the time came. She knew Declan would argue with her about it, but she didn't care. Her thoughts raced as she considered an appropriate place for them to meet. One quickly came to mind. The thought of returning there made her stomach hurt, but she knew it was the best choice. A few well-placed phone calls would give her the access she'd need, plus it had all the amenities she'd require.

"You got a pen handy?" she asked Sarah. "Let me give you an address."

**

Listening from the hallway, Julian heard Sarah talking on the phone.

After leaving Julian's office the previous evening, Sarah had disappeared upstairs. Julian had kept his eyes and ears open in the event that he was needed, but Sarah had stayed in her room for the rest of the evening. The next morning, Julian had prepared breakfast and Yates had eaten, but Sarah remained out of sight. After breakfast, Yates had returned upstairs and had stayed there for almost an hour. When he eventually came back down, he'd asked Julian to check in on Sarah later if she was still in her room. He'd then retreated into his lab.

Once his employer left, Julian had made his way to the second floor, thinking he would inquire if Miss Sarah would like anything light to eat, or possibly something to drink. As he neared the bedroom, he noticed the door cracked open and he leaned in, not wanting to disturb her if she was asleep. He raised his hand to knock but stopped when he heard talking. He hadn't meant to eavesdrop, but he couldn't help but be curious. He heard Sarah mention an address. He pulled out a pen and paper from his pocket and copied the information down. Having worked for Mr. Yates long enough, Julian knew the man valued information. Julian was smart enough to know when to provide it and, in rare instances, when to hold it back. Although usually eager to give Mr. Yates the knowledge he sought, Julian had made one exception when he'd gone to retrieve Miss Sarah's items from her home and found that they were at Ramsey's house instead. Julian saw no need to divulge that news to Yates. Some information was best kept hidden.

Julian didn't know if what Miss Sarah spoke of was important, but he suspected that the more he knew, the better.

**

Yates sat downstairs at his desk, studying the computer monitors. He'd made excellent progress over the last several days, and the formula lay close to completion. Within twenty-four hours, he planned to begin the preparations to create the serum in his lab. There'd been a slight delay when Sarah had come down with a stomach bug the previous night. He'd gone to check on her and found her curled up in bed, looking pale and tired. She'd insisted he eat dinner since she'd spent a good portion of the afternoon preparing the meal. Not wanting to upset her, he'd agreed and had left her to rest. He'd checked her again after dinner and found her asleep.

He'd wondered if perhaps this was more than just illness, but he could read nothing from her. If she were pregnant, then they'd know it soon enough. He'd stayed upstairs with her in case she'd needed him, but she'd had no problems during the night. Letting her sleep the next morning, he'd gone down for breakfast, but found her awake when he'd returned. She felt better, but had little appetite. He debated whether to discuss the subject of pregnancy, but decided against it, choosing to let Sarah figure it out on her own. Seeing that she was strong enough to get up and shower, he'd left her in their room and returned downstairs.

Now as he sat and reviewed his work, he presumed he had little time left. If she was carrying his child, then any number of changes could happen. The pills she took could be less effective or any energetic shifts in her could escalate, causing her to remember sooner than expected. He'd have to be cautious. He couldn't afford to lose her now. And he couldn't allow any interference either. Ramsey and his crew would not sit by for long. In fact, Yates was surprised he'd not sensed their interference already. He'd planned for it and expected he'd have to scare them off, if not worse. The incident with Marco had helped, but that had been short-lived. Their involvement didn't worry him too much, though. They were a nuisance, but little more. However, if they managed to make contact with Sarah at the wrong time, then they could create a bigger problem. He made a mental note to keep an eye on Sarah and her whereabouts.

After taking another quick look at the screen in front of him, he stood and walked to the center console. He pulled the required equipment out of the lower bins, placed it on the counter, and opened the cabinet to locate the ingredients and chemical substances he would require. If he had the time to work on the serum, then he would use it. It had to be ready the moment he sensed Sarah could take it. If Sarah was indeed pregnant with his child, then no amount of lost sleep, hard work, or intrusive Gray-Lines would stop him from resorting to any means necessary to protect himself and his family.

CHAPTER SEVENTEEN

....

HANNAH MADE THE necessary phone calls. After the last one, she'd called Sarah to confirm their meeting time and date since she'd been allowed a certain time to access the office. Considering who she'd had deal with to use the facility, she knew she was lucky to get in at all. But considering the cards she'd had up her sleeve, she'd refused to back down, and it had been the mention of those cards that had finally gotten her in.

She'd explained little to Declan, Ramsey, and Leroy, telling them only what Sarah had requested and that she had made arrangements through her connections at the hospital. Now, a few days after speaking with Sarah, she approached the office door of the location where they would meet. She read the name-plate at the entrance. *Dr. Marshall Maxwell, Obstetrics and Gynecology.* A shiver ran through her at the sight of that name. It had been two years since she'd been here, but standing here, it felt like she'd just left.

Dr. Maxwell had been an admired and respected professor in nursing school. After graduation, she'd agreed to come work for him as a nurse in this office. Two years later, she'd married him. After three miserable years as his wife, she'd divorced him and left the job. Hannah tried to forget the painful memories as she pulled a key from her pocket and opened the door.

The office was dark, so she flipped on the lights. The place was closed on Mondays, the only time Marshall would allow her to use the space. She had to agree it was better to do this without having to worry about bumping into him. If he'd been okay with her using an exam room during regular hours, then she would have endured it. But now that she was here, she breathed easier knowing she would not see him. She walked through the waiting room and into the back hallway, passed Marshall's office without interest, and made her way into the first exam room.

She hit the lights and looked around. It would certainly meet her needs. She didn't know exactly what Sarah had in mind or what concerns she had, but Hannah had the basic medical equipment at her disposal if she needed it.

"Hannah?"

She walked out to the waiting area. "Sarah?" she asked as she rounded the corner and saw Sarah in the waiting area. "I'm back here."

Sarah took off her jacket. "Where is everybody?"

"We have the place to ourselves," said Hannah. "I pulled a few strings to get in on their day off."

"You must have good friends."

"That's one way of putting it."

Sarah clutched her jacket uncertainly.

"How are you?" Hannah asked.

Sarah smiled nervously. "You must think I'm crazy."

"No, I don't. I'm just curious."

"I know. Sorry. I just didn't know who else to talk to." Sarah flipped her jacket over her forearm. "I know this is unconventional," she added, continuing to fidget, "but if you suggest I seek a doctor's medical advice, then I will."

"Come on back," said Hannah.

Sarah followed her to the exam room. Throwing her jacket and purse into a chair, she studied the room.

"So," Hannah said, "why don't you tell me why we're here?"

"Before I forget," said Sarah as she reached into her purse, "here's the pill." She pulled out a plastic bag and handed it to Hannah, who took it and observed the small yellow disc inside.

She didn't recognize the medication, so she placed it on the counter to take back with her. "Okay," she said, "I'll get it analyzed."

"Good. Thanks."

"What else?" asked Hannah.

Sarah continued to stand and stare as if distracted. But then she winced and held her head.

"Why don't you sit up on the examining table?" Hannah motioned toward the usual padded table, with its paper covering. Sarah stepped up and sat on it, the paper shifting and crunching beneath her. She rubbed at her temples again.

"You feeling all right?" asked Hannah.

"It's my head. I've had this headache since yesterday, but I followed your advice."

"What's that?"

"I took some aspirin, and not one of those darn pills."

"Is it helping?"

"It takes the edge off, but the damn thing hasn't gone away." Sarah dropped her hand. "It's one of the things I wanted to ask you about."

"What?"

"I'm wondering if I should be taking the pills."

"The yellow ones?" asked Hannah.

"Yes. I wasn't getting headaches before. Now I am."

Hannah debated how much to say. She suspected Sarah's headaches were due to her body attempting to regain its equilibrium without the medication. "How do the pills make you feel?" she asked.

"Fuzzy. Hard to focus. It's why I don't like them."

"How long have you been taking them?"

"Every day since..." Sarah made a face.

"Since..."

"This is where my memory issues kick in. I remember taking them since just before I got married, although I've apparently been taking them since the accident, but I don't remember."

Hannah nodded. "There's another possibility to consider."

"What's that?" asked Sarah.

"You stopped them cold turkey, and your body is adjusting."

"You mean I'm hooked on them?"

"Well, not hooked, as in addicted, but you've taken them long enough that, now that you've gone off them, you need to give yourself time to adjust. It's like quitting caffeine."

Sarah seemed to relax. "I didn't consider that."

"A few more days, and your headaches should ease."

"You think it's that simple?"

"Have you had any other problems?"

"Problems like what?"

"Dizziness, blurry vision, nausea?" asked Hannah.

Sarah looked at her hands and didn't answer.

"What?"

"I, uh..." said Sarah, still playing with her fingers. "That's the other thing I needed to talk about."

"What is it?" asked Hannah. "Are you sick?"

Sarah hesitated. "No, not sick."

"Sarah, it's hard for me to help without more information."

"Nausea," said Sarah.

"Nausea?" asked Hannah. "You've been nauseated?"

"Yes."

"How often?"

"It started four days ago. The afternoon after we met, in fact. It's happened every morning since."

Hannah's eyes widened, but she didn't voice her suspicions.

"And I'm late," said Sarah, her face furrowed.

"Sarah—" said Hannah.

But before she could finish, Sarah hopped off the table, the paper ripping beneath her, and she began to pace the room. "I don't know how this happened. I've been careful."

"Are you sure about this?" asked Hannah. "Have you taken a pregnancy test?"

"No, but I can sense it. It's why I wanted to see you. Imagine my surprise when you asked me to meet you in an Ob/Gyn's office. Quite the coincidence, huh? I thought maybe you knew something before I did." She kept pacing. "Funny, huh?"

"Yeah, funny." Hannah didn't know what else to say. She just watched as Sarah moved around the room. "Does Yates know?"

"No. I haven't said anything. I've been doing my damnedest to keep it from him. I guess I just wanted final confirmation."

"But you said you sensed it."

"I did, but I want the whole pee-in-a-cup or blood-test thing. Whatever you do to confirm it. I'm a Red-Line, so I don't know how that might affect things. If I tell Yates, he'll drag me to one of his doctors, and I don't know how I'm going to handle that. I needed to talk to someone first. Someone I feel comfortable with and I trust." She rubbed her temples again. "Damn this headache."

"Sarah, why don't you sit?" Hannah motioned her to a chair in the room.

"No, I'm too restless. I've been dealing with this for days, trying to figure out how this happened and how I feel about it."

"How do you feel about it?" asked Hannah. She had to be careful how she handled this. Hoping the discussion might trigger any emerging memories, she wanted to draw Sarah out, but she didn't want to push too hard.

"That's just it. I don't know. I mean, shouldn't I be happy? Gushing with joy?"

"I don't know. Should you?"

"I should, but..."

"But what?"

"Something's not right."

Hannah held her breath. "What's not right?"

Sarah stopped pacing and stared at Hannah, folding her arms in front of her and clenching her hands into fists. "I had a dream last night," she said.

"A dream?" asked Hannah, unsure where Sarah was headed.

Sarah turned and started moving again, her arms still crossed. "Yes."

"About what?"

She paused. "About him."

"Him?" asked Hannah. "Him, who?"

Sarah let out a deep breath. "Ramsey. John Ramsey."

Hannah froze her face into place and shut down whatever emotion that wanted to surface. She couldn't let Sarah read her.

"I know you know him, and I don't want to disparage him, but I know what he tried to do."

Hannah had no idea what Sarah meant. "Tried to do?"

"He tried to take me from Yates. Tried to hide me. Wouldn't let me leave after my Shift ended."

"Sarah..." Hannah started.

"He's the reason I had my accident, my memory loss..." Sarah looked even more anxious now as she continued to pace. "Which is why the dream was so disturbing."

"Disturbing?" asked Hannah. "What do you mean?"

Sarah hesitated, and Hannah could see the concern in her eyes. "Because," she said, "in the dream..."

"Yes?" asked Hannah.

"I was with him."

"You were with him?" asked Hannah.

"Yes," said Sarah, shutting her eyes. "In his bed."

"Oh..." said Hannah. "But it was just a dream." Sarah resumed her movement, her back rigid and her hands on her hips. "Wasn't it?" Hannah recognized that Sarah's mind was finding subtle ways of remembering.

"I don't know. I mean, yes, it was a dream, but...it was so real. It felt more like..."

"Like what?" Hannah almost crossed her fingers behind her back.

"Like a memory," said Sarah, and she kneaded her temples again.

"A memory?" asked Hannah.

"Yes, but how can that be? I didn't sleep—" She stopped, her eyes widening.

"What?" asked Hannah. "Sarah, what is it?" She waited to see which, if any, of Sarah's memories had returned.

"Oh my God," said Sarah. She pushed her hair back with her hands and stared into space. "What if I did?" She looked at Hannah with focused eyes. "What if I did and I don't remember?" She dropped her hands and hugged herself.

"What are you saying?" asked Hannah.

"Hannah, what if I did sleep with him? And I don't remember? What if...?"

Hannah struggled to keep up. She'd expected that any returning memories of Ramsey would make Sarah happy, but Sarah only looked stricken, as if she'd just heard the worst news. "What if this isn't Yates's child?" Sarah found the chair then and did sit, with her hands on her head. "Oh God. This can't be possible."

Hannah was at a complete crossroads. She had not anticipated this. Sarah feared carrying Ramsey's child. She reminded herself that until all of Sarah's memories returned, this was to be expected. Hiding her concern, Hannah decided that her best course of action now was to comfort her friend.

She kneeled next to Sarah's chair. "Hold on there, Sarah. Just relax. You're getting ahead of yourself."

Sarah took several deep breaths and wiped at her eyes. "You think so?"

"You had a dream. That's all."

Sarah blinked a few times and shook her head. "I don't think it was a dream."

"Okay, so maybe it wasn't. Maybe something did happen between you two."

"But how could that happen? I mean he...he..."

"He what?"

"He held me against my will."

"Did he force you to do anything in the dream?"

"No. No. It wasn't like that."

"So you were a willing participant?"

"I...I...I don't know." Sarah rubbed at her head. "Yes. In the dream I was. Very willing, if I'm honest."

"Okay."

"Okay, what?"

"So maybe there's more to discover."

"More to discover?" Sarah stood. "Like what? That I slept with another man who is not my husband and I may be pregnant with his child?"

"Whoa, slow down," said Hannah.

"I can't. I'm freaking out."

"How about we take this a little slower?"

"What do you mean?"

"What did you come here to ask me for in the first place?" asked Hannah.

Sarah shook out her hands with nervous energy. "I wanted to give you the pill."

"And?"

"I wanted you to confirm that I'm pregnant. Make it official."

"Okay, then. Let's start there."

"Where?"

Hannah walked over to a cabinet of medical supplies and opened it. She pulled out a plastic cup with a lid. "Here," she said, handing the cup to Sarah. "The facilities are outside the door to your left."

Sarah stared at it. "All right," she said, visibly calmer as she took the cup.

"And when you come back, I'll take some blood."

Sarah stood, holding the cup. "What then?"

"After we make it 'official,' as you say, then we'll decide what to do next."

"How long will the tests take?"

"Couple of days."

"Then what?"

"You come back here. In fact, let's plan on you coming back here next Monday, and we'll go from there."

"Next Monday? But if you get the results sooner?"

"I'll text you when I have the results, and you call me when you can. Either way, we'll meet here next week to talk. Unless you want to meet sooner, then call me and we can meet somewhere else. We don't have to meet here if you don't want to."

Sarah nodded and let go of a shaky breath. "You'll text me as soon as you know something?"

"Yes."

"And we'll meet again?"

"Yes."

"And what then?"

"Let's just take one step at a time."

"But how do I know who the father is?"

Hannah could see Sarah start to tense up again. "Hey, don't forget who you're talking to," said Hannah, trying to keep her calm. "I worked in this office for five years, and I've dealt with a lot of expectant mothers. I may not be a Red-Line, but I've got a few tricks up my sleeve."

"You do?"

"Don't worry, Sarah. When the time comes, you'll know everything you need to know. I promise."

"I just hope it's the news I'm hoping for," said Sarah.

"Me, too," said Hannah, praying that Sarah would remember Ramsey by then. "Me, too."

**

Yates walked up from his lab and into the kitchen. "Sarah?" he asked, but didn't see her. He headed up the stairs, calling her as he went. Not finding her there either, he walked to the back of the house, where he saw Izzy dusting a set of candlesticks.

"Izzy, have you seen Sarah?" he asked.

"No, sir. I haven't," she answered.

He grunted as he walked past her and found Julian in his back office. "Julian?"

Julian looked up from the desk and stood. "Yes, Mr. Yates?"

"Have you seen Sarah this morning?"

"She went out, sir."

"Out?"

"Yes."

"But I thought I saw Nelson out by the garage."

"You did, sir. She drove herself."

The answer surprised Yates. "She did?"

"Yes. I saw her leave."

"What time?"

Julian looked at his watch. "About two hours ago."

"Did she say where she was going?"

"Not directly, sir."

Yates cocked his head. "Not directly?"

"No, sir."

"What about indirectly?"

Julian took a second. "I'm not sure I should say."

"Why not?"

"It's something I overheard. I doubt I'm supposed to know."

Yates's gripped the door frame. "You overheard Sarah?"

"Yes, sir."

"When?"

"The day after she became ill. A few days ago."

"Was she on the phone?"

"Yes."

"Who was she talking to?"

Again, Julian hesitated.

"Let me make one thing clear, Julian," said Yates. "My wife is the most important thing in the world to me. And if something were to happen to her that could have been prevented by you, believe me, you'll wish you'd never heard my name."

Julian swallowed. "I believe her name was Hannah, sir."

Yates narrowed his eyes. "Did you say Hannah?"

"Yes, sir."

Yates stared, gauging Julian's truthfulness. Finally, he turned to walk away.

"Excuse me, sir?" asked Julian.

Yates glanced back. "What, Julian?" He clenched his fists.

"I heard Miss Sarah mention an address. Would you like to have it?"

CHAPTER EIGHTEEN

....

ANNAH DROVE HER car up the long driveway to Morgana's home. Leroy's car was already there, and she watched in her rearview mirror as Declan pulled up behind her. She'd left Sarah thirty minutes ago, and Declan had called and told her that Morgana had requested an update and to meet at Morgana's house. She shut off the ignition and got out of her car as Declan did the same.

"How'd it go?" he asked.

"I'll fill you in when we get inside."

Walking up the driveway, he asked, "You gonna tell me who the guy is?"

She stopped her approach to the front door. "Excuse me?"

"The guy. Dr. Marshall Maxwell." He rolled his eyes. "It sounds like someone in a soap opera."

"You went to the office?"

"I walked up to the door. I wanted to see where you were."

"What for?"

"Makes it easier in case I have to come help you to actually know where you are. It's sort of a basic rule of protection."

"And you're sort of an ass." She moved to walk past him.

Her annoyance didn't thwart him. "You dating him?" he asked.

That stopped her again, and she couldn't help but laugh. "Are you worried about my safety or my relationship status?"

"Both, actually."

Hannah resumed her walk to the front door. "Well, don't be. You have nothing to worry about in either case."

Her answer seemed to mollify him, and Hannah couldn't help herself when she added, "But there's a good-looking plastic surgeon across the hall," she said. "Now him, I've got my eye on." She grinned when she noticed his shoulders bunch and knew she'd irritated him.

"What's his name?" Declan asked. "Dr. Bradley Breechcloth?"

"No," Hannah answered as she rang the bell. "It's Dr. Henry Heart-Throb." She reached her hand beneath the top of her shirt and thumped her fingers against her chest, simulating a heartbeat. "And he lives up to his name," she said in a sultry voice.

Declan frowned. "You think you're pretty funny, huh?" he asked as the door opened.

"I do," said Hannah, dropping her hand. "Hello, Ronald," she said to the man who opened the door.

"Please come in," said Ronald, who stepped back. "They're in the office."

Hannah and Declan walked down the long hallway, passing the living area and kitchen, and headed into Morgana's office. Seeing Leroy and Ramsey already seated, Hannah dropped her purse on the chair and sat, and Declan took the seat next to her. Morgana was at her desk, her usual air of authority in place.

"Welcome," she said, "Thank you for meeting me here, especially since I know we've all been somewhat preoccupied."

Ramsey made a grunting sound. "You always did have a way with words." He spoke to Hannah. "What happened?" he asked. "Is she okay?"

Hannah pulled out the bag from her purse. "I got one of the pills. She wants to know what it is."

"As do we," said Morgana. "I'll arrange for the analysis."

Ramsey took the bag from Hannah and studied the small pill through the plastic. "This is what she's been taking?"

"Yes. It's probably some sort of anti-anxiety drug mixed with a mild sedative, if I were to guess."

"Great," said Ramsey, dropping the bag on the coffee table. He looked worn and tired. "Anything else? Any progress?"

"She's experiencing headaches."

"Headaches?" asked Leroy.

"Yes, since she stopped taking the medication."

"What does that mean?" asked Ramsey.

"I think she's trying to remember, but her mind's not giving in just yet."

"Is there any indication that she's remembered anything?" asked Morgana.

Hannah hesitated.

"Hannah?" asked Ramsey.

"Yes," she said.

Ramsey leaned forward. "Yes?"

"She had a dream."

"A dream?" asked Declan.

"About what?" asked Ramsey.

Hannah eyed him. "About you."

"Me? What kind of dream?"

"The kind you don't tell your mother about."

Ramsey frowned, and Hannah rolled her eyes. "A sex dream."

His eyes widened. "She did?"

"Are you sure she didn't use the term nightmare?" asked Morgana.

Hannah dropped her jaw and the men looked just as surprised.

"My God," said Leroy, "did you just crack a joke?"

"I rarely joke, Leroy," said Morgana. She stood, made her way to front of her desk, and leaned back against it. Ramsey shook his head at her.

Hannah managed to continue. "She believes it's more than a dream. She thinks, or knows, it actually happened."

"That's good news, then," said Leroy. "Sounds like she is remembering."

"There's a 'but' coming, though, isn't there?" asked Ramsey. "Don't tell me. I'm not going to like it, am I?"

Hannah didn't mince words. "It terrified her."

He sat up. "Why?"

"Because..." Hannah found it harder to say than she thought.

"Because why?"

"Because she's pregnant."

Ramsey sucked in a breath and clenched his eyes shut.

"She is?" asked Declan. "You're sure?"

Hannah nodded. "Yes."

Ramsey dropped his head into his hand. "This is actually happening."

"Yes, it is."

He looked up with weary eyes. "And why is this terrifying her?"

"Because she's afraid it's your baby."

"She's what?" asked Declan.

"Why is she afraid of that?" asked Leroy.

Hannah slipped off her jacket and rested it on the back of her chair. "Because she still doesn't remember Ramsey. She still thinks she loves Yates. Right now, she's thinking she had some sort of fling with the man her husband hates and may be carrying his child."

"Hell." Ramsey hung his head.

"That's excellent news," said Morgana.

Ramsey's head shot up. "What? How is this good news?"

"Because she remembered something," said Morgana. "That's a good sign."

"I think Morgana's right," said Hannah. "Right now, it's her only logical interpretation, but as she remembers more..."

"Then she'll figure out the truth," said Leroy.

"But what is the truth?" asked Ramsey.

"What do you mean?" asked Hannah.

Ramsey fell back against his seat. "We know she's pregnant."

"Yes," said Hannah.

Ramsey couldn't hide the look of dismay in his eyes. "But how do we know it's mine?"

Hannah held his gaze. "Because it is."

He made a sad smile. "You don't know that."

"Yes, actually I do," she said.

He didn't look convinced.

Hannah gauged her next words carefully. "Listen. I worked as an obstetrician's nurse in that office for several years, Ramsey," she said. "I may not have Declan's sensitivity or your gut instincts, but what I do have is a damn good barometer."

"Barometer?" he asked.

"Yes. I did a general physical exam on her before she left. I've done it a million times with expectant mothers over the course of my employment there. And there's one thing that happened every time, without fail."

"What's that?" asked Ramsey.

"While I had my hands on them during the exam, every time I mentioned the father, or mother, for that matter, I could feel the baby flutter."

Ramsey paused. "Flutter? What are you talking about? She can't be more than two months pregnant."

Hannah shook her head. "It doesn't matter. It has nothing to do with a baby's size. It's about the energy I feel transmitted from them to me. I feel it every time."

Ramsey's fear-filled eyes glimmered with hope. "And you felt this with Sarah?"

Hannah didn't waver, projecting all the confidence she could to convince him. "I did."

"And you say you felt it 'flutter'?"

"Both times."

"Both?"

"I made a point of mentioning both Yates and you while I did the exam. I did it a few times, just to be sure."

"And you felt it when my name was mentioned?"

"Yes. Easily."

"And when Yates was mentioned?" he asked softly.

"Not even a whisper of movement." She watched quietly as he sat unmoving across from her and tried to digest what she told him.

"You're not lying to me, are you?" he asked. "You're not just trying to make me feel better?"

She didn't take her eyes off his, knowing how much he'd struggled with the doubt, no matter how much he'd tried to hide it. "No, Ramsey," she said. "I'm not. That baby is yours. I'd swear my life on it."

Anchors of weight seemed to drain from his shoulders, and she saw his eyes well with emotion. He sighed and dropped his head back into his hands. "You promise me?" she heard him ask.

"I promise you," she said, feeling her own emotions surface.

"You okay, Sherlock?" asked Leroy.

Ramsey exhaled a deep breath.

"Perhaps you should focus more on the silver lining and less on the cloud," said Morgana. "It helps."

"Thanks for the advice," said Ramsey, wiping at his eyes and composing himself.

"It's not my advice," said Morgana. "It's your grandmother's. She said it to me more than once."

Ramsey nodded at her with shiny eyes, but she held his gaze only briefly before she turned back to Hannah. "So, what's next?"

Satisfied she'd convinced Ramsey, Hannah answered Morgana. "I told her I'd contact her once I have her test results confirming her pregnancy."

"How long will that take?" asked Morgana.

"Shouldn't take more than a couple of days. I told her we could meet up again next Monday, or sooner if she wanted to."

"Has she told him?" asked Ramsey.

Hannah assumed he was referring to Yates. "About the pregnancy? No, not yet. She's still processing it. It took her by surprise."

"How was she when you left her?" he asked.

"Better. Calmer. I told her we'd figure everything out. We'd just take it slow." She thought back on the conversation. "I just hope she remembers more soon, before I have to tell her who the father is."

"We'll just have to figure that out when the time comes," said Declan. He regarded Hannah. "She hasn't said anything to Yates about you?"

"No," said Hannah. "Not that I know of. She somehow knows that he won't approve."

Declan gripped the arm of his chair. "Let's hope she keeps it quiet."

Ramsey was clearly frustrated and he bounced his knee. "All this waiting...I don't know how much more I can take."

"We can't wait too long," said Morgana.

"What do you mean by that?" asked Leroy.

"Has Sarah made any reference to the Mirror?" Morgana asked Hannah.

Hannah shook her head. "No, but I haven't mentioned it either."

"What is it?" asked Leroy. "Something we should know?"

"It's the Mirror," said Morgana. "It's beginning to cloud."

"Cloud?" asked Ramsey.

"Older mirrors can begin to cloud over, begin to lose their reflectivity. We noticed it last week."

"But the Mirror was fine when Sarah tried to read it," said Hannah.

Morgana crossed her arms. "We don't understand it either, but there is definitely a discernable difference."

"And what is the significance if it clouds?" asked Declan.

"It can become unreadable," said Morgana.

"You're kidding," said Ramsey.

"I wish I were," said Morgana. "It's why I asked you all here. Is there any way we can speed this process along?"

"We're not playing Twister here, Morgana," said Declan. "We can't just walk up to Sarah and ask her to hold John's hand, oh, and by the way, please read this Mirror and tell us where our serum is."

"I appreciate your ability to point out the obvious, Declan," said Morgana, "but at the rate the Mirror is clouding over, we may have few other options."

"It's happening that fast?" asked Leroy.

"Apparently," said Morgana, "it's doesn't take long."

"How much time do we have?" asked Ramsey.

She tipped her head. "I'd say a week, maybe less."

"A week?" asked Declan.

"Yes." She observed their looks of concern. "It's better than twenty-four hours," she said.

"I'm glad you're optimistic," said Declan.

Morgana remained unflappable. "I have found that once given a deadline, the odds of success tend to improve."

Ramsey grunted. "Especially if missing it means we're all going to die a lot sooner than we want to."

"That helps, too," said Morgana.

"Well, I hate to deepen the hole here," said Declan, "but if Yates gets wind of our plans, and at some point he will, reading the Mirror is the least of our worries."

"And I thought we were already under pressure," said Ramsey.

"Guess I'll be canceling my pleasure cruise this weekend," said Leroy.

"Pleasure cruise?" asked Ramsey. "What? You weren't going to invite me?"

"I said 'pleasure,'" answered Leroy.

Ramsey made a face. "You're all heart."

"So worst-case scenario," said Hannah. "Sarah hasn't remembered by next week. What do we do?"

"Maybe exactly what Declan suggests," said Morgana.

"What? We ask her to sit down and read the Mirror with me?" asked Ramsey.

"Why not?" asked Morgana.

"Well, first of all, she'll have all kinds of questions which will require an explanation," said Hannah.

"Yes," said Morgana. "She probably will."

"But that would mean telling her everything," said Ramsey.

"Yes, I suppose it would."

"But that could hurt her," said Ramsey.

"Maybe. We don't know for sure."

Ramsey objected. "Morgana, I am not going to put her at risk like that."

"You don't think she's at risk right now?" asked Morgana. "You think if she knew the situation, she'd want you to do any different?"

"We may not have any other choice," said Declan.

"We can't do that to her," said Ramsey.

"What are our options?" asked Declan. "If we leave her as she is and do nothing, we lose the opportunity to read the Mirror. Maybe she eventually remembers and, if we've managed to do away with Yates, we all still die within the next twenty-four months and she's left alone. Or worse, we don't manage to do away with Yates and he either kills us or he just waits us out until we're all dead, leaving Sarah to fend for herself."

Hannah scowled at him. "You are definitely not optimistic."

"Or," said Ramsey, offering an alternative theory, "we tell her everything and she falls apart. She refuses to see me and won't read the Mirror, in which case we die anyway and she's left dealing with whatever part of her mind is left intact, Yates or no Yates."

"Or," said Hannah, shaking her head at Ramsey, "we tell her everything, she remembers, she agrees to read the Mirror, she falls back in love with you, we get rid of Yates, she has your baby, and we all live happily ever after."

"I like Hannah's version," said Leroy.

"So do the seven dwarves and Cinderella," said Ramsey.

"And me," said Morgana.

"That explains a lot," said Ramsey.

"It could be any of those scenarios or anything in between," said Declan. "We don't know."

"Exactly," said Morgana. "Stop thinking it to death. We'll do what we have to do and hope for the best. Besides, we have no idea what the week will bring. Everything could change in a heartbeat." She studied Hannah. "I doubt that last week you thought you'd be using your ex's office space again, right?"

"Never crossed my mind," said Hannah, avoiding the look she felt from Declan.

"Of course, it didn't," said Morgana. "We all have to deal with the unexpected. The key is to trust that destiny is on our side. Without that, then we are doomed to fail."

They went quiet and Hannah suspected they were all considering where they would be in a week's time. Ramsey broke the silence. "Did anyone ever tell you that you'd make a great Councilwoman?"

She raised an eyebrow at him. "Is that a compliment?"

He smirked. "Don't get used to it."

"Perish the thought," she answered.

Declan eyed Hannah. "Soap opera guy is your ex, huh?"

Hannah glanced over but didn't respond.

Declan turned his attention back to Morgana. "You're right about one thing."

"What's that?" she asked.

"This week is gonna be full of surprises."

CHAPTER NINETEEN

··

THE WARM WATER soothed Sarah's muscles as the voluminous bubbles almost spilled out over the tub, creating a slightly comical scene. Sarah realized that the only body part of hers visible was the top of her head. Returning home after meeting with Hannah, she decided that she needed to relax. Not seeing Yates and feeling worn and drained, she'd headed upstairs and run the deep-jetted tub, and now, dropping her shoulders deeper into the water and closing her eyes, she began to unwind and tried to gather her thoughts.

The last few days had been troubling, and her mind had been in overdrive, and now she was pregnant and didn't know what to do about it. It wasn't that she didn't want to be a parent. She'd planned to have children, but she'd assumed it would be a decision she would make in the future, not six weeks into her marriage. And now, the possibility that she was carrying another man's child loomed over her, making her almost physically ill. She wished she could remember the circumstances surrounding her relationship with John Ramsey. If she could, then maybe it would shed some light on her current situation.

She heard a noise over the popping of the bubbles and opened her eyes to see Yates standing at the doorway of the bathroom, watching her.

"There you are," she said.

"Yes," he said. "Here I am." He paused. "Where have you been?"

She closed her eyes again, maintaining her calm demeanor. "I went out. I had some things to do."

"Went out? Without Nelson?"

"Yes."

"Why?"

She opened her eyes again. "Because it's silly for him to drive me."

"You said you would use him. We made an agreement." He leaned against the doorframe, his posture rigid.

"We did. I agreed to use Nelson and you agreed to make an appointment with that doctor."

"He's been out of town."

"And when he's back and I've seen him, then I'll use Nelson."

"Sarah..."

She groaned in frustration. "Please stop talking to me like I'm a petulant child."

He walked into the bathroom, grabbed her vanity chair and pulled it up, facing backwards, next to the tub. He sat and draped his arms across the back of it.

Sarah closed her eyes and rested her head against the tub.

"Where'd you go?" he asked.

"Out. I told you I had some things to do."

"Out where?"

She sighed and cracked her eyes open. "Now I have to tell you where I go? Is that why you want me to use Nelson, so you can keep track of me?"

"I'd like to know where you are, yes."

"So do what every other husband does, and call me."

He studied her as if gauging how far to go with the subject. "And if I'd called, would you have answered?"

"What do you mean?"

"Do you not want me to know where you were?"

She tensed, and the water sloshed gently against the sides of the tub. "I had an appointment," she said. "Can we leave it at that?"

"I'd rather we didn't. What appointment?"

Sarah sighed. "Please, Yates. I'm tired, and I don't want to talk about this right now. I'm trying to relax."

"I can see that. But I'd still like to know where you were."

Her energy shifted, and she sat up. "Damn it. Can't I just have a moment of peace without you interrogating me?" She stood and the bubbles slid down her body as she grabbed for her towel. Wrapping it around her, she stepped out of the tub and moved around him.

"How's Hannah?" he asked.

She froze and swiveled to face him. "How did you know?"

His face was as hard as the granite countertop in the bathroom. "It doesn't matter how I know. I just want to know why you saw her."

She felt his tension and knew he was unhappy, even angry, and her own anger grew. "Because she's my friend. And I wanted to see her. You have a problem with that?"

He rose out of the chair. "When it means my wife lies to me to spend time with a woman who'd rather I didn't exist and who is friendly with Ramsey, then yes, I have a problem with that."

"Oh, stop being suspicious. Hannah has never said one word against you. Nor has she said anything to sway me toward Ramsey's side."

"All the more reason to suspect her."

"You can worry about nothing if you want to, but she's my friend and I enjoy her company, so I will continue to see her whether you approve or not. You're my husband, not my father."

"Then go see Rachel," he said, his eyes steely. "She's a friend. But not Hannah."

"You don't understand, Yates. Hannah's been extremely helpful. I can talk to her about things I can't talk to Rachel about."

"Like what?" he asked. "What could possibly be so important?"

Sarah tried to hold her temper, but it was like holding back the water of a draining tub, and she didn't have the patience for it. "I'm pregnant."

He went silent at her words, and his eyes rounded. "You're what?"

"You heard me." She turned back to the mirror and studied herself. "I'm pregnant."

"But I thought..."

"That I was using birth control? I was."

He took a few seconds before he spoke. "I don't believe it."

"Join the club."

"That's terrific."

She eyed his reflection and saw him grinning. "You think so?"

"Of course, I think so." He walked up behind her and put his hands on her shoulders. "We're going to have a baby?"

A tingle of discomfort radiated from her belly. She tried to ignore it, not understanding its source. "Yes," she said. "We are."

"I'm so happy." Moving closer, he wrapped his arms around her, but she tensed, and he felt it. "What?" he asked.

"That's why I saw Hannah. I wanted to talk to her about it. Have her confirm it."

"Confirm it? What's to confirm? I'm sure you're right if you can sense it." He dropped his arms but remained behind her. "And she's not a doctor. We need to find you an obstetrician."

She tightened the towel around her. "I will. I'm sure Hannah can recommend one."

"Hannah?" he asked. "No. I don't want you to see her anymore."

Sarah turned. "Excuse me?"

"You're carrying my child, Sarah. I will not let you put him or her at risk."

"Risk?" she asked. "What risk? You think Hannah's a baby snatcher?"

"Don't be naïve.'"

"Don't be an idiot."

"Sarah, listen to me..." He reached out to touch her, but she pulled away.

"No," she said. "I may be having your baby, but I am not your toy. I will go where I please and see whoever I please."

He stared, and she sensed his surprise at her outburst, and she waited for him to say something. "Did you take your pill today?" he asked.

The unexpected question made her pause, and as she was considering her answer, he took her hand and began to knead it with his fingers. His touch soothed her, and her mind went quiet, but a sudden flare of irritation erupted, and a burst of energy surged down her arm and shot out through her palm.

Yates yanked his hand back when the electric pulse buzzed through him and massaging his hand and fingers, he stared at her in shock.

She gazed back at him as if she'd just handed him the toothpaste. "I'm going to get dressed now," she said. The matter decided and the discussion over, she turned and walked into the closet, leaving him alone in the bathroom.

**

Hannah turned the knob, stopping the flow of water, and opened the steam-covered shower door. After grabbing a towel and drying her body, she wrapped the towel around her head and stepped onto the tile, feeling better after a long night where she'd dreamed of evil Red-Lines chasing her with syringes in their hands.

It had been two days since she'd last seen Sarah, and she hoped the test results would be ready today. Since their conversation with Morgana, she'd been on edge. She'd been nervous anyway, but now every noise made her jump and her imagination wouldn't calm. She told no one, especially Declan. He worried enough about her, and she knew her feelings were completely normal, considering her situation.

After applying moisturizer to her face and body, she pulled off the towel and rubbed it over her head to remove the excess water. She pulled a wide-tooth comb through her hair, applied some deodorant, threw on some sweatpants, fuzzy socks, and a spaghetti-strapped fitted camisole, and headed into the kitchen. Wanting a cup of tea, she grabbed the teapot, filled it with water, and put it on the stove. She figured if she had to wait for the test results and worry about the unknown, she would at least do it comfortably.

The doorbell rang, and she stopped in mid-movement. Rubbing her arms against a sudden chill, she moved into the front room and stared at the door. She couldn't help but remember the time she'd answered the door to Yates back at the safe house and how her lungs would not inflate. It made her shiver.

A knock sounded, and she jumped. "Hannah, it's me," she heard from the other side of the door. "It's Declan."

Her shoulders slumped in relief, and she let go of a held breath. She went to the door and opened it.

He leaned an arm against the door frame and looked her over. "You okay?" he asked.

"Yes, I'm fine." She didn't miss his appraisal. "Is something wrong? How's Ramsey?"

"Everything's fine, relatively speaking. Can I come in?"

She debated for a moment, wondering why he was there, before she stepped back. He walked in, and she closed the door behind him.

"What is it?" she asked. She could tell something was bothering him.

"I put a security team outside your building."

"You what?" she asked. "What for?"

"Because something's nagging at me, Hannah, and I don't like it. It usually means something."

"Maybe it means that you're overly protective." She headed into the kitchen. "You want something to drink?"

"No, thanks," he said. "I'm just being cautious. I don't like knowing you're here alone."

She took a seat and waited for the water to boil. "I live here, Declan. I've lived alone for a while now."

He joined her at the kitchen table. "You know what I mean."

"You really think I'm at risk?"

He put his elbows on the table and clasped his hands. "I think we all are, but you're the one talking to Sarah."

"Just a few more days, though. Then we'll see what happens."

Declan sighed. "I want you to consider something."

"What?"

"Backing out of this. Disappearing for a while."

That surprised her. "I can't do that. What about Sarah? What about the Mirror? And Ramsey? I can't do that to him."

Declan fiddled with a napkin on the table. "I know. But is it worth it if you end up dead?"

"We'll all end up dead without the serum."

He bunched the napkin in his hand.

"And what's the point of living if you sacrifice your self-respect at the same time?" She leaned in closer. "Besides, I suspect there's more to this than just my safety." She hesitated before she asked, "What's this really all about?"

He tapped on the table. "You mind if I ask you a personal question?"

"As long as you don't mind if I choose not to answer it."

He took a second. "What happened between you and Dr. Marshall Maxwell?"

The teapot began to scream. Hannah took advantage of the distraction to turn off the stove and grab a teabag. "You want some tea?" she asked, trying to look busy.

"Please."

She prepared a second cup and brought them over. "You want any sugar? Cream?"

"No, this is fine." He waited as she played with the teabag, lost in her thoughts.

"It's the usual story," she finally said. "Student falls for professor from afar. I went to work for him after graduation, and we were involved six months later. Eighteen months after that, we were married." She continued to play with her teabag.

"And then? What happened after that?"

She shifted in her seat but didn't look at him. "Let's just say it became apparent I wasn't the only nurse he liked." She picked up her mug but didn't drink from it. "He had other student admirers as well, only there was nothing 'afar' about his relationship with them."

Declan made a quiet noise of understanding.

She glanced up, the uncomfortable memories swirling. "Unfortunately, it took me three years to finally start listening to my instincts, but I eventually dumped the bastard."

He nodded, and she knew he could feel her pain. It was just too hard to hide. She took a sip of her drink.

"We're not all like that, you know?"

Hannah could feel herself tighten up. She clenched her mug, but didn't answer.

"And you're right about what you said."

She did look at him then, but with confusion.

"There is another reason why I'm here. Why I want you to leave."

"What's that?" she asked.

"Our conversation with Morgana. It hit me then."

"What did?"

"This week. A lot could happen over the next few days, Hannah. Things that could alter our lives forever."

"I know."

"And I don't want that to happen without telling you how I feel."

She put her cup down. "How you feel? What do you mean?"

"I like you, Hannah."

Her heart thumped against her chest and she stood, arms crossed, and he stood too, not willing to let her walk away. "Declan—" she said.

"Listen," he said. "Before you freak out on me, I'm not saying this to make you do anything. If you want nothing to do with me or the feelings are not mutual, I'm fine with that, but I have to tell you how I feel. I've never been one to sit back and say nothing. It eats at me if I do. And right now, I'm feeling pretty chewed up that I haven't said anything sooner."

She turned away, knowing full well that he could feel every emotion coursing through her. Despite her attempts to distance herself, she couldn't deny that she liked him too, and there was no way to hide it. He'd given her an out, though, and she appreciated it.

Chills broke out on her skin. She wanted to shut him out and not open herself to heartbreak again because she felt sure that a betrayal from him would wreck her forever, but she couldn't ignore how his words made her heart skip.

"Hannah?" he asked. "You going to say something? I could use a little feedback here."

Turning back, she met his gaze but couldn't bring herself to talk.

He waited, but when she still didn't say anything, he took a step toward her. She fought the urge to retreat, and her mind warred with her body as to how to handle this. Taking another step, he reached for her hand. His warm fingers closed over hers, and she let him clasp it.

"I don't know if I can do this," she heard herself say.

Her hand now in both of his, his warm energy radiated through her. "Do you want to try?" he asked. "We can take it slow. If you feel rushed, just tell me to back off."

His fingers on her skin and his words made a piece of her heart that had been hardened by her divorce melt. Desire welled up within her, no matter how hard she tried to prevent it.

"You realize," he said, "that whatever you resist, persists." Declan pulled gently at her hand, drawing her closer to him until their bodies almost touched.

Her breathing picked up, and her heart raced. She found herself staring at his lips and then his eyes. It had been a long time since she'd felt this way and a long time since she'd felt desirable, but watching him watch her, the locks and walls she'd erected began to crumble. It scared her, and she tensed, fighting the urge to pull away from him.

"If it helps," he said, "I'm scared, too." He reached up and touched her jaw, trailing his fingers along it. "In case my actions haven't made you fully aware by now, I'm slightly crazy about you."

Her heart picked up its frantic pace, and the energy of his touch coursed through her like a tidal wave. Something about the way her heart was pounding made her pay attention, and she tuned into it. It had a pattern that she recognized. It was the same frequency as the familiar energetic flutter of an unborn child. She'd used that flutter to discern the connection between a child and its parent, but now the realization of what it truly meant occurred to her: she could sense the connection of one heartbeat to another. She sucked in an audible breath as she understood then that her heart knew Declan's, and their winding paths had both led them to find each other.

Her last reserves of doubt falling, she moved in close, and he slid his hand behind her neck. Dropping his head, their lips met, and she let go of her fear, opened up, and let him in.

CHAPTER TWENTY

....

"**Y**ES," SAID LEROY, phone to his ear, as he walked into his kitchen. He saw Sherlock at the sink, rinsing a glass and placing it in the drainer. "No," he continued. "We're here." Leroy sat in one of the kitchen chairs. "Okay. I'll let him know." Leroy hung up and put the phone down.

"Who's that? Hannah?" asked Ramsey, drying his hands. "Has she gotten the test results?"

"No," said Leroy. "It's not Hannah. I haven't heard from her yet. It was Morgana."

"Morgana?"

"Yes, she'll be here in a few minutes."

"Here? Why?"

"She wouldn't say. She wanted to be sure you were here."

"Me?"

"Yes."

Ramsey moved and sat next to Leroy. "What is it now?"

"No telling."

Ramsey rubbed his neck. "You heard from Declan today?"

"No, he's been uptight over Hannah. He's probably hanging out at her place."

Ramsey chuckled softly. "You think he realizes it yet?"

"Realizes what?" asked Leroy.

"That he's fallen for her?"

Leroy smiled. "Well, if it's apparent to us, then it sure as hell should be obvious to him."

"Poor Hannah," said Ramsey.

"Poor Declan," said Leroy.

Ramsey couldn't help but grin when the doorbell rang. "She was in the neighborhood, wasn't she?" he asked as Leroy stood and walked out of the kitchen. Ramsey heard the door open and close, and seconds later, Morgana stood in the doorway of the kitchen.

"Ramsey," she said. She wore a navy-blue pantsuit with a white silk scarf, and she stood with her hands in her pockets, her stance serious yet striking.

"Long time, no see, Morgana," he said. "We keep meeting like this, people might begin to talk."

"Don't flatter yourself."

He shifted in his seat. "What can I do for you?"

She spoke to Leroy, who stood beside her. "You have a place where he and I can talk?"

Leroy glanced at Ramsey, who looked back with surprise.

"Don't worry," she said. "He'll be perfectly safe."

"One never knows with you, Morgana," Leroy answered. "You can use my office."

"Thank you."

Ramsey stood with a bit of apprehension but then led the way to Leroy's office as Morgana followed. Once inside the room, he turned and closed the doors. Leroy watched from the living room.

"If you hear me scream," said Ramsey, "please rescue me."

"What, and risk my life too?" asked Leroy. "Olivia would never forgive me."

"For God's sake," said Morgana. "Shut the door."

Ramsey did as she asked and turned to face her. "So," he said, "what requires my undivided attention?"

Walking to the other side of the office, she turned to face him as if debating what to say. She took her small purse off her arm and dropped it onto Leroy's desk. "I wanted to discuss a few things."

"What?" Ramsey had never known her to beat around the bush, so her apparent hesitation surprised him. "Something on your mind?"

"Quite a bit, actually, as I'm sure there's quite a bit on yours."

"You could say that."

She walked over to Leroy's plants and regarded them. "I spoke with the Council yesterday. We talked about our discussion the other day."

"About the Mirror?" asked Ramsey.

"Yes, as well as Sarah and Yates."

"And what was discussed?"

"It is our hope that after you pull Sarah out, we can find a way to remove Yates."

Ramsey nodded. "I know that's the hope, but we still don't know how. I don't think the guy is going to go down easy."

"There's a way," she said, still studying the plants.

"And what is that?"

"He has a weakness," she said as she turned from the plants. "The serum."

Ramsey sat on the couch, feeling weary. "We know that, but he's not going to hand it over to us."

"Which is why we'll have to take it from him."

"Any ideas how we'll do that?"

"The less you know, the better."

That made Ramsey sit up. "What do you mean?"

"Once you get Sarah out of there, if Yates has not been subdued, you will need to take her away from here."

He straightened. "Take her away?"

"Yes. She won't be safe, and neither will you as long as Yates lives."

"Where do you suggest I take her?"

"Anywhere. But you can't tell anyone where."

"You mean go into hiding?"

"Yes. If you are able to bring her out, assuming her memories are intact, you will both need to disappear. The Council has arranged for monthly deposits into your account. You can take her anywhere. But you will have to be smart about it. Yates will do his best to track you. If we—"

He raised a hand. "Whoa, wait a minute, you mean leave here? For good?"

Her expression did not change. "That's exactly what I mean."

"But what about Leroy? And Hannah and Declan?"

"Their lives will be at risk if you tell them where you are."

"They'll be at risk regardless."

She disagreed. "Yates won't come after them if they don't know where to find you."

"Wrong. He'll use them to draw us out."

"He can't use them against you if they can't locate you to do it."

He got up from the couch. "We can't run forever, Morgana."

"Nobody is saying you should. You just need to give us time."

"Time?"

"The Council is not as ill prepared as you may think. We have a few skills and abilities. Our goal will be to find a way to get to that serum and bring him down."

"But the best way to do that is through Sarah," said Ramsey. "She's been in that house. She may even know where it is."

"I acknowledge that, and I hope that's the case, but in the event that fails and he escapes, then you must take her away. Her safety and that of her child are of extreme importance."

Ramsey started to argue with her, but stopped himself. Was she right? He hadn't considered what would happen after they'd saved Sarah. He'd always pictured the two of them just going home, but he had to admit that Morgana had a point. If Yates still lived, he would stop at nothing to get Sarah back, and if he knew the child she carried belonged to Ramsey, then he could attempt to end the pregnancy.

Something else about Morgana's statement made Ramsey curious. "But once she reads the Mirror and we find the serum, assuming we do, then what exactly is her role? She's no longer necessary to the Council."

Morgana walked over and sat on the edge of Leroy's desk. "That's where you're wrong. She holds the key to not only finding the serum, but to contacting our people. And so does her child. And so do you, for that matter."

"Contacting our people?"

"Yes. Don't you think we'd like to reconnect with our host planet?"

Ramsey's head swum with the unexpected possibilities. "Why?"

"Why?" asked Morgana. "Why not? We used to travel between our worlds with regularity. We lived among Red-Lines and engaged in all manner of scientific discovery and exploration. We'd like to do that again. Who knows? Perhaps they've been trying to reach us as well."

"And you think Sarah can facilitate that?"

"Yes, we think she can. Red-Lines were the branch between our worlds. She is one, and she will give birth to one. And you are the grandson, great-grandson, and the father of one. That puts the odds on our side."

Ramsey had not considered it that way. "You think our child will be a Red-Line?"

"Why wouldn't it be?"

"Because I'm not a Red-Line."

"But you carry the genes of one. Sarah's overcome all sorts of problems already. I suspect she'll handle your shortcomings as well."

Ramsey smirked. "Thanks."

"You're welcome."

He tried to come to terms with what Morgana asked of him. "Let me get this straight," he said as he walked over to the window and looked out. He seemed to think better staring at Leroy's lawn. "If we get Sarah out and her memories return, but Yates is still alive, you want me to disappear with her. Go into hiding."

"Until such time that the Council successfully deals with Yates, yes."

"And we can tell no one where we are?"

"No."

He looked back at her. "And how will we know Yates won't follow?"

"He will, but Sarah should have learned enough by now to cloak herself so he can't sense her."

"And you don't think Declan, Hannah, and Leroy will be in danger?"

"Not if you go deep enough into hiding."

He paused. "What about the Mirror?"

"You mean reading it?"

"Yes. Where does that fit into this plan of yours?"

She joined him at the window. "You'll have to read it fast, I suppose, and then get out of town."

"And how do you suppose we do that?" He asked. "It's not like I can hand it to her and say, 'Here you go. Read fast, 'cause we've got to run.'"

Morgana hesitated, eyeing Leroy's backyard. Then, with a determined step, she walked back to the desk. Ramsey watched as she picked up her purse, opened it, and pulled out a red velvet pouch. She held it out to him. "As a matter of fact," she said, holding the bag, "you can."

He stared at the pouch. "That's not what I think it is, is it?"

She didn't answer.

He walked over and took the bag from her hand. After loosening the opening, he gently pulled the Mirror from it, noting the elaborate engraved D etched on its surface. "I can't take this." He ran his thumb over it.

"Why not?" she asked. "It belonged to your grandmother."

He held the object in his hand, feeling its weight. Twisting the lid, he felt it give way and he removed it. The Mirror within reflected his image, although its clouded surface marred his reflection. "This is it?"

"It is," she said.

"This little thing is what everyone's talking about."

"Funny how such a small object can hold so much power."

Feeling nothing from it other than his grandmother's warm energy, he replaced the lid and returned it to the bag. "I'm supposed to carry this with me? And when Sarah and I reunite, she reads it, we convey the location of the serum to you, and then disappear until the Council disposes of Yates?"

"If Yates still lives, then yes."

"And the Council's in agreement with this?"

She paused, putting her purse down. "The Council has no idea you have the Mirror. I took certain liberties."

"You mean you took the Mirror without their consent?"

"I did. I agree with the saying that it's better to ask for forgiveness rather than permission."

He shook his head. "You've got balls, I'll give you that."

"I think having a uterus is all that I require, thank you."

He didn't argue with her, and slid the Mirror into his jacket pocket. "I take it you don't want me to tell anyone I have the Mirror."

"I would appreciate it if you didn't."

"Okay."

Morgana returned to the window, and he joined her. The fountain in the yard bubbled, but he hardly noticed as another thought came to mind. "Can I ask you something?" he asked.

She glanced at him. "You've never been one to ask permission either."

He watched a robin drink from the fountain. "How did my grandmother die?"

Morgana stilled at the question.

"It wasn't a heart attack, was it?" Ramsey recalled the phone call from his mother three years ago, telling him that his Nana Rose had been found dead in her bed, apparently the victim of heart failure.

Morgana studied the yard. "She ran out of serum."

Ramsey's heart sank. After learning that his grandmother was a Red-Line, he'd begun to wonder if that had been the case. He let out a held breath, wondering how many years he'd lost with her.

"I knew it was coming," Morgana continued. "I suspected Destine didn't have enough." She set her jaw. "She never told me specifics, but when she started to show the signs...I knew."

He heard the tightness in her voice and realized how much his grandmother had meant to her. They'd both been profoundly affected by her death.

Morgana cleared her throat and shook off the memories. She turned and moved toward the desk, picking up her purse and preparing to depart.

"You know," he said, seeing that Morgana had returned to business, "the likelihood of Sarah wanting to leave and disappear with me is slim. She has ties here, too."

"Then it will be up to you to convince her."

"And if I don't?"

Morgana drew herself up, her body language leaving little to the imagination. She walked right up to him. "You are the great-grandson of Varalika, the grandson of Destine, Sarah's mate, and the father of a future Red-Line. Figure it out."

Her vehemence took him by surprise, and he found himself at a loss for words.

"And for that matter," she added, "considering your lineage, if you could manage to pull your head out of your ass once in a while, you might actually make a good Councilman."

Ramsey wasn't sure he heard right. "Should I take that as a compliment?"

She walked to the office door and opened it. "Don't get used to it," she said, and she left the office without looking back.

"Perish the thought," he said as he watched her walk away.

CHAPTER TWENTY-ONE

....

THE FOLLOWING DAY, the test results arrived. Sarah's phone pinged when she received the text message. The weather warming, she ate breakfast on the patio as she read the note from Hannah.

Results in. It's official. Congratulations. Also, received analysis. Can you meet?

She quickly typed back. *Tomorrow? PM?*

Her phone pinged with Hannah's response. *4:00? At the Dr.'s office? They're closed Friday pm, so it will just be us.*

Perfect. See you then. She put the phone down and heard the back door open.

"Good morning," said Yates, sitting at the table.

After their argument, they'd spent the last two days saying little to each other. Yates had stayed hidden down in his basement while she'd remained upstairs, choosing not to leave because it would only make him more suspicious if she went out. He maintained a calm, even pleasant, demeanor, but she knew it was forced, and although she thought perhaps she should apologize to him, she couldn't bring herself to do it.

"Good morning," she answered.

He helped himself to a croissant as Julian brought him a plate of scrambled eggs. "Thank you, Julian."

"Of course, sir. Enjoy your breakfast."

Sarah sipped her coffee. Her eggs sat half eaten on her plate. "Not hungry?" he asked.

She grimaced at the eggs. "No. Breakfast is iffy with me."

"Morning sickness?"

She nodded.

He buttered his croissant. "So, how long are we going to stay mad at each other?"

She eyed him across the table. "I'm not mad anymore. I'm just frustrated."

Finished with the butter, he put the knife down. "I know I can be demanding, but there are certain things I won't compromise on."

Her back stiffened, and she prepared to defend her point.

"But before you get upset," he said, "I'm willing to discuss it."

That surprised her. "Discuss it?"

"I won't compromise the safety of my family, Sarah."

"Neither would I."

"I'm just worried you're placing your trust in the wrong hands."

"I told you, Yates. Hannah has never given me any reason to distrust her. I'm a Red-Line. Give me some credit."

He speared his eggs with a fork. "Point taken. But I would like you to see a doctor."

"I know that."

"Do you want me to find one, or are you going to ask Hannah?"

She stilled. "You're willing to let Hannah recommend someone?"

"As long as I can check him out and he meets with my approval, I'll concede that much."

She knew Yates's acquiescence didn't come easy, but she appreciated that he made the effort. "Thank you."

He sipped some coffee. "Are you going to see her again?"

She met his eyes and held them. "Yes."

"I don't suppose I can change your mind?"

"No."

"Very well."

"What? No interrogation?"

"As you said, Sarah. I'm your husband, not your father. I can't monitor everything you do, or everyone you see, nor do I wish to."

"I'm glad you see it that way."

"But if her involvement harms you or the baby in any way, then I will insist that she disappear."

"Disappear?" Sarah asked. "You mean no longer see her?"

"Yes. That's what I mean. Can you concede that much?"

"Yes. I'll concede that much, but you have nothing to worry about."

"Thank you." He took a bite of his eggs, and stared out over the water. He picked up the paper that was sitting on the table and scanned the headlines. "I told you I'll be gone for the day tomorrow?"

Sarah debating drinking some coffee, but put her hand on her stomach when it gurgled. "Yes, you told me. Meetings, right?"

"Yes. I'll be meeting with various people during the day, and then I have our board meeting tomorrow night. I won't be home until late."

"That's fine." She blew out a breath.

"You okay?" he asked. "You look a little pale."

"Excuse me." She jumped up from her seat and ran into the house.

"Of course," he said.

**

After she left, Yates waited several seconds as the breeze blew his hair and he listened to the waves of the surf. After putting the paper down, he took another bite of eggs and a swig of juice. He wiped his mouth with a napkin, reached over and picked up Sarah's phone. He typed a few buttons and smiled as he began to read her text messages.

**

The coffee machine beeped, and Hannah grabbed the pot to fill her mug with coffee. The smell perked her up, and she took a sip, appreciating the taste of the fresh brew. Returning the pot to its base, she sat at the table. She'd slept like a recruit during hell week, closing her eyes one moment and opening them again eight hours later having barely moved from her original spot. She hadn't slept like that in weeks, probably months. It didn't hurt that Declan slept by her side; his presence made her feel safer than she had in a long time. She knew he slept well, too, because he was still in her bed; the man who routinely woke at the crack of dawn had not stirred.

She thought back over the course of the last twenty-four hours, still dumbfounded by all that had happened. The memory of the previous day elicited a silly smile, and she almost giggled. She couldn't imagine now what she had been so afraid of. Declan and Marshall were polar opposites. Everything Marshall lacked, Declan exuded. She didn't know why she hadn't seen it before.

Her stomach growled, and she stood to open the refrigerator when her phone buzzed with an email from the lab. Accessing it, she read the lab report and the attached corresponding analysis of the pill. Nothing unexpected in the results that she could see. She opened her text messages and sent one out to Sarah, who responded back soon after, and they set their meeting for the following day.

She put the phone down, turned back and jumped when she almost bumped into Declan. "How is it you can sneak up on me in my own place?"

He grinned. "I don't know. Maybe you were distracted."

Hannah shook her head, stepped around him and opened the fridge.

He came up behind her, slid his arms around her waist, and nuzzled her neck. "Maybe you were thinking of me."

She smiled and leaned back into him. "That is a distinct possibility." She let her hands find his, and she squeezed them. "There's a fresh pot of coffee, Romeo, if you want some. You hungry?"

"Just for you, my dear."

And before she knew it, he'd turned her in his arms and sought out her lips. She kissed him, despite her coffee breath, but he didn't seem to mind.

Pulling back, but still held by him, she met his eyes. "How'd you sleep?"

"Like a baby. You?"

"Like a hibernating bear."

"Feeling better?"

"Better than I have in a long time."

He hugged her close. "Good. You look great first thing in the morning, by the way."

"Thank you. So do you."

He glanced at the refrigerator. "Were you planning on making something?"

"I think I have some eggs. You want some?"

"Hmm," he said, finding her neck with his lips. "Maybe in a little while."

She sighed and tilted her head back as he nibbled her skin and his soft lips caressed her, and she struggled to think. "I heard from the lab," she said, trying to focus.

"You did?" he asked, continuing his ministrations.

"Yes." Her breathing picked up. "It's confirmed. Sarah's pregnant."

"She is?" His tongue flicked against her neck.

"Yes, she is." She gripped the back of his shirt and tried to think of the next thing to say. "We're going to meet again tomorrow."

"You are?" His lips moved to just below her ear, and his hot breath sent chills through her.

"Yes." She closed her eyes, enjoying every sensation. "And the pill..."

"What pill?" He worked his way down her neck to her collarbone.

"You know." She bit her lip. "The yellow pill."

"What about it?" He slid one hand up behind her neck and the other down her back and pulled her closer.

Hannah tightened her arms and pushed against him. "It's what I thought."

He trailed his lips back up and found her ear. "And what was that?" he whispered. His teeth nipped at her lobe.

Her mind wouldn't engage. "I have no idea."

He slid his lips over her cheek and found her own, and all thoughts of breakfast and lab reports vanished.

**

"So," said Leroy. "How do you want to handle this?"

Ramsey was sitting on Leroy's living-room couch with his elbows on his knees. It was Friday morning. After a long night, he'd been up early, considering his options. Leroy had joined him, having slept little himself. Hannah had informed them yesterday afternoon that she would be meeting with Sarah today at four o'clock, and asked how Ramsey wanted to proceed. They knew they had little time left to read the Mirror, but there had been no indication that Sarah's memories were returning, so they'd left it to Ramsey to decide if it was time to confront her with the truth.

"I don't know, Leroy," said Ramsey. "Much as I'd like to end this, I'm worried about how this will affect her. It hasn't been a week yet. We still have some time."

"Morgana said a week at most, Sherlock. We may not have another opportunity like this without Yates around."

"I know."

Leroy sat on the couch with him and waited. "I think you know we have to do this."

Ramsey rubbed his temples. "I know. I guess I'm just scared."

"Of what?"

He sighed. "What if she doesn't remember me?"

"What if she does?"

Ramsey hung his head, torn by indecision.

"But if she doesn't," said Leroy, "then we'll deal with it. We'll figure it out. We always do."

Ramsey studied the floor. After several long seconds, he lifted his head. "Okay," he said. "Call Hannah. We'll meet them at the doctor's office." He stood and walked to the closet to grab his jacket.

"Where are you going?" asked Leroy.

"I can't sit here all day thinking about it. I've got to get out of here."

"You want company?"

Ramsey picked up his keys. "Thanks, Leroy, but I need some time on my own."

"You call me, let me know where you are."

"I will." Jiggling his keys nervously, Ramsey opened the door and left.

CHAPTER TWENTY-TWO

··

SARAH RUBBED HER belly. It had been a quiet morning. Yates had left an hour earlier, after breakfast, and she'd been preoccupied since, thinking of her appointment with Hannah that afternoon. She'd had another bout of morning sickness earlier and had skipped the oatmeal Izzy had made. But now, her stomach had settled and she felt a little hungry. Looking at the pantry, she considered what her stomach might be able to handle. Nothing was off limits. Last night, she'd had the strangest craving for green beans, and Yates had offered to summon Julian to go to the store to buy some fresh ones, but she'd wanted them right out of the can. She'd seen them in the pantry weeks ago, and she'd suddenly craved them. He'd gone downstairs for her, dumped them in a bowl, and brought them up to her, and she'd eaten every one of them. She'd had no idea why. They weren't even a favorite vegetable.

Now, as she sat at the table, she peered at the open pantry door. As her stomach rumbled, she stood and flipped on the light. There were numerous items to choose from, but none that beckoned her. She ignored the cereal and chips, didn't want any nuts, and none of the canned veggies interested her. She saw a box of crackers just as she was eyeing the peanut butter. Another flare of hunger made her grab at both, deciding that would satisfy her.

She placed the items on the counter, grabbed a plate and knife, picked up the peanut butter and unscrewed the lid. Reaching for the knife, she stopped when her eyes caught sight of the open jar. Wincing as her head flared, she gasped when a picture swam in her mind of her holding another jar of peanut butter, but one with her finger inside, then pulling out a scoop, bringing it to her mouth, and eating it. No, not eating it—sucking it right off her finger. Her body warmed, and her belly stirred, but it had nothing to do with hunger. Then another picture, this time of John Ramsey with his finger in the jar. Only he didn't suck the peanut butter off his finger, he'd reached over and wiped it across her...

Her vision blurred, and a wave of pain sliced through her skull, making her double over. She tried to gain her balance, but she knew if she stood upright, she'd fall over. Her mind continued its journey, and she saw herself in a bed, with John Ramsey's lips on her, moving over her body while she shivered and clutched at him, pulling him closer.

Sarah could barely breathe. The pictures swam in her head, and she closed her eyes, but they wouldn't stop. She saw herself in the shower with him, on the floor, on the couch. It all came back to her—his touch, his caress, his kiss, and her reaction to him, her cries of pleasure, her excitement, her lust.

She dropped down to her knees, and the peanut butter fell. It hit the ground, and a portion of it escaped the jar and splattered across the floor. The pain in her head began to subside, but she fought to suck in air and her vision still swirled. Keeping her eyes clenched shut, she waited for the spinning to slow. Trying to regain her equilibrium, she forced herself to take long, slow breaths. Her mind slowly stopped its replay of events, and she opened her eyes, happy to see that the room had stopped moving.

"Miss Sarah? Are you okay?"

She heard Julian's voice but didn't answer him. She tried to grasp what had just happened and he kneeled next to her.

"Miss Sarah?" Julian shook her shoulder. "Please tell me. Are you all right? Do I need to call Mr. Yates?"

That snapped her out her shocked state, and she moved her head to look at him. "No," she said. "I'm fine, Julian." She wiped at her forehead and pushed the hair away from her face. As she breathed deeply, her dizziness eased.

'Are you sure? You're very pale, Miss Sarah. Is it the baby?"

She stared, surprised that he knew. "You know I'm pregnant?"

He gave her an uncertain look. "Yes. Mr. Yates told me. He asked me to watch out for you."

Sarah steadied herself and sat back on her heels. "Of course, he did." She moved to rise, and Julian held her by the elbow. Gaining her footing, she managed to stand upright on shaky legs. She grabbed at the counter for support.

"You're sure you're okay?" asked Julian.

"Yes, I'm better now. Thank you."

"You want to go lie down?"

"No. No. I'm fine."

Julian eyed the peanut butter on the floor. "Are you hungry? Can I make you something?" he asked. He reached for a paper towel and began to clean the sticky mess from the ground.

Sarah's stomach flipped again, but she didn't know now if it was due to her pregnancy or John Ramsey. Groaning inwardly, she finally accepted that she had indeed had a relationship with Ramsey, and a passionate one at that.

Finding she could stand without assistance, she let go of the counter. Julian was still cleaning when she made up her mind.

She turned and left the kitchen. "I'm going out, Julian."

Julian spoke behind her. "Why, Miss Sarah?"

She moved into the entryway and found her jacket. "Because I want to."

"Where are you going?"

"That's of no importance." She picked up her purse and slung it over her shoulder. "Thank you for cleaning up."

"But Miss Sarah, you shouldn't leave."

Sarah stopped before reaching the side door that led to the garage. "Why not?"

Julian hesitated for a moment. "Mr. Yates wanted you to stay in today. He told me he was worried about you."

She felt the pulse of unease come from him and realized he was nervous. "Well, then, Julian," she said, swinging the door open. "I guess he should have discussed that with me instead of you, huh?"

Julian didn't say a word as she closed the door behind her and headed for the garage.

**

The dishwasher engaged as Hannah turned the knob, hearing the sound of the water begin to spray from within. She'd showered, changed, and had breakfast, all with Declan beside her. They planned to go to his place to let him get a change of clothes and wait there until her meeting with Sarah that afternoon. Leroy had called a little while ago to let them know that he and Ramsey would meet them at Marshall's office. She knew Ramsey had struggled with the decision, but she could see no other way. If they wanted Sarah to read the Mirror, they had to do it this weekend, and they could not pass up the opportunity to talk to her outside the house and away from Yates.

She heard footsteps and saw Declan approach.

"You ready?" he asked.

"Yes." She grabbed her bag and walked up to him. When he didn't move, she noticed his subdued face. "What?"

He hesitated. "I think we should reconsider."

"Reconsider what?"

"This meeting."

"What? What for?"

"Something doesn't feel right, Hannah."

She sighed. "You've been saying that since this started. I know you don't like this, but I'll be fine. Heck, I've got all three of you there today. The only thing to worry about is Sarah and how she handles it."

Not looking convinced, he walked into the dining area and rested his hands on the back of a chair. "Still..."

"Still what?"

"Something... I don't like it."

She walked over to him. "I can't abandon her. I have to be there for her. She'll be looking to me for reassurance. And if this goes badly and she doesn't remember, then we'll need to be there for Ramsey, too. I can't leave right when I'm needed the most, and neither can you."

"It's not me I'm worried about."

"I'm aware of that, but you'll be there. I won't be alone."

He studied his hands resting on the chair. "Fine." He straightened. "But you get the hell out of there if you get the slightest inkling that something's not right. Don't stop to worry about me."

Hannah couldn't imagine running away and leaving Declan behind, but she didn't tell him that. "I'll be gone so fast you'll wonder if I was ever there." His eyes narrowed and she knew he didn't believe her. "Can we go now?" She waited while he stood there. "I'm sure you'd like to get a change of clothes."

"What for? I've barely worn these." Grinning, he arched an eyebrow at her.

"Yeah, well, you stay here any longer, and people will talk."

"I think it's too late for that, especially after last night."

Hannah's cheeks warmed at the memory. "Great. I'll be the talk of the building." She walked to the front door, and he followed.

"We could stay in, give them more to talk about." He stopped at the threshold and waited.

"Come on, Casanova." She took his hand, opened the door, and pulled him through it. "Stop stalling. We've got a busy afternoon in front of us."

"Yeah," he said as she closed the door and locked it. "Let's hope that's all it is."

**

Ramsey unlocked the door to his house. He'd been driving for a while, but needing to reconnect, he'd decided to stop at home. He closed the door behind him and perused the familiar rooms and smelled the familiar smells. It didn't take long before the expected impact hit him. Sarah. Feeling her everywhere in the house, he took a second to adjust, but he couldn't help but wonder if they would ever return here together again. After this afternoon, she would either be lost to him or they would be back together and in hiding, provided he could convince her to leave. The thought of deserting Leroy, Declan, and Hannah haunted him, and he wished he could tell them, but he knew doing so would only put them in jeopardy. Until Yates was gone, he would have to do everything necessary to keep them, and Sarah, safe. He put his hand to his jacket, feeling the object within his pocket. The Mirror remained where he'd placed it after his conversation with Morgana. He hoped Sarah would be able to read it that night before they left.

Walking into the living room, he saw the cracked coffee table and couch. The memories surfaced, but he closed his eyes and forced himself to think of something else. His clothes. He would need a few items to take with him and he moved toward the hall closet to retrieve his overnight bag. Ramsey was about to open it when he heard a noise from the other room. Letting go of the closet door handle, he listened. All was quiet for several seconds before he heard it again. It sounded like a footstep, muffled by the carpet, but still a footstep. He wasn't sure at first, but as he tuned in, he felt certain someone was there. Remaining where he was, he reached out with his senses to pick up on whatever he'd heard, and continued to listen. His hair stood on end when he realized that he was not alone; someone was in his bedroom.

His breath turning shallow, he tried to constrict his energy, although he didn't know why he was bothering, since he felt sure that whoever was in his house already knew he was there. Finally deciding that he'd never been good at the waiting game, he stepped back out into his living room, trying to peer around the partially closed door to his bedroom.

"Who's there?" His heart thumped. No one emerged, but the feeling didn't leave him. Someone was on the other side of the door.

"I know you're in there," he said, deciding to be bold, "so do us both a favor and come out. If you're going to kill me, let's get it over with. I could use the relief."

Another few seconds passed, and he suppressed the urge to walk to the door and slam it open when he heard movement. The door began to swing inward, and he stared in shock and disbelief when he saw who stood there. Sarah.

Everything muffled and his heart stopped. Ramsey could only stand mute, not believing his eyes. Looking equally uncertain as she watched him from across the room, she didn't move.

"Sarah?" he finally made himself say.

Her eyes widened, and she took a step out. His gaze moved over her, taking in her hair, body, and face. He took a step forward, but she moved back, and he stopped, unprepared for her reaction. She didn't retreat into the bedroom, but instead sidestepped along the wall as if to back away without getting too close.

"Wait," he said when he understood that she meant to leave. "Where are you going?"

Sarah stopped, and he felt the conflict within her, as if she couldn't decide what to do.

"I'm leaving," she said. "I'm sorry. I shouldn't have come here." She edged closer to the door.

"Why?" he asked. Something told him not to approach her, or she would bolt. "Why did you come?" It took all the self-control he could muster not to run and stop her.

"I..." She hesitated, her face clouded. "I thought I remembered something. I'm sorry. I should go."

"What?" he asked. "What did you remember?" Holding his breath, he waited for her response.

She shifted her stance, and she gripped her purse. "I..." Her other hand came up and rubbed at her temple.

She wouldn't or couldn't say it, so he tried to help her. "Us? Do you remember us?"

His words made her suck in a breath and she held her stomach. "Was there an 'us'?" She said it so quietly, he almost didn't hear her.

It took him a few moments while he considered various answers, but settled on the truth. "Yes, Sarah."

She took a step back and moaned. "Oh, God," she said. "How? Why?"

"Sarah, please..." He tried to approach, but she stepped back, and he stopped again. "Listen. You and me..." He didn't know what to say.

She waited. "You and me what?"

The words popped into his head. "We love each other."

She made a nervous laugh. "We what?"

"We love each other. We fell in love during your Shift."

Her mouth fell open. "No, we didn't. That's not possible. I love Yates."

The words hit him like a brakeless two-ton truck, but he held it together. "No, you don't, Sarah. You only think you do."

Her eyes narrowed. "I what? How can you say that? You don't know how I feel."

She was closing up on him, and he knew he had to act fast. "Listen, Sarah, please. Let me tell you everything. You're a Red-Line, and so is he. He's always wanted you, but when he knew you loved me instead, he plotted to take you away. He gave you something to cloud your memory. He made you believe that you loved him instead. You never had a car accident. You were never in the hospital. He implanted all those memories in you. He's not who he says he is, Sarah. He never was."

Sarah didn't move, but her face contorted as if nothing made sense and she couldn't possibly imagine that anything he said was true.

Ramey fought to find the words that would convince her. He looked down at his wrist. "Look," he said, showing her his wristband with the word 'Relax' etched into the band. "You gave this to me. In the hospital. Remember?"

Her gaze moved to observe the band, and she held her head. "I was in the hospital."

"No," he said. "Not you. Me. Yates almost killed me."

"Almost killed you?" She scoffed. "It sounds like quite a story, Mr. Ramsey. Suddenly you're the injured party here, not me."

"That's what happened, Sarah. He used my illness, which he caused, in order to get you close to him. He gave you serum for me in exchange for your blood, which he used against you to make you forget."

Her features hardened, and her hands clenched. "Serum? Blood? You've got quite the imagination. Yates would never hurt me."

He pushed back the rising panic and forced himself to calm down. "But he has, Sarah. He's hurt all of us. You, me, Hannah, Leroy, Declan. He'll hurt all of us to keep you where you are."

"And where exactly am I?"

"You're married to a man you don't love, while the man you do love is doing his damnedest to get you back."

She stilled. "You've been trying to get me back?"

"I showed up at your door, remember? But you didn't remember me. You wouldn't leave. And then..."

"Then what?"

"You married him."

She squinted back at him.

"It was kind of hard to sweep in and take you away after that. Plus, I didn't know how it would affect you. We don't know what he gave you."

She dropped her head and rubbed at her eyes.

"That's why you have the headaches, Sarah," he said. "You're trying to remember."

She groaned. "I don't believe any of this. You're just trying to get me back. You loved me, and we had some sort of relationship, but when I said no and wanted to leave, you wouldn't let me. I had to run and escape, which is why I had my car accident."

"No, Sarah. None of that is true. You chose me. You Binded with me. You made me your mate."

"I what?"

"All female Red-Lines, when they choose a mate, go through a binding ceremony. You did it with me. That's what you remember.

Yates somehow found a way to mimic that with you, but it's not him you want. It's me."

She didn't answer for several seconds, and he could barely stand the waiting. He didn't know what else to say to get through to her.

"You're saying that I Binded with you? Is that what you call it?" she finally asked. "That I made you my mate?"

He let out a long-held breath. "Yes, you did."

She smiled, but not from happiness. "My, you are all full of stories, aren't you?"

Slumping his shoulders, Ramsey grasped for anything else he could use. "What about the mirror? That's not a story."

"The mirror? What mirror?"

"The mirror we want you to read. To find the serum. To save the Gray-Lines."

"Serum. What do you mean?"

He pulled the mirror from his pocket and took it from its pouch. "This mirror. Do you remember, Sarah? Morgana asked you to read it. It contains the location of the serum that will save our line from dying out. That means me, Hannah, Declan, Leroy, Morgana—all of us—will not survive the next two years without the serum. You tried to read it once, remember?" He opened the lid and held it out for her to see.

She winced again.

"Take it," he said. "Feel it. You'll remember, Sarah. I know you will."

Continuing to hold it, he waited and forced himself to take steady breaths, praying that this would work and that the mirror would finally break the chain on her memories.

She started to reach out, but as her hand neared the object, she stopped, her posture straightening, and pulled back, as if she knew that touching it would reveal too much. "I can't," she said, stepping away. "I won't."

"Sarah, no."

"You're crazy," she said. "None of this is true." She continued to step back toward the door. "Yates loves me and I love him. We're going to have a—"

Desperate to think of a way to keep her from leaving, he finished the sentence. "...a baby?"

She made a muffled sound. "Yes," she said. "We are."

Ramsey swallowed, knowing he should stop but unable to do it. "That's not his baby, Sarah." Her backward progress halted. "It's mine."

Her face blanched, and he felt the shock wave from her pierce him.

"That's my family you're referring to, not his," he continued.

Her face changed from pain and fear to anger and resentment, and in that moment, he knew he'd lost her.

"Don't you dare say that," she said. "You're a liar and a coward. Don't you ever come near me or Yates or my child. You hear me?"

Her words crushed him. His chest constricted, and he realized that he would not be able to convince her. "Okay, Sarah." He watched in silent agony as she turned for the door and opened it. He warred with himself about running forward and preventing her from leaving, but he knew he couldn't. He had to let her go. "Just know that no matter what happens, I'll always love you."

Sarah didn't even look at him as she walked out and slammed the door shut behind her.

CHAPTER TWENTY-THREE

....

S IPPING HER CUP of tea, Morgana dropped the folder on her desk. Looking at the pile of work she'd planned to complete that morning, she sighed and sat back in her seat, dissatisfied by her lack of progress. She'd hoped the effort to keep busy would distract her from the day's events, but that plan had proved unsuccessful. Now after a quick lunch, she eyed the time. Three hours, she noted to herself. Three hours until Hannah met with Sarah and Ramsey attempted to revive Sarah's memory. Three hours until the fate of their people was determined. Her nervousness inched up a notch. Knowing that worrying about it accomplished nothing, she stared at her desktop full of paperwork. She put down her cup, picked up the folder again, and began to flip through it, reading the contents. The doorbell rang, but she ignored it, knowing that Ronald would turn away any unwanted visitors and welcome anyone she needed to see.

Rereading the page she'd held for several seconds, she glanced up when her office door opened. "Yes, Ronald?" she asked. "Anyone important?"

A man entered the room, and she stared, transfixed. The folder fell from her hand.

"Morgana," said Yates, stopping at her office door. He was dressed in a tailored chocolate-brown suit and a blue-and-yellow striped tie. "You don't mind if I stop in for a chat, do you?"

Her mind went blank. Then she thought of her valet. "Ronald," she said. "Where he is?" She stood.

Yates took a few steps into the room. "The gentleman who answered the door?" He glanced at his sleeve and straightened the cuff. "Just taking a short break." He looked back up. "I'm sure he'll come around soon."

She sized him up, determining how best to handle this unexpected visit. Directness being her usual method, she decided to stick to what she knew. "What do you want?"

He took a few more steps into the room. "You're not going to offer me any tea?"

"It seems my valet is indisposed." She watched him move through the office. "You'll have to help yourself."

He smiled. "So much for hospitality."

"I doubt that's why you're here. You want hospitality, there's a hotel three blocks away."

He didn't answer, but instead continued his meandering. He stopped and looked at her walls, studying the few pictures and diplomas displayed there.

Morgana slowed her breathing, intent on staying calm.

"You're right, of course." He turned away from the wall. "Hospitality is not why I'm here."

She felt it then. Enmity drifted off him like heat waves on hot asphalt, and she stiffened before she could stop herself. "Then why are you here?" Although she knew he could feel her discomfort, Morgana could do nothing to stop it.

He took a few steps toward her desk, and she fought the urge to step back. "I came to send a message."

"A message?"

"I came to cut the head off the snake."

She knitted her brows. "Excuse me?"

He stopped in front of her desk. "What do you do, Morgana, when you want to stop an army?"

She didn't answer, but she knew what he meant.

"You remove the leader," he said. "Takes the stuffing right out of them."

She straightened her shoulders. "Or it makes them fight that much harder."

He cocked his head. "I considered that, of course, but then I figured it didn't really matter." He paused. "It's hard to fight back when what you're fighting for is lost to you, never to return."

"All the more reason to fight," she said. "Sometimes removing the enemy is destined, no matter what the cost."

His gaze never wavered. "Perhaps." His fingers trailed over her desk. "But I find I actually enjoy a good fight. I'm planning on it, in fact."

She didn't move, but her mind raced. "You're wasting your time if you think messing with me is going to stop them. I think you overestimate my importance. I'm more an annoyance to them."

"No, you're more of an annoyance to me. To them, however, you offer guidance and motivation, no matter how misdirected it might be. You're the one who misinterprets your importance."

"So," she said, "you're here to kill me?"

He smiled again. "Don't be so dramatic. No. I'm not going to kill you. Where's the fun in that?"

"It didn't prevent you from killing Marco."

His smile dropped. "An unfortunate incident, but a necessary one." His hands slid into his pockets, and he maintained his relaxed demeanor. "I have different plans, though, for you, Ramsey, and his merry bunch of miscreants." Her expression must have conveyed her contempt for him, and he frowned. "Please," he said. "Did you really think I was going to let you take Sarah back? That I didn't expect you to come for her?"

"She can't remain the way she is. She'll remember."

"That's where you're wrong. You've all underestimated just exactly what I'm capable of."

"And what is that?" she asked.

"Sarah will never return to Ramsey. She'll never remember any of you. After I'm finished, she and I will be together and she will deliver my child, and Ramsey won't be but a speck of dust in her mind."

Morgana didn't hold back. "I think you underestimate what she's capable of."

He smirked. "No, I know what she's capable of. But I've planned for it. I know exactly how this will play out."

Morgana ticked up an eyebrow. "How impressive. Can you do magic tricks as well?"

One side of his mouth lifted. "Mocking me?" His hands came out of his pockets, and he leaned forward, his palms on the desk. "Do you think I don't know what you've got up your sleeve?"

She narrowed her eyes.

"Hannah's been meeting with Sarah, trying to help her remember. She's analyzed the pill Sarah's been taking, right?"

A cold shiver ran up Morgana's spine.

"Yes. I know all about that. She's meeting with Sarah today, in fact." He looked at his watch. "At four o'clock?" Morgana swallowed. "And poor Ramsey, what's he going to do? Oh, wait. Don't tell me. He's planning on confronting her, hoping to rekindle her love for him. Oh, and of course, have her read the Mirror."

Morgana sucked in a breath at the mention of the mirror.

"Yes," said Yates. "I know you want her to read that mirror, and I know you're in a hurry, too. Probably why you gave it to Ramsey, huh? So he could have Sarah read it before it's too late? Before it clouds over?"

Morgana couldn't help but react. "How did you know?" No one other than a few privy Councilmembers and Ramsey's group knew of the mirror's condition.

Yates grinned. "Who do you think caused it to cloud?"

Her eyes widened. "How...?"

He chuckled. "Who do you think you're dealing with here? You think I haven't had access to that mirror? I have for some time now. My sperm donor fathers snuck me and my brothers in to read it years ago. We wanted to take it, but they wouldn't let us. They had some overriding fear that messing with that thing would lead to their downfall. So we let it be. But we knew where it was and we could get to it whenever we wanted to. None of us could read it, but we didn't see the point, really of taking or destroying it. I mean, to be honest, I've always been curious to see if Sarah could read it. What if she did find the serum?" He held out his hands. "We had nothing invested one way or the other." His voice lowered. "Until you decided to stick her with that half-wit Ramsey during her Shift. Then, well, you pissed me off." His posture turned rigid, and he exuded the first signs of anger.

"I can see that," she said.

"If you'd stayed out of it," he continued, "things might have been different. I could have helped her read that mirror, maybe have even found that serum for you. But now..." He leaned back in, his arms crossed. "I'm going to enjoy watching you all drop like flies while Sarah and I sit back and live happily ever after."

Morgana forced herself to remain passive. "I'm glad we can be a source of entertainment for you."

"Oh, you have indeed. But you've also been a source of irritation, especially now, which is why I have to take a few precautions."

"Precautions?"

His arms dropped back to his sides. "Precisely. Given your incessant need to retrieve Sarah, I've had to concoct a whole new serum. One which will ensure her total and complete acquiescence and her absolute loss of any memory of those who've sworn to take her from me."

Morgana couldn't believe his words. "What do you mean, another serum? You can't do that to her. You have no idea how it will affect her or what it will do to her unborn child."

"Again, you underestimate me. I would never put the child at risk. I've seen to that. But I agree, it would be wise to test the serum first in order to ensure Sarah's safety."

Morgana heard the warning tone in his voice. "What are you planning, Yates?"

"I'd love to fill you in, Morg, but..." He tapped his watch. "...unfortunately, time is running short, and I've got a few more errands to run before the ill-fated meeting at four o'clock."

Morgana had to warn Hannah but realized Yates would anticipate that. "Why are you here, then? You just needed to waste some time?"

He eyed her desk. "I figured you could use a break, seeing as how you have so much work to do." He looked up. "Plus, I couldn't help but do the pop-in. I love the expression on someone's face when I'm the last one they expect to see."

"I have no doubt mine was rewarding."

"One of the best. But I expect it to be eclipsed."

"Really?"

"Oh, yes. First when Hannah sees me, and then when Ramsey does." His features darkened. "It's going to be a fun afternoon."

Morgana's heart raced when she comprehended Yates's plans. She needed to find a way out of this. "Yates..." She hesitated as she tried to think of something to say. "Surely there must be a better way. If you truly care for Sarah, then let her be."

"The time for a better way has long since passed." His posture relaxed, and he stepped away from her desk. "And what I'm doing with Sarah is in her own best interest. Had you not interfered, she'd be with me anyway, so what's the difference?"

"You don't know that."

"Yes, I do."

"Destiny will find its way. No matter what you do."

He faced her. "Well, then, we'll see just exactly what destiny has up its sleeve. The question is, on whose side will it fall?"

Morgana's heart rate was rapidly accelerating. "I suppose we'll find out today, won't we?" She glanced at the clock. "Don't you have somewhere to be?"

His lip crooked up again, and he advanced. "You're right. Much as I'm enjoying our chat, I suppose I have to cut it short."

"You know where the door is."

He laughed and chills broke out on her skin.

"Just one more thing before I go." He stepped towards her.

She tensed at his approach. "You've overstayed your visit as it is." He didn't answer but instead began to walk around the desk. She began to back away as he encroached on her space.

"I admire your courage, Morgana." He moved to the corner and then around to the side of the desk. "But you know I can't let you warn them."

"Why even come here then?" she asked, still moving backward as he advanced. "Why not just do what you plan to do and let me hear about it after? What's the point?"

"The point?" He slowly moved closer. "The point is to have fun."

"Fun?"

"Where's the fun if I can't see what it does to you to know that all you've planned has failed? That your people are in trouble and you have no ability to help them? To know that I know everything and you know nothing?"

"You think this is fun?" She retreated, but knew she had nowhere to go. "You're insane."

He leered at her. "Insanity is underrated and misunderstood. My insanity keeps me sane. It guides me, teaches me, molds me, and serves me. It's my greatest asset." He closed the distance between them. "And it's your total undoing."

Morgana's back found the wall, and she did the only thing left to her—prayed he wasn't right.

**

"I'm telling you, it's weird." Izzy stood in the library as she held a dust cloth in her hand and waved it. "Don't you think this whole thing is off?"

Julian busied himself with pulling books from a large bookshelf and dusting them before returning them to their proper place.

"I mean, do you really see her with him?" she asked.

Julian glanced back at her. "I don't know what you mean. Miss Sarah and Mr. Yates make a handsome couple."

"That's not what I'm talking about." The dust rag flapped. "There's a vibe there that doesn't match. I don't think she even likes him."

Julian replaced the book he'd just dusted. "She married him, didn't she?"

Izzy looked at him as if she was speaking to someone who couldn't count to ten despite using his fingers. "So what?" she asked. "Women do stupid things all the time when it comes to men." She stared at a wedding photo of Sarah and Yates that hung on the wall. "A woman knows when something's not right, and I know something's not right."

"I'll tell you what's not right," said Julian. "You're snooping. You need to stay out of it. That, and you haven't rearranged the pictures as they were." He picked up a smaller wedding picture on the shelf and switched it with another on a lower shelf. "Pay attention to detail, please."

Izzy rolled her eyes at him. "What do you think I've been doing since I've been here?" She put her hands on her hips. "And now you say she's pregnant? I don't buy that at all."

Julian shot her a look. "You don't believe she's pregnant?"

"No, I believe she's pregnant."

"Then what's not to buy? It tends to happen after a couple gets married, if not sooner."

She gave him that same dull look. "You really are blind, aren't you? She didn't want to have his baby, or at least hadn't planned on it."

"And how in the world do you know that?"

She huffed at him. "A woman knows these things."

Julian grunted. "Does this woman know how to finish her work and mind her own business?"

"And him spending all that time in that room downstairs? What's that all about?"

"It's called an office, Isabelle. He's working. How do you think he affords this house and pays us?" Julian grabbed at another book and swiped at it.

"That's not just an office. He's got test tubes and microscopes and God knows what else down there."

Julian sighed. "It's a laboratory."

"It's weird is what it is. Why doesn't he use the fancy labs at his work? I mean, he could cause a fire or something."

"I think Mr. Yates is quite capable and you have no need to worry. Now, would you mind getting back to the dusting?"

Izzy picked up another picture and swatted it with the rag. "I wonder if I should try to talk to her."

That made Julian stand and look at her as if she'd just stepped out of a clown car. "Have you lost your mind?"

"No. I think the lady could use a friend. She's holed up in this big house by herself half the time. She must get lonely."

Julian raised his eyebrows. "You're the *housekeeper*, for heaven's sake, not a member of the Junior League. Do yourself a big favor and say nothing, or Mr. Yates won't hesitate to find a replacement for you."

Izzy put her hands on her hips. "And you are just a bit too enamored with him, by the way."

"Excuse me?"

"Mr. Yates this and Mr. Yates that."

"He's my employer, you crazy woman."

"That's right. Your employer. Not your confidante, not your mentor. You're not his 'right-hand man.'" The dust cloth flapped again.

He stiffened at her words.

"Wait a minute," she said. "That's what you want, isn't it?" He could feel his face pale at her question. "You want to be his little go-to guy. You want to be the Igor to his Dr. Frankenstein, don't you?"

Julian turned and grabbed at another book, pulling it from the shelf and dusting it, although it was one he'd already cleaned.

Izzy studied him. "Do you know something?" Julian ignored her. "You do, don't you?" Julian continued to dust. "What?" she asked. "What do you know?" When he still didn't answer, she kept trying. "Is it about Mr. Yates? What he's up to?" She crossed her arms, thinking. "Is it about that man who came here that day? The one who tried to talk to Sarah?"

Julian slammed the book he was holding on the shelf and faced Izzy. "You need to get back to work, Isabelle."

Her face fell. "It is, isn't it? I knew it. That's the man she loves. He came for her, didn't he? I could tell there was something between them."

Julian debated whether to grab a book and throw it at her. "Something between them? She didn't even know who he was. She loves Mr. Yates."

"The hell she does." Izzy moved to a painted picture of sunflowers on the wall and smacked at it with her cloth. "A woman knows these things."

"I hope a woman knows when to keep her mouth shut if she wants to keep her job," answered Julian.

Izzy stopped her smacking. "Depends on the job."

Hearing the distant sound of a door closing, they looked down the hall, staying quiet, concerned that they might have been overheard. Seconds later, they watched as Sarah emerged in the hallway. She turned the corner, heading away from them and toward the front of the house, but not before they caught sight of her tear-stained face and noticed that she was wiping at her eyes.

Izzy looked at Julian, dropped her cloth, and headed into the front room. Julian followed.

**

Sarah walked through the house and entered the kitchen. Sniffing, she grabbed at a tissue and dabbed her eyes, then blew her nose, her emotional conversation with John Ramsey still playing in her mind. She sat at the kitchen table and dropped her head into her hands.

Sarah heard a noise and looked up at Izzy peering at her from around the corner. Julian was behind her.

"Miss Sarah?" Izzy asked. "Are you okay?"

Sarah sat up and composed herself, but not without sniffing again. "I'm okay, Izzy."

Izzy walked into the kitchen with Julian. "Can we get you something?" asked Julian. "Have you had any lunch?"

Sarah started to say no, wanting only to be left alone to think through her altercation with Ramsey, but she couldn't deny that her stomach was growling.

"We have some leftovers from last night," said Julian. "I can warm them for you."

"That would be great. Thank you, Julian." Sarah sighed and saw Izzy looking worriedly at her. "I'm fine, Izzy, really."

"You want to talk about it?" asked Izzy.

Sarah missed Julian's warning glare. "No," said Sarah, "thank you. It's just something I need to work through." She studied the table, thinking of Ramsey's stricken face when she'd left him. "I'll figure it out."

Julian placed a plate of leftovers he'd pulled from the refrigerator into the microwave and turned it on. "It will be ready in just a few minutes. Would you like some water?"

"Please," said Sarah.

"Isabelle," said Julian, pulling a glass from a cabinet. "I think Miss Sarah would like some space. Why don't you return to the library?"

Izzy frowned, but spoke to Sarah. "Miss Sarah, if you ever need to talk, I'm a good listener."

Julian cleared his throat as Sarah answered. "I appreciate that, Izzy. Thank you."

Izzy nodded and walked away.

Sarah sniffed again. Julian placed the glass of water in front of her, but she barely noticed. Snippets of her conversation with John Ramsey continued to replay themselves in her mind. She and Ramsey had fallen in love? Yates had made her forget? Ramsey had been the one in the hospital? She'd Binded with him? Made him her mate? None of it made any sense. The only things that did make sense were that Ramsey was crazy and that he'd fabricated the entire outlandish scenario. But who would go to all that trouble for her? Why would Yates want to force her to love him? Because they were the last two Red-Lines? And the mirror? What was all that about? She had read a mirror?

She dropped her head back into her palms as the microwave dinged. Julian removed the plate and set it in front of her along with a napkin and silverware. She looked up, smelling the pasta and hearing her stomach growl again.

"Thank you, Julian," she said.

"You're welcome, Miss Sarah." He turned to leave, but stopped. "Are you sure you're all right? Would you like me to call Mr. Yates?"

Sarah recoiled at the thought of that, but managed not to react outwardly. "No, Julian. I'm fine. Thank you."

"You'll be in for the rest of the day?"

Sarah remembered her appointment with Hannah and checked her watch. "No, Julian. I have to be somewhere at four o'clock."

"Are you sure you wouldn't rather stay in and rest?"

"No. I'll be fine. Really."

He waited for a moment before he nodded and left.

Sarah began to eat, wondering if she would be able to stomach the food, considering her emotional turmoil, but after a few bites, she found she was famished. She devoured everything on the plate and began to feel a little better. After wiping her mouth with her napkin and swallowing some water, she pushed her plate back, her mind racing again. No matter how hard she tried, she couldn't put the images of her in bed with Ramsey to rest. They wouldn't leave her. There had definitely been something between them. She knew that. But she also knew she had never been the type of person to have a fling with someone. And according to Yates, she'd already been romantically involved with him before she'd ever met Ramsey. So why would she have begun a relationship with someone else? Her head hurt from thinking about it.

She had a few hours before meeting with Hannah and Sarah considered calling her and meeting earlier. She needed someone to talk to, and she knew Hannah would help her through this. Maybe Hannah had some knowledge of her history with Ramsey that would shed some light on the situation. That was what she needed. A third party's opinion. Someone else who knew Ramsey. But could she trust Hannah? Yates had warned her that Hannah would try to coax her away from him and toward Ramsey, but intuitively, Sarah didn't believe that was true.

She brought her plate to the sink and leaned back against the counter, wringing her hands together, feeling the conflicting emotions. Now another clear image sprang into her mind. Another memory of her lying in a bed, but for a different reason altogether. She'd been sick. She'd been worried and confused, just as she was now, but she hadn't been alone. Someone had held her hand. A flare of pain in her head made her wince, but then it faded and she focused in on who had been with her. Warmth spread through her stomach, and a warm and loving energy moved through her. It spread from her hand, up into her arm and chest, and she got a clear glimpse of the man who had been with her—Ramsey.

Sucking in a deep breath, she wrapped her arms around her midsection as the encounter took shape in her mind. He'd comforted her, helped her, and protected her. She felt the first stirrings of emotion and moaned almost audibly as she realized for the first time that she'd had feelings for him. She'd cared for him. Something stirred in her gut, and her heart thumped, but she shoved it away, unable to comprehend this new influx of sensation. What was happening to her? Could she have loved two men at one time?

Pushing back from the counter, she left the kitchen, intent on going to her room. She needed to get her mind off John Ramsey. The more she thought of him, the more confused she became. Moving to the stairs, she caught sight of the door to Yates's office.

An image of her mother came to mind. She hesitated, but then realized that her mother was urging her, prompting her to follow her instincts. She stepped back off the stairs and walked to the door to Yates's lab. Placing her hand on the knob, her mind yelled at her to leave it alone and go to her room, but her heart prompted her forward. She opened the door and flipped on the lights. Considering her options, she waited for several seconds before making up her mind. She took a few steps, closed the door behind her, and headed down the stairs.

Reaching the bottom, she approached the locked door. She trailed her hand over the lock, feeling the cold hardware against her skin. Focusing, she centered her energy and moved it through her body, letting it expand. It made her skin tingle as it passed from her and into the bolt, and in her mind's eye she saw the lock mechanism sliding open. The metal vibrated in her hand, an audible click sounded, and she turned the knob.

She hit the switch, the lights flickered on, and she took in the room. It looked the same as it had when Yates had brought her down here. The room was clean, with the only color being the ocean green of the walls. She saw the large stainless-steel cabinet and the wide island with the sink and cabinets and various lab equipment sitting atop it. The door to the small bedroom was closed. The large desk with the computer still sat adjacent to the wall, but now without the folders which had cluttered it before. She eyed the computer, then walked up to the desk and stopped, brushing her hands over the back of the desk chair. The large monitors that spanned the tabletop seemed to stare back at her in warning. After a few moments of internal debate and her mind encouraging her to leave, she determined that she would do exactly the opposite. She pulled out the chair and sat. The hidden keyboard beckoned her, and she took it from its hidden space and placed it on the desk. The keys felt familiar beneath her fingers. When she depressed one, the computer began to whir and the monitor came to life, displaying exactly what Sarah had anticipated: a password request.

She knew Yates would never be lazy enough to use a birthdate or a pet's name for a password. She deliberately exhaled, calming herself. Closing her eyes, she cleared her mind, forcing all thoughts of Ramsey, Yates and her situation out of her head.

Yates had worked with her on increasing her sensitivity, but with her pregnancy, she'd found that her abilities had heightened even further, making this exercise possible. Taking several deep breaths, she began to feel the calm of her empty mind. She sat still for several minutes, and when she felt ready, she opened her eyes. Her hands rested over the keys as she anticipated the signal she knew would come. Letting go of all outside distractions, she focused, reading the keys as if she would read a person who stood beside her. As her mind relaxed, she moved her fingers over the keyboard.

The sensations gained strength, and she opened a shallow drawer, found a pen and pad, and began to write down each key that spoke to her, not with words, but with the energy of the molecules that bound them together. When she felt complete, she put down the pen and looked at the letters, numbers, and symbols she'd noted. She held the paper, feeling for the order, and as the sensations moved through her, she began to type, one keystroke at a time. When she finished, she looked up and saw the password display populated with the black round circles indicating the keys she'd typed. She put down the paper and dropped her hands back into her lap. Her mind, once cluttered with indecision, now felt clear. But despite that clarity, she knew that if she continued, there would be no turning back, potentially imperiling her future with Yates.

She stared at the screen, letting her mind play out all the various scenarios. Deciding it was now or never, she raised her hand, hit the enter key, and sucked in a breath when the computer let her in.

CHAPTER TWENTY-FOUR

··

"**Y**OU NEED TO relax," said Hannah. "Everything is going to be fine." She and Declan had arrived at his place, and he'd changed clothes and made them sandwiches. They sat at the kitchen table.

Declan bounced his knee and stared at the clock, waiting for the time when they would depart to meet Sarah. "I'll relax when this meeting is over."

"Well, you're making me nervous."

"Sorry. That's not my intention." He reached over and grabbed her hand. "How are you?"

She squeezed his fingers. "I'm fine. You heard anything else from Leroy?

"Just that he and John would meet us there. I should call him." He picked up his phone and dialed a number, then hit a button and set the phone down in speaker mode.

Hannah listened as the phone rang and Leroy picked up. "Hello?"

"Leroy?" said Declan. "It's Declan and Hannah."

"Hey."

"Everything still a go for four o'clock?"

"Yes. We'll meet you there."

"How's John?"

"He's a nervous wreck."

"Can't say that I blame him."

"Nor I, but he's hanging in there. He left a little while ago. Said he needed to get out of here for a while."

"He left?"

"Yes. He's over at his place. Said he'd be back in time to head over for the meet-up."

"Okay." Declan paused. "Have we thought about what happens if she doesn't remember?"

They heard an audible sigh across the phone. "Honestly, Declan. I don't know what happens. I guess it all depends on how much of her memory returns and her reaction. We'll just have to play it by ear."

"I guess so."

"Hannah there?"

Hannah leaned in. "I'm here, Leroy."

"How do you want to handle this?"

"Handle it?"

"Yes. You want us all there?"

"Not at first, no. I think that would be a bit much for her."

"Where do you want us to be then?" asked Declan.

"I think I should go in and see her first. Which is what she's expecting. Let me talk to her. Gauge her emotional and mental state. When I think it's time for you to join us, I'll text or call you."

Declan spoke into the phone. "Did you get that, Leroy?"

"Yeah, I got it. We'll meet up with you, Declan, in the garage outside the office, and then we'll wait for Hannah's signal."

"That'll work."

"Okay, we'll see you then."

Hannah's phone buzzed. "It's a text from Sarah," she said, picking up the phone.

"Hold up, Leroy," said Declan. "Hannah's getting a message from Sarah."

"What is it?" asked Leroy.

"She's asking to meet at three o'clock instead." Hannah said. "Can you do that, Leroy?"

"Meet at three o'clock?" Leroy asked.

"Yes."

"I'll have to get in touch with Sherlock, but it shouldn't be a problem."

"Three o'clock?" asked Declan. "Did she say why?"

"No, she didn't. I'm telling her that's fine. The office closes at two, so we'll still have the place to ourselves."

Declan stared at the phone. "Then I'll guess we'll meet you..." Declan looked at his watch. "...in about an hour and a half. Sound good?"

"Okay." They heard Leroy take a breath. "To be honest, I'm glad. This waiting is torture."

"We hear you," said Declan. "I'll be happy when this is over."

"Even if she remembers," said Hannah, "it still doesn't mean it's over."

"No, but your part is vastly reduced, which will make me feel a lot better," said Declan.

"I'm gonna call Sherlock," said Leroy. "Tell him to get his butt back here. I'll see you two soon."

"All right, Leroy," said Declan. "See you outside the office."

"Yup. See you."

Declan disconnected the call and sat back. "An hour and a half."

"Ninety minutes," she said, still holding his hand. "And then you can stop worrying."

**

Leroy hung up the phone with Declan and searched for the number to contact Sherlock when there was a knock at the door.

Phone to his ear, he walked up and answered it, thinking perhaps it could be Sherlock returning.

He froze in place when he saw Yates standing on his doorstep. Sherlock answered just before the line went dead. Leroy's blood ran cold as he stared at the man who'd wreaked havoc on all their lives in just a few short months.

"Why, Mr. Leroy," said Yates, who stood impeccably dressed, as if on his way to a photo shoot. "You mind if I come in?"

Leroy was tongue-tied.

"I'll take that as a 'yes,'" said Yates, walking into the front foyer.

Leroy shook himself out of his daze and lowered the phone from his ear. "What the hell are you doing here?"

Yates took a moment to look around the living room, kitchen, and den. "Nice place you have here. It's...cozy."

"Get out."

Yates glanced back toward the entry and the door handle was yanked from Leroy and the door closed with a slam.

"Not just yet," said Yates. "You and I have business."

Leroy glared. "You and I have nothing to discuss. You can't just walk in here and expect me to be at your beck and call."

"Oh, but I can. And I do."

Leroy slipped the phone into his pocket, knowing it was useless to him. His mind whirled. He didn't need Sherlock walking in and seeing Yates. "Then tell me what you want and get out."

"My. Your manners are deplorable."

"What the hell would you know about manners?"

Yates moved into the den. "You get more flies with honey. Is that the saying?"

"Flies being the operative word."

Yates smiled. "Yes, I suppose I'm a bit of a nuisance."

Leroy lowered his voice. "You're a bottom-feeder. A person who survives off the misery of others."

"Careful, Sampson," said Yates, turning back. "You may hurt my feelings."

"I'd hurt a lot worse if I thought it would accomplish anything."

Yates trailed his fingers over the leaves of Leroy's plants.

"I'll ask you again. What do you want?"

Yates looked up from his study of a leaf. "You have a green thumb, I see."

"You didn't come here to chat about my hobbies."

"No, I didn't." Yates noticed the empty office adjacent to the den. "I take it Ramsey is not here?"

Leroy took offense at the question. "Leave him alone. You've put him through enough, don't you think?"

Yates shook his head. "Oh, not near enough."

"What is it with you?" asked Leroy. "With your obsession? Why not just leave him and Sarah alone? They never did anything to you."

Yates sneered. "He exists. That's enough to annoy me. And he thinks Sarah belongs with him. He will soon learn otherwise."

"Sarah doesn't deserve this either."

"Sarah is fine. She's happy and well taken care of. She wants for nothing."

"Except for the man she loves."

Yates stared hard at Leroy. "She's with the man she loves."

"No, she's not."

Yates seemed to shrug off the comment and resumed his stroll through the room. "You can't win this."

"Win what?" asked Leroy.

"This game you're all playing."

"What game?"

"Don't be so obtuse. You know what I'm referring to. This plan of yours to save Sarah." Yates waved a hand in the air. "It's pathetic, really."

"The only thing pathetic is you," said Leroy. "Trying to make a woman love you by poisoning her mind against the man who truly loves her. Don't you find it sad that you have to make a woman want you by tricking her into believing that she does? How in the hell is that good enough for you? How do you sleep at night?"

"I put my head on a pillow and roll over." Yates set his jaw, and Leroy knew he'd angered him. "Plus," he continued, "it doesn't hurt that I curl up next to my lovely wife."

Leroy's anger bubbled up. "Don't get used to it. That won't last much longer."

"On the contrary, it will." Yates walked up closer to Leroy, and Leroy took a step back. Yates noticed the movement and stopped. "Don't worry," he said, holding his hands out. "Nothing in my hands."

"Pardon me if I think you're full of shit," said Leroy.

A grin broke out on Yates's face. "I can see why you two are friends."

Leroy held his breath, wondering how to get this man out of his house. "Are we about done here?"

Yates appeared smug. "We're just getting started."

"Then get to the point. I've got places to be."

Yates tilted his head. "Oh, that's right. You're supposed to meet up with my wife. Is that right?"

Leroy widened his eyes at Yates's revelation.

"Yes. I know all about that," said Yates. "You don't mind if I crash the party, do you?"

"What are you planning?"

"Planning? I'd thought you'd never ask." Yate's face turned stony. "You better warn Ramsey to stay out of my business. He tries to take Sarah from me, and that knife in the belly will feel like a flesh wound compared to what will happen to him. That goes for

Declan and Hannah, too." He watched as Leroy glared at him. "You still have time to back out."

"Back out?"

"Yes. Don't show up at the meeting with Sarah. Leave her to me."

"No."

"Either way, you lose. I'll keep her by my side regardless, but if you choose to interfere..."

Leroy maintained his composure. "Is this where you threaten me?"

Complacent, Yates wandered over to the mantel. "You?" he asked. He perused the pictures displayed there. "No, not you. But if you come after my wife..." He paused as he picked up a picture of Leroy and Olivia. "...then I reserve the right to come after yours."

The blood drained from Leroy's face. "You son of a bitch." He clenched his hands into fists. "You touch a hair on Olivia, and I swear to God I'll yank out your insides, wrap them around your throat, and hang you with them."

Yates put down the picture. "My, how colorful," he said. "I'm sure Ramsey has had the same thoughts, and yet I find myself to be in perfect health."

"You leave him alone, Yates. Leave all of us alone. Or you're going to find out what retribution feels like."

"Retribution?" asked Yates. "Really?"

"You can't survive all of us. When Sarah remembers..."

Yates turned from the mantel. "Perhaps I haven't made myself clear." He took a step toward Leroy, and his eyes narrowed with ire. "Sarah will never remember. I will make sure of that. And you and your pitiful group will all pay the consequences of your interference. I didn't come here to warn you. I came here to promise you. You take action against me, and you all will reap what you sow. So think long and hard before you show up this afternoon. Because I do not take prisoners, Sampson. I'll crush Declan, destroy Hannah, cut Ramsey off at the knees, and then I'll come here." He moved a few steps closer. "And I'll take everything you love." His blue eyes turned dark as his body exhibited the extent of his malice. "Just as you try to take it from me."

The rage in Yates's words made Leroy's own ignite. Before he could stop himself, he took a step toward Yates, intent on wrapping his hands around his neck. But as he lunged and raised his arms, Yates lifted one of his, and before Leroy could reach him, he felt a sharp pain in his head, his ears popped, his legs gave out, and he fell to the floor.

**

Ramsey dropped the phone onto the tabletop. He was sitting outside on his back porch, recovering from his encounter with Sarah, when Leroy had called. He'd answered reluctantly, because he dreaded the conversation that would follow. He didn't want to have to explain that he'd failed in stirring Sarah's memories and that he may have, in fact, pushed her even further away. He'd sat in stunned silence for several minutes after she'd left, and then he'd moved outside, needing some fresh air to help clear his head. The ringing phone had interrupted his miserable thoughts. When the phone had disconnected, he didn't bother calling back. He anticipated Leroy's return call, but was in no hurry for it.

Sarah's presence in his home and the conversation they'd had still played in his mind. He imagined other possible reactions or responses he could have made and berated himself for not making them. He should have never told her about the baby. But her defense of Yates had forced him to push back, and he'd gone too far. Now he sat in silent regret and mental chaos as he considered what to do next. Had he lost his chance with her? Would she still show up to see Hannah? Even if time ran out for the mirror, it didn't mean Sarah was lost to him. If at some point she remembered, they could still make a life together. Although the time left to them would likely be spent in hiding if Yates couldn't be handled. And what kind of life would that be, to spend his remaining months with her on the run?

The questions plagued him, and he had no answers. He resigned himself to the fact that he didn't know what would happen next. The only thing he knew for sure was that he would fight for her until his last breath. It was the only thing he had left.

He rubbed a hand over his face and starred out over his barren yard. He would go with Leroy to meet with Sarah, and if she showed, then he would try again to get through to her. And if she didn't show... He shut his eyes. Would it be worth the risk to return to Yates's house and force her to leave, knowing Yates would fight to keep her? Leroy, Declan, and Hannah would want to help, but he could not ask them to endanger themselves any more than they already had. Opening his eyes, he spied his phone on the table. He decided then that he would not mention to Leroy his conversation with Sarah. If Sarah showed that afternoon, then it wouldn't matter anyway. He checked the time. He still had at least an hour before he needed to return to Leroy's. His mind preoccupied with thoughts of Sarah, Leroy's phone call faded from his mind.

CHAPTER TWENTY-FIVE

··

ARAH SLIPPED OUT of Yates's office, closing the door behind her and relocking it. Standing outside the door, she tried to process what she'd learned. After flipping through several files on his computer, she'd found most of them to contain formulas and equations that made little sense to her, but she had also found descriptions of those formulas included with some of the files, detailing exactly the intended symptoms and effects his discoveries would create, and it disgusted her. Everything from headaches and stomach pain to heart attacks and aneurisms could be induced based on the information she'd found. Why would Yates need or want that? It made no sense. But aside from that, she'd learned that Yates's company was disturbingly irresponsible. That upset her the most. Everything from tax evasion, utilizing child labor in foreign countries, and even blackmailing his own staff seemed within Yates's purview. She moved to the stairwell and sat on the first step. Who was this man she'd married? How could someone she loved be so ruthless?

She sat for several minutes, wondering how to handle this new information. Should she confront him? Should she leave him? Her mind traveled back to John Ramsey and what he'd said to her. Did she carry his child? And what if she did? Her mind fuzzy and her eyes fatigued, she dropped her head into her hands. She didn't know what to do. Thinking of the time, her head shot up. She was supposed to meet with Hannah, and she had to leave soon. She stood and made her way back up the stairs.

She'd talk to Hannah. Then she'd decide what to do.

**

Declan parked the car in the quiet parking garage. Hannah sat silently in the passenger seat. "You ready?" he asked.

She nodded. "As ready as I'll ever be."

He reached over and took her hand. "You be careful. If something feels off, you get out of there."

She rubbed her thumb over his wrist. "I'll be fine. I've done this before, you know."

His gaze held hers. "Things are escalating. I can feel it. We need to be alert. I still feel uncomfortable about this."

"I know, but you're right outside the office. And Ramsey and Leroy will be here soon. Nothing is going to happen."

"Well, let's hope Sarah remembers. It's going to be hell on John if she doesn't."

"She's already started to recall things. It will happen eventually, if not today."

"Our window of opportunity is closing, so if you can coax it out of her now, that would be ideal."

"I know." Hannah stared out the window at the office building. "I should go."

"Don't you want to wait for Leroy and John?"

"It's three o'clock now. She could be inside as we speak. I don't want to keep her waiting."

Declan sighed. He eyed the silent garage. All of the early departures had left, and workers leaving at the usual five o'clock hour were still inside. "Okay," he said. "I'm right out here if you need me."

She clenched his hand. "I know you are."

"You contact me as soon as you're ready. I'll be waiting with John and Leroy."

"I will." He continued to hold her hand as she reached for the door and she looked back. "Hey."

His wary gaze met hers. "Hey, what?"

"Stop worrying."

"I'll stop worrying when you're out of there."

She leaned in and kissed him. They held the kiss until she pulled back. "I'll be back in this seat in no time."

"I'd rather have you back in my bed." He cocked an eyebrow at her. "We could go there now. Forget this whole meeting thing. I'm sure Sarah wouldn't mind."

She laughed, pulled her hand away from his, and placed it on his cheek. "Tonight." She rubbed her thumb over his skin. "I promise I'll take all your troubles away."

His moved his hand to her knee, and he squeezed it. "That's a date." He shifted closer, smelling her scent. "I look forward to finding that special spot again, the one that made you—"

She sucked in a breath, blushed, and put her hand over his mouth. "You're a bad boy, Declan." Dropping her hand, she reached again for the door handle.

"You have no idea," he said, and she got out and closed the door. She leaned over and waved at him through the window before she walked away.

He watched her approach the double glass doors, open them, and disappear inside. He couldn't see the door to Soap Opera guy's office, but he could see the hallway that led to it, and he kept his eyes on it. Glancing at the time, he expected John and Leroy to arrive at any moment.

The next few minutes felt like hours. Nobody moved in or out. It bothered him that Leroy and his brother had still not showed, and he was reaching for his phone to call them when something cold moved through him. His insides constricted when he recognized the sensation and his alarm bells went off. He'd cracked his window earlier, and he listened now, attuned to the energy around him. Staying alert, he reached for the door handle and popped the door open, viewing his surroundings. He stepped out, watching and waiting, seeing nothing but parked cars, but feeling something vastly different. It didn't take long before he heard the sound of footsteps.

Yates stepped out from between a parked van and a cement support post. Walking to within six feet of Declan, he stopped, and the two men eyed each other.

"I thought I smelled something funny," said Declan, his heart thumping.

"Took you long enough," said Yates. "I thought you were considered advanced." He flicked at something on his suit. "I'd use the term lightly."

Declan gathered his energy and concentrated it, building up whatever wall of protection he could. He thought of Hannah inside the building. "Where's Sarah?" he asked.

Yates smirked at him. "Back at the house, I suppose. She's not due here till four."

Declan tightened his jaw when he realized what Yates had done. "You sent the text message."

Yates's expression did not change. "Indeed. I can't very well have my wife meet up with you two. She needs to know who her true benefactor is." He read his watch. "She'll be here in an hour, only to find no Hannah. She'll be disappointed, but I'll explain to her that Hannah never had her best interests in mind."

Declan stayed calm, although adrenaline coursed through him. "Don't be stupid, Yates. Sarah's not dumb. She can sense you better than anyone. She'll know you're lying. Probably already does."

Yates shrugged his shoulders. "Maybe. Maybe not. Either way, it won't matter."

"And why is that?"

"Because by the end of this day, I'll be back in her good graces, you and Hannah will be out of my hair, and Ramsey will know he's lost the war." Yates took a deep breath and smiled. "It's a good day."

"You plan on all of that?"

"I do. In fact, I just came from Leroy's. He sends his apologies, but he'll have to miss this little meet and greet."

Declan's stomach fell. "What?"

"Yes. I warned him, of course, but he's a terrible listener and he does have a temper."

"Where is he? Where's John? What did you do?"

Yates's slid his hands into his pockets and shook his head. "You really should be more worried about what I'm going to do to you."

"Me?" Declan pulled at whatever energy he could use to prepare himself. "You got something against me?"

Yates leaned sideways against the car next to him and chuckled. "Yes, actually I do. It's been simmering for a while now. But I'm good at simmering. I like the anticipation."

"You've lost me," said Declan. "Oh, wait a minute. This isn't about Edward, is it?" He knew this approach would anger Yates, but he hoped that any distraction might buy enough time to make Hannah suspicious. He prayed that if she came out and saw Yates that she'd run like hell. On second thought, she'd more likely stay and help him. He cursed himself that he'd not listened to his instincts and kept her from coming here.

Yates's eyes were like a cat's observing its prey. "You know what happens when you play with fire, Declan?" He paused. "You get burned."

Declan didn't back down. "Funny. I don't feel hot." Despite his fears, he kept a calm facade. But a kernel of warmth flared in his midsection. The kernel's intensity grew and he began to feel uncomfortable.

"Feeling it now?" asked Yates. He cocked his head as Declan grabbed at his belly and sweat popped out on his brow. "How about now?"

The warmth turned into a bed of hot coals, forcing Declan to double over. He had to suck in a breath and grab onto the side of his car to keep from falling over in agony. Holding back a moan, Declan gritted his teeth as the coals became a white-hot poker in his stomach.

Yates began to walk closer. "Hmm," he said, nearing Declan. "Not so cocky now, are you?"

Declan tried to muster whatever strength he had left to control the pain, but he realized how ineffectual it was against Yates's abilities. How had they ever expected to get rid of this man? He gripped his stomach harder as he fought to stay on his feet and forced the air in and out of his lungs, although it hurt to breathe. Managing to turn his head at Yates's approach, he said, "So you got my attention. Big deal." He grimaced again when another lance of heat moved through him, dropping him to his knees.

"Oh, I want much more than your attention," said Yates, leaning over Declan. "In fact, I've already taken one thing from you." He straightened. "And..." he said as he glanced at the glass doors to the office building. "...in a moment, I plan to take another."

Declan understood what Yates intended. He had to keep him talking, and he prayed Hannah would notice what was going on and get away. "Leave her alone, Yates." His voice shook from the pain.

"If you'd left Sarah alone, I would have. But you insist on taking her away from me, so therefore, I insist on taking Hannah away from you. An eye for an eye." He paused before adding, "Just like I did with your dad."

Declan heard the words but didn't understand. He forced himself up despite the pain. "My what?"

"Your father," said Yates. "You took mine." His eyes glittered like snow in the sun. "So I took yours."

The world tilted, and Declan shut his eyes at the blind rage that overtook him. Momentarily forgetting his pain, he reached out for Yates and tried to grab his pant leg, wanting to slam his fist into Yates's midsection, but Yates sidestepped him and he found himself grasping at the air and falling hard onto the cement ground. Another lance of pain seared through him and he struggled to lift himself but couldn't do it. "You bastard." Sweat trickled down his face. "You killed my father?"

Yates moved around to Declan's side. "With the same toxin I used to poison Ramsey. Only your poor dad was older and weaker. Didn't take him long to succumb."

The anguish ripped at Declan's heart. "No."

Yates squatted next to him. "Oh yes."

Declan wrapped his arms around his middle as another round of heat assailed him and he struggled to breathe. "I'll kill you," he whispered.

Yates nodded. "Yes. I'm sure you want to, but you'll understand if I'm not too worried." He looked around the quiet garage. "You know, I considered killing you right here and having Ramsey find you like this." His eyes shifted, as if imagining it. "I mean, I'm not done with him either. He took my brother, so it's only fair I take his. Don't you think?"

Declan could not suppress a moan. He blinked up at Yates and tried to stay conscious.

"But the thought of you lying here while I go to see Hannah, well, that just gives me a thrill."

Declan reached out again, but Yates stepped away.

"Don't," said Declan.

"Besides," said Yates, "I can always kill you later. Perhaps right in front of Ramsey. Now that would be entertaining."

Spots began to form in front of Declan's eyes, and he strained every muscle to try and stop Yates, but his strength had evaporated and he fought to suck in air. He watched with unfocused eyes as Yates straightened his tie and peered down at him.

"I hope your last words to her were good ones," he said, and walking up, Yates stepped over him, and Declan felt his last reserves vanish as he succumbed to unconsciousness.

**

Hannah paced the waiting room. She kept looking at the clock, expecting Sarah to arrive at any time. The office sat empty, and the familiar astringent smells and sterile environment did nothing to calm her. She moved back into the exam room for the second time, checking and rechecking supplies she knew were there. The clock in the room said ten after three. She knew if Declan didn't hear from her soon, he'd be out of his car and in the office in a heartbeat, so she reached for her phone, hoping to contact Sarah. As she typed, she heard the door open and close in the waiting area and she breathed a sigh of relief. Putting the phone back in her pocket, she walked out to greet her friend.

"Sarah?" She turned the corner and stopped cold. It was not Sarah.

"Sorry, Hannah," said Yates. "Sarah is delayed. Looks like you'll be talking with me. You don't mind, do you?" The door closed behind him, and Hannah's heart slammed in her chest. Her mind went to Declan.

"Unfortunately," said Yates, reading her, "he will not be able to save you. He'll be lucky if he can save himself."

She swallowed and took a step backward, heading back into the hall.

"You really should have minded your own business, Hannah," he said, advancing as she moved backward into the exam room. "I hate it when I'm forced to make a point."

Hannah continued to retreat, but she knew she had nowhere to go. "Where's Declan?"

"He's lying in the garage. Guess you thought he might rescue you instead of taking a nap. Looks like you chose poorly again."

"Don't hurt him."

"It's too late for that. It's too late for all of you. You should have stayed out of it."

She looked around for anything to help her, but saw nothing. "But Sarah doesn't love you. I couldn't stand back and do nothing."

"Yes, you could have. You just stay away. Simple, really."

"It's not simple at all. You don't deserve her."

"That's not a decision for you to make."

"It's not yours, either." Her back hit the wall of the exam room.

He stood in front of her. "Tell me," he said, eyeing the room. "What did you and my wife talk about?"

Hannah tried to focus. "What?"

"Don't play stupid, Hannah. You're far from it. What did you two talk about?"

"I...uh..." She struggled to find the words.

He crossed his arms in front of him.

"We talked about...um...her headaches."

"Her headaches?"

"Yes."

"What about them?"

His questions flustered her. She couldn't think what to say.

"Come on, Hannah," he said. "We don't have all day."

"She...she didn't like the pill she was taking."

"Oh, yes. The pill. The yellow one?"

"Yes."

"And what did you advise her?"

"I..."

"Tell me," he yelled, his face furrowed.

She jumped. "I told her to stop taking it."

His eyes turned to dark blue specks. "Did you now?"

She nodded. "Yes."

"Why would you do that?"

She realized how angry he was, and she began to wonder if she'd leave this room alive. Her head spun with regret. She didn't want to die. There was too much she'd left undone and unsaid. "Because I knew why you wanted her to take it."

"And why is that?"

"To keep her memories at bay."

He seemed pleased. "Much better, Hannah. You'll find I'm much less impatient if you simply answer my questions."

Hannah's own anger began to grow at the thought of her possible demise. If she had to die, she wouldn't go down cowering at this man's feet.

"And she stopped taking it, didn't she?" he asked.

Hannah straightened. "Yes. And she wanted me to have it analyzed."

"There you go," he said. "Now you're starting to show a little fire."

She set her jaw and glared at him. "She told me she was pregnant."

"She did?"

"Yes."

"Do tell. What was her reaction to the news?"

"Less than ideal."

His eyes narrowed. "Really?"

"She didn't expect it."

"I'm sure she didn't."

She warned herself to shut up, but her mouth ignored her. "'Course, the dream didn't help."

"The dream?" His brow rose.

"About Ramsey. The one where she remembered sleeping with him."

His face stilled, and his eyes turned to slivers resembling black coal.

"You didn't know?" she asked. He stood in silence in front of her. "Guess you're not as all-seeing and all-knowing as you think you are."

She waited for the reprisal, certain it would be ugly, but his shoulders came down, his face relaxed, and that same smug look returned. "You enjoyed that, didn't you?"

"Oh, yes," she said. "Very much."

His mouth quirked up. "She remembered him?"

Hannah realized that he meant to continue on with the conversation, and she tried to keep up. "Bits and pieces, yes."

"Small bits and pieces, I'm sure."

"Bigger than yours, I suspect."

He paused. "You're a brave lady, Hannah."

"Or a stupid one."

"That, too." He paused. "But she didn't remember everything?"

She debated not answering any more of his questions, but she didn't know what good it would do. "No, not everything."

"And me?"

"You?"

"Yes. Her feelings for me were still intact?"

"Sadly, yes."

He quirked another grin at her. "Oh, Hannah. I'm going to miss these interactions. I find you quite amusing."

"The feeling is not mutual."

"I'm sorry to hear that."

She pressed back against the wall. "No, you're not."

"You're right. I'm not. I do need your help, though."

A new twist of fear curdled her belly. "My help?"

"Why, yes." He reached into his jacket and took out a vial of fluid.

She held her breath. "What's that?"

"It's more serum for Sarah."

"What?" she asked, staring at the liquid.

"Because of your interference, I find I have to administer something new. Something that will keep her memories from returning."

"No." She shook her head. "You can't do that."

He jostled the vial. "Yes. Actually, I can."

"But the baby..."

He rolled his eyes. "The baby will be fine."

"But what about her? Please, let her be. She deserves to know the truth."

"Whose truth?" he asked. "Yours or mine? Who's to say which one is better?"

"She is. Let her decide."

"Why? So she can end up with that fool, Ramsey? No, that can't happen." The liquid danced within the vial. "But I have to be sure."

"About what?" asked Hannah.

"About the serum." He looked Hannah up and down. "I don't want to give her too much or too little. It has to be just right."

Hannah felt ice water move through her veins. "What are you going to do?"

"Well," he said, reaching into his pocket and pulling out a small syringe-like device with something that looked like a trigger on it.

He popped the vial into it and held it like a gun. "I need to test it first."

True fear bubbled up when she comprehended what he meant and she began to tremble.

"You're about her size and weight." His eyes glimmered at her.

"No," she said.

"Just relax, Hannah. You won't feel a thing."

She whimpered. "Please don't."

He stepped up and raised his arm. A scream welled up in her throat, but no sound emerged.

"Memories are overrated anyway." He pressed the device against her skin and pulled the trigger.

CHAPTER TWENTY-SIX

....

SARAH DROVE UP to the front of the building, parked her car, and got out. Checking the time as she walked up the front steps, she saw she was five minutes late. She entered and headed to Dr. Maxwell's office, near the back of the building. Turning down the far hallway, she found the door to his office on her right, located near the parking garage, and reached to open the door. Her progress stopped when the door did not open. It was locked. She looked at the time again. It was just after four o'clock. She knocked, but there was no answer. Holding her ear against the door, she listened but heard nothing.

Her nerves on edge, she stood outside the office and waited, assuming that Hannah would arrive soon. Her phone showed no new messages. Thinking that Hannah might be in the lobby, she walked down the hall and peered toward the front entrance of the building. But it was quiet. The elevator opened, and she watched as workers, holding their briefcases and purses, left for the weekend.

She returned back down the hall, but stopped at the doors to the parking garage. She pushed the doors open and took a few steps into the enclosed area. It was quiet, with cars parked in random spots. A couple emerged from the doors behind her, and she stepped aside as they headed toward their vehicle.

She couldn't place what had her on edge. It was something in the air, like having the sensation of someone standing behind you, but when you looked, no one was there. Sarah stepped further out into the garage, as if the signal originated from somewhere among the parked cars, but she couldn't place it.

Feeling on edge, she returned to the building and went to wait outside the doors to Dr. Maxwell's office. After a few more minutes passed with no word from Hannah, she began to worry. Accessing her phone, she sent a text to Hannah and waited for a response. None came. As she stood at the door, the sensation that had prickled her skin came again, and she studied the door. Looking both ways down the hallway, she took a hold of the knob and held it, feeling the energy within her build, and within seconds, she heard and felt the lock click open. She opened the door and poked her head in.

"Hannah?"

The office was dark and empty. Sarah stepped inside and listened. It felt the same to her as it had the first time she'd been there, only this time, she sensed something else. Centering in on the feeling, she tried to figure out why it was familiar to her. She walked back to the exam rooms, following the sensation, and entered the first room, where she and Hannah had originally met. Her skin broke out in chills when a wave of fear washed over her.

Hannah. She'd been in here, and she'd been afraid.

The impulse to leave was almost overwhelming, but Sarah ignored it, knowing she was only feeling what Hannah had felt. Shaking off her nervous energy but fearing for her friend, she tried to focus. She took a breath, relaxed, and tuned in. What had scared Hannah? Her mind reaching out, Sarah closed her eyes, connecting with the energy in the room. It felt constricted, as if she were cornered, with nowhere to go. The fear escalated when the presence of a man drew near. A scream in her throat threatened to erupt, and Sarah opened her eyes. She reached for the wall and took several breaths to steady herself. Someone had wanted to hurt

Hannah, but who? The feeling in the room struck Sarah again, and she zeroed in on it, intent on determining who had been here. A gasp escaped when the familiar energy struck her and she recognized its source. *Yates.*

She clutched at the wall, confusion and anger sweeping through her. What was he up to? How had he known? Thinking of the possibilities, she pulled her phone from her pocket and studied it. Could he have? It was the only way he would have known. She realized her stupidity. If she could access his computer, then he could easily access her phone. Cursing herself and him, she left the room and exited the office, closing and locking the door behind her. Marching through the lobby and back out to the car, she considered her options. Contact him now and confront him, or wait? Calling him now would serve no point. He'd likely not answer or he'd lie to her, and reading him over the phone would be difficult. No, her best shot at getting the truth was to wait until she could talk to him face to face.

She decided she'd deal with him that night. And there'd be hell to pay if he'd hurt Hannah.

**

"Leroy? Leroy?" Ramsey shook his friend's shoulder as Leroy lay prostrate on the ground. "Can you hear me?"

He'd returned twenty minutes ago expecting to see Leroy waiting for him, but instead he'd found him unconscious on the floor. He'd been trying to rouse his friend ever since, but had only managed to garner a few groans and faint eye movements as Leroy moved in and out of consciousness.

Holding a cool cloth against his friend's head, Ramsey debated whether or not to call an ambulance. Leroy's breathing and heart rate appeared normal, and he had no outward signs of injury, but

Ramsey knew that any number of internal issues could be just as harmful. The clock on the kitchen wall told him it was a little after four. He'd tried again to reach Declan or Hannah, but neither of them picked up, which worried him almost as much as Leroy's condition did.

Leroy moaned again, and his eyes slowly opened.

"Hey, Leroy. Can you hear me?" He patted his friend's face. "Don't pass out on me again. You there?"

Leroy rewarded him by keeping his eyes open and focusing, which was more than he'd done since Ramsey had arrived. "That's it," said Ramsey. "Look at me."

Leroy blinked and grunted, but his eyes stayed alert. Ramsey observed his condition to ensure that Leroy didn't deteriorate, but he seemed to be coming around.

"Sherlock?" Leroy managed to say.

"Yeah, it's me. You okay?"

"My head." Leroy winced and shut his eyes.

"Easy. Take it easy." Ramsey pressed his fingers around Leroy's skull, but he could find no bumps or bruises. "I'll get you an ice pack." He began to get up, but Leroy grabbed his arm in a surprising show of strength.

"Wait," said Leroy. "Where's..." He looked around the room as if looking for someone.

"Where's who?" Ramsey had picked up on the odd sensation in the house but Leroy's condition had prevented him from investigating. "Who did this?"

Leroy found his gaze and managed to hold it. "Yates."

The unpleasant feeling made sense then. "What?" he asked. "Yates was here?"

"Yes, he was." Leroy struggled to sit up.

"Careful," Ramsey said, watching Leroy grimace and hold his head. "Go slow. We don't know what he did to you."

Leroy pushed himself up despite his obvious pain. "Where's my phone?"

"Your phone?"

"Yes. My phone, damn it. Where is it?"

Ramsey looked around, surprised by Leroy's insistence. "I don't know." He patted at Leroy's pockets. "Here it is." He pulled it from Leroy's jacket, handed it to him, and Leroy dialed a number. "What's wrong?"

Leroy didn't respond as he waited for the call to connect. "Olivia?" he said, breathing a sigh of relief. "You all right, honey?"

Leroy talked to his wife for a few minutes and then hung up, hanging his head as he did so.

"Leroy, what the hell happened?"

Leroy grunted and tried to stand. Ramsey helped him to his feet, but then sat him on the couch when Leroy swayed and almost fell back on the floor.

"I'll get you some water," said Ramsey, but Leroy stopped him again.

"No. I don't need any water. Where's Declan?"

"That's a good question. We should be meeting him right now, but I can't reach him."

Leroy's eyes darkened.

"What the hell happened, Leroy?"

Leroy fought to catch his breath. "Yates. He was here. He knew about the meeting with Sarah. He threatened all of us. Told us to stay away or else. He said he'd come after Olivia."

"What?" asked Ramsey. "Is she okay?"

"She's fine." Leroy darted his eyes around the room. "What time is it?"

"It's a little after four. You say he knew about the meeting?"

"Yes, he did." Leroy tried again to stand. "We have to get over there."

"I'll go, Leroy," Ramsey said, supporting Leroy as he swayed again. "You're in no shape to handle this."

"Call Declan."

"I did. He doesn't answer. Neither does Hannah."

"What time did you say it was?"

It was obvious Leroy still needed some recovery time. "It's just after four."

"Dammit."

"What?"

"The meeting was at three."

Ramsey shook his head. "No, it wasn't. We were meeting at four."

"Sarah moved it up an hour. I was calling to tell you when Yates showed up."

Realizing the implications, Ramsey gripped Leroy's wrist. "Declan and Hannah."

"I know. We have to find them." With Ramsey's help, Leroy started to walk, but he stumbled and almost went to his knees until Ramsey pulled him back up.

"You're not going anywhere," said Ramsey, sitting Leroy down in the nearest chair. "You can barely stand."

"You can't go alone, Sherlock. He's coming after you, too."

"Well, I doubt you'll be much protection. Most you can do right now is sit on him."

"That has its merits."

"Not from where I'm standing." Ramsey grabbed Leroy's arm and pulled it over his shoulder, then lifted him to his feet. "Come on."

"Where are we going?"

"Back to the couch. Then I'm going to find Hannah and Leroy."

"Not without me, you're not," said Leroy, and he attempted to hold himself up, with little success.

Ramsey maneuvered him back to the couch, and Leroy slumped into it. "You need anything before I go?" asked Ramsey.

Leroy slumped his shoulders. "Sherlock, be careful."

"I will." Ramsey waited to be sure his friend didn't try to follow him and then turned and headed for the door. He pointed at Leroy. "You stay put. I'll be back soon as I can."

Ramsey opened the door and was almost knocked backward when Declan fell at his feet. His head bleeding, he curled up on the floor with a grunt.

"Declan... Oh my God." Ramsey dropped to his knees. He looked over his brother and noted his sweaty features, bloody face, and the way his hands were gripping his midsection. "Declan. What happened?"

"Sherlock? What is it?" he heard Leroy ask.

"It's Declan." He tried to get Declan's attention, and Declan threw his arm out, knocking Ramsey's away. He was shaking and a deep moan escaped him.

"Declan, it's me. It's John." Ramsey put a hand on his brother's shoulder. "What happened?"

"Declan?"

Ramsey looked to see Leroy leaning against the doorframe.

"Is he okay?"

"Would you go sit down?" said Ramsey. "I don't need you passing out on me and hitting your head."

"I'm fine," said Leroy, looking pale despite his dark skin. "How is he?"

"Not good. He's barely coherent."

"How did he get here?"

"How the hell do I know?"

Declan grunted, and his face contorted in pain as his arms tightened around his belly. "Declan, what is it? What's wrong?"

Declan sucked in air and mumbled something.

Ramsey leaned in to listen. "What?"

"He killed him..." said Declan, barely audible.

"Who?" Ramsey asked.

Declan blinked and managed to focus on Ramsey, but his eyes still looked glazed. "He killed him...he killed my dad," he whispered shakily.

Ramsey didn't understand. "Who killed your dad?"

Declan trembled and blinked. "John?"

"Yes, it's me. I'm right here." He gripped Declan's shoulder. "What happened to your dad, Declan?"

Declan clenched his eyes shut against whatever pain assailed him. "Yates," he said. "Yates killed him. He killed Dad."

Ramsey's heart dropped. "What?"

"Poisoned him," said Declan.

"No..."

Declan started to say something else, but paused when a shiver racked his body. His knees came up, his head turned into the floor, and he moaned.

Ramsey held on to him. "I'm going to call an ambulance."

Declan's head shot up, and he grabbed at Ramsey's shirt. "No. No ambulance."

"Declan, you're in pain. You're injured."

"Hannah..."

"What?" asked Ramsey, feeling Declan's fear. "Where is she?"

Declan struggled to speak, but he twisted and cried out.

Ramsey had no idea how to help. "Declan..."

"Yates..." Declan finally said, his voice raspy. "He took her. He took Hannah." Declan stared up in complete anguish. "We have to find her."

Ramsey glanced at Leroy, whose face reflected equal shock, then sat back on his heels, his hand finding Declan's, which still clawed at his shirt. Waves of acrimony began to build as he thought of what Yates had done to each of them. The bastard had taken Sarah and stripped her of her memories, stabbed and poisoned him, threatened Leroy and his wife, hurt Declan and killed his father. And now he'd gone after Hannah. His fury building, Ramsey resolved then and there that it would stop. One way or another, they would deal with Yates.

Setting his jaw, Ramsey leaned in close to Declan, hoping to provide some measure of comfort. "We'll find her, Declan,' he said, squeezing the hand that clung to him. "I promise you. No matter what it takes. We'll get her back. We'll get them both back."

**

Sarah walked into the house, hearing only the sound of the surf. She threw her purse into a kitchen chair and began to pace, walking back and forth between the counter and island, wondering what to do. After all she'd learned that day, she prepared herself to confront Yates. Why had he scared Hannah away? Did Hannah know something Yates did not want her to reveal? And what about John Ramsey and her relationship with him? Had Yates told her the truth about her supposed accident? She began to question everything. How far did his lies go? The information she'd discovered on his computer told her the lengths to which he would go to protect himself.

Making up her mind, she walked out of the kitchen and toward the back of the house. She didn't know when Yates would return, but she wanted privacy when she spoke with him and she didn't need Julian poking his head into their business. The man was nosy, and she didn't like it.

She entered Julian's small office at the back of the house, but when she looked in, the room was empty, although a small TV was on, with the volume turned low. A TV show was on but she paid little attention as she made her way over to his desk and pulled out a pad of paper. She began to write, telling Julian that he could leave for the day. As she wrote, she glanced at the television. The actress Lynda Carter appeared onscreen, and Sarah watched as her character sprinted away from a man with a weapon. Managing to find a secluded spot, she twirled and transformed into Wonder Woman, wearing the small red, white, and blue outfit that left little to the imagination.

Sarah stopped writing. Something about the program had her complete attention. She continued to watch Wonder Woman fight her adversary, deflecting gun shots with her wristbands and ultimately lassoing the bad guy with her golden rope. As Wonder Woman took care of business, a flash of light went off in Sarah's head and she dropped the pen.

Something let go, and a hot stab of pain hit her behind her forehead, forcing her to lean over and drop to her knees. Sarah shut her eyes, praying it would pass, but it continued for several seconds before the agony began to ease. Feeling better, she stood slowly and left the office without finishing the note, needing to find a place to lie down. Moving from the back of the house and into the small sitting area, Sarah felt the pain hit again. She grabbed at the back of a chair but found herself back on her knees as a spark of memory emerged. In her mind's eye, she saw herself standing, looking down and seeing herself in the same red, white, and blue outfit. As the vision played out in her head, she watched herself move toward John Ramsey. She'd backed him up against a wall and pressed up against him, telling him she wanted him.

Her body shivered at the memory, and she moaned. Another flash flared, and she recalled his response—he'd backed her up in return, pushing her up against a wall, and then he'd kissed her as his hands moved over her, and she'd kissed him back. And then...

The visions came fast, and she held her head, clenching her eyes shut. She remembered their weekend together. She'd stayed, bringing her things to his house. Then the bookstore. Seeing him in the aisles. The diner, as she sat with Rachel. Spilling coffee on him. Her apartment—he'd knocked on her door. Their lunch. Waking in a strange house to find him there with her, telling her who she was. He'd held her hand, and his energy had raced through her. A brief flash of her lying in a heated tub, bubbles popping around her. Then Hannah, and Leroy, and Declan.

She moaned again. The memories came fast, and she struggled to keep up with them. She saw herself leaning over Leroy, her hands bloody, healing him with the little energy she'd had left. Hiding in a dark closet, tears running down her face while Ramsey sat with her, holding her hand. The second house. Her lost abilities and arguments with Ramsey. Meeting Morgana.

Sarah sucked in a breath at the memory of meeting Yates. She'd met him in a coffee shop. Her skin prickled, recalling his handshake. The memories swirled, rushing through her head. She remembered shopping at the mall with Ramsey, meeting his gaze through a mirror. The bar, and Ramsey leading her out of it after two drunk men had hit on her. The stabbing. Seeing Ramsey taken away on a gurney. Sitting at his bedside while he fought to survive.

Her hand clamped over her mouth at the memory of the text from Yates, her desperate need for the serum that would save Ramsey, and offering her blood in exchange. She recalled her collapse and waking up in Yates's bed the next morning. More memories surfaced from the hospital. Ramsey's sickness, but not from infection. Yates had poisoned him. She'd saved him by pulling the toxin from his body. Then the joy of knowing he would live. She felt the relief of lying next to him in the hospital while he'd slept, and she remembered his attempt to pull away from her and her refusal to let him, leading her back to that moment at his house, with her wearing a Wonder Woman outfit.

Her stomach twisted as it all came back. She had to force herself to stand, grabbing at the wall to steady herself before she found her way to the bathroom, where she vomited into the toilet, her nausea overtaking her as she realized what she had done. Married Yates. Left Ramsey. Said and done terrible things. Defended Yates. Slept with him. She gripped her belly and gagged again at the thought that she was possibly carrying his child. Another round of retching hit her, and she leaned back over the toilet. She clutched the basin for several seconds, waiting to see if she had finished, still reeling from the memories and her disgust. Emotion welled up in her, and a sob escaped her. How could this have happened? How could she have believed all that he'd told her? How had she been so easily fooled? How could she have forgotten John? The man she loved?

The tears slid down her face, and she sat back against the wall, angry and mortified. Another memory surfaced. This time, she saw herself holding the Mirror, the Council in a circle around her, watching to see if she could read it. The Mirror. She needed to read it to save Ramsey. And Hannah, Leroy, and Declan.

Sarah couldn't get up for several minutes, fearing she would not have the strength to stand if she tried. But then the realization that she was sitting in Yates's house, as his wife, and knowing he would return soon, spurred her into action. She had to get out of there. She would find Ramsey and beg his forgiveness and pray he would take her back. She found her balance, splashed her face with water, and rinsed her mouth in the sink.

Her hummingbird necklace reflected in the mirror, and she fought the urge to rip it off, feeling as if she'd betrayed the dignity of the women who'd worn it before her. She stared at her reflection and could almost hear her mother tell her that she could feel sorry for herself later. Taking her mother's advice, she stopped her mental abuse. Already thinking about what to pack, she left the bathroom and headed to the front of the house.

Before she reached the stairs, though, she hesitated, realizing her mistake. It wouldn't work. She couldn't leave. Yates would only come for her. He'd hurt John, maybe kill him, to keep her at his side. She couldn't risk that. She couldn't hurt John anymore.

Sarah hung her head, realizing the futility of trying to run, knowing the only way to protect John was to stay. But she couldn't do that either. Living a life with Yates was not an option. She dropped down and sat on the first step of the staircase. There had to be a way out, a way to get back to John and read that mirror. Something in her told her she would be able to read it. That it would speak to her. But how to handle Yates? She could never live a life with John if Yates remained a threat. But what could she do? How could she stop him? There was no way to—

She stopped as an idea occurred to her. Thinking hard, she stared off into space, letting the idea take shape. Could she do it? Closing her eyes, she felt the energy of her mother join hers. Hugging herself, she considered her options. There were few others to consider. If she wanted Ramsey, she'd have to do whatever it took.

Glancing at the clock, she saw it was just after five o'clock. There was little time to waste. Yates would return home sometime after dinner. Sarah jumped up, then raced up the stairs. Searching through her bedroom closet, she felt the shock begin to wear off and the flames of anger begin to take its place. All that Yates had done to her raced through her mind, fanning the fire. She remembered her encounter with him when he'd drugged her at the restaurant, and then her waking with him next to her, filling her head with stories. Her marriage to him. All the lies he'd told her, the pills he'd given her, the way he'd manipulated her and used his energy to distract her, to keep her from remembering. His seduction. She fought the urge to be sick again and let her hatred build. When she found what she needed, she quieted for a moment, waiting for the confirmation she needed to continue. Once she received it, she headed back down the stairs, praying she had enough time.

Approaching the door leading down to Yates's office, she heard a noise and jumped. She turned and saw Julian.

"Miss Sarah?" he asked.

Sarah made no effort to hide her outrage. She could only assume that Julian had played a part in Yates's deception. "What, Julian?"

He hesitated. "That's..."

She took a step toward him. "That's what?"

He made a noise in his throat. "That's Mr. Yates's office."

Taking another step, she said, "That's right."

His face furrowed, as if he'd caught Sarah shoplifting. "It's his private office."

Sarah narrowed her eyes, feeling his energy constrict when he realized that perhaps he had said too much. "His private office?" She edged closer, and he took a step back. "Let me explain something, Julian." She crossed her arms. Having found a suitable target for her fury, she had to hold herself back from launching him into the driveway. "I am Yates's wife. If I want to go to into his private office, then I will."

He nodded, his nervousness evident.

"Do you have a problem with that?"

He shook his head.

"Good." She dropped her arms and started to turn but then remembered what she'd wanted to tell him. "And you are dismissed for the weekend."

He dropped his jaw. "Excuse me?"

"Mr. Yates and I have some things to discuss. You and Isabelle can take the weekend off."

"But Mr. Yates—"

"Mr. Yates what?"

"He wouldn't approve."

"He wouldn't?"

Julian shook his head again.

"Julian," she said, walking toward him.

He managed to hold his ground and did not move back, but he leaned away as she neared.

"Right now," she said, stopping within inches of him, "you need to be much more concerned about what I approve of." She saw him swallow. "So pack what you need and get the hell out of this house. Or I promise you I'll escort you out myself, and believe me, you'd rather you do it on your own two feet."

He made no movement. "Yes, ma'am."

She scrutinized him, gauging his honesty to do as she asked. "And do me a favor. Find Isabelle and tell her, too."

He nodded his head and scurried around her.

"Oh, and Julian?" she said.

He stopped and looked back.

"You make any effort to contact Yates, and I'll know it." She held his gaze. "You understand?"

He took a second before he nodded again.

"Good. Now get out."

He disappeared. She doubted he could've moved faster if he'd had wings.

Sarah checked the clock and headed back to the office door. She opened it and headed down the stairs, knowing she had no time to waste.

**

"I'll go tonight, after dark," said Ramsey, holding a towel against Declan's bloody forehead. He'd managed to get his brother on the couch and get a pillow under his head.

Leroy was sitting in a chair and doing better with staying upright unassisted. "You're not going alone, Sherlock."

"I have to, Leroy. Neither of you are up to it. As it is, you both should be in a hospital."

"I'm doing better now, and you can't do this by yourself," argued Leroy.

"I don't have a choice. You have Olivia to think of. She'll kill me if something happens to you."

"And Sarah will kill me if I let you walk into an ambush. He knows you'll be coming. It's what he's expecting."

"Exactly, Leroy. He wants me. Why give him the satisfaction of taking us all down?"

"Because you have a better shot at success if you have help. I can't stand back and watch you commit suicide."

Declan shifted beneath him, and Ramsey pulled the cloth away. Declan's eyes were open.

"He's right," said Declan. "You're not going in alone. I'm going with you."

Ramsey couldn't help but chuckle, considering the circumstances. "In case you haven't noticed, Declan," he said, "you're in no shape to go anywhere."

Declan winced. "Just give me some time. I'll be okay. A few hours is all I need."

"Yeah, and pigs are flying through a frozen hell. You're a mess. How are you going to break into a house after dark, after running across the grounds, without collapsing?"

Declan breathed out slowly. "I got back here, didn't I? I can control it long enough to get myself from one spot to another. I just need to focus." Another wave of pain hit him, and he clenched his hands into a couch pillow.

"I'm not convinced," said Ramsey.

"How did you get back here?" asked Leroy.

Declan waited for the ache to pass and exhaled heavily. "Yates left me on the garage floor. I must have passed out. When I came to, I summoned enough energy to control the misery and made it to the office." He paused and rode another flare of pain. "The door was locked, and I couldn't get in, but then I found a maintenance guy and convinced him to open the door. The place was empty. Hannah was gone." He stopped then, but not because of any physical pain. "I made it back to the car and drove back."

"You *drove?*" asked Ramsey and Leroy in unison.

"I can't believe you didn't kill yourself and somebody else on the way over," said Ramsey.

"I told you," said Declan. "If I can get focused, I can control the pain."

"You didn't look too focused when you fell at my feet," said Ramsey.

"I fell in the driveway. Hit my head on a planter. My focus pretty well dissolved at that point."

Ramsey dabbed Declan's forehead with the cloth. "You're still in no shape to go charging after a Red-Line. Especially the one who did this to you in the first place."

"I'm already better than I was. If we go tonight, that'll give me enough time to pull it together." Declan sucked in another sharp breath and held it.

"Easy," said Ramsey. "Try and relax. Breathe through it."

Declan gritted his teeth. More sweat popped out on his skin. "Besides," he said, his voice trembling. "How am I going to get over whatever this is if I don't face him?"

"How do you know he won't make it worse?" Ramsey blotted Declan's face again. The gash in his head appeared to have stopped bleeding.

Declan blinked weary eyes. "I have to go. He's got Hannah."

Ramsey dropped the towel next to Declan. "Like Leroy said, that's what he wants. He'll be ready for us."

"I don't care," said Declan. "Even if it means he gets to us, if we can get Hannah out, then I'll do it. You want the same for Sarah."

Ramsey couldn't deny that. If he could find an opportunity to get Sarah away, memory or no memory, then he'd sacrifice himself to do it. And in his heart, he knew the likelihood of leaving Yates's house in one piece was slim. But he had no other choice. If Yates's wanted a showdown, then he'd give him one. He'd have to trust the only thing left on his side: destiny. "You two sure about this?" he asked. "You know the odds are not in our favor."

"Since when are they ever in our favor?" asked Leroy. "Besides, the bigger the struggle, the greater the reward."

"Then we're set for life if we make it through this," said Ramsey.

"So we all go," said Declan, gasping through another lance of heat. "And if we go down, we go down together, but not without a fight."

"And we don't leave without Sarah and Hannah, or there's no point in leaving," said Ramsey.

"Agreed," said Declan.

"That doesn't apply to you, Leroy," said Ramsey. "If this goes bad, you get out. Grab a hold of Olivia and don't let go."

"I'll decide that when the time comes," said Leroy. "But for now, we're all in this together." Leroy leaned forward, his eyes appearing much clearer than they had earlier. "We go tonight." He looked at the clock. "If he's expecting us, let's not make him wait." He turned back. "How about ten o'clock?"

"Yates's house at ten o'clock?" asked Ramsey. "That long enough for you to pull it together?" He grabbed the cloth and wiped a trickle of sweat from Declan's neck.

Declan released a long breath with a moan and a nod. "Ten o'clock," he said. "Don't worry. I'll be ready."

CHAPTER TWENTY-SEVEN

··

THE WARM SEA breeze blew in the through the open windows, rustling the curtains and carrying the scent of the ocean. Sarah sat in the living room, waiting. Darkness had fallen, and Yates had not yet returned home. She'd finished her preparations two hours earlier, jumping at every sound, fearing Yates would walk into his lab at any moment to find her there. But he'd never showed. Once she'd finished, she'd closed up his office and gone upstairs. She'd packed a bag, anticipating that she would not remain in the house that night. She took only her essentials and the few clothes she herself had purchased. The thought of wearing the clothes he'd bought for her made her physically ill. She'd placed the bag under the bed and returned downstairs, where she sat on the couch, listening to the sound of the surf, and thought of John. Images of her leaving, finding him, and throwing herself into his arms drifted through her mind, but she knew she couldn't seek him out yet. Her happiness would be short-lived. If Yates still posed a threat she'd never sleep, knowing she would always be looking over her shoulder, expecting his retaliation and fearing for John and anyone close to her. She couldn't allow that. Yates had to be dealt with, and she was the only one capable and well suited for the job.

As she considered her plan, she evaluated and re-evaluated her approach, never settling on any one path. She knew most of it depended on Yates and his reaction. Taking a long breath, she closed her eyes and made herself relax. Sarah remembered her mother's words. At times of crisis, stay calm and have faith. She did her best now to follow that advice.

A flash of light caught her attention, and she opened her eyes. The headlights of Yates's car reflected on the front windows as he drove up the driveway. Glancing at the clock, she saw that it was nine forty-five.

She sat and waited, listening for the sound of the side door to open. Five minutes, then ten, passed. She wondered what was delaying him. After fifteen minutes, she almost got up to go find him when she heard the door open and close, and then the sound of footsteps. She let out a held breath and closed down, contracting her energy, keeping all signals that could alert Yates—especially any that pertained to Ramsey—at bay.

The footsteps neared, and she turned her head, catching sight of him as he entered the front of the house. He noticed her in the living room, turned, and walked over, then paused at the entrance. His tie was loose, and he held his jacket over his shoulder.

"I'm surprised to see you up," he said.

Her face revealed nothing. "It's a nice night. Thought I'd enjoy a little air."

"You're usually curled up with a good book by now."

"Guess I didn't feel like reading."

"Hmm." He loosened his tie some more and pulled it off.

"Long day?" she asked.

"Yes, very. All sorts of problems to deal with." He rested his jacket and tie over his forearm, unbuttoned his sleeves, and curled the cuffs up.

"Anything interesting?" she asked.

"Nothing you'd want to hear about. Just a bunch of meetings with VPs and potential investors." He stretched his neck. "You already eat?"

"What, you haven't?"

"No. Been stuck in a board meeting all evening."

"You want something? I think we have some pasta."

"That sounds great." His gaze followed her as she rose. "I can get it. You head up to bed."

She left the living room and walked into the kitchen. "I'm not that tired. You sit. I'll get it."

Following her, Yates rested his jacket and tie over the back of a dining chair.

Sarah walked to the refrigerator and pulled out the pasta. She scooped out a serving on a plate and placed the plate in the microwave and turned it on. She put the pasta back in the fridge.

"How was your day?" he asked, sitting at the table. "Do anything fun?"

The microwave hummed, and she watched the food move in slow circles. "Not really, no."

He tested his elbow on the back of the chair. "Really? The whole day to yourself, and nothing planned?"

Sarah felt his stare, but stayed centered. "You want some wine?"

"Yes, please."

She reached for a glass in one of the cabinets and placed it on the counter. "As a matter of fact, I did have something planned, but it fell through."

The microwave dinged, and she pulled out the plate and stirred at the pasta.

"Fell through?" he asked. "What was that?"

She carried the plate over and placed it in front of him.

"Thanks," he answered.

She opened a drawer and grabbed some silverware and a napkin and set it next to his plate. "I was supposed to meet with Hannah today."

A brief moment of stillness in him caught her eye, but he didn't hold it for long. "Really?" he asked.

"Yes, but she didn't show." A bottle of red wine sat on the counter, and she picked it up, using an automatic opener to pop the cork.

"I hate to say this," he said. "But I told you so." He smelled the pasta and stirred it, letting it cool. "She's not who you think she is."

Sarah held the open bottle, picked up the wine glass, and carried them to the table. "Maybe so." Standing next to him, she poured the wine. The liquid splashed into the glass. Continuing to pour, she moved the bottle and directed the liquid straight into Yates's lap. Jets of red wine spilled and sprayed up, covering him and his plate of food.

He jumped up and yelped. "What the hell are you doing?" he asked, smacking at himself with the napkin, but to little avail. His suit had taken a direct hit.

She put the wine bottle down, and the glass with it. "Board meeting, huh?"

He dabbed at the liquid. "What the hell is the matter with you? You ruined my suit."

"You've got three dozen of them."

"That's not the point."

"You'll live."

His head shot up, and he glared at her. "What's gotten into you?"

She leveled her gaze at him. "I called the office today."

"You what?"

"I called the office."

"What for?"

"To talk to my husband."

"Why not call my cell?"

"Why did you go see Hannah?"

The question stopped him in his tracks, and a flicker of unease moved across his face. "What?"

"Don't play dumb, Yates," she said. "I walked into that room and I could feel you all over it. You could use some work on cloaking yourself."

Sarah could tell he was gauging what to say. Finally, he dropped the napkin, losing interest in his suit. "My, I had no idea my presence was so obvious. Your sensitivities are impressive."

"Not when it comes to choosing a husband. I could use some work in that area."

Annoyed, he pulled his shirt tail out of his pants. "I hardly think you're suffering," he said.

"Answer my question. Why did you scare her away? What are you so afraid of?"

"I told you. I don't want you to see her."

"Why not? You told me later it was okay. Did you say that just to get me to back off?"

"It seemed like a good idea at the time."

"What the hell is going on?" she asked. "I can't believe that one woman could instill so much fear in you. What does she know that you don't want her to tell me?"

His eyes flared, but he remained cool. "Sarah, why don't you just relax? You're overwrought, and with the pregnancy—"

"Stop patronizing me," she said. "You're afraid she'll tell me the truth, aren't you?"

His jaw set, and she could feel his tension. "The truth?" he asked. "What truth?"

"The part where I never had an accident. The part where you lied to me to make me your wife. How about that part?" She closed up as much as she could, preventing him from reading her.

"So," he said, "we've had some developments, I see."

"Developments? Is that what you call them? You drugged me. You lied to me. I never had a head injury. You gave me something to cloud my mind. You fed me stories. You told me I loved you!"

He listened to her rant. "You're overreacting."

Her anger mounted. "Overreacting?" she asked. "You're a bastard. I never loved you, and I never wanted you."

"I beg to differ. You're pregnant, aren't you?"

Furious, she picked up the wine glass and splashed the contents into his face.

His cheek took the worst of it. Wine poured down his neck and wet his hair. He grabbed the discarded napkin and wiped at his face. "You need to calm down."

"I'm leaving you," she said.

"No, you're not."

"Yes, I am. I won't stay with a man like you. You disgust me. You're worse than the lowest form of vermin. I will never spend a day longer with you than I have to."

"Sarah..." His voice pitched low. He threw the napkin back on the table.

"I never want to see you again."

She made to move from the kitchen, but his calm demeanor evaporated, and he stepped in front of her before she could leave. He stood so close she took a step back.

"Listen to me," he said, grabbing her wrist and pulling her forward. "I understand you're upset, but you need to realize something."

She tried to pull away, but she didn't have the strength to break free of his grip. "Let go of me."

His grip tightened further, making her wince. "I will never let go of you," he said. "You are my wife, Sarah. You carry my child. That makes us a family." His eyes were hard bits of ice. "You will never leave. You will stay by my side, and we will raise our child together."

"The hell we will. I won't stay here."

"You did it before and you'll do it again."

"What do you mean?" She struggled against him. "Let me go."

"Stop it." He barely moved as she tried to free herself. "You're not leaving."

While fighting him and feeling the pain of his grip on her wrist, she felt the energy within her begin to build. The pressure mounted when he pulled her forward and dragged her through the kitchen door. He yanked on her again, and something in her snapped. Raising her free hand, she placed it against him, and the pressure released as a surge of power moved from her core and down her arm.

The air turned electric. Yates shot back from her as if hit by a cow prod. He landed hard against the ground and lay flat against the marble tile, looking dazed and shocked at what she had done. Her fury did not abate. She sneered at him and the emotion within her bubbled up and refused to be ignored.

"I don't love you, Yates," she said, shaking from adrenaline. "I never have, and I never will. You took my memories and you took my life. You took everything." The past flooded in, and her heart ached with all that had happened. She couldn't hold back. "I love John Ramsey, Yates. And I always will."

His face contorted, he lay on the floor with one hand on his stomach. The electric current that had knocked him backwards and had bounced off the walls dissipated, and the room's energy turned cold. He did not bother to hide his contempt or the truth. "So now we get to the point," he said, trying to sit up with a grimace. "You remember him."

"I remember everything."

Moving slowly, he lifted himself into a sitting position. "You're so stupid."

"You're so arrogant. I love somebody else. Get over it."

He managed to get to his knees, and took a moment to collect himself. "That's not why you're stupid. You miss the point."

She didn't understand, but before she could tell him that, he was up on his feet and within two steps of her. Then he was on her, grabbing both hands and shoving her up against the wall. She grunted when her head hit the hard surface.

"You should have taken the opportunity when you had it, Sarah. Never give an opponent time to recover. Especially this opponent." He held her hard in his grip.

Her fingers tingled from the constricted blood flow to her hands. "Stop it, Yates," she said. "You accomplish nothing by holding me against my will."

He pushed up against her.

She held her breath and tried to summon the energy she'd gathered a moment before, but she found herself weakened, unable to mobilize it.

"It doesn't work like that, Sarah," he said, sensing her attempt to strike back. "It takes a while for the energy to build. It won't happen again, at least not for a while." Stepping back from the wall, he pulled her with him. "Which gives me just enough time." Yanking hard, he pulled her forward, and she fell against him.

Sarah struggled as he dragged her. "Let me go," she pleaded. Her body did not respond when she tried to gather any amount of energy to give her some leverage.

"Come on, honey," he said, pulling her. "I have just the thing you need." Making it to the door of his basement office, he dropped one of her hands, grabbed for the doorknob, and turned it. He stepped forward, and she yanked back, but he was able to get her down the stairs. She barely managed to keep her feet under her.

"Stop it, Yates," she said, desperate to reach him. "You can't win this. I remember. I want to go home."

He got her down the stairs and pulled her to the office door. "But you are home, sweetheart." He reared back, lifted his foot, and kicked the door. The frame gave way with a crack, and the door flew open.

Sarah dropped to her knees, and tried to break free from his hold, but he dragged her through the doorway, ignoring her protests.

"No," she pleaded. "What are you doing?"

"What I should have done in the first place," he said, his face rigid as he slid her hard to the back wall.

She bounced into it, her side taking the brunt of the hit. Looking up at him, she pressed back, seeing his look of malice.

"I'm going to wipe every memory of that man from your mind." He yanked hard on her wrist, and his face came down to meet hers until their noses were almost touching. "And after I do that, I'm going to destroy him."

Sarah shook her head in denial. The fury in his eyes made her shiver.

"And the only thing left to you will be me." Grinning, he watched her face. "And I promise you, my dear," he said as his other hand came up to stroke her cheek, "you will love me forever."

**

Barely visible in the crescent moonlight, three figures moved across the front lawn. One of them stumbled, and the other two slowed, grabbing the fallen one by the arms and assisting him up to the beach side of the house, near the front entrance. The outside light illuminated the front entry, making it an unlikely entrance point. Ramsey leaned back against the brick wall. They'd never planned on entering through the front door anyway.

He observed Declan who was standing against the house as Leroy bolstered him. "You okay?"

Declan managed to maintain his veneer of control, but Ramsey knew he was in pain. "I'm all right," he said. To his credit, he had gotten himself this far. They had been lucky that the back gate to the property had been unlocked. Ramsey didn't know what they would have done if they'd had to scale the eight-foot wall with Declan in tow.

"Can you keep going?" Ramsey asked.

Declan shut his eyes and held still, finding his focus. After a second, he opened his eyes again. "Yes. I'm ready."

His sweaty face and shaky frame indicated otherwise, but Ramsey didn't argue with him.

"Sherlock," said Leroy. "Let's check out the back of the house." Leroy glanced at Declan, who nodded his head, and Leroy let go of him. He moved past some bushes, ducking under windows. Using the wall for support, Declan followed along with Ramsey.

Reaching the back courtyard, Leroy stopped and scanned the area. Ramsey could see the pool, surrounding courtyard, and the raised patio, but the lights were off and no sound could be heard save the pounding of the surf. Leroy kept going, passed the pool and outdoor-living area, and headed to a back door. Declan and Ramsey followed. Nearing the entry, he stopped and crouched down. He peered inside the windows.

"See anything?" whispered Declan.

"Nothing," said Leroy.

"Let me ask you something," said Ramsey, who squatted next to Declan. "If he's expecting us, why don't we just knock on the door?"

"It's called the element of surprise," said Declan. He held a breath and grunted.

"What surprise?" asked Ramsey. "He's a Red-Line. He's probably watching us right now."

"Sherlock," said Leroy. "If you want to go ring the bell, feel free. I, for one, would rather try it this way. If there's the slightest chance that we can gain the upper hand, then I'd rather sneak in." He reached up and tried the knob, but it didn't turn. "No luck. It's locked."

"Well, then how about the windows?" asked Ramsey.

"Windows?" Leroy studied the back of the house. "We can try. But they're likely locked, too."

"No, those windows," said Declan, and he inclined his head toward the other side of the house. Lights blazed from the main floor and the curtains blew inward from the breeze.

"I think that's a good sign they're open," said Ramsey.

Leroy gave him an annoyed glance and stepped away from the back door. He found stairs leading to the raised patio and climbed them. Declan and Ramsey stayed behind him. As they approached the open windows, they moved cautiously, listening for any sounds, but it remained quiet. Leroy looked within and Ramsey did the same. He saw the living room. It was much as he remembered from before, when they'd located this house and confronted Yates. Leroy glanced back at the two men behind him. "You ready?"

They both nodded, and Leroy stepped in through the window, going slowly. He raised the window slightly in order to ease his entry, and to Ramsey's relief, it made no sound. Lowering his torso, Leroy dipped below the pane. He pushed a chair aside and turned to help Declan, who stepped inside with a grimace, and then Ramsey. Once all three were in the house, they moved over to the wall leading from the living room and out into the foyer. They stood still for a moment, feeling exposed in the lighted room, but hearing nothing, they collected themselves and prepared for whatever came next.

Sweat trickled down Ramsey's back. He reached inside his jacket pocket and grasped the small pouch containing the Mirror. He slid it out and moved it to the side pocket of his pants, then took his jacket off and threw it over a nearby chair. He eyed Declan and watched as a trickle of sweat ran down his brother's pale face. Declan was gripping his midsection, yet was still holding himself upright.

Leroy leaned into the foyer and then leaned back. Ramsey met his eyes and nodded. Leroy took a step out of the living room. Declan followed, and Ramsey took the rear. They all moved into the entryway, seeing the large staircase and empty kitchen. A jacket and tie hung on a dining chair, and what appeared to be a large pool of red wine covered the floor and table. A plate of pasta, doused with a healthy dose of red liquid, sat untouched on the table.

In the silence, Leroy stepped further into the foyer. They heard no activity upstairs. Ramsey pointed, indicating to the others to head toward the back of the house, which from their view, sat in darkness. They moved past the staircase. Nearing a short hallway that led to the back part of the house, Leroy paused at the threshold. Their eyes adjusted to the lower light and Ramsey looked from behind Leroy and saw a large den and sitting area. Before Leroy could step into the room, though, Declan touched Leroy's arm and Leroy jumped. Declan held several fingers in the air, giving them the signal to wait. Both Ramsey and Leroy watched as Declan walked to a door across from them, located beneath the stairwell. He put a finger to his lips. The door stood partially open, and a light was on beyond it. Declan approached and edged the door open. It made no sound, and Ramsey gave more silent thanks that the door and windows were well oiled. Ramsey and Leroy moved up beside Declan. The door swung in, and a staircase came into view.

At that same moment, they heard talking and froze. Ramsey picked up on Yates's animated voice, and then—his heart stopping—Sarah's. Then came a loud bang, as if metal was hitting metal, and Sarah cried out, and then they all moved instantly, heading down the stairs.

CHAPTER TWENTY-EIGHT

....

R EACHING FOR SOMETHING in his pockets, Yates drew back from Sarah, but still held her wrist in his grip. Patting his pockets as if looking for something, he cursed and turned to the large stainless-steel cabinet beside him. With his free hand, he turned the combination lock.

"Please, Yates," said Sarah, attempting to pull away, but Yates held fast. "Don't do this. Just let me go."

Yates completed the turns on the dial, grabbed the handle, and pulled the door open. Sarah saw the same items inside: the large covered bin at the bottom of the cabinet, the binders and folders, and the small box on the top shelf containing Yates's serum. Yates grabbed the syringe-like device he'd used to inject himself. It carried a vial within it. He popped it out and placed it back on the top shelf next to the box.

Sarah moaned.

"Don't worry, dear," he said, placing the device down and reaching into his pants pocket to pull out a different vial. "This will all be over in a second." With his free hand, he snapped the new vial into the device.

"Yates," said Sarah, beginning to comprehend. "You can't do this. You don't know what you're doing. Whatever that is, you could hurt me, or worse, hurt the baby."

"Who do you think you're dealing with here? I'm not an idiot, Sarah. You should know that by now. I have no intention of hurting you. You will simply cease to remember much of what has occurred up until this point. I, of course, will happily fill in the details and nurse you through recovery."

"No. You can't," said Sarah.

"Oh, but I can."

"I don't love you," she screamed.

Yates slammed his foot against the open door of the cabinet, and it banged hard against a metal trashcan.

Sarah couldn't help but shriek at the sound, and tried again to pull away, but Yates held on.

"You will in about twenty-four hours," he said, and he approached her with the syringe. "I can wait."

Sarah pressed back as he loomed over her. Desperate to save herself, she reached for anything she could grab with her free hand to stop his approach. Backed against a cabinet, she rubbed her fingers over its smooth surface but found nothing to use as a weapon. She'd run out of time. She braced herself, prepared to fight, but stopped when Yates slowed his advance, then stilled.

Straightening, he swiveled toward the door to the office, which stood ajar after being kicked in. "Well, well. Looks like we have company."

Sarah followed his gaze just as Declan, Ramsey and Leroy flew into the room.

**

They stopped when they caught sight of Yates. His shirt and pants stained red, he was standing over Sarah, gripping her wrist and wielding a small gun-like device in his hand.

Sarah's eyes widened. "John..." she said.

His gaze found hers. "Sarah..."

Yates looked between the two of them. "Well, isn't this nice," he said. "A little reunion before I take her away from you again."

Leroy held on to Declan who was too weak to stand and leaned him against the center island.

"You came early," said Yates. "I didn't expect you for a couple of hours."

"Let go of her," said Ramsey, eyeing the item in Yates's hand.

"Where's Hannah?" asked Declan.

Yates smiled. "Oh, this is fun. The two heroes here to save the day. I couldn't have planned this better if I'd tried." He regarded Leroy. "Too bad Olivia couldn't be here to join us."

"Shut up," said Leroy.

Yates dropped his smile and raised a brow at Declan. "How you feeling? Looks like you're holding together."

"Where is she?" Declan asked again, his body trembling.

"Hannah?" asked Sarah. She stared at Yates. "What did you do?"

Yates scowled. "Like I said, I'm not stupid. I couldn't risk wiping all of your memories clean." He waved the device in the air. "I had to test the serum before I used it."

"What?" asked Sarah.

"Where is she?" asked Leroy.

"It worked," said Yates, leering at Declan. "I lowered my dosage. Didn't need as much as I thought."

"You son of a bitch," said Declan. He moved toward Yates, but Yates grabbed at Sarah, hovering the device closer to her.

"Don't" said Ramsey, taking a step closer.

**

Sarah fought to stay centered and calm. Tendrils of energy were returning, but not enough to confront Yates. Fighting the urge to struggle, she hoped Yates would relax his hold. With Yates distracted, she'd managed to slide her free hand into a low cabinet door, and searched for anything to use against him. But he yanked her back just as she'd thought she'd felt something solid to grab onto.

"Just stay where you are, Declan," said Yates. "Besides," he tipped his head, "you're in no shape to put up a fight."

Declan gasped, grabbed at his stomach, and crumpled to the floor.

"Declan," said Leroy, dropping to Declan's side.

"Leave him alone," said Ramsey. "It's me you want. Let Declan, Leroy, and Hannah go."

"It's not you I want," said Yates. He yanked Sarah's wrist, who continued to pull away from him. "The only thing I want from you is your death."

"No," said Sarah.

"But not before I make you suffer." He smiled, observing Declan's crumpled form. "I'll take your brother." His gaze shifted to Leroy. "I'll take your friend." He pulled at Sarah's arm. "And I'll take Sarah." His gaze found Ramsey's. "But who goes first, I wonder?"

Ramsey stood still. The only indication of his fear was his white fingers, which were gripping the countertop. Hatred wafted from Yates, but Ramsey held himself together. "Think about this, Yates," he said. "You can't get away with this. The Council knows about you. They'll stop you."

"The Council?" Yates laughed. "They're a bunch of old buffoons. About as effective as a tent in a hurricane. What are they going to do, bore me to death? Besides, I made my point with Morgana this morning. They won't be coming around any time soon."

"Morgana?" asked Ramsey.

"Yes," said Yates. "I've had a busy day. Lots of holes to plug."

Ramsey's face turned stony. "No matter what you've done," he said, "you can't expect to kill all of us, dispose of the bodies, poison Sarah's mind, and live happily ever after. You've gone mad. Marco alone has caused suspicion."

"Marco?" asked Yates. "The suspicion lies with you. The police may have asked me a few questions, but they were easily swayed."

"Police?" asked Sarah. "Marco?"

Ramsey's gaze lingered on Yates's hold on Sarah's wrist. "Yates killed him."

"My God." She stared up at Yates. "Why?" Yates's hold on her eased, and she moved her hand further into the cabinet. She found the object again and wrapped her fingers around it. She had no idea what it was, but could only hope it would be sturdy enough.

"He got in the way." Yates paused. "But enough about Marco. It's time we get down to business. It's been a long day."

"Yates..." said Ramsey.

"You choose," said Yates.

"What?" asked Ramsey.

"Which one first?"

Ramsey didn't move. Leroy crouched next to Declan, who lay curled inward, taking shallow breaths. Ramsey stared at both of them. "I can't choose." His gaze returned to Yates's. "I'll do whatever you want. Just let them go." He took a small step forward. "Don't hurt her."

Yates made a mournful face. "That's sweet," he said. "But time's up. Guess I get to decide."

Sarah's eyes locked with Ramsey's.

Yates noticed the exchange. "You're making it easy for me. Guess we'll go with Sarah first."

"No," yelled Ramsey, his hand raised.

Yates lowered his arm to bring the device down as Sarah pulled and swung up with the object in her hand. It made contact with his wrist, knocking the device from his hand and into the wall. The vial popped out, hitting the counter, and shattered on the floor. The syringe device dropped and skittered across the ground. Sarah's momentum carried the weapon forward until it impacted Yates just above his left eye, splitting the skin. Bright red blood spewed from the wound and the blow knocked him backward, causing him to release his grip on Sarah's hand.

Ramsey lunged forward, grabbing her around the waist and pulling her back as Yates fell, hitting his head on the floor.

The object she'd wielded, which she discovered was a microscope, flew from her hand and slammed into a shelf full of beakers, breaking and shattering them, and then dropped and bounced against the floor. Leroy jumped up, grabbed it and held onto it as Yates went still where he lay.

Ramsey yanked Sarah back, away from Yates. They fell against the island and dropped to the floor beside each other. Ramsey held her close, and breathing hard, she gripped his shirt. They looked over at Leroy, who was standing over Yates, holding the heavy microscope.

"You okay?" asked Leroy.

"We're okay," said Ramsey. "He moves, bash his brains in."

"With pleasure," said Leroy.

Sarah sat further up, assuring herself that Yates hadn't stirred before she turned toward Ramsey, who sat up next to her. His eyes met hers, and the feel of him against her made it hard to breathe. Seconds passed as they studied each other, unable to move until he brought his hand up to her face and his palm cupped her cheek. She shivered at his touch.

"You're all right?" he asked.

Her vocal cords had locked, and she could only nod her head. Tears sprang into her eyes and she lifted her own hands and cupped his face, running her thumbs along his cheeks. She forced herself to breathe. "You're here," she whispered.

Ramsey's eyes roved over her face, as if for the first time. He took a deep breath and let it out. "You remember?" he asked, his voice hopeful.

"Yes." She nodded. "Yes. I remember." She stared, not believing he was there, and a tear escaped and fell down her cheek. "I'm so sorry."

His own eyes filling, he shook his head. "No. This isn't your fault."

"I should have known."

"Sarah, stop. It doesn't matter." He stroked her face and held her close. "You're sure you're okay?"

She wiped at her face. "Yes. Are you?"

"I am now." Emotion threatened to overtake him, and he took shallow breaths. She moved her hands down and over his chest, and his body trembled at her touch. His other hand came up, and rested over hers. "I love you."

A small sob escaped her, and she smiled. "I love you, too."

Sarah felt the energy between them begin to build, filling the cracks created by their separation. It was almost hard to remember where they were, but a moan from Declan brought them back.

Ramsey blinked and refocused. "We have to get out of here."

"Agreed," said Leroy.

He stood. Taking Sarah's hand, he helped her up. As she stood, Sarah's fingers grazed against the pocket of Ramsey's pants and she stilled.

Ramsey froze. "What's wrong?"

Tingles moved up Sarah's arm. "You have the Mirror."

"What?" asked Leroy.

Ramsey didn't deny it. "Yes. I do."

"You have the Mirror?" asked Leroy.

"Morgana brought it to me," said Ramsey. "In case we needed to read it fast."

"Of course, she did," said Leroy.

A movement from Declan got their attention, and Ramsey dropped next to him. "Declan," he said. "Can you hear me?" Declan grunted and tried to uncurl. "Can you move?" Ramsey asked. "We have to get out of here."

Declan grimaced. "Hannah..."

Ramsey looked at Sarah. "We have to find Hannah. Any ideas where she might be?"

Before Sarah could answer, a soft chuckle wafted through the room.

Leroy jerked, bringing the microscope down only to have it bounce off an invisible barrier, as if hitting a trampoline. The microscope shot up and out of Leroy's hand, then hit the wall and bounced off Yates's desk. Yates began to stir, and Leroy took a step back, but he moved forward once more, prepared to strike at Yates.

"Leroy, no," yelled Ramsey, just as Leroy was lifted off his feet. He shot backwards, landed on the island and was dragged along it before being pushed off the end and hitting the wall behind it. His back hit first, and he leaned over, fighting to find his breath.

"Leroy..." Ramsey rushed over to him.

Crouching next to Declan, Sarah watched as Yates rose slowly. Blood flowed down over his eye and nose from the gash in his face. The rivulets of red traveled down his neck and onto his shirt, staining it with blood as well as wine. Dazed, he held his head for a moment, but then righted himself.

"You didn't listen, did you?" He wiped at his face with the arm of his shirt. "Never give your adversary time to recover. I thought you were a better student than that."

Feeling her energy return, but uncertain as to how long it would sustain her, Sarah stood. "I think you're going to need a few stitches."

The blood poured down his face and Yates wiped at his cheek again. "You're proving to be quite the annoying little wife."

Sarah faced him. "And you're quite the murderous, deceitful, dishonorable husband. What did I ever see in you?"

He grinned at her, and the blood that smeared his lips gave him the appearance of a homicidal clown. "Oh, as I recall, we had more than a few satisfying nights. Something about me turned you on." His gaze found Ramsey's, and he winked at him.

Ramsey started to rise, but Leroy held him back.

Sarah held her ground. "About that," she said, her anger growing. "You should know every time we were together..." She paused, feeling her energy flicker to life. "...whenever I looked at you, I saw brown eyes instead of blue." His posture turned rigid, and she straightened. "That's right," she said, feeling his hatred bloom. "When I was with you, I was thinking of him." She inclined her head toward Ramsey. "Every time."

The energy in the room vibrated as Yates's resentment and hostility magnified. Yates couldn't help but steal a glance at Ramsey, who offered a satisfied smile and winked back at him.

Yates set his jaw. "You should watch your mouth, dear."

"Sarah..." Ramsey said in warning.

"What are you going to do, Yates?" she asked, ignoring Ramsey. "Drug me? Make me your pathetic little wife again?" She looked down at the broken vial. "Looks like you need some more juice."

He took a step forward, but she stayed put, feeling the enmity within her build. "How about you try being a man for once?" She crossed her arms in front of her. "Or don't you have the balls?"

Yates blinked through bloody eyes, and the room's taut energy continued to build. Declan had managed to uncurl, and his eyes were open to watch the showdown. Leroy and Ramsey sat coiled, ready to spring at the slightest movement.

"Oh, Sarah," said Yates. "You still have no idea who you're dealing with, do you?" He glanced at Ramsey. "Looks like I'm going to have to show you."

For a brief moment, the room went silent, but then something seemed to shift in the air and suddenly Ramsey lurched and gasped.

"Sherlock." Leroy tried to hold him up. "What's wrong?"

Ramsey turned white, and his face was strained. "Can't breathe," he sputtered. Kneeling, he leaned forward, gripping his midsection.

"No." Sarah rushed to his side. "John."

Ramsey doubled over on himself. His fingers curled into his shirt as he fought for air.

"John..." Declan tried to move closer. "Yates," he said. "Stop."

"Sherlock..." said Leroy.

Ramsey shut his eyes. His mouth moved, but no sound emerged. He lowered his forehead to the ground, and sat back on his heels. He dropped his hands and his fingers clawed at the floor beneath him.

"Stop," said Sarah, clutching at Ramsey. "I'll do whatever you want. Just stop."

Yates smiled, and Ramsey forced out a meek "no." But then the air in the room changed, and Ramsey sucked in a rush of air, his color returned, and his grip eased. "No," he said.

"Too late," said Yates. "You lose. I win." He eyed Sarah. "You ready to take your medicine?"

"Sarah, no..." said Ramsey, still recovering.

She found his hand and took it. "I can't let him hurt you."

Ramsey groaned. "He'll kill me anyway."

Yates sighed from across the room. "I'm waiting, Sarah."

Ensuring that Ramsey's breathing had returned to normal, Sarah stayed beside him before speaking to Yates. "Can I make one request?"

Yates wiped at his bloody face. "You really think I'm in the mood to grant you a favor?"

"Depends on the request."

He paused. "What is it?"

She paused. "Let me read the Mirror."

Yates started to say something, but then hesitated. He crossed his arms in front of himself.

Ramsey sat up, holding his stomach and taking deep breaths.

"You have it?" Yates asked.

Ramsey didn't move for a second, but he let go of Sarah's hand, reached into his pocket, and pulled out the pouch.

"Oh, lookey, lookey. The sacred Mirror." Yates looked between the Mirror and Sarah. "I do admit I'm a bit curious." He raised his eyebrows. "I wonder if you really are *The One*." He bent his fingers into quote marks.

"Let's find out," she said.

Yates put a hand out and found the countertop to steady himself. Looking sideways, he spied his office chair, pulled it over, and sat. "What the hell. I could use a break." He eyed Ramsey. "Let's see what she can do."

Sarah nodded at Ramsey, and he opened the pouch. The Mirror slipped into his fingers, and he handed it to her. Leroy and Declan remained quiet as they observed the exchange.

Sarah pulled the lid off and placed it on the ground. She frowned when she noticed the cloudy glass.

"Still readable, I hope," said Yates. "I hear it's clouding over."

Viewing her foggy reflection, she felt the pull of the Mirror's hidden secrets, waiting to be discovered. After glancing at Ramsey for reassurance, she raised her hand, and touched the cold surface.

She sat transfixed, waiting, but frowned when nothing happened. She could feel the Mirror's energy, but yet the message still eluded her.

Yates sat back in his chair, looking satisfied. "Nothing?" He chuckled. "What a shame. So much for old wives' tales."

Sarah stared down at the Mirror, expecting at any moment for the answers to come. She shut her eyes in frustration.

"Sarah," said Ramsey, and she opened her eyes. He reached over and took her hand, wrapping his warm fingers around hers. At the moment of his touch, the light switch went on, her outer vision went dark, and the Mirror illuminated, granting her access.

CHAPTER TWENTY-NINE

· ·

THE CONTROL PANEL blinked a kaleidoscope of colored lights and boxy screens displayed layered bits of information, transmitting data to the pilot as the ship descended and entered Earth's atmosphere at a vigorous rate. Varalika observed the changing numbers, gauging the timing and tracking her position from her chair on the bridge. Her mind focused, she watched the ship's altitude continue to decrease and near her targeted destination. She flipped off a beeping indicator that notified her of the ship's approach. She lifted her hand and hovered it over the panel, stopping over one button, her fingertip grazing it. Watching the clock as the digital display of seconds ticked down, she depressed the button at the precise time necessary and watched the screen. An object ejected from beneath the ship, which continued to fly, never stopping as the projectile plunged downward until it hit the shores with a tremendous splash and then sank into the murky water.

Varalika sat back in her seat, her eyes staring past the panel of lights, and startled when someone placed a hand on her shoulder. She hadn't heard the door slide open behind her. Seeing her husband, she smiled, and she slid her hand over the one that squeezed her. "She asleep?" she asked.

He moved to her side and sat next to her in the copilot chair. "You kidding? She's on her mom's ship. I can't get her to relax. She's back there playing pilot with her dolls."

Varalika smiled at him, her eyes appreciating his strong build and muscular arms. She reached across and took his hand. "Guess I shouldn't be surprised."

"No."

**

Tevnor watched his wife's attention drift. He knew by her actions that something was troubling her, but her fear worried him most. He could feel it within her. "So," he said, "you going to tell me what this is all about?"

She glanced at him.

"This isn't like you, V. Why the sudden exit?"

They'd left Eudora a day earlier after Varalika had arrived home and asked him to pack a bag for them and Destine. When he'd pressed her for more information, she'd only said that she would explain later and to trust her. He'd done as she'd asked, and they'd left that night. His wife, an experienced pilot and gifted Red-Line, made frequent trips between Eudora and Earth, and he'd figured this would be another routine flight, but her uncharacteristic nervousness and her vigilant presence at the bridge made him think otherwise.

She stood and neared the panel, the flickering lights illuminating her face.

"What's going on?" he asked.

She swiveled toward him. "I can't tell you, Tev."

"Can't tell me what?" he asked.

"It's complicated."

"I'm your husband."

"All the more reason."

He stood and walked up to her. From the window on the bridge, he could begin to see the terrain of the earth below as they continued to descend. Their radar veil in place, they could not be detected by any human technology. He'd been to earth once before, staying here for six months. It was here he'd met V six years earlier. A year after that, she'd Binded with him, and Destine had been born nine months later. They'd made their home on Eudora, but Varalika's work took her away from them often, and he'd wondered if perhaps she dallied in more than just aviation.

"Does it have something to do with why we left?"

Her fingers tapped a dial. "Yes."

He took her by the arm. "What is it? Are we in danger?"

Opening her mouth to speak, she stopped when an alarm sounded. Varalika scanned the controls, reading the data that ran across her screens. The alarm continued to sound as she raced her fingers over the panel.

"What's wrong?" he asked.

She continued to type, punching at various indicators.

"V?" he asked.

Her eyes on the instruments, she said, "Get Destine."

"Destine?"

"Bring her up here. Buckle her in."

He started to ask why when the ship lurched and he stepped to balance himself. Another alarm blared.

"Go," said V. "Go and get her. Now."

He left the bridge as another jolt made him reach sideways to prevent from falling. The door opened, and he ran out.

**

Varalika punched at the panel, running diagnostics to ensure her readings were accurate and trying to find the cause of the ship's malfunction. Despite her efforts, the ship continued to pitch in its attempt to maintain altitude. She shut down the alarms, not wanting to scare Destine when Tev brought her forward. Her daughter had always had a fascination with her work, and Varalika had brought her to the bridge many times, letting her play with the various buttons and keys, watching her face light up as the lights twinkled on the screens.

Moments later, Tev returned, carrying Destine in his arms. Her daughter's brown hair disheveled, her dark eyes caught sight of her mother.

"Mommy!" She reached out, a small purse swinging on her arm. "I want to play with the lights."

Varalika smiled at her daughter, hiding her fear. "Not right now, sweetheart. Daddy needs to strap you in."

"Are we landing?" she asked.

Tev sat Destine in a seat, securing her with the seat belt.

Varalika answered. "We will soon, dear."

The ship dropped then, causing Varalika to grab at the console to keep from falling. Tevnor grabbed at Destine's chair.

"Get to your seat," said Varalika.

Getting Destine safely secured, Tevnor moved up to the copilot chair and managed to sit before another violent shudder rocked the ship.

"What's happening?" he asked. He snapped his belt over his shoulders and waist and watched Varalika do the same. She leaned over and continued to work the display. "What's wrong?"

"We're going down," she said.

He gripped his armrests. "We're what?"

"I can't stop it. I don't know what's causing it. The ship's diagnostics aren't functioning." Another lurch made them both grab on before the ship righted itself again.

**

Tev looked back at Destine, who was playing with her purse. As the ship dipped again, the purse slipped and an item fell from it, hit the ground and rolled along the floor.

"Mommy," said Destine. "My mirror fell."

"It's all right, honey. We'll get it after we land." V's gaze never left the indicators that were flashing on the panel.

"Are we going to crash?" asked Tev, speaking low. Another steep drop made him suck in a breath.

Varalika's hands worked the panel. "I'm trying to slow our descent. Hopefully, when we hit, the impact will be minimal."

"Hopefully?" he asked. Sweat broke out on his skin, and he stared out the front window. The terrain loomed larger than before. "Where are we going to land?"

She glanced over, reading his mind. "I'll put us in a remote spot. Our distress signal will alert our people." She noted his worried face. "We'll be okay," she said. "We won't be found."

He bit back a retort and let her return to her frantic attempts to control the ship. Another lurch made his stomach drop, and he looked back at Destine to ensure she was okay. His stomach dropped further when he realized she was no longer in her seat. He searched for her and saw her crawling toward her lost mirror.

"Destine!" he yelled, and he reached for his seat belt to release himself.

Varalika turned her head at his shout. "No," she said.

"I'll get her," said Tevnor, pulling at his belt. But it would not release. He struggled with the buckle, but it held fast. He watched Varalika undo her buckle and leave her chair.

"V," he yelled.

The ship jerked hard, and Varalika slid into Destine sideways and hit the wall. At the last moment, Varalika turned to protect her daughter and took the brunt of the impact.

Tevnor continued to pull at his belt, but it had jammed and he could not get free. "Get back to your seat," he yelled.

Varalika gained her balance as Destine began to cry. Frantic, Tevnor watched as his wife pushed up from her knees and carried Destine back to her chair, grabbing on the armrest for support when the ship tilted again. Destine clutched at her neck, but Varalika pulled her daughter's arms away and pushed them back up underneath the restraints so she could buckle her back in.

"Mommy," Destine cried.

A loud pop sounded in the ship, and smoke began to enter the cabin. Tevnor felt the ship careen just as it lost lift.

"V," he screamed. "Hurry. Get back in your seat."

Destine now secure, Varalika pushed back. She lost her balance and fell but managed to reach out for her chair, grabbing at the base to gain enough traction to pull herself forward, but the force of the ship's fall worked against her and she struggled. Their descent slowed, and for a brief moment, she found her footing and pushed herself into a sitting position as the ship briefly stilled, almost hanging in mid-air. She gripped the arms of her chair, and pulling herself up and getting her legs beneath her, she scrambled into her seat and was reaching for her belt when the ship suddenly tilted at a sharp angle and dropped again.

Tevnor shouted as his wife bounced up and out of her chair, and then the hard hit came. The cracking and tearing sounds of metal and breaking glass and the blaring of alarms blasted the air as they rolled upside down. The ship's momentum took over, and they rolled again, ripping the earth beneath them as smoke bloomed within the cabin. The controls sparked and the bridge window shattered, showering them with glass.

The interior lights winked out and everything went dark, but then an emergency light went on and the ship's movement slowed and then stopped. The lights from the bridge sparked again and went out as smoke billowed, following the current of air that now drifted through the remains of the bridge from the broken window. After a world of noise deafened them, all became quiet, with only the sounds of falling debris interrupting the silence.

Tevnor opened his eyes and saw the destruction of the ship. He shifted in his chair, feeling for any physical injury. His chest was sore from the impact, but he could move. Scanning the area, he searched for Varalika, but saw nothing. He grabbed at his belt again but unable to undo it, he dug is hand into a pocket, and found his knife. Grabbing the belt, he cut it, freed himself, and dropped to his knees. The shock of the crash hit him and his body trembling, he breathed deeply to calm himself. Smelling smoke, he jumped into action.

Destine was still in her chair, crying softly to herself. He crawled over to her and checked her. There was blood on her head and arm, but it didn't look serious and they appeared to be her only injuries. Reaching for her buckle, he stopped when he heard a moan.

Squinting in the dim light, he turned when he heard a noise. He could hear the sound of broken glass crunching on the metal floor. Leaving Destine in her seat, he crawled forward and gasped when he saw his wife. She lay crumpled at the front of the ship, and as he approached, she tried to move, and a large piece of glass imbedded in her leg scraped against the ship's floor.

Tevnor saw that her eyes were partially open and she was semi-conscious. She lay on her left side, with her left arm splayed outward and her right arm covering her belly.

"Oh, God," he said, reaching her. "V." He touched her face.

Her eyelids fluttered, and her gaze found and focused in on him. She moaned as blood spilled between the fingers of her right hand. The fingers of her left hand moved, and he could now see the object she was grasping. Destine's mirror. He gripped her hand, the mirror still between them.

"No," he said. "Please..."

"Tev?" she asked.

"I'm right here, sweetheart." He squeezed her fingers. "I'm right here."

She made a whimper but stayed focused on him. "Destine?"

"She's okay. She's fine."

Varalika managed to nod her head. "Tell her I love her."

"You can tell her that."

"Tev?"

The pool of blood collected beneath her, and he swallowed a lump in his throat, fighting back panic and tears. "Just relax. I'm going to get some help."

"No."

"V..."

"Listen."

He could feel her losing strength. "Don't talk..."

"Take Destine," she said.

"What?"

"You have to take her and hide."

He leaned in close. "Hide? Why?"

She sucked in a strained breath. "...not an accident."

Tev's stomach twisted and his skin prickled. "What do you mean?"

Her eyes closed for a moment. "Protect Destine."

"V...please. Don't die." His vision blurred with unshed tears, and he felt her energy wane. "Don't leave me."

"Protect Destine." She coughed, and blood speckled her lips. "Don't know who to trust." She gripped his hand with a brief show of strength. "Promise me."

A tear escaped and trickled down his face. "I will. I'll take care of her," he whispered.

"They'll come for you," she moaned. "Stay hidden." Her eyes faded again.

He cupped her face with his other hand. "V. No." He couldn't contain his anguish as her energy dissipated.

"I love you," she whispered.

A sob bubbled up as he caressed her face. "I love you, too."

The light in her eyes dimmed, and her body went limp as her life force slipped away and then winked out. Emptiness filled the air. A kernel of grief ignited and flared in his belly, and a groan of agony ripped through him. Taking her in his arms, he wailed, and rocked her as he sobbed.

**

A flash of light popped in Sarah's mind and the vision shifted away from the turmoil of the ship. She saw an open heavy wooden door in front of her at the end of an empty hall. Light blazed around it and from within it. Sarah walked forward, but the door began to swing inward. She increased her speed, eager to reach it before it closed, but just as she neared, the door hit hard against the frame and slammed shut with a bang. Startled, Sarah opened her eyes. Blinking, she looked around. Becoming aware of her surroundings, she felt hot tears sliding down her cheeks and the hard floor against her back, and saw Ramsey's worried face looking down at her.

CHAPTER THIRTY

....

"**S**ARAH?" HE ASKED, feeling relief at her return. Tears ran down her face, and he wiped them away. She'd collapsed moments after he'd taken her hand, and he'd lowered her carefully down while she'd reacted to whatever she saw that no one else could. She'd moaned, and he'd thought he'd her heard her say, "Destine." Her hand clutched his, and she'd begun to cry.

No one else said a word as Sarah processed the Mirror's message. Even Yates could not help but watch in curiosity. After several minutes, Ramsey leaned over her, trying to rouse her, when she startled. Her eyes were still teary when she opened them.

"You back with us?" he asked. Her eyes lost, she stared, almost as if not recognizing him. A curl of fear traveled through him at the thought that she'd forgotten him again.

"Tev?" she asked, but then she blinked and he saw the recognition return.

"Sarah?' he said. "It's me. It's John."

"John?"

"Yes. Are you okay?"

Her eyes filled with tears again, and she reached up and touched her head. "So awful..."

"What?" he asked. "What's wrong?"

She put her hand over her eyes. "She died in his arms. It was heartbreaking."

"Sarah, what happened?"

"Yes. Do tell, my dear," said Yates, turning in his seat. "We're all waiting."

Sarah lowered her hand, and Ramsey could see a fresh tear escape the corner of her eye. "Can you sit up?" he asked. He pulled on her hand, and she raised her torso as he supported her. She leaned against him, and his free hand came down and rested against her stomach.

**

Sarah still felt partially connected to the world she'd just left, but a flutter within her belly helped to ground her in the here and now. She placed her fingers over Ramsey's, and her head began to clear. The flutter came again and she focused in on it and realized what it meant; her child had reacted to his father's touch. The visions in her head dissipated, and when she met Ramsey's eyes, the movement came again. The sensation confirmed for her that she was carrying his child. Her eyes filled again, but for a different reason.

"Hey," said Ramsey. "What's wrong?"

She sniffed and tried to collect her thoughts. "Nothing," she said. "Nothing's wrong."

"I wouldn't go that far," said Yates, eyeing them with displeasure. "You care to tell us what you learned before I wipe it all away?"

Ramsey's arms tightened around her, and she gripped his hand, trying to reassure him.

"Eudora to Sarah," said Yates. "You there?"

"I know where it is," she said.

"The serum?" asked Leroy.

"Where?" asked Declan.

"Really?" asked Yates. "Do tell. Don't keep us in suspense."

Sarah closed her eyes. Her mind returned to the ship, seeing it through Varalika's eyes. She remembered the screen and the location of the dumped cargo. She recognized the map and zeroed in on the exact site where the projectile had splashed into the dark water.

She opened her eyes. "The Great Lakes. She dumped it over the Great Lakes."

"The Great Lakes?" asked Ramsey.

"I hope you can narrow it down a bit," said Yates.

"It's was over Lake Superior. In a remote area on the North side."

"Where?" asked Leroy.

Sarah shook her head, trying to recall the location. "There was a small town nearby." She closed her eyes again. "It hit the water, not far from shore."

"What town?" asked Ramsey.

Her eyes opened. "Pan...something. Pan..."

"Panama Bay?" asked Yates. "Quaint little town," he said, swiveling in his chair, the blood drying on his face. He looked like a character fitted for a haunted house. "Terrible food, though."

Sarah didn't understand. "What?" she asked.

Ramsey eyes widened and then narrowed. "You found it, didn't you?"

Leroy couldn't hide his disbelief. "You know where our serum is?"

"Oh, I know exactly where it is," said Yates. "Have for some time now."

"You knew?" asked Sarah. "How?"

"You're serious?" he asked. "A mysterious mirror holds the secret to a lost serum that could save the lives of hundreds, maybe thousands, in our Community?" He gave her a dull look. "My brothers and I were all over that. What's a bored Red-Line to do when he's stuck in a house, staring at the walls?"

"But you couldn't read the Mirror," said Sarah.

"Not for lack of trying. Our fathers gave us all a crack at it, but no. No such luck. Looks like you get the gold star for that. But we did the next best thing."

"What?" asked Leroy.

"We went there." Yates glanced over at him. "To the ship itself."

"The ship?" asked Declan.

"You think the ship is gone?" asked Yates.

"Where is it?" asked Ramsey.

"Hidden very deeply beneath the earth. The Council knows how to hide something it doesn't want found. Fortunately, my brothers and I had easy access. Once we knew the location, we came and went freely."

"But the ship crashed," said Sarah. "It was destroyed."

"True," said Yates. "It no longer functions, but it's still readable."

"Readable?" asked Leroy.

"Yes, of course. It took me and my brothers months to do it. There's a lot of energy to sift through on a ship that's carried multiple passengers and been flown by various pilots, but we eventually found what we were looking for."

"What were you looking for?" asked Ramsey.

Yates sighed as if he was talking to a kindergarten class. "The indicators are there—Varalika's energy pattern, the approximate date, the movement of her fingers over certain keys, the ship's instrumentation, the crash site. We put it all together to find a location. It was a terrific challenge, one our fathers would have been proud of."

"They didn't know?" asked Sarah.

"No. We kept our project to ourselves. We were grown men by then, coming and going as we pleased. We thought we'd surprise them."

"And did you?" asked Leroy.

"No. By the time we'd found it, let's just say our relationship had become..." His gaze shifted. "...chilly. We kept it to ourselves."

"You know where the serum is?" asked Sarah.

"Oh, indeed I do." He stood, using the counter for balance.

"Was it in the water? Did you find the cargo?" asked Ramsey.

Yates steadied himself, then rubbed his head with the fingers of one hand. "The water was a bit of a challenge. We told the locals we were researchers, scuba diving for scientific evidence of a rare form of lake algae. They were suitably bored."

"You got it out of the lake?" asked Declan.

Yates smiled at him. "Oh, we did much better than that." He walked to the large open cabinet and pulled the trunk from the bottom shelf. Despite its bulkiness and apparent weight, he slid it out with ease. "In fact, you're within ten feet of it." He pulled off the covering to reveal a camouflaged crate.

"It's here?" asked Leroy.

Yates released the locks and swung the lid open, revealing the contents within. They shifted collectively to look. Inside were two large clear containers. They were settled inside foamy material and inside each one was a murky brown substance. "There are eight vials total," said Yates. "I'm sure the serum is in concentrated form." He shut the lid, and they all sat back. "Enough to keep you all around for quite some time, I'm sure."

"How could you hide this?" asked Sarah.

He shrugged. "Not that difficult, really."

"You could have saved lives," said Declan.

"I'm not interested in saving lives." His hard eyes found Declan's. "I find taking them to be much more interesting. Your dad was a highlight."

Declan paled more and attempted to get to his feet, but another lance of pain shot through him. "So was yours," he managed to stammer before he went down hard.

Ramsey moved toward Declan.

"Stop it, Yates," said Sarah.

Yates's glare eased. "It's time to get the ball rolling, honey. You've done what you wanted. The Mirror is read and the serum found. Congratulations. Now do me the favor of lending me your arm." He walked over to the island and opened a drawer, then pulled out another vial. "Good thing I have a spare."

Sarah watched him pick up the gun-like syringe from the floor and pop in the new vial. "I'm waiting," he said.

"Sarah, no," said Ramsey.

"Let her alone, Yates," said Leroy. "Stop this. We have the serum. You can stop all of this."

Yates pretended to ignore Leroy, but Leroy grimaced and doubled over, grasping at his head.

"Leroy..." said Ramsey.

Sarah raised a hand. "Don't, Yates. Stop."

"Then I suggest you join me before it's too late."

"Sarah, don't do it. He'll kill us anyway," said Ramsey.

Indecision tore at Sarah. She wanted to reach out to Ramsey, but his face turned white, he curled inward, and gripped his chest.

"No," yelled Sarah.

"Time's a wasting," said Yates. "I give him about two minutes."

Watching the men around her, Sarah stood and took a step forward. The energy within her was anxious for release, like rising water behind a dam, but she questioned whether to use it. She didn't want to make the situation worse.

Yates watched her with satisfaction. He twirled the device around his finger, confident of his success.

Sarah thought of her mother, wishing she had more time, but the sensations around her told her that there was no time left. Ramsey was struggling to breathe, Leroy gripped at his head, and Declan was shuddering as his insides turned to mush. Asking silent forgiveness, her gaze found Ramsey's. Despite his battle to survive, he looked back at her with anguish. They held their gaze for as long as they could before she turned back to Yates and offered her arm.

"That's a girl," he said, and he reached for her and pushed up her sleeve.

Sarah's heart raced as she prepared for the inevitable. Watching Yates bring the syringe down, she swayed when her vision spun. An unexpected heat bloomed in her midsection and a wave of energy pulsed within her. As Yates brought the device to her skin, Sarah had a clear vision of the female pilot, Varalika, standing behind Yates. Varalika's eyes flashed and Sarah's fear evaporated as a beam of energy projected from Varalika, passed through Yates, and entered Sarah at her core. The fire within Sarah flared and surged through her body.

Without thinking, Sarah shot out her hand and made contact with Yates's midsection, sending a wicked dose of electric wattage into him. Before he could depress the trigger, his body shot backwards and hit the counter behind him, breaking more beakers. The impact brought him to his hands and knees, the device fell from his grasp, and the vial of liquid popped out, rolling near Sarah's feet. Sarah watched it spin and sucked in air as the newfound energy coursed through her. Varalika's image faded away, and Sarah considered her options as Yates, reeling from the blow, sat back on his heels, his forehead on the ground. Making a decision, Sarah raised her foot and brought it down on the vial, crushing it beneath her heel.

"Oops," she said, grinding it into the ground. "Looks like it broke."

The energetic onslaught on Yates caused him to lose focus, and Sarah could feel the pressure lighten in the room. Ramsey took a shallow breath, Declan uncoiled, and Leroy shook his head, but she kept her sights on Yates.

Sarah moved up to Yates's side as he rose up on his knees, trying to breathe himself. "I think I've learned my lesson now." She reached down and touched him, and another river of fire shot from her hand. Yates grunted and fell sideways to the ground.

She heard Ramsey take another relieved breath and Yates stared up at her with pure malevolence. "You okay, dear?" she asked. "You don't look so hot."

Breathing hard and holding his side, he said, "Looks can be deceiving."

"Maybe," she said, leaning over him. "But I doubt it in this case."

His eyes turned feral and she sensed the hidden energy within him just as he lunged up at her and his hands found her throat. Gaining his footing, he stood, pulling her with him, and pushed her backward until her back hit the stainless-steel cabinet. His hands squeezed her throat tighter and her airway closed, Writhing, she clutched at his fingers, trying to hold him off.

"Care to reconsider?" He squeezed even harder as her fingernails dug into his wrists. Ramsey shouted from behind, but then grunted and crumpled to the ground again as Yates reengaged his attack.

Sarah struggled against Yates, but couldn't speak.

"What's the matter, my dear? No more energy left to fight with?" He continued to squeeze. "Pity. We made a cute couple."

Sarah saw stars as her lungs fought to expand, but despite his grip on her throat, something inside her flicked on, and instead of feeling the drain of lost fuel, she felt it re-engage. She let go of

Yates's wrists and dropped her hands to his chest. Another powerful electric pulse surged out of her and into him.

Grunting, he released his hold on her neck and staggered backward.

Sarah gasped at the rush of air and dropped to her knees, her throat burning. She coughed as she tried to breathe.

Ramsey sucked in a breath and clutched at his side. His face was white and he attempted to sit up.

Yates grabbed at the island, fighting to stay upright. Wiping at his eyes, he watched Sarah recover from his attack while he tried to recover from hers.

"You seem to be harnessing some impressive energy," he said. "I'm surprised." He shook his head, breathless. "But don't count me out yet, sweetheart. I may be down, but I'm not out."

Moving slowly, he bent down to pick up the empty gun-shaped syringe off the floor.

Sarah waited, still holding her throat as the coughing began to dissipate.

Yates walked toward her, and she stilled, preparing for another battle, but he passed her and went to the cabinet. He reached up through the open door and found the unused vial of serum he'd removed earlier and had left on the shelf. He popped it back into the syringe and retreated until his back hit the island. Holding the device up, he eyed the room, taking in Sarah's kneeled position, Ramsey's shallow breaths, Declan's slumped form, and Leroy gripping his head.

"Just give me a few seconds," he said, holding the device against his exposed arm. "And I'll be good as new."

He depressed the trigger, and the liquid within the vial slowly dissipated. Once the vial was empty, he dropped the device on the island counter and took a deep breath as he waited for it to take effect. As the seconds passed, Yates's features changed, and a look of discomfort clouded them.

Her throat still burning but her balance returning, Sarah slowly stood. "What's the matter, Yates?" she asked, her voice rough. Yates's face began to pale. "Not feeling too good?"

Yates grabbed the counter. His knees quivering, he blinked, A few seconds passed and he swayed and dropped to his knees.

Sarah approached him. "Feeling sick?" she asked. "Dizzy?"

His skin turned red, and Yates dropped his hands to the floor.

"Hot?" asked Sarah. "That's probably the fever."

Yates's rested his forehead on the ground and gasped.

"Doesn't feel too good, does it?" Sarah asked as she watched him falter. "Don't worry. It won't last long." She leaned over him. "Right now, your body is going into shock. Your temperature is rising rapidly and in a minute or two, you'll have organ shut down. You'll slip into unconsciousness. And then it will all be over."

Yates dropped sideways onto the floor and curled up. Chills shook him, although beads of sweat popped out on his skin. Sarah picked up the device from the counter and squatted next to him. She popped out the empty vial and held it in her hand as Yates grunted and looked up at her through pain-filled eyes.

"That's what you wanted, right?" She held the empty vial out to him. "For Ramsey?"

Sarah reached over to a covered trashcan under Yates's desk and pulled it closer. She reached inside and pulled out an empty syringe. She held it out to Yates. His eyes widened when he recognized the Y written in black marker on the side. It was the syringe of serum he'd given to Sarah to save Ramsey.

"I took the liberty of injecting this into your vial for your next dose." She stared into his wary eyes. "What?" she asked. "You mean you were lying?" She studied the empty piece of plastic. "This isn't what you said it was?" She dropped her hand. "Pity." Sarah shook her head. "Looks like you've killed yourself with your own toxin."

A wave of pain passed through him, and he gripped his midsection. His body arched from the strain of the poison, and a quiet groan escaped him.

She kneeled next to him. "Hurts, doesn't it?"

His body was convulsing with the effects of the drug, but he managed to speak. "You bitch," he said.

Sarah watched him writhe. "Oh, I'm not done. There's more," she said. "I also accessed your computer." His eyes flared, and he rolled his head on the ground. "Yes," she said. "You're not the only one who can read keys." She sat back against her heels. "Imagine my surprise at what I found there. Corruption, blackmail, a total lack of social and corporate ethics and responsibility. Not to mention a few nasty cocktails you created to hurt good people."

His eyes narrowed, and he gritted his teeth.

Sarah remained unfazed. "I made sure to wipe the computer clean of anything I deemed unnecessary. Your toxins and potions are destroyed." She leaned closer. "Don't worry. I found the backup files, too."

He turned redder, even though his skin already glowed from the heat on his skin.

Sarah continued. "And as your widow, I intend to turn your company around, provided it still survives after the government gets involved." She pulled a flash drive out of her pocket. "I have all the evidence I need of your involvement, from blackmail to tax evasion. They'll be most interested."

He puffed out a breath. "They'll take you down, too," he uttered.

"Who, me?" she asked. "Your unsuspecting wife? Who turned over all the evidence to them? And who is willing to cooperate in every way? No, by the time they're through with your little company, they'll be asking me to save it."

Another shudder moved through him, but his shimmering eyes remained on her.

Sarah looked around. "And this house?" she asked. "I'm going to sell it. And all the proceeds will go to the Council, to assist them with helping the Grays who've suffered without the serum and to help with distributing the new serum. It's going to help a lot of people."

The glaze of pain in his eyes began to ebb and was replaced by a dull lethargy, but he still focused intently on Sarah.

"And when I'm done with that," she said, getting down close, ensuring he could see her, "I'm going to marry Ramsey. And we're going to raise our child together, as a family."

Yates gathered his few remaining tendrils of energy and glared up at her. "You live in your pathetic fairy tale, but it's my child you'll have to raise," he said, forcing a grin.

Her gaze drilled through him. "But that's just it, honey. It's not your child." She rubbed her belly. "It's his."

Fury flickered in his eyes but did not ignite, and the pulse of heat blazing from him began to subside even as he fought to stay conscious. He blinked, trying to focus.

Sarah leaned closer and spoke into his ear. "Karma's a bitch, isn't it?"

They were the last words he heard before it all went dark and the fire went out.

CHAPTER THIRTY-ONE

··

HOLDING HIS ACHING side, Ramsey sucked in a breath when the pressure on his lungs released. Feeling his strength return, he inhaled deeply, ignoring the pain of what he suspected were two or three cracked ribs. He looked to see Sarah kneeling over a fallen Yates and speaking into his ear. Grabbing at the counter, he pulled himself upright with a groan. The heavy air in the room suddenly lightened, and he swayed but caught himself. Sarah put her finger to Yates's neck, and he realized Yates was dead. When Sarah slowly stood on shaky legs, relief flooded through him. They stared for an imperceptible second before they both stepped forward and wrapped around each other, her face buried into his neck. He smelled her hair and her ear pressed against his cheek, and the pain in his ribs barely registered. The energy they shared flooded back, swirling and settling, as if finding its home again.

"Sarah..." he said, turning his face into her hair. "You okay?"

She squeezed him. His ribs protested, but he didn't let go. He felt her nod against his neck. "You?" she whispered.

"Nothing a few days of rest can't heal," he answered, but couldn't prevent a groan when she pressed against him and his ribs flared.

She pulled back. "You're hurt."

"Just my ribs. I'm fine." He gave her a look of reassurance before he searched for Leroy, who'd managed to sit up, but was still holding his head in his hands, and Declan, who lay curled in a ball on the floor. "They need more help than I do."

Before he could go to check on them, Sarah placed her hand on his chest and held it there. He started to protest, telling her not to worry, when the pain vanished and he stood in doubt, wondering if his mind was playing tricks on him.

"Better?" she asked, and he realized she had healed his fractured ribs with the touch of her hand.

"Yes." He didn't know what else to say, because she turned then and dropped next to Leroy.

"Leroy?" she asked, reaching for his hands. "How are you?"

Looking sweaty and uncomfortable, Leroy popped his head up. "Better than before," he said. "But I've got one hell of a hangover." He rubbed at his temples and winced.

"Sit back," she said. Leroy lay back against the wall. She raised her hand, placing it on the top of his head, and brought the other to the back of his neck. "Relax," she said.

Leroy took a breath, and after a second, his eyes popped open wide and his shoulders came down.

"How's that?" she asked.

"Better than aspirin," he said. "Much better. Thanks." He massaged his neck.

Sarah turned and went to Declan's side next. Ramsey crouched next to her. "Declan?" she asked.

Declan shifted and moaned but did little else. His eyes were half slits, and he was breathing carefully.

"Declan," said Sarah, leaning close. "I'm going to put my hands on your stomach. Lie still." She addressed Ramsey. "Help me lay him back."

Ramsey took Declan's shoulders and pushed him back. Declan moaned again and tried to curl up, but Ramsey held the pressure. "Take it easy," said Ramsey. "You'll be fine in a second."

Sarah shifted and put both hands on Declan's stomach while Ramsey held him still. She quieted herself, took a breath, and closed her eyes.

Ramsey and Leroy watched as she sat silently, her hands on Declan, for several seconds. She grimaced for a moment. "He's a mess," she said, her eyes still closed. "His insides are twisted." She took another calming breath. "This will take a few minutes."

Ramsey and Leroy shared a look. "Take all the time you need," said Leroy.

Sarah continued to work on Declan. After a couple of minutes, Declan stirred and his eyes became more alert. He winced, but began to focus.

"Stay still," said Sarah, eyes closed. "I'm almost done."

Declan seemed to hear what she said and didn't move. Ramsey felt his brother's body relax. He began to breathe easier, and his arm unwound from his torso.

Sarah opened her eyes and sat back.

Declan, his face no longer furrowed in pain, started to sit up.

"Go slow, Declan," said Ramsey.

"Hannah," said Declan, his voice stronger. "We have to find Hannah." He raised himself into a crouch and stayed there, waiting for his head to clear. Lines of fatigue and worry etched his face, and he looked pale. He stared at Sarah with quiet determination. "Where could she be?"

"She's got to be somewhere in the house," said Leroy. "We'll find her."

Sarah's gaze traveled through the room and stopped at the door leading to the small bedroom.

Declan noticed and stood in a heartbeat. "Hannah?" he asked. He grabbed at the door and turned the knob. The door swung inward, and he stopped. The rest of them followed, and froze when they saw the single twin bed and Hannah's still form lying on it.

"No," said Declan, rushing to the bedside.

Hannah made no reaction to his presence. He sat beside her, but her half-open eyes did not flicker. Declan took her hand, but she did not grip his fingers.

"Hannah?" he asked, stroking her face. "Can you hear me? It's Declan." Her expression did not change. "Hannah, please." The fear in Declan's voice was audible.

"Let me look at her," said Sarah, putting a hand on Declan's shoulder and attempting to calm him.

Declan tried again. "Hannah..."

Ramsey and Leroy stepped forward. "Declan, let Sarah help," said Leroy.

"Step back," said Ramsey, taking his arm.

The words seemed to penetrate his consciousness and Declan pushed off the bed, letting Leroy and Ramsey guide him. "Please help her."

Sarah sat on the edge of the bed. She placed one hand on Hannah's head and the other over her heart, feeling and listening. Several minutes passed as Sarah worked with no sign of improvement.

"Sarah," said Declan. "What's wrong? Why isn't she coming back?"

"Let her finish," said Ramsey. "Give her time."

"Just wait," said Leroy.

Sarah shook her head, and Declan stepped closer. "What is it?"

"I can feel it," said Sarah.

"What?"

"What he gave her. It's worked its way into her system, and she's frail, but there's still time."

"Time? How much time?" asked Declan.

Sarah didn't answer him. She pointed at Ramsey. "I need you on the other side of her." Ramsey let go of Declan and moved toward the bed. Sarah spoke to Leroy. "You keep him back."

"What?" said Declan. "Why? Let me help." He tried to approach, but Leroy stopped him.

"You can't," said Sarah. "Your energy is too erratic right now. I need someone to help me balance her. You can't do that. The best thing for you to do is wait."

Ramsey crouched on the other side of the bed, and Declan shut his mouth in frustrated silence.

"What do you need me to do?" asked Ramsey.

"Keep your hands on her head and heart. I need you to keep her steady while I pull the poison out of her." Sarah rubbed her hands together and took a breath. "You okay with this?" she asked.

"I'm cool as a penguin. Let's do this."

Sarah shifted her position and kneeled on the side of the bed. Ramsey placed his hands on Hannah while Sarah put a hand on her sternum and another on her belly. Dropping her head, Sarah closed her eyes.

Ramsey focused in on Hannah's energy, but found there was little to grab onto, so he made sure the little energy he did feel stayed even. No more on one side than another.

They stayed like that for several minutes. As time passed, Declan's taut energy made him pace the room, waiting for any indication of Hannah's return.

After more time passed, Ramsey began to feel a buildup of energy beneath his hands. He worked to keep it balanced as it continued to grow.

Sarah took several deep breaths. When her head came up, she held a worried look. "It's too fine. I can't gather it in one place."

Declan shot forward. "What is it?" he asked. "What's wrong?"

"Whatever he gave her," said Sarah. "I can't pull it out of her like I did with John." She stopped as she thought.

"We have to do something," said Declan. "There has to be a way."

Sarah spoke to Ramsey. "I'm going to guide it into her lungs."

"What? No," said Declan. "You'll kill her."

Sarah didn't acknowledge him. "We don't have much time. When you feel the movement, focus it toward her chest."

"No, don't," said Declan. He tried to move forward, but Leroy held him back.

Sarah spoke. "You have to trust me, Declan."

He stopped at her words, and she turned away and began to work again on Hannah. Declan forced himself to stand still and wait.

Ramsey concentrated, waiting, and after a few minutes, began to feel shifting currents of movement beneath his hands. He pulled inward, directing the energy toward Hannah's lungs. Hannah began to show signs of activity. She blinked, and he heard her make a small noise in the back of her throat. Her hands began to open and close, and she coughed.

Sarah moved her hands away and sat back. "Sit her up," she said. "Declan, get behind her. Hold her up."

Declan was there in a second to support her from behind as Ramsey helped lift Hannah into a sitting position. Hannah coughed again, and a spray of red particles spewed into the air and floated down.

"Turn your heads," said Sarah. "Don't breathe this stuff." She moved sideways to Hannah to avoid the red mist.

Hannah continued to cough, releasing red puffs of powder into the air. She fought to suck in oxygen as her lungs forced the toxin out.

"That's it, Hannah," said Sarah. "Keep coughing."

Hannah's alertness improved the more she coughed. Her eyes opened, and she grabbed at Declan's hands, which encircled her.

"Keep going. Cough it out. That's it," he said, holding her.

Her body shook with the effort to remove the debris from her airway. She began to tire, but Sarah wouldn't let her stop. She held her hand against Hannah's back, feeling for the remnants of the toxin.

"You have to keep coughing," said Declan. "I know you're tired, but we have to get it out of you."

Hannah clutched at his hands and trembled, but continued to expel the poison. As the coughing and amount of red mist began to subside, she moaned, took another deep breath, and exhaled through another deep cough. The amount of red she released was minimal.

Sarah dropped her hand from Hannah's back and nodded at Ramsey, who nodded in return.

Hannah slumped, but the light was back in her eyes. "Declan," she said.

"I'm right here," he said, coming around to sit in front of her. "I'm here." He took her hands in his.

"Where am I?" she asked, her eyes weary but aware.

"You're safe," said Declan, his hand finding her cheek. He looked at Sarah in gratitude, and she smiled back.

Hannah reached for him, and he took her in his arms. "We're safe," he said. "We're all safe."

CHAPTER THIRTY-TWO

....

RAMSEY OPENED THE door to his house and stepped back, letting Sarah walk in first. She took a few tentative steps forward, then paused at the threshold before stepping inside. Watching her move into the entry way and stop, he followed her in and closed the door behind them, resting the bag he was carrying for her on the floor.

The previous sixteen hours had been tumultuous ones. Once they'd collected themselves, they'd made a few phone calls and their people had arrived not long afterward to take Yates's body and the serum, then clean the area as the four of them took Hannah to the hospital to be examined. Unable to reach Morgana, Leroy had contacted Drake. He'd learned that Morgana had been found earlier, unconscious and unresponsive, in her home and that she was also at the hospital.

Leaving Declan with Hannah in the emergency room, Ramsey, Sarah, and Leroy had found Morgana's room. She was comatose, and the doctors could provide no explanation for her condition. Once alone with her, though, Sarah had reached out and touched her, and within minutes, Morgana had stirred and regained consciousness. Despite her ordeal, Morgana insisted she was fine and she listened as they updated her on the situation, telling her that not only had the serum been located, but they had it within their possession and it was currently on its way to a discreet laboratory to begin the proper preparation and distribution procedures. The three of them left shortly after, happy to leave after listening to Morgana argue for her release with a weary nurse.

Declan stayed at the hospital with Hannah while Ramsey, Leroy, and Sarah returned to Leroy's house around three in the morning before all of them collapsed into bed and slept until almost noon. When they awoke, they shared a quick meal and discussed the story that Sarah would have to tell over the next few weeks to explain Yates's disappearance and her exit from the mansion.

Now, a few hours later and back home, Ramsey watched Sarah take in her return to his house. She was quiet. Perhaps too quiet. "Sarah?"

**

Sarah absorbed the familiar sights and scents. She spotted the coffee cup she'd drunk from that last morning, still sitting in the drainer. She saw the couch and cracked glass coffee table, and the memories surfaced. She noticed that certain items were missing—pictures from the mantle and wall, a few decorative pieces from a set of shelves. When she looked closer, she could see bits of debris in the carpet along the walls, and she saw clearly in her mind's eye John shattering whatever he could grab. She swallowed, feeling the remnants of his outburst, but said nothing. She walked further into the living room and then into the bedroom, and Ramsey followed.

In the bedroom, Sarah stopped at the sight of the bed. Visions of their last moments together played through her mind. She trailed her fingers over the bureau of drawers, then walked into the bathroom and paused to look into the now uncovered mirror, re-calling her hand against it, with John's hand over hers, as she pressed her body into his. He'd turned to face her, taking her in his arms and telling her she was beautiful. And then another image joined the first. One of Yates holding her, telling her the same thing.

She stiffened, wrapping her arms around herself and shutting her eyes. Feeling Ramsey's hand on her shoulder, she pulled away.

"What's wrong?" he asked.

Her turbulent emotions swirled and she turned, not wanting to face him, and wiped at her face as a tear fell.

"What is it, Sarah?"

More memories surfaced, and Sarah swiped at another tear. It was as if that one recollection had opened the door to a room she would have rather kept closed. She stepped back, feeling that Ramsey would hate her, should hate her, if he knew what she had done. She didn't know what to say. But he wouldn't give up, and he stepped in front of her and reached out to comfort her.

"Don't," she said, waving a hand.

He stopped his advance. "Sarah," he said. "Don't pull away from me. Tell me."

She shook her head.

He sighed. "Are you blaming me?"

Her gaze met his. "How can you ask that?"

"I should have been there," he said. "I should have stopped him."

It was then that she realized that, while she'd been torturing herself with guilt, he'd been doing the same. "No, that's not true."

"Yes, it is."

"There's nothing you could have done." She sniffed. He grabbed a tissue from the counter and handed it to her. "It's my fault," she continued. "Not yours."

"No, it isn't."

"Yes, it is. I should have known that he couldn't be trusted. I should have felt his presence. I...I..."

Ramsey tried to take her hand. "Sarah, it's not your fault."

"But it is. I was weak and foolish." She wiped at her eyes with the tissue. "How could I have allowed myself to think I loved him?"

"He gave you something—"

"I don't care." She turned away again. "I still should have known. How could I have forgotten you?"

"He was a smart man. He took your blood, studied your body chemistry..."

"Still," she said. Ramsey came close again, and faced her, trying to meet her eyes. "I should have sensed it," she added, "felt it, suspected it, anything."

"You probably did, but he was prepared for that. He made you take those pills."

"I am so stupid."

"Don't say that," he said. He took her arm, not letting her pull away. "Do you blame me for getting sick?"

That made her look up. "Of course not."

"Then why blame yourself?"

"Because it's different."

"Why? Just because yours was mental and emotional, and mine was physical?"

"I should have stopped him. He...he...we..." She shut her eyes.

"It's okay," he said.

Her eyes flew open. "It's okay?" she asked. "I slept with him." The anguish of saying the words rippled through her. "How can you even stand to be around me? You should hate me."

"Hate you?" His mouth fell open. "Never. I couldn't hate you." He moved closer, and when she couldn't meet his eyes, he lifted his fingers to her chin and tried to get her to look at him. "You could sleep with a Eudoran football team, and I still couldn't hate you."

She did look at him then. "Don't make jokes. This isn't funny. What I did..."

"What you did was what made sense to you at the time. You believed you loved him." He held her gaze. "I would never fault you for that."

Sarah shook her head. "Maybe you can forgive me, but I don't know if I can forgive myself."

His face fell, and she could sense his own warring emotions. "I've got to work on that one too." She started to object, but he stopped her. "It will take some time for both of us." He stroked his thumb over her wet cheek. "How about we just be patient with ourselves? There's no rush to solve everything right now."

His touch helped her to relax and she raised her hands and rested them on his chest. "You promise you don't hate me?" she asked. "You're not angry?"

"Oh, I'm angry," he said, letting his fingers find the bruises on her neck and wrist, "but not at you."

They held still for a moment, each of them taking a moment, and the energy in the room begin to race.

His nearness made Sarah warm and she moved her palm over his sternum and held her breath when she felt his appetite for her engage. "I'm so sorry," she said, stepping closer.

He stared at her lips and she knew he wanted to kiss her, but was holding back. "It's not your fault," he said. "I'm the one who's sorry."

Taking another step, Sarah slid her hand from his chest and around to his back, and she heard him inhale. Moving her other hand lower, she found the edge of his shirttail, and pulled it up. Finding and touching his skin, her heart pounded as she trailed her fingers up his stomach and caressed his chest. "It's not your fault either."

"Sarah..." he said, his breathing picking up and his cheeks flushing. "You're sure? You're in a vulnerable state right now."

She lowered the hand on his back and slid it up underneath his shirt to join the other one and she pressed against him, her mouth hovering near his. Her desire surged as she teased him, but she understood his reluctance. "Listen," she said, so close she could feel his hot breath on her cheek, "we can talk about what went wrong and what we might have done to prevent it, but the fact remains that I gave my body to someone else." She froze when she voiced the words, but kept her eyes on him, watching for his reaction. Feeling relief that he hadn't pulled away, she rubbed her thumbs over his ribs. "And I need to get past that." Another lump of emotion surfaced. "And I need you to help me do it." She blinked back unshed tears. "I need your hands on my body and your lips on my skin. You're the only one who can help me heal."

Her words broke through any resistance he held, and a muffled groan escaped his throat. Unable to deny her, he pulled her in with his hands, found her lips with his own, and met her urgent kiss. Her arms tightened around him, and her entire body responded to the feel of him against her. He ran his hands into her hair while their lips expressed the building intensity between them. As their tongues met and the kiss deepened, she felt him reach down beneath her clothes and pull at her shirt. They broke the kiss as he pulled it over her head. She pulled at his own shirt, and he helped her yank it off, both of them breathing hard as they tried to get at each other. Continuing to kiss and touch, they removed their shoes and jeans. Their clothes discarded, she hugged him against her and ground her body against his, and he moaned into her ear. Naked, they continued kissing and touching until he lifted her, his arms around her torso and hers wrapped around his shoulders, to the bed and lay her down on it.

The energy between them burned hot as they explored each other's bodies, relishing in the feel of being together again. Unexpectedly, Sarah broke away, breathless.

"What?" he asked.

"Do Eudorans play football?" she asked.

He stared as if confused, but then broke into a smile. "Hell if I know," he said before he reached down and tickled her, making her squeal and grab at his hand. "Maybe one day we'll find out." And he leaned down and found her lips again.

She responded, pulling him down against her.

**

That evening, as the sun began to set and the light began to dim, Sarah opened her eyes. She'd dozed for a little while, and she heard John's soft snore behind her. Their energy had reengaged, and they'd found themselves unable to stop touching each other, as if their bodies demanded to catch up on lost time.

Deeply content, she sighed and then smiled when she felt him stir.

He moved and pressed himself up behind her, his arm moving across her waist and resting on her belly. His mouth found her neck, and he kissed her below her ear. "You awake?" he asked.

"Hmmm," she said. His hand trailed over her stomach, and she closed her eyes, enjoying the feel of him next to her.

"Penny for your thoughts," he said.

She smiled. "They're all about you."

"Good." He continued to kiss her neck. "What's really on your mind?"

She didn't answer at first, but then snuggled against him. "You're getting pretty good at reading people."

"I'm good at reading you." He paused. "What's bothering you?"

"Just thinking." She moved her hand to cover his.

"About what?"

"I'm going to have to explain his disappearance."

"We talked about that."

"I know, but I can't stay here while my husband is missing."

"You can stay at your place. Just until the dust settles."

"I want to stay here."

"Don't worry. You're not getting rid of me that easily."

She rubbed her fingers over his hand and felt the flutter in her belly.

"What was that?" he asked.

"Did you feel it?"

"Something moved."

She laughed. "That's your daughter."

"You can tell it's a girl?"

"No. I'm just taking a guess. But you deserve a daughter to keep you on your toes."

His fingers lightly touched her stomach. "Maybe it's a boy. I can teach him all about baseball and camping."

"You could do that with her, too."

He chuckled. "I would love that." He paused. "If it's a girl, I'd like to name her Destine."

"And if it's a boy, we'll name him after your dad."

"I'd like that."

Her fingers intertwined in his and he rubbed his jaw along her shoulder. "Can I ask you something?"

"What?"

"How did you know?"

"Know what?"

"That he would take the serum."

"Yates?"

"Yes. How did you know he would inject himself?"

She shook her head. "I didn't. All I knew was that if I could find a way to upset him enough, rile him up, injure him in some way, that the likelihood that he would take it was high. But even if he didn't, I knew he'd take it eventually."

"How did you know it was poisonous?"

She thought back. "Once my memories returned, I recalled that I still had the syringe that he gave me. My sensitivities have improved since becoming pregnant. The moment I held it, I knew it would kill him."

"You could have erased his memory instead."

"When?"

"He dropped that injection device with the vial still in it. It fell at your feet. I expected you to pick it up and shoot him with it."

She nodded. "I considered it, but I couldn't be sure it would even work on him. I didn't want to take the risk of injecting him and have nothing happen, or worse, have his memories disappear and then have to worry about when they would return. No."

"No?"

"It had to be final. We'd never be rid of him otherwise. Plus, by that point, I knew he was close to taking the serum."

"He was also close to killing all of us."

She stilled at the thought, but then relaxed. "Someone told me a while back to trust destiny, so I guess that's what I did."

She heard him laugh, and he pressed up against her. "That someone's pretty smart."

"He is." She sighed as he let go of her fingers and stroked the skin between her breasts. "I had to be sure he survived," she said, "so I could beg for his forgiveness."

"Did you say beg?" He dropped his hand and slid it down to her bellybutton and then moved it lower until she sucked in a breath and arched against him.

"Oh, you'll beg all right," he said, moving around to face her. He peppered her skin with kisses and moved his lips down to her stomach, following the trail of his hand. "But it won't be for forgiveness."

Sarah bit her bottom lip and, minutes later, discovered he was right.

CHAPTER THIRTY-THREE

··

THE HALLWAY LED down to darkness, but she walked down it anyway, feeling as if she was being pulled through the murky corridor. She didn't know where she was, or how she got there, but it didn't matter. She only knew she had to continue until she reached the end. As she walked, she became aware of light stretching out from beyond the shadows, and she moved faster, eager to reach it before it faded. Nearing it, she saw light peek out from behind the edges of a large closed wooden door. She reached out to graze her fingers over the soft wood, and the door opened. Light streamed over her, and she could see the figure of a woman. The glare from the light dimmed, and she made out the face of the person within: Varalika. Sarah felt compelled to take a few slow steps forward. Walking through the threshold, the light enveloped her and the door slammed shut behind her.

Sarah's eyes flew open and she sat up in bed, seeing the morning light pierce the curtains.

Ramsey, who had been sleeping beside her, awoke. "What is it?" he asked, his voice groggy.

"Get up," she said. "We have to go." She hopped out of the bed, ran into the bathroom and flipped on the shower.

He sat up, still half asleep. "What's going on?" he asked, rubbing at his eyes.

Sarah poked her head out of the bathroom. "Hurry. We don't have much time."

He threw off the sheets and stood. "What are you doing?"

"Come on," she said, hopping into the shower. "I'll explain on the way."

"On the way where?" he asked, stepping into the bathroom.

She stepped out of the shower and grabbed his hand. "Hurry up."

**

Sitting beside Ramsey as he drove down the road, Sarah hung up the phone after having talked with Drake. "Head to Morgana's," she said.

"Morgana's? She's in the hospital."

"She checked herself out. Drake's calling an emergency Council meeting. We're meeting there."

"Are you going to tell me what is going on?"

"I'll discuss it when we all get together. Here," she said, handing him his phone. "Call Leroy. Tell him to meet us at Morgana's. I'll call Hannah and Declan."

"Hannah's still at the hospital."

Sarah put the phone down and put her hand to her forehead. "That's right. Okay," she said, thinking. "We'll wait on them for now."

Ramsey hit a button and called Leroy, telling him to meet them at Morgana's immediately, at Sarah's request, and that no, he had no idea what it was about.

Hanging up, he glanced over at her. "Is everything all right?"

She looked over at him but didn't answer.

Several minutes later, they pulled into Morgana's driveway and got out, moving quickly up the front walk as Ronald, with a bandage on his head, met them at the door. Sarah rushed in, and Ramsey pointed her in the direction of Morgana's office. They both entered the room to see Morgana seated at her desk wearing a gray pant-suit, with her hair pulled up in its usual style, looking as if she'd just returned from a day at the spa. Drake was sitting on the couch along with Daphne, the councilwoman whose acrimony toward Sarah had been obvious since their first meeting. Two other men and another woman were also in the room, but their names escaped Sarah.

Morgana stood when they entered. "Welcome," she said, waving at the room. "You have a captive audience, as you requested."

Sarah regarded the faces that were staring at her.

"You mind telling us what is going on that requires such urgency?" asked Morgana.

"Is this everyone?" Sarah asked.

"Not everyone can drop everything to be at your beck and call," said Daphne.

"Be quiet, Daphne," said Drake. "Charlotte and Benjamin will be here in a few minutes. Anderson is on the speaker phone. He's out of town but was able to call in."

Leroy walked into the room. "I'm here," he said. "Charlotte and Ben are right behind me." He saw Ramsey. "What's going on, Sherlock?"

Ramsey shrugged. "Your guess is as good as mine."

Sarah advanced farther into the room, her mind racing. She paced back and forth.

"Anyone care for a refreshment?" asked Morgana, sitting back down, revealing the fatigue she felt. "If we're going to throw a party, we might as well relax and enjoy it. Ronald?"

Ronald appeared at the door just as the two remaining Council members appeared and entered the room.

"A pitcher of lemonade, if you don't mind?" asked Morgana.

"Of course, madam." And he disappeared, closing the door behind him.

Charlotte and Ben found seats amongst the extra chairs provided, and Leroy and Ramsey remained standing. Sarah continued to pace quietly and surveyed the room.

"Well," said Drake, "you going to tell us what is so urgent?"

Sarah wrung her hands together, debating what to say.

"What is it, Sarah?" asked Morgana. "Does this have something to do with Yates?"

"No," said Sarah. "No, not Yates. I..." She hesitated, unsure where to begin.

"You what?" asked Daphne. She rolled her eyes. "Please tell me you have something to say and that you didn't just drag us over here to gush over your success."

"Oh, shut up, Daphne," said Drake.

"Don't tell me to shut up, Drake."

Drake glared. "She found the serum, for God's sake."

"She didn't find it. Yates did."

"What, you want to congratulate him instead?" asked Drake.

"Shut up, both of you," said Morgana. She sat tall in her seat. "Tell us, Sarah. What do you know?"

Sarah quieted herself before answering and then looked over at Ramsey, who gave her a reassuring nod. "I saw something when I read the Mirror."

"And what was that?" asked Morgana.

"I think it's called your overactive imagination," answered Daphne. When the entire room looked at her with irritation, she crossed her arms and went quiet.

Sarah ignored Daphne. "I didn't understand it at first. It was a closed door. I didn't have access to it."

"What closed door?" asked Ramsey.

"When I read the Mirror," she said, "I saw Varalika, her husband, how she died. And then a door, but it shut on me."

"What about it?" Ramsey asked. "Did you see something?"

"Yes," she said, allowing his presence to calm her. "This morning. I had another dream and I saw the door again, but this time, it opened, and I saw her."

"Saw who?" asked Leroy.

"Varalika," said Sarah. "She was standing there, on the other side."

"She did?" asked Ramsey. "What did she say?"

Sarah's gaze met the eyes of those around the room. "The serum is no good. You can't use it."

"What?" asked Drake. Similar shocked comments could be heard by others in the room.

"Do you even know what the hell you're talking about?" asked Daphne.

"It's poison. It's been tampered with," said Sarah. "It was designed to destroy you, not save you."

No one said anything as what she said and what it meant sank in.

"Explain," said Morgana. "Are you saying we are back to square one?"

"No, not at all," said Sarah. "Quite the opposite."

"I don't understand," said Ben, sitting forward in his chair.

"Please enlighten us," said Charlotte.

"I'll explain," said Daphne. "She's nuts. She's having delusions, and you're all eating right out of her hand."

"Daphne," said Ramsey, scowling. "Either you shut that trap of yours or I'll grab one of those lemons Ronald is presently squeezing and I'll juice it between your teeth."

Nobody argued with Ramsey. Daphne sat back in her seat and huffed, and Ramsey looked at Sarah. "Tell us what you mean."

Sarah sighed. "I saw what Varalika knew. What put her life at risk."

"What was that?" asked Morgana.

"She knew about that serum. She dumped it before the ship had any problems. She deliberately got rid of it because she knew."

"She knew?" asked Drake.

"She knew it was compromised." Sarah rubbed her forehead, remembering the dream. "It was a conspiracy."

"A conspiracy?" Daphne snorted, but then Ramsey glared at her and she went quiet.

"The serum," said Sarah. "You never needed it in the first place."

"What?" asked Drake.

"At first you did," said Sarah, now pacing. "When the Grays first arrived, earth's frequency was too harsh and a serum did exist, but the longer you stayed, the more you adjusted, and in time, you no longer required it."

"Then why did we keep taking it?" asked Leroy.

"Something happened. Something on our home planet. There was a division, a faction of Red-Lines that split from the reigning Council. I don't know what caused it, but they created their own group, their own party. They were covert, and they planned some type of overthrow. I'm not sure."

"But what does that have to do with us?" asked Morgana.

"They used you." Sarah glanced around the room. "All of you, as some sort of experiment."

"Why?" asked the Council member on the phone.

"You were a perfect test group. Using a serum you thought you still needed, but didn't. They took over as earth's controlling research team. Unbeknownst to anyone, they began to experiment with Grays. Sending down various types of serums just to see the effects it would have on the population as a whole. They were testing you, experimenting with you."

"My, God. What for?" asked Drake.

"I think they had some sort of plan to eradicate the Grays, but they had to do it without being discovered. You were the perfect test subjects to do that. They had Red-Lines on earth who were part of the scheme, who helped with their plans. But something went wrong. The secret got out, and they knew if they were discovered, their group would be banished. Varalika had somehow learned of their plans, and she was on her way to reveal what she knew. She took her family with her, knowing if she left them behind, they would be at risk. But they got to her first."

"But that doesn't make sense," said another councilman whose name escaped Sarah. "We've been taking a serum for years. You're saying we never needed it?"

"Not for a long time," said Sarah. "And it was doing you more harm than good."

"But our people have been dying," said Charlotte.

"The older ones have," said Sarah. "The ones who've had more exposure to it. Those who've had the least amount, mainly the younger group, will have the fewest effects."

"But the Reds died off without it," said Leroy.

"The Reds still needed their serum. They never adapted," said Sarah.

"You're saying the serum is useless?" asked Morgana.

Sarah nodded. "Yes. You will all live long and happy lives without it." Morgana raised a brow before Sarah broke the eye contact.

"I don't believe this," said Drake.

"Neither do I," said Daphne. "You sure you didn't smoke something before you went to sleep last night?"

"You must be thirsty, Daphne," said Ramsey just as Ronald opened the door to the office carrying a tray of lemonade and then placing it on the coffee table. Daphne met his eyes but then looked away.

"Where is the serum now?" asked Sarah. "You have to destroy it. You can't distribute it."

"It's at a local lab," said Morgana.

"Dear God," said Drake, standing.

"What?" asked Morgana.

"This morning. Declan called me. Asked me if he could get some."

"Get some?" asked Ramsey. "Get some what?"

"Some serum," said Drake.

"For what?" asked Sarah.

"For Hannah. He thought it would help."

"He what?" asked Leroy.

Ramsey reached for the phone, hanging up on the council member who was listening in, and immediately dialed Declan.

"You gave him some?" asked Morgana.

"I didn't give it to him," said Drake. "He merely wanted to know which lab he could get it from."

"Damn it," said Ramsey, listening as the phone rang, but Declan didn't pick up.

Sarah walked up beside him and pulled out her phone. "I'll phone Hannah," she said.

Leroy pulled out his cell as well. "I'll try the hospital," he said.

Ramsey disconnected the line and dialed again. The phone rang over the speaker. "Come on," said Ramsey. "Pick up, Declan."

**

Declan opened the door to Hannah's hospital room carefully so as not to wake her. He'd spent the last two nights here, sleeping little on the short couch in the room but not wanting to leave. Hannah's condition had not worsened, but her lethargy and fever continued, and the doctor, suspecting the flu, suggested an additional night in the hospital. She'd had a fitful sleep, waking when the nurses did rounds and then after a nightmare where she'd dreamed of a man chasing her with a syringe, but Declan had sat with her, helping her to relax.

Waking early that morning, Declan had contacted Drake. He'd asked about the serum and learned the name of the lab which had begun to process it. He didn't know if it would help Hannah heal from Yates's toxin, but he figured it was worth a try. He'd found the lab, and watched as a technician measured out a dose, diluting it to the necessary proportions, and gave him the prescribed amount.

Now, watching her sleep, he gave silent thanks that she was alive and would recover. The thought of a future without her made his insides quiver. He wanted her well.

Sitting beside her, he drew the syringe from his pocket and pulled off the plastic-covered tip, planning to inject it directly into her IV tube while she slept. He didn't think she'd be too keen on seeing any needles right now.

Declan placed the syringe at the tip of tube. Before he could inject her, though, he caught her staring up at him. "Hey," he said, moving the needle away from the IV.

"Hey," she said, sounding drowsy but alert.

"Feeling better?" he asked.

"I am. Tired, though." She shifted on the bed. "When can I get out of here?"

"Soon as the doctor clears you. Shouldn't be long."

She eyed him with a worried look. "You look terrible."

"Yeah, well, worrying about you is not conducive to an overall pleasant appearance." She slid her hand out from the covers, and he took it in his. "You scared the hell out of me."

"I know." She squeezed his fingers. "But I'm good now. The bad guy's gone, and we're all alive and well." She paused. "Mostly well, at least."

"About that," he said. "I brought you something."

"What?"

He lifted the syringe in his hand.

She pulled back. "What the hell is that?"

"Serum," he said, smiling.

"Serum?"

"Yes."

"*The* serum?"

"Yes. *The* serum."

"Sarah found it?"

"Yates had it all along."

"He did?'

"Yes," said Declan. "He'd found it and had it hidden in his office. I just got back from the lab. They gave me a dose."

Hannah's eyes widened. "They did? What for?"

"For you."

"For me? Why?"

He looked at her surroundings. "I think that's obvious."

She eyed the syringe and frowned.

"What?" He raised the syringe. "We're all going to get some eventually anyway."

"I don't know. It's just weird. Why should I get it first?"

"Well, considering you were instrumental in its recovery and you risked your life to save us all, I think it's only fitting."

"You're sure about that?"

"Of course."

She hesitated.

"I promise," he said. "It won't hurt a bit."

She peered up at him with uncertainty. "Okay," she said, "if you think it will help." She offered her arm with the IV.

"It will. We'll get you back on your feet in no time." He brought the tip of the needle to the IV tube just as the phone in the room rang. He considered ignoring it, but something urged him not to. He sighed, lowered the needle, and answered the phone.

**

Three weeks later, the police found Yates Reddington's body two hours outside of the city, at a remote cabin owned by his corporation. The cause of death was unknown, although an autopsy revealed he'd suffered severe internal hemorrhaging. He'd been on a missing persons list since his wife had filed a domestic violence report not long after he'd gone missing. On the day of his abuse, she had confronted him about her discoveries regarding his questionable business practices and his lies about his whereabouts. After turning over the evidence she'd found on his computer to the police, she'd moved out of the house and back into her apartment. She'd cooperated with the authorities, giving them all the information she could, as had those who worked in the home. And although there were suspected issues between the couple, they were only suspicions and nothing concrete.

After searching the records provided and the cabin in which Mr. Reddington had been found, they discovered files on a man named Marco, also reported missing. A knife had also been found in the cabin, along with Marco's ID. Having questioned Reddington previously about Marco's disappearance, police could only speculate that he'd had some involvement in Marco's case. But without Marco's body, there was little they could prove. And with Reddington dead, few business partners grieving over his absence, and with no physical evidence to connect his wife to any suspicious activity, the case went cold.

EPILOGUE

....

THE PARTY HUMMED with activity. A small ensemble group played a soft jazz number, and guests mingled at the open bar and the buffet, enjoying the food and especially the drinks.

Ramsey stood with a drink in his hand, watching the guests. He saw Sarah's friend Rachel standing with her boyfriend Todd. They were in conversation with Sarah's Aunt Gerry, who held hands with her own date whose name Ramsey could not remember. Sarah had introduced all of them four weeks earlier, and his ears were still ringing from Rachel's shriek of excitement when Sarah had told her of their impending nuptials and her pregnancy.

Glancing around the room, he saw his Aunt Marge and Uncle Phil, drink in hand, as they spoke to his mother. He caught sight of Sarah, who was mingling with one of the Council members. He considered walking over, grabbing her by the hand, and leading her out, taking her home and into his bed.

Leroy and Olivia interrupted him. "Having fun, Sherlock?" asked Leroy, chuckling.

"You know me, Leroy. I love parties," he said.

"But it's your party," said Leroy. "And Morgana's hosting it."

"I think she did it on purpose to torture me," Ramsey said.

Leroy grinned. "Probably."

Sarah made eye contact with him, and he winked at her. She said something to the councilman, who smiled, and she headed over to Ramsey, her belly showing the early signs of her pregnancy. He didn't think she could look more beautiful.

She came up and took his hand. "Having fun yet?"

He leaned over and spoke into her ear. "I'd have more fun if I could get you home and out of those clothes."

She smiled and squeezed his fingers. "Appreciate the anticipation."

"Anticipation is overrated." He put his arm around her. "Let's go."

"We haven't even been here an hour," she said, staying put. "And this is our engagement party. You think Morgana's given you hell before? You leave now, and you'll never hear the end of it."

"She's right, Sherlock," said Leroy, watching Olivia walk away to talk with someone he didn't know. He pointed. "Who's that?"

"Hell if I know," said Ramsey. "How is this my engagement party when I don't recognize half the people here?"

"You're marrying a Red-Line," said Leroy. "Makes you kind of important."

"I don't see why," he answered.

"Me, either," said a voice behind them. Ramsey turned to see Declan walk up to them, with Hannah beside him.

"There you are," said Ramsey. "Where the hell have you two been? Or should I bother asking?"

"You shouldn't bother," said Declan, his arm around Hannah. Hannah blushed.

"There's food and drinks, you two," said Sarah. "Help yourself."

"Where's our hostess?" asked Ramsey. "I saw her for two minutes when we came in, and that's it. I think she's hiding."

"Morgana hide?" asked Hannah. "I don't think so." She eyed the room. "My, who are all these people?"

"Exactly my point," said Ramsey.

"Stop complaining, Sherlock," said Leroy. "Think of all the wedding gifts."

"We don't need any wedding gifts," said Ramsey. "I've got a wealthy fiancée, if you recall."

Sarah nudged him in the ribs, and he grunted. "That money is going into a trust for our son."

"Or daughter," said Ramsey.

"What about the business? What's happening with that?" asked Leroy.

"It's so deep in debt and back taxes, I don't know if it can survive," said Sarah. "It's being run by an appointee right now. I wouldn't want his job for anything."

"When does the house close?" asked Hannah.

"Next month," said Sarah. "Provided everything goes smoothly."

"It should," said Declan. "The people buying it are loaded."

"They can have it for all I care," said Sarah.

"If I'd known you were all going to congregate in a corner and keep to yourselves, I'd have made a shorter guest list," said a voice from behind them.

They turned to see Morgana, dressed in a flowing purple gown that emphasized her lithe frame and elegant features.

"You should have considered that anyway," said Ramsey.

"Do yourself a favor and mingle, Ramsey," said Morgana, holding a glass of champagne. "You could use a few friends outside your social circle."

"What social circle?" he asked.

"Exactly," she said. "Besides, you never know who you might meet."

Ramsey cocked an eyebrow at her. "Unless Elvis Presley walks out of this crowd, I could do without knowing more people."

"Sarah," said Morgana. "You still have time."

"Time?" asked Sarah.

"To get out while you still can. You can call this whole engagement off right now." She took a sip of her champagne, and Ramsey wondered if she was a bit tipsy.

Sarah leaned into Ramsey. "You're right," she said. "It's tempting, but I think I'm stuck with him."

"You're a brave woman. I admire your courage." Morgana met Sarah's eyes. Sarah held the look for a moment, and Declan narrowed his eyes. Ramsey wondered what his brother was picking up on.

"Have you considered our offer?" Morgana asked Sarah.

"What offer?" asked Ramsey, distracted from his observation.

Sarah nodded. "I have, but for now, I think I'll decline. I just want to spend time with my family."

"What offer?" Ramsey asked again.

"I'm disappointed, of course," said Morgana, "but if you change your mind, the offer stands."

"I know," answered Sarah. "Thank you."

"And you..." said Morgana, staring at Ramsey.

"What?" he asked.

She leaned in. "You've done a good job despite your shortcomings." She swiped at a piece of lint on her sleeve. "See that you do the same as a husband and father."

Her sentiment reminded him of someone else. "You sound like my grandmother."

She sipped some more champagne. "I know."

"Speaking of her, I still have the Mirror," said Ramsey.

"Keep it," said Morgana.

"Keep it?"

"It was Destine's. It belongs with her family. She would want you...or her great grandchild...to have it."

"You don't need it for some strange council ritual?" asked Ramsey.

Morgana put her empty champagne glass on a nearby tray. "Contrary to what you may believe, Ramsey, we do not dance naked and howl at the full moon during the Solstice."

"Just between you and me," said Ramsey, "you guys could use some of that. You're all looking a little bored."

She leaned in. "I said the Council didn't do that. I never said I didn't."

Ramsey didn't know what to say to that, but Morgana didn't give him time to answer. "Now get out there and socialize," she said. "These people are here to meet you."

"Why?' asked Ramsey.

"Because you and Sarah are the future of our people, whether you like it or not."

"Future?"

"Yes," she said, walking away. "Better get used to it."

"Terrific," he said. "And what offer?" he asked, but she was gone, disappearing into the crowd.

"You think she was serious?" asked Hannah.

"About dancing in the moonlight?" asked Leroy.

"Don't forget the naked part," said Declan.

"Yes," said Leroy. "I think she's serious."

Ramsey eyed Sarah and she sensed his unspoken question. "She asked me to be a member of the Council," said Sarah.

"She what?" asked Ramsey.

"Really?" asked Leroy.

"Not surprising," said Declan.

"You're not going for it?" asked Hannah. "Can't imagine why not." She smirked. "I mean, who wouldn't want to hang out with that crowd?"

"Well, after that comment about howling at the moon, there may be more to them than meets the eye," said Ramsey. "You're sure?" He asked Sarah. "You don't want to join the ranks of the Head Honchos? You could wear fancy robes, and I'll get you some jewels or a crown or something."

"They don't wear that," said Declan.

"You could be a trendsetter," said Ramsey.

"No, thanks," said Sarah, her thumb tracing the back of his hand. "I'd rather spend my time with you." She rubbed her belly. "And this little bundle of joy we're going to have."

"You don't know what you're having?" asked Hannah.

"No, not yet," said Sarah.

"You don't?" asked Declan. "You can't tell?"

Sarah patted her baby bump. "Strangely, no. I can't. Sometimes I think girl, but then other times I think boy. I think I'm trying too hard."

"I could tell you," said Declan.

"What?" asked Ramsey.

"You can?" asked Sarah.

Declan held his chest. "My accuracy is astounding."

"Sure it is," Ramsey scoffed.

"You doubt me?"

Ramsey shot back. "Does Morgana live to irritate me?"

"You should let him try," said Hannah. "Aren't you curious?"

Ramsey considered it. "Okay, smart guy. Give it a shot. But if you end up being wrong, you owe me a steak dinner."

Declan and Leroy chuckled. "You're on," said Declan.

"I'm guessing a boy," said Leroy.

"I think it's a girl," said Hannah.

Ramsey and Sarah shared a glance. "Care to wager a guess?" he asked her.

She smiled back. "I'll be happy either way. You?"

He thought for a second. "I think it's a girl."

"You do?" she asked.

He nodded. "That, or I want a girl. I can't be sure. Either way, though, I'm happy."

Sarah regarded Declan. "All right, Mr. Wizard. Do your magic."

Declan dropped his hand and placed it lightly on Sarah's stomach, and he stilled, closing his eyes. After a few seconds, he dropped his hand, his face guarded.

"Well?" asked Ramsey. "What'd you get, Captain Marvel?"

They all stared, waiting, as Declan stayed quiet for several seconds. "Well," he said.

"Well, what?" asked Ramsey. "Did we stump you?"

"No, no," he said, shaking his head. "Not that."

Ramsey groaned. "Then what?"

"Congratulations," said Declan. "You're all correct."

"What do you mean?" asked Ramsey.

Declan placed his hand on Ramsey's shoulder. "Nothing gives me more pleasure than to tell you this."

"What?" asked Ramsey.

Declan grinned. "You're having twins."

Sarah froze, and Ramsey stared, openmouthed, at his brother.

"You're kidding," said Leroy.

"Really?" asked Hannah.

"I think that means you owe me two steak dinners," said Declan. "Don't you?"

And for one rare moment, Ramsey was speechless.

ACKNOWLEDGEMENTS

....

None of these books would be here if it weren't for the support of my family and friends. Words cannot express how grateful I am to have to the amount of support that I've had throughout this journey.

Much love goes to my parents, who've always believed in me. Thank you for your guidance and all your help as I found my way.

A BIG shout out to my brother and sister, Cathy and Nick. You are always there for me and I couldn't ask for better siblings.

A BIG group hug to my besties – Christine, Gwen, Fay, May, Paula, Laura, Kim, all my coworkers at Emler, and Artur and the awesome staff at Aboca's Italian Grill. Thank you, thank you, thank you. Your support, assistance, and faith in me makes this process so much easier.

To the extended family – Jessica, Alex, Suzzie, Jack, Anne – thank you for spreading the word and all your help. It is greatly valued and appreciated.

And of course, to my wonderful nieces and nephews – Taylor, Alex, Sydney, Colson and Leighton – You are all rock stars in my book. Watching you all grow up has been so damn fun and I'm so proud and happy to be your aunt.

ABOUT THE AUTHOR

Born and raised in Dallas, TX, J. T. Bishop began writing in 2012. Two years later, the Red-Line trilogy was complete. She's not done though. J. T. continues to create new characters and story lines to entertain her fans.

J. T. loves stories that explore characters' unique abilities and origins. It's a theme she finds intriguing and provides a wealth of inspiration for her books. Drama, angst, passion, and humor all add to the fun. A little bit of romance doesn't hurt either.

J. T. loves to spend time with family and friends, traveling whenever she can, and spending time in nature (despite the heat in Texas). Getting up in the morning with a cup of coffee, ready to write is the start of a perfect day.

When J.T. isn't writing, she's enjoying her time with friends and family. She loves good movies, good books, good food and good people to share it with.

Connect with J.T. at:

http://jtbishopauthor.com.

ENJOY AN EXCERPT FROM

CURSE-BREAKER

··

THIRTY MINUTES LATER, Grayson re-emerged from the bathroom feeling better, but still moving slowly. He walked back into his living room and squinted from the bright light. Sunshine flooded the room and he raised his hand to block his eyes. Franklin had opened the shutters and the ocean came into view. The room had been cleared of trash and his dirty clothes were now gone, presumably in the laundry. Glancing into the kitchen, he saw the clean countertops and empty sink. He had to admit, it looked better. He considered grabbing a beer from the fridge, but he knew he'd regret it and he walked to the back door and opened it. The sea breeze hit him and he breathed deeply. He heard a bark and Max ran across the porch and met him, jumping up for a pet. He ruffled the dog's head and stepped outside. Walking to the balcony, he smelled the sea and listened to the waves. Franklin was nowhere in sight. He stood for several minutes with his eyes closed. Only the beach could calm him when he needed to relax. It was why he lived here now. After all he'd experienced, it was the only place he'd found peace, until the demons reared their heads, and then he'd learned that only bourbon could quiet those voices. And they seemed to speak to him more and more often lately.

The sound of talking reached his ears and he opened his eyes to see people below on the shore, staring and pointing. He looked down the beach as Franklin joined him on the porch.

"There you are, sir...Mr. Steele. Your pizza is here."

Gray continued to stare. "What's going on down there?'

"What do you mean?"

"Down there." He pointed where the beach walkers had and Franklin looked. Red lights flashed in the distance and Gray could see emergency vehicles. It was hard to make out what was happening.

"I don't know, sir. Perhaps an accident?"

A police cruiser joined the scene.

"I hope it wasn't a drowning," said Franklin.

Gray moved toward the stairs. "I'm going to find out."

"Wait, sir."

Gray turned toward Franklin. "What?"

Franklin turned and went inside. He came back out with a paper towel and a piece of pizza in his hand. "At least eat something while you walk."

Gray almost turned him down, but then his stomach growled and he reached for the food. "Thanks." He turned and headed down the stairs as Max joined him.

"Sir?"

"What, Franklin?" He glanced back.

"You mind if I clean your bedroom?"

Gray considered it. "Have at it, Frank. Just watch out for the spiders." He grinned when Franklin gave him a worried look. "Come on, Max. Let's go find out what all the excitement is about." Max ran towards the water's edge and Gray took a bite of his pizza. Franklin disappeared into the house.

A few minutes later, Gray came onto the scene. An ambulance pulled away as he neared and a policeman began to roll out yellow tape to keep bystanders away. A fire truck with flashing lights waited nearby and a second police cruiser joined the fray. Gray assumed the ambulance carried the victim until he moved and got a better view and saw what looked like a blue tarp on the sand. He froze when he realized it was a body. Policeman milled around and he could hear the muffled voices of radio communication coming from their vehicles. Other people had stopped and they all stared from behind the tape as the police worked the area.

He'd finished his pizza on the walk over and he curled the paper towel into his fist. Another vehicle drove up and he saw the words, "Coroner's Office," printed on the side. The car stopped and two men stepped out and walked up to the covered form. Two other men with badges met them. They spoke, but Gray could not hear what they said over the sound of the waves. Max barked at a seagull, but remained at Gray's side.

"Any idea what's going on?"

Gray turned at the voice and saw a woman. Dressed casually with sunglasses perched on her head, she stood next to him, but she watched the police as he did. Her long dark hair blew in the wind.

"No. No idea."

"Doesn't look good."

"No, it doesn't."

They watched the men from the coroner's office pull equipment from their vehicle. The policemen began to question the crowd.

"Do you know who it is?"

He looked back at her. "What?"

"The victim?" she asked. "Do you know her?"

"It's a her?"

"Yes. I saw her before they covered her."

"You did?"

"Yes."

"What'd she look like?"

"Blonde. Pretty. About all I could tell. You're a local, though, aren't you?"

"Excuse me?" he asked.

"You live here? Grew up nearby? Right?"

"How do you know that?"

"You're Grayson Steele, aren't you?"

He groaned, but didn't answer her.

"My name's Gillian. Gillian Fletcher."

He continued to watch the men with their equipment. It was not the first time he'd been approached by a woman on the beach, but at a crime scene?

Still watching the activity, he answered her. "Listen, Miss Fletcher. I'm not interested, okay?"

He could feel her looking at him. "You're not interested in what?" she asked.

"There's a dead body over there. Now is not the time for a hook-up."

"A hook...what, you think I'm hitting on you?"

He looked over at her. She was attractive, and under different circumstances, he might have made the effort, but he was not that man anymore. "Aren't you?"

She smiled. "No, I'm not."

"Then what do you want?"

"Excuse me?"

"You know my name? Know I live nearby? Know I grew up not far from here?" He looked back at the scene. "What do you want?"

She didn't answer for a second. "I'm a reporter."

He chuckled. The men on the beach lifted the tarp, but they blocked his view. "Looks like you've got quite story on your hands. First on the scene."

"I'm not that kind of reporter."

"You're not?"

"No. I work for *Lifestyle* magazine."

"*Lifestyle*, huh? What lifestyle are you interested in?"

"Yours."

He looked at her again. "Let me get this straight. You want to interview me and you're approaching me at a crime scene?"

"How do you know it's a crime scene?"

"There's a dead woman over there."

"Doesn't mean it's a crime."

He paused. "You want to do an interview?"

"I do."

"On me?"

"Yes."

"Why?"

"Why not? Everyone wants to get an interview with you. You're a millionaire playboy who's become a recluse. The Howard Hughes of our time. You're a huge scoop."

"Scoop?"

"Yes."

"No thanks."

"Why not? Don't you want the world to know the truth?"

That intrigued him. "Truth?"

"Yes."

"What truth?"

"That you're not as messed up as they say you are. That you're not a drug user or psychotic. That you're not building sandcastles in your bedroom in your free time. Or tying up seagulls and eating them for lunch."

He grimaced. "Is that what they're saying about me?"

"Depends on the magazine."

He shook his head. "I'm obviously not keeping up on current trends."

"So tell them the truth. That you don't do any of those things."

He stared at her. "And how do you know I don't?"

She didn't say anything, but her eyes moved back to the beach and he looked back as well. The men were moving the body into a zippered bag. They tried to keep the bystanders from watching by holding up a blanket, but a strong gust of wind blew and the blanket moved and he got a quick, but clear view of the woman. A chill shot through him when he realized he recognized her. He knew the victim.

"Oh my God."

"What?" she asked.

He felt the blood leave his face and he looked down at the sand. "You okay?"

He looked for his dog. "Max?"

"Mr. Steele?"

Max ran up to him and shook out the water on his coat. "Let's go, Max."

"Please, Mr. Steele. Would you consider it?"

He didn't answer her. His wooden legs didn't want to move, but he forced them over the sand, the face of the victim echoing in his mind. He blinked and tried to think back. When had he seen her last? Calculating the time in his head, he grimaced when he remembered. Three days. It had been three days since he'd slept with her. He felt the urge to lose his pizza, but he held it back. Picking up his pace, he walked fast through the sand and ignored the reporter behind him.

"Mr. Steele? Are you okay? Can I follow up with you later?"

Leaving the scene, he said nothing and headed back to his home.

Made in the USA
Columbia, SC
06 December 2020